DIPLOMATIC RECRUIT

DIPLOMATIC RECRUIT

THE EMPRESS' SPY™ BOOK ONE

S.E. WEIR

MICHAEL ANDERLE

LMBPN Publishing
PMB 196, 2540 South Maryland Pkwy
Las Vegas, NV 89109

Version 1.01, June, 2021
eBook ISBN: 978-1-64971-821-1
Print ISBN: 978-1-64971-822-8

DEDICATION

To all those who have supported and encouraged me every step of the way. This is as much your book as mine.

- S.E. Weir

To Family, Friends and
Those Who Love
To Read.
May We All Enjoy Grace
To Live The Life We Are
Called.

—Michael

QBBS *Meredith Reynolds*

Phina nudged Alina toward the door of the apartment. "Come on, let's go. Just remember to tone down the squeals when you see all the guys."

Alina smacked Phina's arm at the ribbing but smiled as she turned to walk out. She raised a fist in the air. "Phinalina is leaving the building!"

Phina smirked at the name. When the two of them were in grade school, the girls were teased about their names rhyming and being together so much instead of playing with the other kids. Rather than being offended, the girls thought it was an awesome moniker and adopted it, using it as their code name for their adventures they had enacted over their many years of friendship. Since they were embarking on Phinalina's last childhood adventure before they both turned eighteen, it was very fitting to use the name now. Phina caught up to her friend outside the door as they began to walk the few miles to their target location within the space station *Meredith Reynolds.* She stuck her fist out.

"Phinalina forever!"

Alina grinned and brought hers up for a fist bump. "Phinalina forever!"

They walked down the lightly traveled residential corridor toward the lifts. People moved through the corridor that crossed theirs ahead.

"Hey, Phina?"

"Hmmm?" She had been thinking about what they would soon be walking into. She wanted to be prepared.

"What about Maxim?" Alina's eyes sparkled, and she gave Phina a smile.

Phina blinked. "What about him?"

"He could be the guy for you. He's super-hot, even if he is a little older, but he's a Were, so that doesn't really matter!" She grinned playfully.

Phina was already shaking her head. "No."

"Ronnie Diamantz? He's super-smart!"

Phina glowered at Alina. "*No.*" They reached the end of the corridor and mixed with the crowd, dodging a Karillian in a hurry. His three eye stalks waved at them in irritation.

"Peter Silvers?"

Phina sighed, wondering how long her friend would keep trying to set her up with other guys. Alina had been trying to convince Phina to relax and ease up on her laser-focused goal of becoming a spy. Phina had told her only someone extremely interesting and talented in their own right would be likely to catch her interest. The likelihood of that happening, to Phina's mind, was as rare as seeing a mythical unicorn. Alina's face brightened; she probably thought she was interested since she didn't respond right away. But...

"No."

QBBS *Meredith Reynolds*, Marines' Workout Area

"Which of you would like to spar first?" The large and obviously well-trained man in front of them smiled as if he knew something that amused him. What he thought he knew, Phina wasn't sure. Probably that what they knew about sparring could fill a teacup. Crumbs, more like a shot glass.

The girls had ended up taking the tram in deference to Alina's lack of athleticism. When they arrived, they had gotten through the guarded door without a problem, thanks to the well-made passes Phina had completed that morning. The armored men had given Phina curious glances and Alina admiring ones, and Alina had looked and flirted back. That was fine with Phina; she was used to it. She generally just did her thing while Alina attracted attention and drew people in. It was a good thing flirting her way into places wasn't required in most of the areas Phina accessed since she would have failed miserably. Alina was masterful even when she wasn't trying.

The two girls were the same height and close to the same weight, but where Alina's weight was in her curves, Phina's was mostly in her muscles. Her body had become very toned from climbing all over the space station and exercising, so any curves she had were more like definitions of her muscles.

Phina wasn't jealous about Alina's looks or the attention she got. In fact, she was relieved when attention was diverted from her. Phina preferred to be overlooked so she could do her own thing, usually something she didn't want others to notice anyway.

Of course, if Phina ever did find that mythical extremely talented, and interesting man, she might change her mind.

She didn't give that scenario very good odds, however.

After a wrong turn past the men on duty, they finally made it into the Marines' and Guardians' workout area. Phina had poked Alina again after entering to remind her not to squeal. They were Marine recruits today, not fangirls. Posing as recruits was the only method Phina had been able to think of to get the two of them into this restricted room.

It was a struggle, but Alina did keep the squeals inside, although her eyes grew wider. There were so many tall, strong, and attractive men in various positions and locations on the mats and workout equipment. There were women in the room too, but Alina's eyes lingered on the men. To her delight, their muscles were exposed, and many had their shirts off, per Alina's hopes. Phina sighed inside since she didn't understand her friend's obsession, although she was happy that she had helped Alina's wish come true.

After being greeted and ushered over to an open mat by Todd, the tall and overly muscled man had asked the question Phina now considered. She looked at Alina, who appeared to be torn between being thrilled to be in the secured room, leering at the men working out across the room, and being terrified she would be called on first.

Phina pursed her lips, then looked at the man in front of them, noticing the neatly trimmed crewcut. "I will." She might as well give Alina a few more minutes before they were found out and escorted out of the area. Alina wasn't equipped for any sort of sparring.

As Alina liked to say, her sport came with shopping bags and a credit card.

Todd moved to the middle of the mat and gestured for Phina to follow. She faced the large man and copied his stance, bringing her arms up and fisting her hands. It felt awkward. Todd's face had turned assessing and distant, and his blue eyes probably saw more than Phina wanted him to. She didn't know what to do next, so she just waited.

He sent his fist toward her head. Without thinking, Phina flung herself back as muscle memory took over, hands reaching behind her for the mat. She completed a back-extension roll and popped up several feet from where she had started.

Phina braced herself for another blow before she realized Todd just stood watching her with a look of surprised interest on his face. She quickly decided his interest wasn't a good thing when he leaned forward and swept her feet with a low kick. Phina almost didn't make it, but she jumped higher and more quickly than he expected. Than *she* had expected, for that matter. Her eyes darted around as she rose in the air, and she found the perfect spot to go next.

She moved her foot forward to vault off Todd's head,

but he grabbed at her ankle. His hand had only just slipped off when she flipped. His quick grab had stalled her motion, though, so instead of landing on the floor behind him, she landed half on his back, pushing him down a little more. She had been lucky to complete the rotation.

Realizing she needed to get off before he recovered, Phina flung herself into an aerial somersault and twisted so she landed facing her opponent rather than away from him. She sighed in relief that she had been able to complete the move since it was tricky to jump off a shifting and precarious base.

From the corner of her eye, she saw Alina smiling and looking amazed, then Phina noted the sudden quiet in the room. She had a feeling all those eyes were now looking in her direction, not resting on Alina as had been her plan. Phina nervously assessed Todd as he straightened after her hasty move. His face appeared surprised, curious, and... determined. Uh-oh! Fudging piles of...

Todd moved even faster to close the distance, and her body barely responded in time. Somehow she blocked the strike to her face with crossed arms, though it hurt so badly she wondered if he had broken something. She failed to block the following punch to her belly and slammed onto the floor several feet away. Fudge in a bucket!

As Phina lay on the mat catching her breath and wishing she had thought to train herself in martial arts as well as the spycraft she had been obsessed with throughout her teen years, she heard footsteps come closer. She lifted her chin to see who was walking up behind her. The view was upside down, but she knew it wasn't the man who had just put her on the floor. She tilted her head to the side when she couldn't comprehend what her brain tried to tell her. When she recognized the giant mountain of a man, she realized she just hadn't wanted to.

Fudging crumbs! Her head dropped back to the mat and she moaned. She was dead.

"Come with me." The huge man watched Phina for a moment before turning to Alina. "Both of you." Alina paled but walked toward him while Phina began to push herself up, wincing when her stomach muscles protested. But when John Grimes told you to move, you complied.

Todd stood above her with his hand extended and a small smile on his face. She took a moment to decide but grasped the offered hand and pulled herself up, cringing at the soreness in her belly and arms. He spoke in a low tone so that only she could hear. Well, there were Wechselbalg around, so who knew what they heard.

"Sorry. I think I hit harder than I meant to, but nice job. Add some good punches into your arsenal, and you'll be doing well."

Phina began to smile but remembered John Grimes was waiting for her. She nodded in thanks, then turned to follow Alina.

As Phina approached the door, she glanced back to find Todd watching her. As her eyes connected with his, a flare of something she couldn't put a name to crossed his face. Phina had a feeling she would see him again. She just hoped it wouldn't end with his fist in her stomach as it had today. She put a hand to her sore stomach with a grimace and followed John Grimes out the door.

· · ·

QBBS *Meredith Reynolds*, Lance Reynold's Office

Alina had been told to head home, and she left with a worried glance back toward Phina. The girl nodded at her best friend and followed the large man to another section of the station. Her eyes began to wander as she noticed the area he led her to seemed more official, which caused her nervousness to grow. As Phina walked into the room John Grimes had brought her to, her eyes darted to the man on the other side of the desk.

Holy crumbs!

General Lance Reynolds. Empress Bethany Anne's father. The man who had almost single-handedly built the Empire's military from the small force of around forty people on Earth to the group of tens of thousands it was today, almost thirty years later. Well, Empress Bethany Anne had done a lot to make that happen too, and Dan Bosse had handled most of the logistics, but it was well-known her father had taken the reins for her in the day-to-day matters.

In short, the General was the second most important and powerful person in the entire Empire. And he was standing...er, sitting right in front of her. Before Phina could gather her wits to leave, the door shut behind her. She was stuck.

General Reynolds pointed with his cigar at a metal ergonomic chair on the other side of his desk. "Sit down, please."

As she walked to the chair he had indicated, Phina realized a poised woman had been sitting off to the side, looking rather elegant in a dress suit. The woman faced the

General, so Phina thought it likely they had been talking before she entered the room.

While Phina sat on the surprisingly comfortable seat, the man put the stub of the cigar back in his mouth and looked at her. She felt uneasy, certain he was assessing everything. She wished she had the ability to read minds Bethany Anne was rumored to possess.

Only in the sporadic and very cryptic files she had found on back channels, of course.

The General took the cigar out again and pointed it at her. "So, Seraphina Grace Waters." He tilted the tip up as he inclined his head and considered her. "'Phina Waters.' 'Sera Waters.' Pretty name."

She sat very still and tried to keep her surprise from showing on her face. Phina wondered if he was trying to point out that he knew all the variations she had used on the identification and passes she had made for herself over the past several years. *If so, touché, General.*

"Thanks, but I can't take any credit for my name. That was all my parents."

The deceptively young-looking man smiled in appreciation. "True." He sobered and looked regretful. "I'm sorry you lost both of them. We do try to keep from deploying both parents at the same time. I'm not sure how we missed them."

Phina nodded, appreciating the thought, then shrugged. "It was what they wanted. They had different last names, and both wanted to serve in the Marines. They knew what they were signing up for, and they could have asked for a reassignment if they had wanted one."

"Well, we appreciate their service and sacrifice." He looked at her sharply but with a note of understanding. "Just as we appreciate that you no longer hold Bethany Anne or the rest of us to blame for any mistakes that were made."

Phina's eyes widened in surprise. Just how much did they know about her? She became even more unsettled. The General nodded and gestured at the woman near him.

"I was going to handle this myself, but I need to take care of another situation. Those damned Leath are on the move again. This is Anna Elizabeth Hauser. She now knows everything I know and will ask you more questions to determine what we should do with you." He gave her a look she could have interpreted as either "Don't screw up" or "You're already screwed, so you might as well tell us everything." Her stomach dropped as she thought of all the possible things they could decide to do with her.

He nodded at Anna. "All yours." He and his cigar left the room, the door swishing shut behind him. Phina stared blankly after the man, wondering what had come up with the Leath. There hadn't been anything serious on her intelligence radar, but she supposed she could have missed something. Her fingers itched to take out her tablet and check.

"This isn't the first time you've been in this office, is it, Phina?"

Her head whipped back to the woman who had taken the General's seat. Her breath caught as Anna's words sank in, and she let it out very slowly. She had heard the General was a very smart and crafty man, but she had not heard much about Anna Elizabeth Hauser. She didn't know what to think. "I'm not sure what you mean."

"By all accounts, you are very intelligent and clever, but there's one thing you forgot when you were doing your research, practicing your skills, and having your adventures."

Phina swallowed. It *was* possible, especially considering where she currently sat—not that she liked to think about failure. It irritated her, causing her to work harder so she didn't fail again.

"What did I forget?"

Anna smiled gently. "That Reynolds, Meredith, and of course, ADAM, are always watching."

Phina blinked. Meredith had been the station's Electronic Intelligence, or EI, since the station was built shortly before Empress Bethany Anne had taken the best and brightest people from Earth into unknown space to fight the Kurtherians. Unknown space for humans, at least. She knew from her privately sourced— read, "hacked"— documents that Reynolds was the EI handling all of the station's defensive capabilities. ADAM she had only heard rumors about, although she had found stray pieces of information while she moved through the systems that made her wonder if the entity was a badly kept secret. She felt stupid, though, for not having taken into account that Meredith might have noticed. She had thought the EI would be too busy running the rest of the station to pay attention to someone as small and unimportant as Phina. How very short-sighted of her.

"ADAM?" Phina asked warily. Perhaps she could find out more about the elusive being.

"Hello, Phina." The familiar voice came through the speakers. Hold on. ADAM's was the voice she had heard early that morning when she was acquiring the passes and official workout gear! That meant the AI had known what she was doing all along.

Phina sighed as she began absently answering the questions the sharp and elegant woman asked her. Being a spy was a lot harder than her dad's stories had led her to believe.

CHAPTER ONE

QBBS *Meredith Reynolds*, Lance Reynolds' Office

"So," Anna Elizabeth Hauser finished, "the question, Seraphina Waters, is what should we do with you?" She lightly tapped her fingertips on the desk as she watched Phina closely.

Phina didn't know what the elegant woman expected to see revealed on her face. She never thought of herself as anything special in appearance, being more concerned about her skills instead. Her mid-length, dark, wavy hair was easy to brush or pull back into a braid when needed. Her startling green eyes, dusky skin, and the chin her aunt had told her often was far too stubborn for her own good gave her character, in her own opinion.

She cleared her throat as Anna clasped her hands together. "Just call me Phina, please. What *are* you going to do with me…uh…ma'am?"

She expected it to be bad news. After all she had only hacked into the system for information, stolen…ahem, *borrowed* the workout clothes she currently wore, created a fake key pass, and broken into the Marine and Guardian workout room with her best friend before being escorted to General Lance Reynold's office by John Grimes for the serious conversation that had just taken place. And that was just in the last twenty-four hours.

Anna winced. Was it something she had said? *All right,* Phina thought. *No calling Anna "ma'am." That's good to know.*

"I thought that answer would be obvious, as smart as you are, Phina. You are a bored hyper-intelligent woman in need of a challenge. You exhibit compassion, loyalty, ethics, and morality in quantities unusual for your age. You obviously know how to hack a system since you did it to ours, you catch on to other languages quickly and in an interesting way and have learned to sneak into various secure places with your skills. You will need to join classes and train hard in several different areas, particularly hand-to-hand and weapons." The woman tilted her head before she went on, spreading her hands as she smiled. "Phina, we are going to give you a job."

"May I ask what kind of job?" Phina's eyes widened, and her heart began to race. She was afraid to hope she could continue to fulfill the vow she had made to her parents' memory.

Anna raised her eyebrows, though Phina saw a twinkle of amusement in her eyes. "I am looking to put together a small diplomatic and intelligence team. With your language skills, I think you would be a perfect fit." She leaned forward expectantly.

"Diplomatic team?" Phina's heart sank. Diplomacy, as in talking to people she didn't know? That wasn't the kind of work she wanted, but it was better than being arrested—or thrown out an airlock. She had heard stories of Empress Bethany Anne's temper and what she did to those who went against the needs of the Empire. Phina shuddered, then let out a breath.

"And intelligence." Anna Elizabeth smiled as if she had read the thoughts floating through Phina's head. "The job comes with some side work that will keep you from being bored."

Hmm, diplomacy and intelligence didn't sound *too* bad. "What kind of side work?"

Anna grinned. "What else? Stealthy information acquisitions. When the team isn't being used for diplomacy, it will gather intelligence for the Empire. Often it will be both."

Phina's eyes lit as she heard her favorite term for being a spy, and she grinned back.

Anna assessed her. "There is a catch."

Her hope withered and her smile dimmed. Phina knew the offer had been too good to be true. "What kind of catch?"

Anna straightened and looked Phina in the eye. "This team needs time to develop, and you need time to learn and train. I see the team coming together sometime after you graduate."

Phina's eyes widened. "Graduate?"

The elegant woman smiled as she nodded, but her face showed the seriousness of the situation. "From the Diplomatic Institute. I would like you to join the Diplomatic Corps prior to joining the team. The Institute is newly revamped as of last year to train our diplomats. The first semester of the new year begins in three weeks."

Anna Elizabeth searched Phina's face. "What do you think? Would you like to join our Diplomatic Corps?"

Phina wondered what would happen if she said no. Would the woman just tell her, "Off you go, angel." as her mother had often done when she was alive? A deep pang twinged in her chest at the thought. Or would Anna get the disappointed look on her face that Phina often saw on her Aunt Faith? Not so fun, but Phina had grown used to it. Or would Anna Elizabeth forget all about being nice and have security escort her to the nearest airlock? That option guaranteed pain as well as death.

Diplomacy still didn't sound like much fun—she envisioned people sitting around an elaborate table, using fancy words she would never use in normal conversation—but if gathering intelligence would still be in the picture, even in the future, it might be worth it.

"What happens if I say no?"

Anna looked thoughtful a moment before she responded. "What do you see yourself doing for the rest of your life, Phina? Finding some way to earn money while you travel around gathering information that *might* be compromising for the Empire, then sending a warning to us?"

Since that had been more or less what Phina had envisioned, her eyes widened in surprise. Still watching Anna, she slowly nodded.

Anna gave her a small smile as she leaned forward. "I understand the Corps isn't exactly what you envisioned. However, if you agree, I think you will find yourself pleasantly surprised, and before too long, you will have a satisfying career ahead of you."

Phina's gaze fell to her fidgeting fingers as she tried to process her disappointment and this new direction. If she wasn't in any avenue related to spying now, how would she have time to search out information harmful to the Empire? Would she still have time around doing all these new diplomatic courses Anna wanted her to learn?

"I'll make a deal with you." Phina started at Anna's words and glanced up to meet the woman's serious eyes. "If you agree and join the Corps, in six months, you can go and do whatever you like with the Empire's full support, if that's what you still want."

Phina's eyes grew huge as she realized that Anna basically offered her a blank check. She just needed to suffer through six months of boring diplomat school, and she would be more than free. She would be set for the life she had dreamed about.

Taking a deep breath, Phina nodded. "All right, I'll give it a try."

Anna's eyes warmed as she smiled. Was that relief in her eyes? Her shoulders did seem to relax. That sent Phina's thoughts whirling until the woman spoke again.

"I'm happy to hear it. Welcome to the Corps, Phina."

Phina blinked, then straightened in her chair. "You are part of the Corps, too?"

The woman nodded, appearing every bit as poised and put together as the first moment Phina had seen her well over an hour ago. "Yes, I'm the Dean of the Diplomatic Institute and the Head Diplomat of the Diplomatic Corp." When she saw Phina still frowning in confusion, she clarified, "Basically, I'm in charge of everything related to diplomacy. You are on the young side compared to most of our students, but I have full confidence you will fit into the Corps just fine."

Phina considered while she absently rubbed her sore stomach, then her arms. Todd certainly punched hard, or maybe her muscles were just soft. Though it didn't hurt as much as it had earlier. Anna's words pulled Phina from her musings. "Which brings me to my next question. How do you think your aunt will react to this news?"

The question caused Phina's arms to drop as she gave a loud sigh. "Honestly? I'm not sure. She responds differently every time I approach her about something. It's like an extreme case of moodiness. Also, even if she initially approves something, she could very easily change her mind later."

Anna's blue eyes showed a sympathy Phina wasn't expecting. How much did this woman know about her and Aunt Faith? She thought back to the General's comment when he'd introduced Anna Elizabeth before he left the room. "She now knows everything I know." Crumbs. Does the General know? If the General knew, then from what they said earlier, ADAM knew. If ADAM knew... Phina stopped that line of thinking. If Empress Bethany Anne knew every tiny factoid about her life, Phina didn't want to know. The Empress had been far too intimidating at her last appearance for Phina to feel comfortable completing the thought.

Her attention was pulled back when Anna sighed. "Unfortunately, I'm not surprised. However, classes are three weeks away, so you will have time to acclimate her to the idea. You can decide when it's best to inform her."

Phina nodded. With her eighteenth birthday only

thirty-six hours away, the smartest move might be to wait until then. That way, Phina would be an adult and her aunt couldn't legally ship her off to Estaria, the rumored new home for those humans who wanted life on an established planet, or somewhere equally in the middle of nowhere and away from everything Phina wanted to accomplish. She *could* come right back after her birthday, but why create unnecessary expense and headache when it was easily avoided just by being patient?

"I'll send you a message on your tablet so you know when and where your classes begin." Anna smiled encouragingly. "Until then, you have time to reassure your friend Alina, break the news to your aunt, and get yourself ready."

Phina understood the first two things. Alina had been sent back to her apartment while Phina had been brought here to meet the General, and she would be a nervous wreck until she knew Phina wasn't in trouble for their adventure this morning. Her Aunt Faith would need some time to get used to the idea, but... "Get ready? Is there something I need to do to prepare?" Visions of new workouts, tests, and acquiring new skills flew through her head.

She received a grin. "Get ready for your life to change. Trust me, Phina, you won't be the same person by the end of your time in the Corps. Better to brace yourself now."

Phina nodded slowly, her thoughts reeling as she wondered just how the woman expected things to be different by the end. She heard a light cough and looked up.

Anna raised her eyebrows, eyes amused, then held out a hand toward the door.

"Oh. Right. Okay, I'll see you later." Phina pushed

herself up and headed for the door. With one last glance at Anna Elizabeth, who still looked elegant and beautiful as she sat in the General's chair, she left the room.

Though Phina remained lost in thought as she walked back down the hallway to the more public areas, she couldn't help noticing John Grimes, the personal guard of the Empress, with his large frame in front of one of the doors, eyes tracking her movements. Her heart began to pound. The Empress must be behind that door.

As she passed him, looking everywhere except at him in her nervousness, she heard his deep voice. "Happy Birthday, Phina." She paused, then turned just in time to see his wink. "Try to stay out of trouble."

Surprised by the whole situation, Phina could only nod and say thank you. She felt dazed. These important and famous people in the Empire all seemed to know about her. She was now joining a group of people that would be pivotal to the future of the Empire. Though not enamored of the idea of diplomatic talks, Phina was aware of how strategically important the Corps could be. No matter what she thought of the work they did when it came to her personally, she knew if the diplomats did their job right, they could shape the future of the Empire, even though most people might never know their names.

Who was Phina to become part of that? Still, she hoped there would be some real spying in the near future, or she might space herself to escape.

She left the office area, and instead of heading straight home, she meandered toward the main deck. The ache in her stomach and arms was easing, and Phina liked to walk around when she had things on her mind and needed to clear her head. As of this morning, Phina had more on her mind than she knew what to do with.

QBBS *Meredith Reynolds*, Lance Reynolds' Office

Anna Elizabeth looked up at the quiet knock that preceded the opening door. Her visitor stepped in and viewed her with a face devoid of expression.

"Is it done?"

She nodded. "It's done."

"What did she say?"

"She explained her thoughts and the motivations behind her decisions, which didn't deviate far from what you suspected. She also didn't admit to anything right away, just as you thought."

The visitor snorted. "Of course not. She's not a cursed idiot."

"No, she isn't. She did forget that ADAM and Meredith watch just about everything that happens on the station." Anna raised her eyebrows, waiting.

She received a wave to continue and watched as her visitor began to pace within the confines of the office. She didn't think the space worked all that well for the activity, though it didn't seem to bother the nondescript person in front of her. "That doesn't concern me since she's not interacted with the digital entities much at all, ADAM especially. It's easy to forget."

Anna nodded in agreement. "She was honestly shocked that we knew everything she had done since she began to learn her spy skills, including everything about her parents' unfortunate deaths and her vow to her parents' memory. Also that she showed the wisdom to see the larger picture instead of casting blame."

"The picture that she knows about, anyway. "

Anna had to strain to hear the mumbled words but decided not to comment on them. "You were also right about why she started spying and sneaking around, the reasons she purposely got Bs in her high school classes as well as failed the Etheric Academy entrance exam—so that she would sneak under the radar of recruitment—and…"

Brown eyes narrowed. "And what?"

"She expected to get caught." Anna's face looked slightly sour as she watched her visitor stop with their head thrown back to laugh. She rolled her eyes.

"How much was it again?"

"Ten." She reached for her tablet to complete the transaction.

"Wasn't it fifteen?"

"It was ten." She spoke firmly as she shook her blonde-and gray-haired head at the familiar interaction.

"So, old friend, what did I get wrong?"

"For heaven's sake, I am not old!" Anna glared at her "old friend" as she set the tablet down harder than warranted.

"I'm old, and you're…what, twenty years older than I am?"

Anna disliked that she so easily reacted to the visitor's taunt since it felt like a loss of control. She much preferred to be in control of herself at all times. Anna took a moment to relax the tension in her shoulders before smiling as sweetly as she could manage. "And you know I had help."

"It's a good gig if you can get it. Having Bethany Anne

give you her blood to regenerate cells and become younger—"

"It was an emergency since I was shot, and as I've told you before, I don't remember any of it." Her eyes narrowed as if daring her friend to say more about it. Anna Elizabeth had been caught by a bullet at a diplomatic event before the Empire had left Earth, and only Bethany Anne's nanocyte-rich blood had saved her. Not only had the blood healed her wounds, but it had also taken twenty years off her body. Years that, in the time since, had been slowly making themselves known again.

Hands raised in surrender. "So, what did I get wrong?"

"She learned her acrobatics from an old neighbor who was a retired Olympian." Her shoulders relaxed more now that they had switched to a less personal topic.

"Gymnastics, and yes, I just found that out this morning. What else?" Intense eyes bored into her as her friend stepped closer.

Anna raised her eyebrows at the news and her resulting impatience. "All right. The other thing you got wrong was that she apologized to ADAM for snapping at him in the heat of the moment this morning."

"Well, he had been a surprising voice in her head through her implant..." Her visitor's lips pursed in thought before smiling. "Excellent."

As her friend walked toward the door, Anna raised her voice. "One question. How did you know she would hesitate to say yes and need me to offer the six months?"

Her old friend winked as they opened the door and stepped through.

"Experience."

. . .

Etheric Empire, Planet of the Baldere

Glaeken felt a presence that sent chills up his spine. He had never experienced such a sensation before and didn't know what it meant. His considerable intellect rejected ignorance and regarded the situation while he continued to walk back to the commune through the darkness.

He had to share what he had just discovered while carrying out his duties with his brothers. The dishonor to their people was too great to ignore. Just a few more blocks and he could mentally connect with those of his siblings who lived with him in the commune.

His mental senses pinged. Another presence joined the first, then a third. The darkness couldn't hide the tremor that froze him in place for a moment, his staff wobbling in his grasp. He wasn't one to succumb to the pressure of fear, valuing critical thought more than emotional outburst, but something about these presences caused his long, lanky body to shiver. When a fourth presence joined the other three, he jolted out of his paralysis and continued walking at a faster pace.

Glaeken bypassed Baldere and other alien life forms as they crowded into and around bars, restaurants, and clubs. Rather than being centered around food or dancing, however, these establishments focused on the main thing the Baldere valued most—fighting. Glaeken would have found shelter with those raucous beings, but he didn't think they would provide any protection for him. He was an alien to them, and he valued life and knowledge over fighting. The Baldere had no reason to help him. He would be better served by finding his brothers.

He sped down the street, turning corners when needed to try to lose his pursuers as well as reach his brothers faster. Though lights hung suspended from the buildings, they were not frequent enough to illuminate the whole street, only creating wide circles along his path. When he reached the end of the next patch of light, there was a noise behind him. He spun, and his cloak flared in the air.

Four Baldere stepped out of the darkness, the light glinting off the tops of their bald, ribbed heads. Their faces appeared fierce and determined, and their purple skin gleamed. The weapons in their hands showed him their actions were not for peace. His two hearts beat faster when he realized these were the four presences he had sensed.

Only now, with these four Baldere so close, did he realize that though their intellects were not high enough to reach his mental wavelength, his telepathy had been warning him of their intentions.

His death.

"Just come with us nice and quiet, hey?"

The Baldere took another step forward with his hand extended. Glaeken's brow furrowed as he tried to deduce what the male reached for and came up with the intention to take his staff or to take him prisoner.

"I'll pass, thank you," he whispered before swallowing roughly.

"He's a polite one, eh, Narvid? Not like that other one." The Baldere to the far right spoke as he elbowed the male next to him.

He received a scathing look in return. "Get off me, Vodin."

Glaeken's eyes narrowed as the three fingers and the thumb of his left hand tightened on his staff. "That other one" Vodin mentioned must have been Dreuved, who had disappeared several days ago. His absence had caused Glaeken to be in his current situation since his task had been to search for his fellow Gleek's whereabouts.

"You have dishonored us by his death." Glaeken's voice at full volume sounded raspy and harsh from disuse since he was accustomed to speaking mentally with his brothers.

The Baldere exchanged glances and shifted their feet, looking uneasy.

"*Vrukk!*" the last Baldere to speak muttered. "He sounds like the dead."

Vodin and Narvid began to whisper to each other in uneasy tones, causing the Baldere in charge to hiss at them. "Quiet, you empty-headed snakes-for-brains! This is what the boss said needs to happen."

First one, then the others nodded and looked more confident, which didn't bode well for Glaeken. In one-on-one combat, Glaeken felt certain he could take them. Though his people did not study weaponry and combat with the zeal of the Baldere, they had developed a fighting style of their own that took advantage of their longer limbs and staff work. However, having dishonored his people once, he had no faith these Baldere would show any honor now.

Glaeken ran with all the swiftness available to him and reached the edge of his brothers' mental range. He hoped the Baldere weren't aware of the capabilities the Gleek possessed. They might not save him, but they would at least ensure his brothers were enlightened with the truth.

The Baldere ran swiftly behind him, the pieces of their body protection clinking against each other the only sounds in the night. Glaeken had just established his mental connection into the collective consciousness of his brothers when a hard impact to his back knocked him to his knees. He gave a cry of pain.

What's going on?

Who did that?

Why are you in pain, brother?

His brothers' voices clamored in his mind, trying to understand what had caused his mental cry to pierce their quiet murmurings. Even as he began flinging words into the mix to explain what happened, he felt pain and his blood seeping down his clothing onto the street.

Glaeken was dead.

The Gleek knew it even before the Baldere leader came up to him and pulled the weapon out of his back. Glaeken's hand slipped off his staff as he swayed on his knees and fell forward, his face scraping the pavement.

Traekor, the leader of their commune, pushed forward in his thoughts. *Brother Glaeken, your thoughts are not clear except for your pain. What has happened?*

As one of the Baldere stood above him, lifted his weapon, and swiftly brought it down, Glaeken had little time for thought before the darkness.

We have been greatly dishonored. Dreuved and I have been killed and our bodies taken—

CHAPTER TWO

QBBS *Meredith Reynolds*, Marine Training Facilities

Maxim threw off the hold Peter had on him and darted back, then dodged left as Todd came in swinging. The punch caught his side but didn't slow him down as he twisted to meet Peter's kick with a knee block.

Then both men came at him with blows and kicks and holds one after the other, so quickly that he reacted more than had a chance to attack. The two were lethal individually. Putting them together felt like a rising tide where he drowned inch by inch.

Finally he called a halt, reached for his water, and downed half the large bottle. As he wiped his mouth with the back of his hand, Peter and Todd came up and clapped him on the shoulder. As tall as Maxim stood, he was eye to eye with the two men he had idolized for years.

Peter gave him a grin as he stepped back. "You have definitely grown into your big hands and feet!"

Maxim raised an eyebrow. "I would hope so since it's

been some years since I rattled around on feet too big for me."

Todd elbowed his best friend with a smirk. "He just doesn't want to get more sentimental. Tears would affect his manly image."

Peter lunged and began wrestling with the large man, finally pinning Todd down due to his larger bulk as a Wechselbalg—a shape changer those on Earth would have called a werewolf, even though the folktales had gotten things wrong. Peter grunted as he let go and pushed himself up. "Manly image, my ass."

Maxim grinned at the familiar ritual. "I'm sure your ass is very manly." He blanched as the others began hooting in laughter. "I mean, I'm sure the women find it so."

Peter gasped for air and pounded Maxim's back in appreciation, which felt more like punishment. "That was priceless. I think you need a woman of your own, my man."

Todd grinned and continued the thought. "A woman definitely would keep your attention off Peter's manly ass."

Maxim shook his head with a grimace. "I hate you both."

"Nah," Peter declared as he reached for his towel to wipe the sweat off his chest. "You love us. We keep you on your toes."

"Need a little help with finding one?" Todd inquired as he picked up his tablet.

"A woman?" Maxim asked in surprise before shaking his head. He reached for a towel of his own as he thought about it. "Finding a woman isn't the problem. You shake a stick on this hunk of asteroid we call a station, and half a dozen women show up."

"Well, if it's a manly stick." Peter grinned, then turned to throw his towel in the hamper at the side of the room.

"And it's not like we are roughing it on the space station with how developed it's become," Todd added, his tone absent as he scrolled through his messages. "So, if finding a woman isn't the problem, what is?"

"The problem is finding one that interests me and is interested in me for more than my...well, manliness. Outer self." Maxim struggled to explain his half-formed thoughts as he wiped himself off before shrugging and throwing the towel in the bin. English still didn't feel like his first language, even though he felt much more comfortable with it in the years since he had come to space from Russia. "Not like I have a lot of time in between assignments."

Todd shot Maxim a piercing glance before exchanging looks with Peter that he couldn't interpret. Todd handed Peter his tablet. Peter scanned it, then looked up with a grin.

"Not enough time to find a woman between assignments? Then I've got the perfect assignment for you. It requires you to remain on the base for the foreseeable future—at least several months. Bound to find a woman in that time if you tried."

Maxim's eyes darted between the two men as he subconsciously changed his stance to be ready for a fight. "What does this assignment entail?"

Peter scanned the tablet again, then handed it back to Todd. "Nothing strenuous. Just teaching a girl how to fight."

Maxim was puzzled and scratched the back of his neck, where he felt a strange tingle. "Why does this person need a Guardian to teach her how to fight? Why not one of your Marines?"

Todd shrugged. "I could assign one, yeah, but she's going to need special training that isn't usually taught to the core Marines. You've taught girls how to fight before, so you have the patience, and you seem to be available." Todd gestured at Peter, Maxim's leader in more ways than one.

Maxim let out a breath that wasn't quite a sigh, then nodded. "Is it all right if I assess her to make sure she's trainable and we work well together first?"

Todd nodded soberly as he tapped the tablet before putting it away. "That sounds like a good idea, though I doubt you will have a problem there."

Maxim's interest piqued. "Oh? Who is this girl?"

The Were and the Guardian exchanged glances again before Todd answered, "The girl from this morning. Her name is Seraphina Waters."

"The one who jumped over you like a grasshopper?" Maxim queried, a small grin on his face.

"The very one." Todd had a faint smile, but his eyes were sending Maxim a message he wasn't quite reading. "So, see how things work between you. I have a feeling she will learn quickly."

Maxim nodded, then straightened and gathered his things. "I'll do my best."

"Yup, see how things work." Peter grinned as he gathered his own stuff. "You can always just shake your manly stick at her."

Sniggering laughter followed him from the room as Maxim yelled back, "I *really* hate you both."

He shook his head as he asked Meredith to find the young woman for him. Peter was right; he did love them, even though they could be royal pains in the ass.

QBBS *Meredith Reynolds*, Secluded Hallways

Phina took the roundabout way home, still weighing everything that had happened. Since Anna Elizabeth had offered the invitation to her, she could be sure ADAM knew about it already. The AI had been silent in the meeting with Anna Elizabeth after everything had come to light. Phina kind of missed hearing ADAM's voice in her head. Given that the first time he spoke to her she had hit her head on a sharp corner of an air vent, that was saying something.

She had been angry about his intrusion and interference at the time, but ADAM had worn her down until she had grown concerned about him and crossed that boundary into friend territory. Since Alina was currently the only name on Phina's friend roster, that thought scared her a little. Still, though he wouldn't be a conventional friend, she thought it might be worth giving him a chance.

"Excuse me."

Phina broke off her thoughts as she noticed a tall, broad sandy-haired man walking next to her. She stopped suddenly and turned to face him, and he did the same. Alina would ogle the handsome man, but Phina felt highly suspicious after everything that happened over the last twenty-four hours.

"What do you want?"

His brown eyes looked startled at her tone, then amused. Phina sighed and tried again more politely.

"Is there something I can help you with?"

A fist flew toward her face.

Rather than the gymnastics moves she had used this morning with Todd, this time, Phina merely dodged to the side. Her adrenaline ramped up quickly as she avoided another punch to her stomach by flinging herself back.

Who was this man, and why would he attack her?

Tall, Blond, and Overly Muscled hardly looked like he was exerting himself; he was almost lazy in his movements. After avoiding a leg sweep, Phina decided she needed more distance, so she quickly did a back handspring sequence that took her down the hall. After straightening, she winced to see the tall man staring after her with a slight smile on his face. Well, winced for more reasons than one. She would be sore in the morning after all the sudden movements without stretching first, and her stomach and arms still twinged from Todd's punches.

Phina blinked as he rapidly approached and stopped right in front of her, her breath catching at how quickly he had moved. Could this man be one of the vampires she had heard so much about? Aside from rumors about Bethany Anne, Phina hadn't yet been able to find any details on those elusive people; she had only found brief mentions of them in the files. Her efforts had been blocked—now that she thought about it, she realized ADAM had done the blocking—so her scraps of information about them came from rumors.

She watched him step closer until he stood within her personal space. She tilted her head and tried to figure him out. He had attacked her but then acted like he wasn't even trying. He possessed better than normal human looks, more on the rugged side than beautiful. He stared at her as if he expected the force of his gaze would cause her to look away. Ah.

"Wechselbalg?" Phina used the official name of the wolf shifters who were often soldiers called Guardians.

Surprised, the crazy man nodded and relaxed.

"What was the point of that?"

He frowned as if something was off. Perhaps he had thought she would be a pushover? If so, he was in for a surprise. "I thought I would find you and assess where your skills are."

Phina raised an eyebrow and crossed her arms as she stood back a step to get more space. "I'm still not understanding who you are or why you would attack me."

Maxim seemed puzzled. "You don't know?" He cursed, then shook his head. "I'm Maxim. I've been assigned to train you. Are you sure you haven't gotten some sort of communication about it?"

Phina narrowed her eyes at the man Alina had always idolized, but this seemed too weird a story to make up. Holding up a finger, she went to pull her small tablet out of her pocket and realized she still wore the same stretchy, body-conforming workout clothes she had dressed in that morning. While they were comfortable, the small pocket that had held her now-confiscated key card had not been large enough to hold her tablet, so that item currently rested on Alina's bed, along with the clothes she had worn that morning.

She let out a sigh. "I don't have my tablet on me. Would I be able to use yours?"

The corner of his mouth curled up before he nodded and pulled his tablet out. As he did so, she strove not to grumble at the man. He had scared her half to death when she thought he would hurt her, and now he was being all helpful. Phina didn't like it but knew she could do little to him that would make any difference. Weres were hard to permanently injure, let alone kill, and more so if they could change into that powerful third form, the Pricolici. The way Phina's luck had gone today, she wouldn't make any bets against him having that scary alter ego.

Phina's fingers flew over the tablet, checking her inbox first and finding nothing. She decided to be thorough and do a search in the servers for all mail containing her name that had been sent today. There were several that piqued her curiosity, but she only opened the message from Anna Elizabeth to Todd Jenkins and Peter Silvers, asking if there was someone they could assign to train her for several months on a semi-permanent assignment. They must have assigned Maxim the job.

Phina wanted to protest on principle or walk away from the man and ignore the directive. However, she recognized this had more to do with her mindset and her stubbornness rising than his actions. She'd just had too many changes and revelations happening in one day. She needed to clear her thoughts somehow before she bit off someone's head.

Bit off someone else's head…as a wolf would…

Phina snorted softly at her musings as she returned the tablet, then stepped back and nodded. He had been silently watching and likely assessing her. Maxim nodded back. Perhaps he realized she felt overwhelmed and needed some space. "Any preference on what time to meet?"

She thought for a moment, then told him the truth. "I usually train in the mornings before breakfast and school, then in the afternoons when school gets out. I've kept that up since graduating."

He raised his eyebrows. "You train?"

Phina raised her eyebrows. "Yes, Man of Few Words. Train. You don't know much about me, so no quips." Never mind that it was agility and climbing she trained herself in more than fighting.

He shrugged, his expression displaying interest but also watchfulness. "I don't need to know much about you personally to begin training you. It's part of the process. Better to find out where your skills are at directly and figure out where to go from there than to assume I know what you need."

She sighed. "Fine, but I need to get back and change. If you still want to talk, you can walk with me, I guess. Otherwise, let me know when to meet you."

When she turned to walk away, he fell into step next to her, so she supposed that was her answer.

They left the quieter back hallways where Maxim had found her wandering and entered the busy corridors that led toward where Alina lived. It was quite a hike since Phina had been distracted and hadn't cared how far out into the station she wandered. She usually avoided the trams so as not to get lazy or to cool down or keep her muscles toned. She didn't hear a peep of complaint from him as she did that now, and she grudgingly wondered about him.

"This is not where the records say you live," he finally remarked as they drew closer to Alina's house.

"No, it's my friend's house. I left my stuff here this morning."

He nodded, amusing Phina with his lack of verbosity. She tended to be quiet and was used to being around Alina, who could talk your ear off if she felt like it. Maxim didn't seem to care that they weren't conversing about the training she needed, the very reason he had supposedly come with her. Odd man. Was he just respecting her need for space?

Leaving the collection of humans and aliens behind when they reached the hall leading to Alina's apartment, Phina began to wonder in what state she would find her friend. Alina had seemed anxious that morning when Phina left to follow John Grimes after being caught in the training room. And even if she had thought of it, Phina hadn't been able to send Alina a message to let her know she was all right because her tablet was on her friend's bed. Fudging crackers. Alina would be pissed. She walked a little faster, not surprised to find Maxim's pace matching hers.

She hesitated for a moment before ringing the bell. The tone had barely died before the door opened and Alina threw herself into Phina's arms, sobbing her heart out. Startled, Phina reflexively hugged her friend back.

"I've...been...waiting...hours!" she finally got out through her tears and ragged breathing. Alina managed to get her crying under control and pulled back, wiping her face with her sleeve, then punched Phina in the arm.

"Ow!" Phina frowned at her friend as she rubbed the rapidly bruising area. Alina was definitely mad, according to the evidence she'd left on Phina's body. The harder Alina punched, the more upset she was—which was, of course, Phina's fault.

"Why did you take so long?" Alina glared at her, eyes sparking with fury.

Phina sighed. "I'm sorry. They were talking to me for a long time, and then I just wandered around, trying to process things in my head. I should have tried to let you know. I'm a horrible friend."

"Yes, you should have." Alina's tone was biting, but Phina knew her well enough to tell that she was softening. They had been friends almost since they were babies. Alina knew her thoughts only wandered when she felt over-whelmed.

Phina glanced over to see Maxim standing a few feet away, dressed in workout clothes only slightly less form-fitting than she wore. Though he looked concerned, he had a small smile on his face as he watched Alina.

Her friend followed Phina's glance to Maxim, and she barely avoided squawking in dismay. Alina grabbed Phina's arm and pulled her into the house as Phina looked back and gestured for Maxim to follow. He did and stood next to the door as Alina shut it, then continued to pull Phina down the hall to her room while she yelled behind them, "Be right back!"

Used to this treatment in a general sense, though not to this degree, Phina knew Alina would be on overload herself. She just kept quiet, letting the girl draw her into the room and shut the door gently behind them. Her friend left her hand in place for a moment as she visibly took a breath to calm down.

Turning to Phina, Alina grabbed her shoulders and looked her in the eye with a funny light Phina had never seen before. "Why is Maxim standing in my living room?"

Phina tried to shrug as Alina's fingers dug in; she felt really uncomfortable. "He walked here with me."

"No. Why. Is. *Maxim. Nikolayevich.* Standing. In. My. Living. Room!" With every word, Alina shook Phina just a little harder until the pain was too bad and she pulled away.

"Ouch! Geez, Alina!" She rubbed the marks and soreness out of her shoulders as she darted confused looks at her best friend. The past day must have been too much for her, and she was going crazy. She'd never seen Alina like this before. She looked up from her shoulder to see Alina staring at the door with a strange mix of emotions on her face. Concern welled up within Phina.

"Alina?"

Her best friend seemed dazed as she stood unmoving, staring at the door. "I can't believe he's here. Do you know how often I've imagined meeting him? He's one of the hottest guys on the station. I just can't believe he's out there in my own living room."

Phina gently touched her friend's arm, startling Alina into motion as she looked down at Phina's hand in dawning horror. "I can't believe I was wearing this ratty thing and Maxim saw me!" Alina shrieked and pulled away, tearing the worn sweatshirt off as she ran toward her closet, stumbling over the heels that had been left on the floor. The blonde tore the door open and dove in. Phina just stood with a bemused look on her face.

Apparently, Alina had finally realized a handsome man stood in her living room while she still wore the ratty but comfortable sweats she couldn't ever seem to get rid of. Phina's smile faded at the thought. Alina only wore her sweats when she hung out at home and worried about something, working herself into a state. No wonder she had been so upset when Phina rang the doorbell.

Rather than watch the stream of color flying out of the closet as Alina muttered and mumbled to herself and tried to decide what to wear, Phina turned her attention to changing into her own clothes. After she finished and slid her tablet into her pocket, she felt better. She pushed her feet into her boots with a satisfied sigh.

She still wore the black jeans and green shirt from yesterday since she hadn't yet been home to get new ones. But still, slipping on her black jacket and wearing her own clothes made her feel much more the thing. She wasn't used to showing as much of her body as the workout clothes revealed since she usually trained in her bodysuit, which, though tight, fully covered everything. Her own clothes were much more to her liking.

Alina finally emerged from her closet dressed in small black shorts, a tight black crop top that sparkled when she moved, and tall black boots that zipped up. Over her outfit, she wore a red satin jacket with a bolero-style top, but the hemline extended down below the shorts. As her friend turned to put makeup on, Phina noticed that from the back, Alina's outfit looked like a minidress.

Less than a minute later, the young woman turned to her, biting her newly reddened lips. She had sprayed on some perfume as well, which joined the floral and fruity scents that already permeated the room.

"What's wrong?" Phina crossed to her and gently held her hands. "You're never like this. Is it Maxim? I'll kick him out if he makes you feel uncomfortable."

Alina looked up in shock. "No, you can't!" She shook her head, then tried to relax and smile. "No, Phina, I'm all right. I just wasn't expecting to see Maxim Nikolayevich standing outside my door." She narrowed her eyes and glared. "With my best friend of all people, who never cares about guys or how hot they are."

Phina shrugged. "I don't."

Alina protested, and Phina shrugged again. "I see it, but I don't really care how hot they are. It doesn't matter to me."

Her friend's eyes widened. "Tell me you guys aren't together!" She clutched Phina's hands. "You're not interested in him, right?"

Phina looked at her with concerned amusement. "No. Not together, and not interested. I don't even know if I like him yet."

Relieved, Alina pointed her finger from her newly heeled height, all of five inches taller—which told Phina how badly Alina wanted to make a good impression on the tall Wechselbalg—and spoke firmly. "You *are* going to like him. He's not just a hot guy, he's kind and caring and takes care of his friends and the Guardians. I've been following news of him for years. He actually reminds me of you in some ways." She narrowed her eyes to show Phina she was serious. "Speaking of which, you *are* going to tell me why he's here with you. Best friends don't keep these secrets from each other."

Phina stared at Alina for a moment, then blandly spoke. "Sure, but can I tell you later? He's been waiting for, like, ten minutes already."

Alina's eyes widened and she squeaked in alarm, threw the door open, and quickly strode out to the living room. Phina followed her and saw Maxim's eyes grow larger before he got control of himself. Phina grinned. Alina always made an impression.

CHAPTER THREE

QBBS *Meredith Reynolds*, Waters Residence

Phina opened her eyes on her first day as a legal adult. *Legal. Adult.* She would no longer be restricted by law or aunt decree in travel, education, or occupation. She could finally make her own decisions. It felt amazing. Fantastically amazing.

Since her birthday was now here, Phina would also tell her aunt she planned to join the Diplomatic Corps. Phina just hoped Faith was in a good mood. Sniffing the air, she thought there was a good chance. Pancakes for breakfast never happened when her aunt was moody, depressed, or pissed off.

Anxious to move on with her plans for the day, Phina showered and quickly dressed. Thinking about spending time with Alina later that day reminded her of the amusing twenty minutes she had witnessed yesterday. Alina hadn't been shy; she'd tried to discover everything she could about Maxim. The trainer had been drawn out of his stoic shell despite himself and seemed to really appreciate Alina.

He had left after finally making solid plans for training, and Phina expressed her surprise that Alina hadn't even tried to flirt. The girl's answer had shocked her. "Phina, when it's someone you want to have something real with, and fate steps in with the opportunity to find out if it could happen, you don't mess it up by being fake." Phina had just stared at Alina, wondering what had happened to her friend. Alina hadn't been this serious about a guy she barely knew in...well, ever.

She shook her head, still not sure what to think. She finished getting ready for the day and went to find breakfast. Her Aunt Faith stood in front of the stove wearing her simple but classic separates, fishing the last of the pancakes off the griddle. "Just a minute, sweetie." The kitchen's dimensions were small but still large enough to take a few steps while preparing meals.

Her aunt deftly placed butter between two pancakes and drenched the whole thing in fruit syrup. Aunt Faith sometimes complained about the lack of real syrup, but since maple syrup trees were scarce in space and her aunt refused to use artificial substitutes, creativity was required. After sliding the plate onto Phina's side of the table with a cup of her favorite juice, Aunt Faith finally looked up, her dark hair framing her brown eyes, and smiled as she gave Phina a hug. "Happy Birthday!"

Phina relaxed a little as she returned the hug. Apparently this really would be a good day. "Thank you, Aunt Faith."

Her aunt stepped back and winked. "You're welcome, kiddo. It's not every day that you turn eighteen and begin your adult life." She turned back to the stove to put together her own plate.

Phina cleared her throat as she sat down. "About that…" She took a drink of the juice to help loosen her throat and got distracted by the delicious fruity taste. She put her cup down to see her aunt sitting across from her, smiling at her niece's enjoyment of her favorite things. Anxious to get it over with, Phina finally blurted, "I'm going to join the Diplomatic Corps and attend the Diplomatic Institute."

"The Diplomatic Institute?" Her aunt hesitated but continued to smile as she cut a piece off her pancake and dipped it in the syrup. "Really? Are you sure you're up for it, sweetie?"

Phina frowned. "What do you mean?"

Her aunt waved her fork. "Well, you did fail the Academy exams. Are you sure this Diplomatic Institute won't be too much for you? Too stressful, maybe?"

Her mouth tightening, Phina stiffened in her seat. "Of course not!"

Aunt Faith delicately rolled the pancake around in her mouth before swallowing and eying Phina doubtfully. "Hmmm. If you say so, then suppose I must believe you."

Phina's face burned with suppressed emotion, though she responded calmly. "I can handle it, Aunt Faith. I'm not in the least concerned. Besides, isn't it my life to worry about?"

"Oh, of course. I just wonder, you know, since you did have trouble before. I promised my brother I would look out for you, and I always do my best for you."

Phina wanted to snort at that, but she kept it inside. "Well, trust me, I'm not worried at all."

"Then I won't say anything further."

"Really?" Phina couldn't believe her ears. Aunt Faith usually drove her point home in multiple ways.

Her aunt raised her eyebrows. "Yes, really. Why not? It could be a great idea."

Phina finally let out the breath and tension she had been holding and smiled. A good day for certain. "Thanks, Aunt Faith."

After finishing breakfast and cleaning up, Phina left for Alina's quarters, but not before eliciting a reminder from her aunt to be back for dinner to celebrate. "Of course, Aunt Faith! I'm bringing Alina, too."

Ignoring her aunt's comments about Alina being a nice girl aside from the way she dressed and her poor excuse for parents, Phina grabbed the bag she had packed earlier and left. Of course, with her aunt, there would be a comment of some kind, but if it had to be something, that one wasn't too bad.

Halfway to Alina's quarters, she was startled by a voice on her communicator. "Hi, Phina!"

She grinned. "ADAM!"

A Yollin clicked his mandibles in irritation next to her. She didn't need to pay attention to know a few choice words were being said. She shrugged and apologized in Yollin, hoping he could see it was genuine. After a skeptical survey of her face, he quickly moved ahead through the crowd.

"We are using your communicator. There is no need to speak out loud when you can subvocalize."

She shook her head at the slight buzzing sound from her communicator but made the correction. "Oops! Sorry,

I forgot. What have you been up to?"

She could hear his amusement. "A little of this, a little of that."

"That tells me absolutely nothing, you know."

"I know. What have you been doing?"

"Don't you know?" She teased the AI. "You do have eyes everywhere."

"Just because I can watch everything doesn't mean I do it every moment. I try to give people their privacy when I am able to do so."

"That's very considerate of you, ADAM, thank you."

"You're welcome, Phina. Are you going to tell me what has happened, or was that a deflection and you didn't want me to ask again?"

"No, it's fine. Are you aware of the rest of Anna Elizabeth's conversation with me?"

"Yes. I'm aware of all the interactions you had outside of the residences. I deemed those inside more private and didn't want to intrude."

"Do you have that policy for everyone?"

ADAM hesitated so briefly she barely noticed. "It depends on the situation. But I try to do be mindful of privacy for those who are my friends."

Phina grinned, not caring that the humans and aliens around her in the corridors could watch her smile for no reason they could see. "Are we friends, ADAM?"

"I think I would like to be, Phina."

"Settled, then."

Phina spent some time telling ADAM about Alina's reactions two days before, going into more detail after he asked questions. She approached Alina's residence as she finished relaying her morning so far with her aunt.

"Interesting."

"Right? I was completely surprised."

"Did you expect her to be mad?"

Phina hesitated as she approached Alina's door. "I hoped she wouldn't be, but yes, ADAM, I expected her to blow up."

Alina had the door open with a huge smile almost before she finished talking. "Happy birthday, birthday girl!"

>>**I'll talk to you later, Phina.**<<

"Stay if you like, ADAM. I'll let you know if it's a problem."

Phina went into the house with her friend and talked through the same events for Alina, with even more dramatic results.

Alina stared at her in shock. "This is your aunt, right?"

"Yeah, I know! I expected her to get super angry and protest more."

Alina shook her head in disbelief. "I mean, I know you joining the Diplomatic Corps is a surprise. I was surprised, and I'm your best friend!" She narrowed her eyes playfully at Phina. "But your aunt never just…agrees without more of a fight!"

Phina shook her head, then nodded. "Sometimes, but it is rare."

She wanted to forget about it and just enjoy the day, so they moved on, though it took Alina a while to calm down. Finally, after retrieving snacks and drinks, Alina moved on to some surprising news of her own.

"I have made a decision!" She sat on the arm of the

couch facing Phina, holding a half-empty glass of Coke in one hand while her other hand fluttered as she talked. Phina faced her friend with one leg tucked underneath her. She couldn't help teasing Alina a little.

"You're going to marry Maxim."

"Yes. No. What?" Alina looked flustered for the first time that day, her glass of Coke drooping to spill before Phina rescued it by reaching out and pushing it back up.

"You seemed enamored with him." Phina shrugged apologetically as she moved back. "It made me wonder what's going on in your head. He is rather on the old side compared to us, and I don't want you to get hurt."

Though Alina looked irritated, that last part deflated her, and she sighed. "I know you don't. But age shouldn't mean that much when you love someone!" She perked back up as she continued. "So, while I might love to answer your question with yes, that's not my announcement."

Phina thought it was a little sudden to be using the word love, but she waved her hand to indicate she was listening. She would have to talk to Maxim about this later. One word of encouragement from him, and Alina would be flinging herself into his arms.

"I've decided to go into fashion!" Alina smiled with excitement, but her posture seemed nervous as her hands fluttered.

"Brilliant!" Phina grinned to think about her friend's future. Alina had always been amazing at choosing fashionable clothing, so this would be a great avenue.

"Really?" Alina squealed, pushing to her feet and pulling her arms tight to her body in excitement. Phina moved just in time to catch the again forgotten Coke before it spilled.

Don't want to waste that. The Empress took Coke very seriously. She put it on the nearby table and gave Alina a huge hug.

"Really," Phina assured her. "You are awesome at putting together outfits and figuring out what looks the best on other people. It's about time for you to do it officially and get paid for it."

Alina giggled and gave Phina another hug, then danced around the room in excitement. When a dance beat came on the speakers in the room, Alina looked surprised but went with it, grinning and throwing herself into the music. Phina watched her friend for a moment, thinking this was the best birthday she had in a long time.

"Thanks, ADAM." Phina subvocalized.

>>**You're welcome, Phina. Would it help if I gave her the name and contact information of one of the designers on the station?**<<

"Alina would love that and probably be your friend for life. Thank you!"

>>**You're welcome. Go dance with her. I almost wish I could dance with you two.**<<

"You don't have a way to dance where you are in the nethersphere?"

>>**Nethersphere?**<<

"Wherever your consciousness dwells? The station is a big place, and I don't really know all of what it is you do, so I figured I would just make up a word for it."

>>**Ah, I see. And I'm not certain. I haven't really tried before.**<<

"You should try it. Dancing is definitely a must."

Taking her own advice, she began moving her body to

the beat of an old song that said everything was all right and to just dance. Dancing with Alina as ADAM made occasional comments and suggestions and her rare laugh when Alina pulled her in to dance around the room with her was the most fun she'd had recently.

After their impromptu dance party, Phina changed into her workout clothes and walked with Alina to the room where Maxim would train her. Afterward, they would head back to Phina's quarters for her birthday dinner. This time when they went through security, she had the appropriate official documentation to show she was allowed to be there. The guards didn't blink an eye about Alina joining her, either—quite a difference from last time, when she felt like they would get caught at any moment.

As they entered the smaller workout room reserved for them, Maxim turned to greet her briefly before lighting up when he saw Alina. It didn't take a genius to see they were interested in each other. The two gave little waves of greeting, then Alina sat down on a bench against the wall to watch, and Maxim turned back to scrutinize Phina as she approached.

Phina stopped a few feet away and stared at him. At this point, she didn't care if his Wechselbalg self saw it as a challenge. She needed answers, both for herself and for the state of her best friend's heart. She could see a mutual attachment forming and was concerned. She knew very little about this man and hadn't had a chance to hack his files yet, given other more pressing issues in the Empire keeping her attention. Not to mention her nervousness about starting a new school. From past experience, she knew there would only be so much his facts and files could tell her about him.

She held up a finger. "I just have one question."

Pausing, she thought about it and then held up two. "No, one question with two parts, and then an additional question."

Maxim stood watching her with his arms crossed and his head tilted just enough that he could watch both Phina and Alina with a flick of his eyes. Flick. Hmm… The man was either extremely situationally aware, or he had it just as bad for Alina as she did for him.

"Go on."

She narrowed her eyes when she heard the amusement in his voice. She wanted to be taken seriously, for fudge's sake.

"What made you chase me down in that empty hallway when I first met you?"

He focused on her and seemed to consider his words carefully before speaking. "I am a Guardian, along with my friends Drk-vaen and Ryan Wagner as seconds. When we are not deployed, I usually help train new Guardians or Marines." He paused before continuing. "That day, I was requested to meet and train a person who not only isn't a Guardian or a Marine but is also a young female with no combat experience at all." He raised his eyebrows. "Tell me, in my position, what would you have done?"

Phina nodded slowly. "I would have been curious and tried to find out more."

Maxim nodded. "Which is what I did. I wanted to find out how you would react and what you would do when you weren't expecting an attack."

"And what did you find out?"

He smiled faintly. "You definitely suck at combat."

Phina rolled her eyes and groaned. "Really? I wouldn't have known that if you weren't here to point it out, thanks." When Maxim merely raised an eyebrow, she moved on. "For the second part, why did you follow me to Alina's place instead of making the appointment and leaving?"

"It follows what I already explained. I have never had a request like this before. I saw you needed space, and I wanted to figure out more of who you are and what makes you tick. You had to be…well, special in some way for the powers that be to make such an unusual request."

Phina felt uneasy again, thinking about all these important people knowing about her. And her, special? She put it away for another time and made a face at the man. "Did you figure out everything you needed to know?"

He smiled mysteriously. "Not yet, but I will."

She gave him her signature smirk. "Well, that's not creepy at all, but fair enough." She adjusted her stance slightly so Alina was directly over her shoulder. No chance Alina could see her ask, even if she was trying. "And the second question is, what are your intentions toward Alina?"

His face turned wary. "I don't know what you mean."

"Lie."

She stood calmly, looking him in the eye. He looked surprised that she would call him on it and froze in place before he lightly sighed. "Fine. She's a nice girl, but she's still young. I would find it inappropriate to act on what is clearly an infatuation she will grow out of."

Nodding slowly, she considered that. "While she's my best friend and I'll find some way to hurt you if you take advantage of her," she gave him her best fierce stare so he knew she was serious, "I think you sell Alina short in thinking that way."

He resumed his stoic expression from earlier. "I'll take that under advisement."

She shrugged and decided to move on. Other people's love lives weren't of interest anyway, and Alina was legally an adult now, so she could do what she liked. "What are you teaching me today?"

Phina didn't think she made up the look of relief in his eyes as Maxim answered. "I thought I would tailor some fighting styles to take advantage of your flexibility and speed. With these moves, you can take down bigger opponents, which you will need with your size." Phina glanced down at her average height and build, then up at the tall, broad, and muscular man in front of her. Well, he did have a point. "Today you will begin learning the first style, which we will build on. Have you ever heard of an Earth fighting style called Sambo?"

Phina narrowed her eyes slightly as she crossed her arms. "That sounds like a snake."

Maxim smiled mysteriously. "Not a bad comparison. Now, for the first move, you stand this way…"

CHAPTER FOUR

QBBS *Meredith Reynolds*, Secluded Hallways

Phina's body shook with anger. Her aunt's reaction had never been this bad before. She stopped to close her eyes and concentrated on breathing in and out. *Just breathe. Just breathe.* Finally, she stopped shaking, but the anger remained. Phina continued walking, then sped up to run from one hallway to the next, always making sure she stayed in corridors people weren't visiting at this time of day.

Now that her body was occupied, her mind began to clear. Last night had been wonderful; she enjoyed learning how to fight a lot more than she thought she would. Then she had a small but fun birthday party with Alina and her aunt and received a few thoughtful presents. She had fallen asleep with positive thoughts.

The trouble started that morning after Phina returned from her early training session with Maxim. She'd showered and had just left her room, on the way out for the day, when Aunt Faith stopped her with a big smile like she had a secret she couldn't contain any longer.

That should have been her first clue.

"Sweetie, could I talk to you?"

"Sure, Aunt Faith."

They entered the living room and sat down. Her aunt immediately got back up and began pacing. As she watched this play back in her head, Phina realized for the first time that she got her impulse to move when she had things on her mind from her aunt. Not the first startling revelation of the day by far, but still worthy of note.

Her Aunt Faith stopped and folded her hands in front of her, squeezing them together in her excitement. "Phina, I've taken a new job!" She smiled, her brown eyes shining with happiness, clearly inviting Phina to be excited with her.

"That's great, Aunt Faith!"

That proved all the encouragement her aunt needed for the rest to come tumbling out. "Isn't it wonderful? It's on a brand-new space station, so new it doesn't even have a name yet, just a number! I'll have my own lab with brand new equipment. I'll even have a new research partner so I can continue my work. We'll have an apartment even bigger than this one. Your room will be bigger, too, with a really large closet! I've seen all the pictures, and it's really amazing. They are even building a new college on the space station and a whole new shopping area, so whether you want to go to school or get a job, you can do whatever you want. Isn't it fabulous?"

That explanation smashed her expectations.

Though her aunt grew more animated as she talked,

Phina's smile dimmed and then disappeared. Yesterday had been so easy that she felt blindsided, but she really should have known. Aunt Faith noticed Phina's frown and narrowed her eyes disapprovingly. "Phina, why aren't you happy? This is an amazing opportunity!"

Phina slowly rose to her feet and smiled carefully at her aunt. "It *is* an amazing opportunity, Aunt Faith. For you. I'm very happy that you've found a great job you will enjoy."

Her aunt scowled. "What do you mean, 'for me?' You're coming with me!"

Phina felt a tiredness that had nothing to do with how well she had slept last night. "No, Aunt Faith. I'm staying here and going to the Diplomatic Institute. I told you about this yesterday, remember? I'm joining the Diplomatic Corps."

Eyes popping out of her face, her aunt scoffed. "You weren't actually serious about that, Phina? What a joke! You think you could go through the Diplomatic Institute when you couldn't even pass the test for the Etheric Academy? What are you going to do, sleep your way through to pass your classes? I raised you better than that! After all, I did what I had to to be a parent to you after my brother and your mother passed away, and you throw this joke in my face when we finally have the opportunity to get out of this small apartment and into a decent place?"

Phina knew the woman didn't care about her wishes. Before her parents and Uncle Simon had died, her aunt had been fun and happy, and Phina had enjoyed spending time with her. When Aunt Faith took care of her while her parents were gone on assignments, her life was an extension of that. Everything had changed for them both after the battle on Karillia. Phina had just turned eleven and celebrated her birthday with her mom and dad before they left.

Phina now realized that since they'd heard the news about their family seven years ago, Aunt Faith had only ever done what she wanted or thought was right, regardless of what anyone else said. After years of suppressing her emotions to try to get along with the only parent figure she had left, Phina felt anger well up that she found difficult to control. She clenched her hands into fists and began to tremble.

Due to the effort to suppress her emotions, Phina could barely speak above a whisper to get the words out. "I'm sorry, Aunt. I'm going to the Diplomatic Institute. I'm staying here."

Her aunt's face turned red and furious. "Seraphina Grace Waters, you ungrateful little brat! You won't even have a place to live after I leave. How many times have I..."

Phina stood there, still trembling with her suppressed anger as she listened to her aunt list every way she had helped Phina over the years and every way Phina had failed to live up to her aunt's expectations and her perceived potential. How it reflected on her aunt and who she was, and what everyone had expected of her niece.

"Really, Seraphina, I'm one of the top scientists in the Empire, working on understanding the nanocytes themselves so we can do even more with them. I told everyone you were sure to get top marks on your entrance exam into the Etheric Academy! Do you know how embarrassed I was when you not only failed the exam but also got Bs in all your classes? You will never understand how hard my life is…"

When the woman finally wound down and moved on to all the ways she wished Phina had been different and how much easier Aunt Faith's life would have been if she had tried even a little harder, Phina was done. She couldn't and didn't want to hear anymore, interrupting her aunt in mid-sentence.

"Aunt Faith, I am following what I believe is the right path for me, and as fun as it sounds on that station, my place is here in the Diplomatic Institute. I'm sorry if this decision brings you pain, but I can't do anything else."

Her aunt's face had grown puffy and red from her anger, with the blood rushing to her cheeks. She glared at Phina. "You mean you won't."

Phina's spine stiffened. This moment felt like a turning point. She could buckle under to what her aunt wanted and apologize, or she could hold firm even if it broke what relationship she and her aunt had. Even knowing the potential consequences, she just couldn't buckle. Not anymore. The rest of her life was too important.

"Fine, then. I can't, and I won't. I do still wish you to be happy."

With a small head bow, she left and closed the door behind her with fingers trembling so badly she fumbled with the latch. She had quickly moved away, hoping to reach an empty corridor as soon as possible.

Now, she stopped running and stood still, her chest heaving with the emotions she had forced herself to suppress while confronting her aunt. She didn't even know what was running through her aside from anger, but she couldn't stop the tears leaking from her eyes.

She had lived with an authority figure she constantly walked on eggshells with for half her life, never knowing which aunt she would experience at any given moment. Phina resolved to stand firm in her decision. Even if her aunt made her miserable for it, she couldn't toe the line anymore. She had to break free and stand on her own.

After wiping away the tears, she slid her tablet out of her pocket, grateful for her habit of always keeping it close. Though she spelled a few words wrong due to her scattered thoughts and still-trembling fingers, she was able to send a message to Anna Elizabeth.

Told Aunt yestrday- seemed happy. Changed her mind todey. It was really bad. She's lesving for new job and wanted me to go. Said I wouldn't have a place to live here. I'm stil staying.

QBBS *Meredith Reynolds*, Anna Elizabeth's Office

Her old friend walked in, eyes blazing with anger. "What has that damned woman done now?"

Anna jerked up from watching her screen. "ADAM told you?"

"Meredith did." He scowled at the ceiling.

"I prefer not to spy on my friends, DS. I told you that."

"I'm not spying on her to get my rocks off, ADAM!"

Anna frowned as she tapped her fingers on her desk.

"Why are we, as you say, spying on her, then? You never told me, just waved your hand and said, 'Make it so.'"

"A classic!" He grinned at her impersonation, but it seemed strained.

She shook her head with a small smile. "You and your movies. Have you forgotten that I'm your boss?"

"You and Stephen, yes." He named the Nacht in charge of counterintelligence. The man sobered at her question, though his eyes remained intent. "We needed this, Anna. We are spying on her for exactly this reason." He waved his hand at the screen.

Anna lost all her humor as she took in the scene that showed Phina getting loudly berated by her aunt. Her heart grew heavy, making her want to reach out and rescue the girl. "How could she say things like this to her own niece?"

The man scowled but his eyes never left the screen. "Yes. How can parents verbally berate or abuse their own children? Yet, it happens all the time."

Anna protested. "Not on the *Meredith Reynolds*, surely? Isn't Meredith programmed to let us know when people are being harmed?"

He turned to her, anger swimming in his eyes as he gritted his teeth. "And what is Meredith's definition of harm? Does it encompass mental and emotional abuse, particularly prolonged abuse? Does she know at what point she needs to intervene and let someone know it has progressed from venting occasional frustration to abuse?"

Anna felt too stunned by his ferocity to remind him again about his behavior. She wondered what drove him to push about this since the intensity seemed unwarranted in the current situation. "I...I don't know. I thought we fixed things like this by offering mental services after that whole debacle with Anne's mom. Meredith?"

"Yes, Anna Elizabeth?"

"Could you provide any insight here that could shed light on Phina's situation and how it got to this point?"

"Apologies, Anna Elizabeth. This behavior from Faith Rochelle exceeds what she has exhibited in the past. Before today, her words could have been categorized as bickering, berating, or heavy nagging. This is the first time Faith Rochelle hit the markers for mental or emotional abuse." She paused. "However, as I review the instances over the past several years, she has gradually gotten worse, though I see no obvious trigger for the change."

"Thank you, Meredith." She barely heard the EI's further response. Her eyes kept returning to Phina's posture, which vibrated a little more with each passing moment. "Grey, are you sure she's the right person? I want to help her, but is this really the best course? You are going to need someone strong. Look at the poor girl; she's trembling."

His eyes were glued to the screen now. "She *is* strong. And she's not trembling in fear so much as anger unless I miss my guess. She just needs to peel off the layers of BS her aunt has heaped on her to find her inner strength. Just watch... There!"

Anna watched Phina's posture change until she straightened to her full height and spoke her final words to her aunt. "Fine then. I can't, and I won't."

She was so relieved Phina had stood up to her aunt that she asked a question she didn't really want the answer to. "Do you ever get tired of being right?"

He grinned, his own relief evident on his face. "Not so far."

They watched Phina walk and then run away through the hallways. Just when Anna began to get antsy to do something as she watched tears falling, Phina stopped and took out her tablet. "What's she doing now?"

"Sending you a message, I imagine."

Sure enough, a new message dinged on Anna Elizabeth's tablet. She read it, then looked at her old friend before shaking her head in exasperation. "How about now? She's still in."

"Excellent. Please give her whatever she needs."

"You don't think that's going a bit far for one person, do you?" Anna felt troubled about where their attention should be focused. There were many more needs than those of one girl, regardless of how much she sympathized.

He turned away from the door and walked back to her, eyes bright with something Anna couldn't name. He stopped just outside her personal space and spoke softly. "Believe me, that girl is worth the time and effort. She is as raw as a diamond in the rough now, but she has all the necessary potential. And when I am finished with her?"

The man she called Greyson Wells was lost in his thoughts a moment before abruptly turning toward the door. She couldn't help calling to him, "When you're finished with her?"

He turned again and gave her that careless grin she couldn't stand, which resulted in her making a face at him.

"When I'm finished with her, she will be the hidden gem of the Empire, shining brilliantly even in the dark."

His grin disappeared when he saw her face, and he sobered. "Trust me, Anna. We will need her."

As he walked out, Anna Elizabeth thought she faintly heard him speak again.

"I've left it long enough as it is."

QBBS *Meredith Reynolds*, Secluded Hallways

Phina closed her eyes and took a few breaths to calm down, but it didn't seem to matter. The anger had cooled, but it was still there. She focused on all the emotions tumbling inside her, then mentally pushed them back. Within seconds, those emotions were gone. Phina was relieved, but she also felt a trickle of disappointment that she couldn't handle them. A few moments later, her tablet indicated she received a message.

Don't worry, Phina, you will still have your home. Keep your chin up. You have friends here.

Phina let all her breath out and nodded. She would be all right. Anna Elizabeth's phrase, "you have friends here," made her think about Alina, and ADAM, and Maxim. Alina's friendship was solid, no doubt in Phina's mind. ADAM had been a great new friend so far, but she didn't want to bother him too often since he was busy with Bethany Anne and the General. Phina didn't know about Maxim as a friend yet, but she leaned toward finding out. At the very least, if she sparred with him, perhaps she could work out some of the adrenaline now coursing through her.

She lifted her tablet and quickly sent another message. She hadn't gone ten steps before receiving the reply.

Absolutely. Meet you there.

Though she still felt unsettled, she began to feel a glimmer of satisfaction. She had friends and would get through this.

CHAPTER FIVE

QBBS *Meredith Reynolds*, Marines' Workout Area

It took Phina some time to traverse the massive space station back to her normal area and reach the training room. Enough time that she chose to use the tram, glides, and lifts instead of walking as she normally did. When she finally entered the training room assigned to her, she raised an eyebrow at the sight of Maxim speaking with a relatively young Yollin, who was around the equivalent of a human in his upper twenties or low thirties. The alien appeared to be very comfortable with Maxim as they exchanged glances after noticing Phina at the door. Ah. Right. Maxim confirmed her conclusion when he turned to her and introduced them as she approached. "Hi Phina, this is my friend and second, Drk-vaen. Drk, this is Phina, my new student."

Yollin - Image by Eric Quigley

Drk-vaen stood tall, as did most Yollins. His family must have been higher in the old caste system Empress Bethany Anne had done away with. Shortly after leaving Earth and entering the Yollin system, Bethany Anne had defeated the old Yollin king. He had subjugated his people in many ways, one of them being segregating them into castes. One mark of the higher castes had been four legs. The lower-caste Yollins were bipedal like humans. The arms ended with hands containing only three fingers and a thumb.

Drk-vaen's feet flared out from the heel into three toes with strong and sharp claws. His broad torso, currently covered in armor, narrowed at the waist. His face showed the typical bony ridges of a Yollin that extended from the nose and brows, with mandibles on either side of his mouth. As Yollins went, the male appeared magnificent and would become even more so with all the armor encasing his body.

Phina bobbed her head and greeted the Yollin in a human's approximation of his tongue. Some of the sounds were difficult for humans to produce since the Yollins used clicks from their mandibles in their language, as well as sounds from their mouths. Phina had practiced until her Yollin verbalizations were as close to correct as a human could make them. "Greetings, Drk-vaen. I am very pleased to meet you."

Drk-vaen abandoned his own greetings in surprise as he jerked his head and clicked his mandibles. "You speak to me in Yollin without the translator!"

She smiled, putting aside her troubles with her aunt for the moment. "Yes. I learned Yollin many years ago and look forward to more opportunities to refine my understanding."

"I look forward to those opportunities as well, Phina." Drk-vaen's alien features approximated a smile before he turned to Maxim, his tone chiding. "From your description, I expected a child, Maxim. She may be young, but she is no child. And obviously very intelligent since most humans don't bother to learn the language and just rely on their translators."

Phina crossed her arms and stared at Maxim with one eyebrow raised and her lips pressed together. Seriously, just because she didn't have curves like Alina didn't mean she wasn't a woman. Maxim appeared uncomfortable as he raised a hand to rub the back of his head. "Well…"

She stuck her tongue out and made a face at him, startling a laugh out of both males. "It's all right. I may be an adult now, but I *am* still young." Phina raised her eyebrows and spoke pointedly. "I hope this is the last time you describe me as if I were a child, though."

Maxim held up his hands in surrender. "Done."

Phina's body drained of tension as she took a breath, then nodded at the two males. "Thank you for the last-minute training session."

"No problem." Maxim gestured to his Yollin second. "Since I was with Drk at the time, I thought it might be helpful to show you how that move I taught you yesterday could be used against a Yollin."

She agreed and stood back to watch the two move to the center of the mat.

Maxim demonstrated the move she had learned yesterday in slow motion. Whether a person got in her face, punched toward her, or had a gun or another weapon in their hand, this move was a fast and efficient way to neutralize the threat. According to Maxim, anyway.

He had Drk-vaen stand in front of him, holding his fist out as if to throw a punch. Maxim glanced at Phina, his muscles bunching in anticipation of the move. "Let me know when you see the problem." He quickly stepped inside the Yollin's reach and caught Drk-vaen's arm with his left hand while reaching out to grab the Yollin's throat with his right. He pivoted, intending to throw the Yollin to the floor as he showed her yesterday, but...it didn't work. It had worked during the last couple of training sessions when Phina had landed on the floor.

"Oh! It doesn't work because he has four legs instead of two, so his center of gravity is different."

Maxim released his hold and turned to her with a nod,

his eyes warming with approval. "Exactly. Any thoughts on the best way to adjust for taking him down with the extra limbs?"

Phina ran her eyes over Drk-vaen, picturing different scenarios in her head but coming up with very little. She noticed the Yollin fidgeting as if he wanted to say something but held it back. Finally, Phina shook her head. "The only direction I see working is forward, but I don't know how that would work with the move you showed me."

She glanced at Maxim to find him nodding with a small smile that made her feel like she was doing something right. "Exactly, Phina. The basic idea is the same, but the hold and takedown are different. Watch and see how it changes."

Returning to their original positions, this time Maxim caught Drk-vaen's left arm while simultaneously grabbing behind the Yollin's neck and flinging his own weight backward and to the floor, pushing his feet into the Yollin's front legs. The combination of the maneuvers pushed the four-footed alien off his center of gravity enough to make a difference. As he fell, Maxim used his leverage to pull Drk-vaen to the side. Once they hit the mat, he rolled on top of his friend, holding him down with a knee to the back and pulling the still-captured arm back at an angle where the Yollin couldn't move much without pain. Maxim's other hand pressed down on his fellow Guardian's neck to make sure he stayed there.

Phina hadn't known if she would like learning how to fight, but she had to admit that looked fun, as well as having the advantage of not being in pain from a fist to the stomach. She rubbed her belly at the thought. Phina didn't feel much pain anymore, but she still had lingering bruises since Todd didn't seem to have pulled his punches much. At least, that was how she felt. Maxim had assured her that if Todd hadn't pulled the punch, she would have needed to go to Medical. It didn't seem like Maxim had pulled his punches just now with his second.

Drk-vaen moaned while lying on the floor. "Come spar with me, he said. Show off some moves to a young girl, he said." He mumbled something after that which sounded suspiciously like a Yollin curse. "May your progenitors never meet, your armor become brittle, and your family be scattered to the wind." He groaned as Maxim let go and they both pushed up off the floor. "I knew I should have worn all my armor!"

Phina giggled, more at the comical expression on the Yollin's face and the memory of the way his back legs had flailed in the air than anything else.

"Sorry, Drk." Maxim gave the male's shoulder a hearty smack in commiseration. "If it helps, Phina here is much smaller than I am, so it should be as soft as landing on a hillcat. Nothing to worry about."

The Yollin turned to stare at his friend suspiciously. "The ones from Skahna? Those had huge claws!"

"They did? You know, I think you're right." Maxim seemed to be holding in a smirk even as his eyes widened in mock disbelief. "Then maybe you *do* have something to worry about."

Phina dissolved into full belly laughs. She didn't know if they were always like this or if it was for her benefit since they could tell she had been upset, but as Maxim called her over to try her hand at the move, she felt a lot more at home. She just had to survive her aunt over the next several weeks until she left and classes started.

Drk-vaen groaned as she walked over. "I definitely should have worn all my armor."

Etheric Empire, Vermott, Planet of the Baldere

Terland glanced around the corner to make sure he had no witnesses to what he was about to do. Since none of the sounds he heard were coming closer, he sped toward the command center, using the key card he had swiped from another guard who was assigned here. After closing the door behind him, he paused to make sure no alarms sounded or guards moved toward his location before he turned to the data terminal.

He had always wanted to make a difference and help the leadership of the Baldere. When Drestin, the previous Jeskir of the Balderian race, had offered him a place in his guard, Terland had jumped on it. He hadn't always agreed with the male, but he could see now the former Jeskir had tried his best to put the needs of the people first.

When Velof had taken over as Jeskir almost ten years ago, Terland had asked to stay, and for a while, life had been good. His duties were easy: guard and patrol, occasionally accompanying Velof or another official while they were out on business.

It took him far too long to realize that half the business he guarded was shady and against the law. For a while he had looked the other way since by then he was already involved, and he needed the money to support his mother.

After he overheard two guards describe how they had

pushed around a little shopkeeper, one Terland liked and who reminded him of his own mother, he realized he couldn't turn a blind eye anymore. He opened his eyes and ears to see what was really going on with Velof and his government, especially with the guards.

What he found made him ashamed to call himself a Baldere.

His current task was an attempt to make it right, or as right as he could. Terland used the password he had surreptitiously gleaned from the guard who worked here to access the terminal.

He had always thought of his computer skills as a hobby, and he thanked his lucky stars that he hadn't thought to make them known to his boss or co-workers. They would have mocked him, saying it wasn't warrior work. He would use his skills now to take them all down. He cracked his knuckles and got to work.

Thirty minutes later, he had a good-sized file filled with as many documents and videos as he could find to support his suspicions and knowledge of what Velof had been doing. His stomach turned as he recalled the brief glimpse of a group of Velof's guards chasing an alien with an elongated body and a funny-looking head. The guards had behaved like a pack of animals chasing prey. He was sick that he had thought those Baldere were his friends and comrades.

He checked his tablet. "Vrukk!" He had no time left. He quickly uploaded the file before frantically burying everything in layers of folders and encryptions he didn't think anyone would be able to find or access without serious skills. He didn't have time to do more. He would have to come back.

He made himself slow down as he covered his tracks to make sure no one would notice his activity. Sloppy work would get him caught as easily as being found in the room. Finally, he was finished and ran a cloth over the keys just in case.

Quietly and carefully, Terland opened the door and shut it behind him. Too late, he heard footsteps striding down the hallway around the corner. Whirling, he knocked on the door he had just exited while trying to calm his breathing. A moment later, Gaudin appeared.

"Hey, Terland!"

Terland turned and feigned casualness. "Oh, greetings, Gaudin. Just who I came to see."

Gaudin scowled, causing alarm to trickle down Terland's body. "What are you doing here? Velof sent for you half an hour ago!"

"He did? I hadn't heard that. Is he in his office?" He tried to calm his nerves. No Baldere would tremble in fear or panic. It just wasn't done. "I'll go find him, hey?"

"Come on, then. I'll take you to him." Gaudin turned to retrace his steps.

"That's not necessary. I'm sure you have plenty to keep you busy, hey?" Terland glanced at the command center door again as he slowly took steps toward the other guard.

"You're wasting time. Let's go."

Terland reluctantly followed, his mind working overtime to figure out a way to extricate himself. Unfortunately, nothing came to mind that wouldn't cause him to go on the run, which was a sure-fire way to get caught and killed. He tried to calm down. Velof might not know what he had been doing, so he might be fine. No need to cause problems when there were none.

He gradually let go of the tension in his body and strove to act normally.

All too soon, Terland realized they were not heading toward Velof's office. They were headed toward the interrogation and torture room Velof had installed when the Governing Center had been renovated to its current glorious state. His nerves ramped up to overwhelm him as Gaudin stopped in front of the door and opened it.

Terland reluctantly entered, still hoping he might be there as guard rather than a participant. Unfortunately, the sight that greeted him rendered his hopes to dust.

"Come in, Terland."

Velof stood tall and imposing in his gleaming armor, which was polished to a piercing shine, and his cape rested flat behind him, as dark as ink. The contrast between them had been chosen to cause Velof's opponents to feel uneasy. The Jeskir was handsome enough for a Balderian male, with his dark fringe of hair around the crown of his ribbed and armored head. Velof held his helm under one arm and his signature hagrund, a stylized battle-axe, in the other.

Terland swallowed hard. Velof didn't dress in his full-body protection unless he was showing himself in public or making an example of someone. Given their location, Terland couldn't mistake this situation for anything else but what it was; Velof intended to kill him. Terland's lack of armor would make it easy. Out of the corner of his eye, he saw that the other guards had lined the wall to watch.

A hand shoved him inside, causing him to stumble a few steps.

Yes, he was going to die.

He had seen the same scene enacted too many times to mistake this for anything else. Terland drew himself up and stood straight. He wouldn't beg or ask for a different outcome since it would make no difference. He would keep his honor as a Balderian warrior intact.

"Where did you find him?"

"Outside the command center door, Jeskir Velof."

The Jeskir's eyes narrowed. "Had he been inside?"

"No, Jeskir Velof. He knocked on the door as I walked up and said he was looking for me."

Terland sighed in relief as Velof waved Gaudin out the door and turned to Terland, viewing him with dark, glittering eyes, his face devoid of expression. When he spoke, his voice was deceptively soft but held sharp menace.

"Do you have anything to say?"

Terland met the Jeskir's gaze, knowing he had nothing to lose now. He only wished he had been able to save more money for his mother. Leaving her was his only regret.

"Only that you're a backstabbing, money-grabbing, honorless excuse for a Baldere, and you aren't worth the homage paid to you. You're no better than a petty crime lord."

Velof's face turned dark as he took a step and backhanded Terland, the spikes on his armored hand connecting with the side of Terland's face before he staggered back. Deep-violet blood dripped to the floor from the punctures.

"I was going to kill you since you obviously haven't the

stomach to align with our goals." Velof hefted the hagrund, playing with the handle as he glared his ire and spoke harshly. "But now, I'm going to take you apart piece by piece."

Terland didn't bother raising a hand to touch his face. Still standing straight, he continued his diatribe. "You want us to see you as this great leader, but you're nothing but a wannabe hack with delusions of grandeur."

Velof's mouth curled in a snarl as he hefted his hagrund and sliced it across Terland's middle. Without armor of any kind, Terland had no way to prevent it. Purple warmth cascaded down his body and over his hand as he pressed it against the wound. Baldere were strong and stoic warriors, but no male wanted to see his insides on the outside of his body. He fell to his knees, but he didn't stop his verbal defiance even though his voice dropped in weakness from blood loss.

"Just like you to be armored with weapons while your opponent has no armor or weapon to defend himself. You'll die as you lived, Velof—a two-bit male that wouldn't know...what to do with a female...if he had one. A trumped-up bully...with no honor."

Velof howled his anger as he rushed forward, swinging and hacking. Darkness threatened to pull Terland under.

"Traitor," he whispered hoarsely and heard Velof bellow. Something hit his head, and he knew no more.

Velof turned away from the broken and mangled body and reached for the towel Torel held out to him. His chest was still heaving from the emotions the filthy maggot had elicited with his spew of words before he had been ended.

The Jeskir's thoughts were still too volatile to put into words. After mopping his face and hands while a guard knelt and wiped the blood off his spiked and armored feet, he hooked his hagrund onto his belt and beckoned to the female to follow.

He strode ahead of her, thinking only of the slurs that had been thrown in his face. Out of all of them, only one accusation haunted his thoughts. So much so that instead of entering his office, he moved past it, heading for another room.

After entering, he turned around to see Torel's eyes light with anticipation, a knowing smirk playing on her lips. Silently, he grabbed her wrist and pulled her forward, then tossed her on the bed. Without taking his eyes off her, he began to peel off his armor, dropping it on the floor piece by piece as he stalked forward.

Wordlessly pulling Torel's armor off and dumping it on the floor behind him, his movements grew rough and hard. She began to moan and move under him as he tried to ignore the name of a different female that pounded through his head.

One he had tried for years to forget.

CHAPTER SIX

QBBS *Meredith Reynolds*, Waters Residence

"Hi, Phina!" Her aunt smiled brightly, seeming eager to see her.

"Hi, Aunt Faith," she responded cautiously as she paused in the doorway, not sure how to react.

"Why don't you come sit? It's been ages since we've talked."

Phina stood staring and blinking at her Aunt Faith in disbelief. The difficult woman had been giving her the silent treatment for the past three weeks. However, the scientist was scheduled to leave the next day, a fact Phina only knew because there had been a note about it on the kitchen counter a week ago. The lack of interaction didn't bother Phina. In fact, she was relieved. Her aunt viewed it as punishment; she wanted Phina to think about what she had done wrong and change her mind. Phina, however, wouldn't change her mind since she didn't think she was in the wrong. Even so, as time ran out with the silence unbroken between them, Phina's stress level had increased.

Although Phina avoided her aunt, she had also celebrated Alina's birthday and being an adult, talked to ADAM, and trained with Maxim. Occasionally, Alina had watched, or Drk-vaen came in to help train. Alina had become busy with her plans to pursue fashion, and Drk-vaen had a few other friends and responsibilities he had mysteriously alluded to, so he didn't hang out with Maxim all the time.

Her workouts had increased as she grew stronger. Maxim had taught Phina that first takedown as a quick way to neutralize someone in self-defense, but now they were "going back to basics," as he called it. She only knew her muscles were tired of repeating the same punch and kick motions over and over, even though she knew it was necessary to learn.

Phina had messaged back and forth with Anna Elizabeth about her new classes. She had grown to appreciate the elegant woman's calm assurances and practicality and found herself looking forward to beginning classes.

She had also spent more time with ADAM, who she discovered to be an amazing fount of old Earth movie and show quotes. Occasionally they watched one he recommended "together" while he explained all the Earth things she didn't understand. Those times were a delight in the middle of the stress she felt at home.

But now, the day before Aunt Faith left and three days before classes started, her aunt finally broke her silence. Phina had come home after another training session to find her aunt sitting in a chair in the living room waiting for her. She had stopped cold, her mouth dry and her heart pounding harder, wondering if Aunt Faith would yell at her again. But she hadn't; she was acting as if nothing had happened.

Aunt Faith frowned at her when Phina hesitated too long. She sat down, then kicked herself for doing so since it showed she might yet follow her aunt's directives. Still, it was only one more day, and then her aunt would be gone for a while. Phina could put up with anything for that amount of time.

"So, tell me what you've been up to, Phina."

"Well, I've been training a lot lately, learning martial arts, and I'm looking forward to my classes starting in a few days."

Aunt Faith's demeanor darkened. "So, you refuse to change your mind about coming with me."

Phina took a deep breath as she shook her head. "I will not be going with you."

That went over like a lead balloon. However, her aunt just pressed her lips together and continued the conversation as if Phina hadn't said a word. Even though this had occurred often over the last seven years, Phina still didn't understand how Aunt Faith could ignore everything and act like it never happened. If only ADAM were here to make random comments about her aunt or joke about how bad things could have been.

Sometime later, she finally escaped to her room.

***

"She just ignored the tension between you? Again?" Alina's disbelief smoothed Phina's feelings, allowing her to move past the present and consider the larger whole she couldn't see before.

"Yes. I think I just need to let this go."

"What? In what world would letting this go be the best idea?" Phina's friend's voice rose in volume and intensity in her implant, and she smiled at the warm feeling she received from Alina's outrage on her behalf. "She's being completely unreasonable! How is tearing you away from everything you know and your best friend what is right for you? I still don't understand how she could think that."

"Because she's leaving tomorrow. If I don't let this go, it will eat at me, and I'll just stew on it. Yes, she hurt me, and yes, I'm angry, and yes, I'm completely fed up with her doing this, but dwelling on it isn't going to do me any good. Nothing I do or say now is going to change her at this point."

Phina didn't know if it was the healthiest decision, but right now, it was the sane one. Alina grumbled about it for a while but admitted Phina had a point.

The next day, Phina helped Aunt Faith by pulling the transport cart containing her luggage to the spaceport. Alina walked with her, chatting amicably with Aunt Faith while they were on the tram to cover over the awkwardness, despite her offended feelings on Phina's behalf. Phina couldn't have loved the girl more if she were her own sister, and this act warmed her bruised heart.

After a quick hug from her aunt with a reminder to behave and message her often, Phina and Alina waved her off. Once they returned to the apartment that was now solely Phina's, she realized a huge weight had been lifted from her. She felt free—amazingly, wonderfully free.

Stunned speechless by this revelation, Phina didn't hear Alina speaking as the young woman sat down cross-legged on the couch.

"What?"

"Are you all right, Phina?" Alina's beautiful face frowned and concern shone from her eyes.

Phina nodded in disbelief as she sank onto the other side of the couch. "I think so. I really do think I am."

"Then what's going on in your head?"

"Do you want to move in here with me?" Phina blinked in surprise since that hadn't been what was in her mind, but since she liked the idea, she didn't correct it.

Alina grew silent and thoughtful. Phina knew it would be a change to move into a smaller place, but hopefully, her friend wouldn't need to bring *everything* with her. Then again, this was Alina. She had two closets and a dresser overflowing with clothes. After another wordless moment passed, Phina shrugged. "Just think about it. I don't see Aunt Faith coming back very often, so it will be open."

"I'll think about it for sure." Alina nodded, her smile wobbling. "Part of me still hopes my parents will pay attention to me if I'm there in the apartment with them. It's a child's dream, and I know I need to let that go myself, but I need a little more time."

Phina nodded and moved closer to give her friend a hug, though she was outraged on her friend's behalf. Alina's parents were successful in their jobs and appeared to love each other very much, but when it came to Alina, there seemed to be a disconnect. Perhaps it was because they were both very serious-minded and didn't seem to know what to do with a girl who loved fashion more than anything practical, but to Phina, that shouldn't matter. A parent should love their child no matter what and show them every day, even if the parent had to adjust their expectations. Phina had avoided Alina's parents as much as possible ever since she'd told them off for missing Alina's birthday for the third year in a row when she was sixteen. She didn't want to make things more difficult for her best friend. "Of course. You can have all the time you want."

Alina flashed her a thankful smile that turned mischievous as she sat back.

"So, who's Adam? Have you been hiding a boyfriend from me?"

"What?" The suddenness of the question caused Phina to freeze in mid-motion, arm and leg sticking out at awkward angles. She imagined ADAM's laugh in her ear if he had heard Alina, which caused her to smile a little too much.

Alina gasped in shock. "Oh, my stars! You *have* been hiding a boyfriend from me!"

The smile dropped as Phina shook her head so quickly she felt like she got whiplash. "No!"

"Why wouldn't you tell me? Don't you think I want you to be happy?" Her friend's face crumpled in hurt.

Phina quickly changed her position, getting her legs under her so she could lean forward and hold Alina's hands. "Look at me." Pained blue eyes did so, and Phina shook her head slowly as she spoke.

"I do not have a boyfriend. I hesitated because I was trying to figure out how you knew about him. ADAM is a great new friend, but a friend only. If I ever do find myself in possession of a boyfriend, you will be the first to know after me and the poor sap himself. All right? Whether it's next year or in twenty years, you will be the first to know."

"Twenty years!" Alina's eyes widened in shock. "You can't wait twenty years! What about kissing? Or…or sex? You can't wait twenty years for that!"

Phina laughed, finding it a welcome release after the past weeks of tension.

Alina giggled and continued long after Phina had gotten hold of herself. "I'm serious, Phina! You can't wait that long! It's unconstitutional!"

Phina shook her head, smiling. "We don't have a constitution, remember? We live in a benevolent dictatorship."

"Well, I'm sure Empress Bethany Anne would agree with me!"

Making a face, Phina shook her head. "That's just what I need. Walking up to Bethany Anne, the Empress of the entire Etheric Empire, and asking her opinion on my sex life. She would probably look at me like I'm crazy."

Alina triumphantly pointed out, "You can't have a sex life if you aren't having sex!"

Phina rolled her eyes as she smiled. "Fine. Can I at least wait 'til I find someone I like first?"

The blonde girl playfully pursed her lips in thought. "Sure. But if it takes too long, don't be surprised if I start throwing guys at you."

Phina shuddered. She didn't even want to think about what those men might be like. Not that Alina had poor taste, but she tended to think more about the aesthetics than the substance, Maxim notwithstanding. "I'll take that under advisement."

She leaned over to Alina and held out her fist. "Phinalina forever?"

Alina laughed, which filled Phina with relief. "Of course, silly! Phinalina forever!" She bumped her fist to Phina's before lifting it and miming fireworks, causing Phina to laugh and Alina to grin before sinking back in her seat.

"So, who is Adam? Oh, and I know about him because I heard you talking to him when you got to my house on your birthday."

"You've known about him for almost three weeks and didn't say anything?" Phina's eyebrows rose high. Alina rarely sat on something that long before mentioning it. The young woman gave her an affronted pout.

"Well, I thought he was your first boyfriend, and I've been waiting for you to tell me all about him! Why do you think I got so upset? Now I know he isn't your boyfriend, but I still want to know who he is, so tell me."

Alina leaned forward eagerly while Phina explained who ADAM was, his part in their adventure, and the support he had given her over the past few weeks. Alina grew more shocked. "Why *didn't* you tell me about him?"

She shrugged. "I don't know. I don't really have a good reason."

Alina eyed her, then nodded knowingly. "I think you just wanted to keep him to yourself for a while. He's really the first friend you've made aside from me, and I don't count since we met when we were babies. I don't think you knew how to handle it, so you just didn't say anything."

Phina stared at Alina in surprise, then slowly nodded. "That's probably true."

"So, can I meet him?"

Not needing any convincing, Phina pinged ADAM as he had shown her weeks before.

>>Hello, Phina.<<

She greeted him, told him the situation, and asked if he had time to talk for a while. He agreed, greeting Alina through the speaker in the room.

"Hello, Alina. I'm pleased to meet you."

She moved past her astonishment quicker than Phina expected. It was one thing to know about an AI in the abstract and quite another to speak to one personally.

ADAM had corrected Phina and said that "artificial entity" was more accurate than "artificial intelligence." She'd frowned and told ADAM that AE just didn't sound right, so he was stuck with the term.

Phina had explained that the contact Alina had received from Mal, the famous fashion designer, had originated with ADAM.

Alina gasped, and Phina winced at the screech when she spoke. "Really? Oh, ADAM, thank you so much!"

Alina stood up and danced around the room while moving her arms everywhere in excitement. "Thank you, thank you, thank you so much!"

Phina smiled as she watched her friend's joy. "See, ADAM? Friend for life!"

Speaking privately through her implant, he sounded amused as he responded. **>>Yes, I do see.<<** Through the speaker, he asked, "Alina, what sort of fashion are you interested in?"

"I just love all of it!" She gushed about various designers and styles for some time. Phina was surprised ADAM followed along with her friend without any hesitation, knowing styles and brands and asking her for her opinion often. Phina was lost. She sat back, bemused and delighted about two people she liked enjoying getting to know each other.

"Now, Alina, what are your thoughts on shoes?"

Shaking her head with a smile, Phina noticed that Alina's eyes sparkled with pleasure. It was one of her favorite topics. She pushed up from the couch and made dinner for the two humans among them, enjoying the rest of the night with her friends.

As she fell asleep that night, Phina thought that even if the Diplomatic Institute bombed out for her, having Alina and ADAM in her life made everything worthwhile.

QBBS *Meredith Reynolds*, Diplomatic Institute

Two mornings later, Phina headed for her first day of class. She had felt like she'd moved from getting her butt kicked repeatedly to only getting her butt kicked most of the time in her morning session with Maxim. She strode toward the coordinates Anna Elizabeth had sent to her tablet a week ago, feeling a little nervous. Phina didn't know what to expect, but she felt ready for anything.

After finally finding the right door, she walked through the entrance to the Institute and stopped when she saw the massive number of people inside. For a moment, she seriously contemplated walking out, but she took a deep breath and slowly wove through the crowd while trying to avoid running into people.

"Excuse me. Pardon me."

Humans and Yollins mainly comprised the crowd around her, but occasionally she saw a Karillian, a Torcellan, or...actually, she didn't know what that alien was called. She tilted her head as she studied the being who looked almost human but was hairless and had something strange going on with its eyes.

When she saw the alien noticed her attention, she averted her gaze and moved to what she thought might be the office door. She squeezed by a few humans and a Yollin who were talking together and peeked through a doorway just as Anna Elizabeth walked out. Phina backed up a step to give the beautiful woman space as Anna smiled in welcome.

"Great, you're here, Phina. I'm happy to see you." Anna's warm eyes sharpened as they turned to the students lounging in the room. Raising her voice, she beckoned them forward. "Please follow me, everyone. We will find somewhere more comfortable to chat."

Phina followed the masses into a larger room off a hallway. As people found seats in the short rows, she realized there weren't *that* many people in the room; it had just felt that way since they were all pressed together. She sat in a chair at the back and counted, estimating around forty people.

Anna Elizabeth stood smiling at the front of the room, silent until the buzz of whispers and movement died down. "Welcome to the second year of the newly revitalized Diplomatic Institute, version 2.0. We are pleased you have joined us. The Diplomatic Institute is in the business of developing the finest diplomats in the universe. You should try your very best to learn the material and work hard. You will learn serious skills and knowledge in a number of topics. It's strenuous but very rewarding. It's possible that up to half of you will drop out or fail the year. However, that will depend on you. If you work hard and learn everything you possibly can, then you will most likely pass. You should now be receiving your copy of the school manual if you are new this year."

Sure enough, Phina felt the buzz from her tablet, notifying her of a message. She pulled her tablet out and accessed the manual. Her ears tuned out Anna Elizabeth briefly as she read the mission and vision statements and other pertinent information on the first page.

The Diplomatic Corp had been established at the beginning of the Empire to facilitate the introduction of alien species into the Etheric Empire, protect Etherian citizens from unknown entities, and prevent the Empress from having to intervene as much as possible.

Phina snickered at the thought of Bethany Anne's intervention. The scene in the Empress' receiving room just before the Karillian first came to the Empire's attention had become a legend. It wasn't often that the Ixtalis, a race of information-acquisition agents who prided themselves over others, were taken to task for their arrogance. Phina appreciated their goals but couldn't bring herself to approve of their morals...or rather, the lack of them. That event had also gained Empress Bethany the loyalty of Addix, the Ixtali she had saved from the painful death her people would have given her. From what she knew about the incident and the people involved—from hacking into records, of course, since it wasn't public knowledge by any means—Phina figured Bethany Anne would put Addix's skills to use at some point if she hadn't already. No grass grew under that woman's feet.

Upon remembering "that woman" was the Empress, Phina coughed, her cheeks flushing, and focused on the manual again.

Diplomatic candidates will enter the Diplomatic Institute, progress through their courses under the supervision and mentorship of an existing diplomat, and graduate when their studies are deemed complete. Completion in the student's course of study will be assessed by the dean.

Phina thought this over. Perhaps some students would be able to graduate early, then, and perhaps some would be slow. Considering the academic skills she had been careful not to expose, Phina didn't know what to think about that one, but the phrasing was clever in its simplicity as well as its implications.

Diplomats will travel where and when the Head Diplomat directs, the position currently being occupied by Anna Elizabeth Hauser. The diplomat's primary allegiance is to the Empress and the Empire, and they will do all in their power to uphold honor and Justice throughout their service. For this reason, it is recommended that Diplomatic Service candidates and graduates remain single for the duration of their service to the Empire. Senior diplomats are the exception to this since they largely have stationary postings at Imperial Consulates.

"Recommended that they remain single for the duration of their service?" Phina whispered as she wondered how many diplomats developed issues about that. Most people were not as boy-crazy as Alina or as stand-offish as she was, but even being somewhere in the middle could cause problems. Good thing remaining single wasn't an issue for her. It would just give her a better excuse to put Alina off about those blind dates.

Imperial Consulates are posted at strategic locations throughout the Empire with the sole purpose of facilitating relationships between the surrounding planetary cultures and the Etherian government...

Phina jerked her head up from reading as Anna Elizabeth's next words pierced her concentration, "Mentors will be chosen and announced next Friday. I trust there will be no attempt at hacking to get the list this year, Mr. Anderson?"

Anna Elizabeth raised her eyebrows pointedly at a man appearing in his mid-twenties who sat in the row in front of Phina and down on the right. She could just see the edge of the grin on his smooth face below a messy thatch of black hair before he replied. "Of course not, Dean Hauser."

"See that you don't." She stared at him another moment in all seriousness, likely hoping to impress on him the importance of following her words.

Mr. Anderson merely widened his grin as he returned the stare. Phina didn't know if it was confidence or arrogance that made him so bold, but she could see that he bore watching. He had troublemaker written all over him.

"Thank you, everyone, for your attention. Please proceed to your classes, and come back here at the end of the day." Anna Elizabeth clapped once and waited for them to leave.

The students moved out of the room in various groupings. Phina could see some were friends already, likely those who had been here last year. Those who were likely new walked by themselves. She was so interested in watching everyone as they left that she didn't realize she had hung back until the door shut.

CHAPTER SEVEN

QBBS _Meredith Reynolds_, Diplomatic Institute

"Hey, new girl." Phina followed the voice to see that Anderson guy staring at her with calculating but playful brown eyes, a raised eyebrow, and a smirk on his face. He seemed to be of mixed heritage, at least half of which was Earth Asian.

She stared back and nodded. No need to be unfriendly, but she didn't want to encourage him either. She was here to learn, not make friends—particularly not with the school troublemaker. Since Phina had tripled her number of friends in the last few weeks, she wasn't in a hurry to add more.

"Go on to your class, Jace." Anna Elizabeth's voice startled him into breaking his stare. Apparently he had forgotten she was still in the room. Phina stifled a snicker at the realization on his face.

Jace turned and saluted their teacher. "Yes, ma'am." By his smirk as he walked away, Phina guessed he knew Anna

Elizabeth didn't like being called ma'am and did it anyway. Cheeky.

Phina stood and walked to the end of the row and toward the doors, her eyes following him out. She sensed that Anna Elizabeth had stopped next to her, though she didn't hear her move. "So, is he arrogant, a jerk, or a fool?"

"You tell me, Phina." She turned her head to see Anna Elizabeth giving her one of those smiles adults wear when they imply, "If you think you're so smart, figure it out for yourself." She didn't think Anna Elizabeth was being mean, but she still sighed. When the realization hit her that she herself was now an adult, she almost snorted. Almost.

Training. This was all training.

If Phina remembered that, she would likely find things much more useful and learn more than they were being taught. This attitude had allowed her to accomplish what she wished to in high school: absorb what they were taught, then seek out what they were not and learn as much as possible. Avoid attention by pretending to know just enough to get by. Anna Elizabeth now knew that tactic, however. Smelly purple eyeballs. Wincing, Phina shook her head. No, that phrase and that tactic weren't going to work here.

"Go on now, you will be late for your class. Do you have your schedule? Yes? Please come find me if you need me or have a problem."

Phina patted the pocket where she had placed her tablet, then nodded at Anna Elizabeth, thanking her before leaving the room. She pulled out her tablet to check her schedule, and several classes were listed: Ethics, Cultural Studies,

Languages, Current Events, and Communications, with a break for lunch in the middle. Following the signs pointing to her first class, she opened the door to find a group of eight students sitting in front of a distinguished older gentleman. Noticing her entrance, the man broke off speaking. Students and professor eyed her for a moment, then the gentleman greeted her with a smile on his dark face.

"Hello. You must be Seraphina Waters?"

"Phina."

"Thank you, Phina. Please take a seat." He gestured at the last seat available, thankfully located in the back. As she sat down, the man spoke again.

"So, to continue, what are ethics?"

"Moral principles?" a casually dressed blond man several years older than Phina answered.

Their teacher nodded, his eyes warm and kind. "Thank you, Derek. Anyone else?"

"Codes of conduct?" This came from a quiet Yollin female. Given the development of her frontal protrusions and coloring, she was only a little older than Phina.

"Good answer, Sis'tael." He leaned against the small desk at the front of the room and held out his hands, gesturing for more.

An older dark-haired student with a shaggy beard answered, "A system for choices."

"Yes. All of these answers are essentially correct. Ethics in its most basic sense is this: what you are willing to do, what you won't do, and any situations where those answers may change. What we will look at over the next couple weeks is different ethical philosophies or ideas and how those apply both to the individual and the culture as a whole."

As the class continued, Phina fully expected to be bored but found herself drawn in. Leaning forward on her elbows, she continued to follow the professor's reasoning and examples. His conclusions intrigued her. Just before the end of the class period, he gave an example using current events.

"How does an ethical system change within a culture? Take the Leath, for example. What we know of the Leath indicates their ethical system is based on the decree of their 'gods,' or as we know them, their Kurtherian overlords. What the Leath's gods dictate, the Leath do. What implications does this give us?"

There was silence in the classroom for a long moment, though the students shifted as if hoping he wouldn't call on them. Phina hesitated, then repeated something she had seen in a report by General Lance.

"It makes them dangerously predictable and unpredictable at the same time."

The older gentleman solemnly gazed at Phina with his dark-brown eyes and nodded. The other students turned back to look at her with varying expressions of confusion, understanding, and concern on their faces. She realized that the human students were of differing ages. None appeared older than mid to upper thirties, but with humans gaining greater longevity, Phina couldn't confidently tell their age based on looks.

"Yes. This is exactly what makes them so dangerous. Their ethical boundaries, or morality, could shift at any moment, based on what their gods tell them. Within their code, the Leath will stick to the letter, but the Kurtherians can change that code at any time."

The students shifted uneasily. Phina didn't blame them. The Leath had attacked the Karillians with fierce determination. It only had been due to the alliance with the Etheric Empire and the Leath's predictable tactics that the Karillians had successfully withstood the massive attack. Since Bethany Anne had brought the Empire between the Leath and their goal, the Leath had now set their sights on the Empire. The idea that the Leath would be even less predictable than before was frightening.

QBBS *Meredith Reynolds*, Diplomatic Institute

Later that week, Phina waited in her seat for the Music Across the Universe class to begin. She sat behind two students, one a timid female Torcellan and the other a young human male who appeared to be in his upper twenties and had blond hair and an arrogant look on his face. Phina had been listening to him brag about himself and loudly criticize certain things about the school.

"...I mean, why do we even have a class about music? What use is that for diplomacy? It's not important like planetary politics, negotiation, or even current events."

"Oh, but don't you think..." The Torcellan female didn't get far before she was interrupted by the teacher walking in.

"Mid-day to you, everyone. My name is Addison Stone." An older but pretty woman who Phina later learned played many instruments spoke to the class with a musical lilt to her voice as she stood at the front of the classroom with a confident smile on her face.

"If you aren't here for Music Across the Universe, then you may be in the wrong room. Everyone supposed to be here? Good. Let us discuss the purpose of this class. You may have wondered, why do we even have a class on music? It's not serious, or a critical topic like planetary politics or negotiation, right?"

Phina felt a smile grow on her face. Their gray-haired teacher might be older, but she was as sharp as a knife and must have been listening in on the conversation before she walked in.

"Wrong. Music is just as important for several reasons, but mainly two. First, if both you and your diplomatic counterpart are familiar with the music at hand, it gives you a point of discussion. If you haven't learned this yet, a diplomat's work doesn't just pertain to the formal talks between you and the other parties. It happens before and after when casual interactions take place, and you will want to have topics and experiences to bring to the conversation.

"You will learn more in your Negotiation class about this idea, but these casual conversations are just as critical, if not more so, than the formal discussions as they will provide a common ground and a reason for the other party to listen to you when it matters. To put it simply, you build relationships through those conversations, and those relationships are critical."

Addison spared a small smile for the arrogant man in front of Phina, who watched his neck grow red. She wondered if the flush was from embarrassment or anger.

Either way, he had been rude and would now hopefully have a more open mind.

"Back to why music is important! There are only three activities that are universal, just appearing different depending on species and culture, which are sports, arts, and entertainment. Almost every species and culture has at least one of each category, though sometimes you will find a culture where some are mixed as one, even all three together. The Baldere are one such species. I'll give you a word of warning now. Never make light of the Balderian games of Rikhar, where they all compete against each other to become the Balderian leader for the next ten years. It is entertainment, athletics, and art form rolled into one, and it is the most serious thing in their culture.

"When you come across a new species, these three topics are some of the first you should inquire about. Which brings me to the second reason music is important to know. When you show that you know, care about, value, or appreciate the music and other aspects of each species' cultural experience, it shows them that the Empire values them as a culture and species. This goes a long way toward bridging the distance and gaps between you and those of the new culture as you forge an alliance or bring them into the Empire."

Addison Stone continued teaching as she segued into sharing music samples throughout the class period. Phina found herself fascinated and eagerly listened as each new sample was played.

"Ladies and gentlemen, we are almost done with our tour of music for today. We will learn more about these music styles over the next several classes. Now listen up.

This next piece of music is a complete mystery, but one your musical experience wouldn't be complete without."

Addison smiled with a tinge of sadness as she drew the words out, causing Phina to tilt her head in puzzlement. A few of the students who had been whispering dropped their conversations immediately to pay attention. Before Phina could ask the questions forming in her mind, the music played.

Phina's breath caught, and she closed her eyes to focus. The tones were not like anything else that had been shared with them so far or like any music from Earth she had heard. Low tones resonated deep within her at a steady rate, almost like a heartbeat. Middle tones wrapped around her and moved her emotions from one to the next so quickly Phina didn't think she could name them all. Through both of those cut a higher lilting tone that moved up and down the scales between the middle notes in a melody she knew would haunt her for days. The harmonies resonated in a way that was beautiful, breathtaking, and heartbreaking.

Just as Phina began to see a pattern to the music and wonder if there was a deeper layer, the music ended. Her eyes popped open in surprise and protest. She wanted to hear more. Had to.

"Where is it from?"

Phina looked up to find many of the students, even the males, wiping tears from their faces. The woman who had spoken seemed a little more put together than the rest, but she still sounded shaken. Phina felt her face and was surprised at the tear tracks, though she felt fine compared to the wrecked appearance of everyone else.

Addison smiled sadly. "I spoke only the truth earlier. It's a complete mystery. The music comes from a planet a short hop inside the current edges of the Empire, but as far as we can tell, no one has ever been able to communicate with the inhabitants there. All anyone who goes to their planet hears are variations on this music. No one has figured out what it means or if it means anything. Now, with this next and last song…"

Phina's mind dwelled so much on the music she had heard that she spent the rest of the day in a daze. The melody kept repeating in her head. There had to be something more to it. She didn't make up the sensation that a pattern twined through the music.

Later that night, she sat on her bed, leaning against the wall with her arms wrapped around her knees. She had talked to ADAM about what she had learned that day and hesitated before bringing up the music class.

"Our teacher Addison Stone played this strange mystery music today. Do you know what I'm talking about?"

"Yes. I have accessed the class curriculum."

"Is there any way for you to listen to it, ADAM? I'm positive there is something more to this music, but I couldn't make it out."

ADAM played the music, and the haunting notes swept through the room, drawing her in. The clip played for almost ten minutes before it finished. She had been drawn forward by the music and now half-crouched on the bed. She frowned, then settled back against the wall. Phina shook her head. She hadn't imagined something just out of her mental reach.

"Do you hear it, ADAM?"

"I hear the notes and the tones, but I'm not certain I hear what you hear, Phina."

She tilted her head back against the wall in disappointment, her eyes closed and shoulders slumped.

"However, just because I or anyone else does not hear what you hear, it doesn't make you wrong."

Phina lifted her head as she perked up. "You think so?"

"One thing I have learned about people is that each person hears and experiences life a little differently from anyone else. So, yes, it is very possible for something to be there, and we all have missed it so far. Your brain works differently than other people's. It's one of the reasons I find you interesting."

Phina smiled as she relaxed against the wall with her head tilted up and her eyes closed. "Thank you, ADAM. And thank you for being my friend."

"You're welcome, Phina."

"Can we play it again?"

Sound filled the room again, and Phina fell into the music.

QBBS *Meredith Reynolds*, Diplomatic Institute

"Communications involved in diplomacy runs differently than in other professions. Normally when it comes to communications, you would take into account the person and who they are, a part of which involves the culture they came from."

Anna Elizabeth spoke from the front of the large room they had started in on Phina's first day. Every so often, the dean would scan the students in front of her, likely trying to see if they were paying attention or not. From her chair in the back, Phina wondered what Anna Elizabeth saw when she looked at them all.

"The person's culture is one of several factors you give weight to when it comes to deciding your approach. In normal modes of communication, the goal is to gain some sort of understanding of the other person, but usually we only pay attention enough to convey the message we want to send once they are finished speaking or listen to understand the message we are receiving.

"However, as diplomats, you aren't merely taking the cultural considerations into account, among many other factors, with the goal of trying to understand or convey a message. In diplomacy, you are first and foremost trying to gain information on the people as a culture so that you understand them on a bone-deep level. This step is needed to assess what the species needs as a people and culture and what they can give the Empire. It is a nuance in viewpoint, but a difference nonetheless."

The elegant woman stepped forward, her blue eyes intent as she spoke. "We aren't merely conveying a message, or we would be a messenger service, not diplomats. We aren't merely trying to understand, or we would be solely anthropologists. We are striving to understand who they are so that we can fill a need and discover how they can fill a need of our own. This is mutual beneficence or reciprocity, which is a hallmark of diplomacy."

Phina listened with rapt attention. She found communications just as interesting as her other classes, if not more so, but much harder to grasp as the content was not merely facts, figures, or bits of history to remember. These were principles to learn in the abstract to be applied in the concrete. Phina found it rather confusing.

Even more confusing was watching Jace interact with his friends, and he had a lot of them. Students from the first and second year were together in the Communications class near the end of the day. Most of the students in their second year seemed to gravitate toward the dark-haired man. Phina didn't know what they saw in him. To her, he appeared arrogant, hot-headed, and quick to make judgments. Though she supposed if she looked at it another way, it could be said that he was confident, passionate, and loyal to his friends and their thoughts.

She shook her head. He would need to get over that arrogance and judgment quickly, as well as be more careful about his defensive reactions. Not that it wasn't admirable to be loyal, but sometimes you needed a certain distance to see things clearly, and it didn't seem like Jace had that.

Class finally finished, and rather than hanging back as she usually did so she was last to leave, she was one of the first out the door. By the end of the day, she needed time by herself to process and digest everything she had learned, as well as to decompress from being around so many people all day.

Phina had just eased out of the Diplomatic Institute and into the flow of foot traffic to head for home when she heard a playful voice behind her.

"Hey, new girl! Wait up."

Turning, Phina saw Jace working his way toward her, a smirk on his face. His messy hair bobbed up and down as he dodged two humans, a Yollin, and a Torcellan. The two humans, a mother and a young girl who might be her daughter, laughed as he made a funny face while he wove around them to try to catch up.

Phina turned around and kept walking. She didn't need to encourage Jace to follow her. He caught up, settled into her pace, and gave her a quick grin, which she ignored. "You headed home?"

"Nope."

"Doing anything interesting?"

"No." Not that she was going to tell *him*, anyway.

"Can I come with you?"

"Why?" Phina furrowed her forehead, trying to figure out his angle. She hadn't been getting any vibes from him that he was interested in her in a romantic or sexual way, so why did he want to come with her?

"I want to get to know you."

"Lie. No, scratch that." She watched his face intently. "Partial truth. Want to try again and tell me the whole truth?"

Phina knew she was spot on when she saw him wince. She shook her head and continued at her quick, even pace. Jace began to sound out of breath and struggled to keep up despite his height advantage.

"Come on, new girl. At least tell me your name?" His cajoling sounded dangerously close to whining, which Phina detested. She didn't need him getting to know her or trying to convince her to open up to him.

She opened her mouth to tell him off when he crossed the line.

"I could just hack your file, so why not tell me?"

Anger sparking, Phina stopped short in the middle of

the hallway, causing a tall guy with a slight beer belly to curse under his breath as he moved around her.

"Sorry!" she called to the man before he disappeared into the masses, then glared at Jace. His smirking face dared her to say something.

"Is this guy bothering you?"

The deep voice behind her sounded unexpectedly kind while possessing a note of steel in warning. She turned to see a large, well-muscled black man standing behind her. He eyed Jace briefly before looking at her with concern.

Phina blinked as her brain worked overtime to try to place the man. He seemed nice even though he appeared to be tacitly offering to beat Jace up for her. Thinking of that visual made her produce the first genuine smile all day. Jace stood next to her, gaping at the man, which seemed rude. Really, he looked like a flapping fish. With a small sigh, Phina turned to the man with a genuine smile.

"Thank you, but I got it."

The large man looked at the two of them and nodded. "All right. I'm sure I'll see you both later." After looking pointedly at Jace, he strode away gracefully for his size.

"Don't you know who that is?" Jace still stood with his mouth wide open, then he looked at Phina with a squee worthy of a fangirl. "That was Darryl! Darryl-Freaking-Jackson! Does he know you?"

Phina blinked in surprise at that information since Darryl Jackson was yet another personal guard of the Empress, but she shrugged it off in light of the current situation. "I seriously doubt it. He was probably just being helpful and considerate, unlike some people who prefer stalking."

"I'm not a stalker. I just wanted to talk to you!"

Phina looked at him in disbelief. "And you thought blackmailing me by telling me to talk to you or you would hack my file was a good way to accomplish that?"

Since they were still in the way and there was a less crowded hall behind him, Phina put her palms on Jace's chest and pushed him back. "Hey! What are you doing?" His eyes rounded, and he arched his back too much and windmilled his arms to compensate as his feet shuffled backward.

Once they were out of the way of traffic, Phina grabbed his shirt to stop his momentum, then stepped back and pulled out her tablet, her fingers flying over the surface.

"What…"

Without looking up, Phina held up a long, thin finger before resuming her tapping.

"Come on, wha—"

She held her finger up again, forcefully adding, "Shush!"

Jace crossed his arms and glowered at her, but since he was silent, she ignored him and continued tapping rapidly for another minute. Finally she relaxed and replaced the tablet in her pocket. Without another glance at the source of her trouble, Phina turned back to the main corridor to go on her way.

"Hey! That's it? What were you doing?"

She turned at his aggrieved tone and glared at him, then walked back to poke him in the chest. "What I was doing was protecting my information so that even if you wanted to hack it, you couldn't." She crossed her arms and tried to shoot laser beams out of her eyes. Sadly, it didn't work. She mimicked him in a mocking tone. "'I could just hack your file, so why not tell me?' Seriously? You don't threaten people with stuff like that. I would have thought you knew better!"

He blinked in disbelief. "You can't do that."

Phina narrowed her eyes at him. "Can't do what?"

"You can't just put that kind of protection in place. That takes major skills and hours of work."

Phina shrugged a shoulder half-heartedly. "I just did, so clearly you can." She turned away again.

"Won't you at least tell me your name?"

His voice sounded almost desperate, and Phina turned back to really look at him. His jaw was clenched, his body tense, and his mouth twisted as if he were not sure whether to scowl or smile. In his eyes she saw curiosity, but more so anger's younger brother, frustration.

She took a step back toward him. "I see what this is."

His face turned wary. "What do you mean?"

Taking a step closer with every few words, Phina ended up in his face. "I mean, you aren't really interested in me. Good job trying to convince me, though. No, you just can't stand that even though everyone else thinks you're the greatest thing since implants were created, I not only don't fawn over you, but I'm not even interested in talking to you."

She laughed as he reddened and looked away, his jaw tightening in irritation. She didn't need to be so harsh. Phina sighed before she patted his chest with a reassuring hand.

"Sorry, pal. It's not you, it's me. I don't have anything against you except your deplorable threat to hack my files. My friend card is just full up."

Turning to go, Phina made it almost to the end of the corridor before he shouted, "Hey, new girl!"

She turned to find him staring at her with a glint in his eyes. "I'm going to find out your name, and it's going to be soon."

Phina smirked then threw back. "You do that, Jace!"

She continued on her way, joining the masses in the corridor before repeating to herself, "You do that."

CHAPTER EIGHT

Etheric Empire, Vermott, Planet of the Baldere

Geirik held his shield up just in time to deflect the blow coming toward him, then thrust his skalax, the twin-bladed weapon he favored, forward. When he saw his blow would be deflected by a shield, he sprang to the side, then stepped forward, this time swinging the skalax to slice into one of the narrow spaces between his opponent's armor.

Blood sprayed as his arm completed the arc, though the wound didn't appear deep enough to be debilitating. Geirik pulled back just in time to miss getting a blade to the chest. He set his shield in the proper place to defend and sank into the battle zone where all that existed for him at that moment were Geirik's opponent and his weapon. After several more minutes of dashing, lunging, and slashing, time was called. Geirik relaxed as he straightened and assessed his injuries, finding two small slices and a large bruise on himself and two long gashes on his opponent, all of which seeped deep-violet blood.

"Good. Very good." With weapon sheathed and shield

hooked on the belt harness made for it, the other Baldere inspected the gashes on his body.

Baldere - Image by Eric Quigley

Geirik lowered his skalax and shield. "Is it enough?"

"Probably."

"Halvad, 'probably' isn't going to do it. Not this time. There is too much at stake, hey?"

His oldest friend and mentor frowned, removing his head protection and running his fingers through the fringe of hair around his bald, ribbed head as he considered the question seriously. He finally nodded. "Aye, you've a fair chance of it. Velof is tricky, though, as well as being quicker and more agile than most. You will need to be at the top of your game to win and become the Jeskir."

Geirik hooked his shield on his belt but still held his skalax as if the weapon had been made to be an extension of his own hand rather than sheathed.

"Halvad, Velof has lied to everyone, risked our status in the Etheric Empire, and abused his position as Jeskir and the leader of our people. He can't be allowed to continue, hey?"

"Aye, I understand. You wouldn't say it unless you knew it to be true. It's one of the reasons I follow you, you bow-legged leatherneck." Halvad grinned briefly before dropping into serious tones. "Just the betrayal of risking our position in the Empire is enough. I admit, I had my doubts, but we've gained more by allying with them than not. One of the better decisions Velof has made, hey? The people love him just for that."

"I know. His popularity has been high since he signed the agreement with them at the beginning of his rule, but that was then, hey? We know what he's done since then, which is why I must win in the Rikhar games. No one would have the position and authority to do anything about his depredations if I do not."

Geirik motioned his friend over to the side of the ring. His bondmate had entered near the end of their bout and now stood with their refreshment, one container in each extended hand. The two warriors downed their cold protein slusher at the same time. Geirik let out a satisfied breath and smiled at the female before him. "Thank you, Fastel. These were just what we needed."

"Of course! I couldn't let my bondmate and future Jeskir go thirsty, hey?" She winked at him before accepting the empty containers.

Geirik put his arms around her and pulled her in for a hug, being careful of his skalax. He ignored her initial hiss of surprise and held her until she wrapped her arms around him, her hands still holding the drink containers. After a moment, he pulled back and rested his ribbed head against hers. Halvad wisely found something else to focus his attention on for the time being.

"Thank you for the vote of confidence, Strength of My Soul, but there's a long way to go 'til I get to that point."

"The Rikhar games test brain, brawn, and strength of will to end up with the best leader for our people for the next ten years, hey? That Baldere is you, Geirik. You almost beat Velof last time, and I have no doubt you will beat him and everyone else at the games this year."

He smiled at her confidence. As she wiggled out of his arms, he couldn't help asking, only partly teasing. "Oh? And what gives you such confidence in my success?"

"Because you have something now that you didn't have last time."

"And what's that?"

"Me."

She winked at him again, then walked out of the ring and back to their dwelling around the corner. He grinned as he watched her leave, admiring her form as well as her spirit.

"You have quite a female." Halvad came back over to stand next to him and watched her leave as well.

Geirik elbowed him none too gently. "Get your own female."

"She was joking, hey?"

"About what?"

"That she's the reason you can be confident about the games—a secret weapon of sorts, it sounded like."

Geirik carefully took his skalax off his hand to stretch

his fingers as he gave his friend an amused glance. "Why do you think I've improved so much in the last few years? We practice together several times a week."

"Really? Is she competing in the Rikhar games as well?" Halvad turned back to where Fastel had disappeared from view. "More importantly, does she have a sister?"

Chuckling, Geirik resettled his skalax, then removed his shield from his belt. "Yes, and she's got a skalax of a cousin who is wild but just as fierce in combat."

Halvad grinned for a moment before his eyes grew serious. "You know Fastel is why Velof has been making it hard for you to succeed these past years. He's always wanted her."

A fierce growl rose in him, startling his friend and deepening his voice. "He'll never have her. She made her choice. Fastel saw through him sooner than I did, and that won't change anytime soon. You ready for more?"

Halvad none too gingerly inspected the cuts he had received from their previous bout. "All healed and good to go."

They strode back to the middle of the ring, where Halvad stopped him with the flat of his blade. "You will introduce me to this wild and fierce cousin, hey? She sounds like my kind of female."

"Of course, Halvad, of course. When you're ready to begin, hey?"

They settled into their positions, his skalax at the ready. As their blades whirled and their shields deflected, Geirik grew even more focused and grim. Others might get close, but Geirik had the best shot at beating Velof. Everything depended on him winning the games and becoming the next leader.

His life, his mate, his city, and his world were at stake.

QBBS *Meredith Reynolds*, Anna Elizabeth's Office

"How is she doing?"

Greyson had joined Anna Elizabeth shortly before classes were let out for the day. Anna tried to hide her smile at the feigned casualness of the question. By the fierce light in his eyes as he spoke, she knew her friend was not casual about anything pertaining to Phina.

"She's adapting very well. I don't think she will want to leave after six months, even if you weren't going to pull her into your world."

He smiled as he lounged in her visitor's chair with cat-like laziness. "Glad to hear it, but I didn't think there would be an issue."

"Of course not. Since you know everything and are always right." She rolled her eyes and shook her head.

He grinned playfully. "And don't you forget it."

"How could I when you constantly remind me?" Anna stared at the man sternly as she tried to hide her smile.

He waggled his eyebrows as he spoke to her in her native German. "You don't fool me, old woman! I know I'm your favorite."

"*Sheisse!*" She glared at the younger man, who appeared to be a few years older than her. "For the last time, I am not old!"

He opened his mouth to respond when ADAM interrupted.

"Excuse me, DS and Anna, but you may wish to watch what's happening in the hallway right now."

They stared blankly at each other before turning to the screen on her desk as Meredith flicked it on.

QBBS *Meredith Reynolds*, Diplomatic Institute

Phina headed toward the exit, still thinking about the reflection question her Current Events teacher had asked the students to write an essay on before the next class.

What quality about the Empire caused the most upheaval in the current systems of the local galaxy?

The louder than normal buzzing of voices throughout the corridor pulled her out of her thoughts. As she moved closer to the door connecting the Institute to the rest of the station, Phina could see a large number of students crowded together, looking down at their tablets. Since the group blocked the hallway, Phina stopped until she could decide how pushy or rude she wanted to be. She wanted to be home decompressing.

While she mentally debated, she felt someone stop next to her and turned to see the young female Yollin she had noticed in Ethics last week giving her a friendly smile. "Hello, I am Sis'tael. I have been hoping to meet you, but you usually leave right away."

"Greetings, Sis'tael. I am Seraphina Waters, but please call me Phina. I am sorry. I was rude to leave so quickly. If I had known you were looking for me, I would have spoken to you earlier."

Phina spoke in Yollin, which caused Sis'tael to light up in surprise and eagerness. Before she could respond, a male student standing in front of them turned with an eager brand of nosiness.

"Did you say your name is Seraphina Waters?"

Belatedly, Phina realized the translation chips in everyone's implants would allow anyone listening to understand what she said. She nodded, thinking he was likely another human who wanted to be her friend. She regretted it when the annoying male yelled, "Hey, here's Seraphina Waters!"

All the students in the hallway, but especially the clustered group in the middle, turned toward her, revealing Jace Anderson at the center, surprise and annoyance warring on his face.

"So, the new girl is Seraphina Waters."

She shrugged, not bothered that he knew her name. "That's me."

"How did you get Greyson Wells as your mentor, Seraphina Waters?"

"What?" Her eyebrows drew together as she frowned in confusion. Honestly, Jace seemed erratic to her most days, and this confrontation didn't correct that impression. Phina fought her instinct to get out of the spotlight since she didn't like being the center of attention and tried to formulate a response. The murmurs of the students around her made her want to leave. Jace walked toward her and showed her his tablet, which displayed the mentor pairings. Right. Friday. The list of mentors must have just been posted.

"Greyson Wells is your mentor."

She stared at the man in front of her, wondering what she was missing. So what if this Greyson Wells was her mentor? "And?"

Jace looked at her in disbelief. "You don't know who he is?"

Whispers filled the hallway as the other students reacted to their conversation.

"No."

The sneer on his face caused her eyes to narrow in displeasure. Apparently, the desire to be Phina's friend had passed with this event, but he still had no right to treat her this way. "Greyson Wells is only one of the most famous diplomats in the history of the Empire! Everyone, and I do mean everyone, has been wanting to have him as a mentor, but he never takes a student. He wasn't even on the list for last year, but now he's finally chosen someone, and it's you? Who doesn't even know who he is?"

The scowl on his face flickered with another emotion Phina couldn't grasp, but the man appeared personally offended for some reason. She shrugged casually while she tried to formulate a response, and thought about saying she wasn't really into following the diplomats. With her current status as a student in the Diplomatic Institute, she didn't think that would go over well. Phina's brain shifted gears and she finally spoke.

"I think you are laboring under a few misconceptions."

Jace kept that flickering gaze on her and raised his eyebrows in a mocking manner. "Please, enlighten me."

"The first misconception is that you seem to think this Greyson Wells would choose instead of being assigned."

"He *would* choose. He wouldn't have it any other way."

Phina raised her own eyebrows at Jace's apparent familiarity with the man as she answered, "Even so, the dean would need to approve the choice, would she not? Here is the second misconception, that you believe a mistake has been made. Do you believe that both Dean Hauser and this Greyson Wells made a mistake? Two highly regarded diplomats who are obviously respected?"

She waited for that to sink in before continuing, "And the third, in all this choosing, the only one that had no choice was me. Yet you are asking as if I knew something about it when I know no more about it than you do."

"Sounds like it's a lot less to me," he muttered.

Phina gave him her signature smirk before dropping all expression on her face. "The last and worst misconception is that you appear to think you know or understand anything of who I am and are able to determine on your own whether I'm deemed 'special enough' to be chosen by this well-regarded diplomat. You think knowing a name makes a person special and magically grants you anything you need to know about the people or situation involved?

"I assure you, you know nothing of me because I have told you nothing, and I have shown you very little up 'til now." She glared at him, her emotions slipping out of her usual stranglehold to add a snap to her words. "Thinking you know someone after barely speaking to them is called 'prejudice.' Not the best characteristic to have when your profession purposely meets new species and cultures all the time. I suggest you straighten that out before you trip over yourself at the wrong time or get yourself spaced."

With that, she pushed past him and headed out the door, ignoring the rising tide of voices she left behind her.

Finally, Phina felt like she could breathe.

· · ·

QBBS *Meredith Reynolds*, Anna Elizabeth's Office

A grin grew on his face as Greyson Wells watched Phina firmly put that Anderson douche-puppy in his place.

"Why is he part of the Corps again?"

He glanced over to see Anna concentrating on the screen as she absently spoke. "Just as I'm to trust you with Phina, I need you to trust me with Jace. He has hidden depths you haven't noticed. Just because he isn't interested in spying doesn't make him less worthy of being a diplomat. I think he will work out just fine once he gets a few things out of his system."

He looked back at the screen in time to see the young man in question sneer at Grey's new potential in human form. His lips curled up in a grimace. "I'll have to take your word for it."

Greyson listened with pride as the girl finished sharing her thoughts on the young scuzz-bucket's misconceptions. Not that Grey had anything to do with it; he just enjoyed watching the girl prove herself to be the right person several times over for what he had in mind. She would do well—very well indeed.

As the girl stormed out of the Institute and into the main area of the station, he turned to the door to follow. "I'll catch you later, old lady!"

His friend shook her head in irritation. "*Wichser!*"

He laughed as he walked out. He really did enjoy pushing her buttons, and she made it so easy for him.

Grey stepped out of the office into the hallway, and the whispering died down as the first people began staring at him. The silence quickly spread.

He sped toward the exit. As he passed the young man in

question and saw the shocked recognition on Jace's face, Grey paused and pursed his lips in thought, then shrugged and pointed over his shoulder at the door Phina had left through.

"What she said."

Greyson watched the younger man's face turn red with anger for a moment before it drained to white in shame and dismay. His eyes showed disappointment, and he was clearly mentally kicking himself. The older man nodded thoughtfully as he watched the change in attitude.

"Keep your chin up, kid. She just might be right about you."

This time he pointed to the office door where Anna Elizabeth had just stepped out. As Anderson turned toward her in confusion, Grey continued out the door, leaving the buzzing students behind.

He had his own future protege to catch up with.

CHAPTER NINE

QBBS *Meredith Reynolds*, Open Court

Phina walked quickly toward the Open Court. After that scene with Jace, she needed to shake off her irritation, and usually only training or talking to Alina managed that. Maxim had told her that morning he would be busy after class, so her decision had been made for her.

As she entered the higher traffic area near the Open Court, she became aware of a man walking up to her with a smile on his face. He appeared to be in his mid-fifties and his clothing had the look of a uniform on his lanky body, consisting as it did of gray dress slacks and a blue button-down shirt with the sleeves rolled up and the collar open on the top.

"Just the girl I'm looking for!"

She stopped and turned toward him, struggling with speaking civilly through the irritation. As her emotions surged up from that inner well, Phina couldn't stop the scowl from forming on her face.

"What do you want?"

"I've been waiting a long time to find someone like you."

She froze at the statement and stared at the man in shock. When she saw a smirk form on his face, she pointed her finger at him. "Fudging crumbs, you're a pervert! I've watched movies about men like you. You're all sick!"

"What?" He looked surprised and taken aback by the accusation. "No! What kind of man do you take me for?"

Phina frowned at him and stood with her feet shoulder-width apart to have a firm base like Maxim had shown her, just in case. "Well, I don't know you, or anything about you! Run those lines you just told me through your head again from my perspective and see what conclusion *you* come to."

He opened his mouth to disagree and stopped, looking up in thought. After a moment, his gaze returned to her and he bowed his head in apology. "You are absolutely right. Savor this moment as it doesn't happen very often."

Wary, Phina shook her head. "Why would I do that when I don't even know you?"

"I'm your new mentor." He waggled his eyebrows in a manner that suggested, "Aren't you the lucky one," and, "So what are you going to do about it," at the same time.

Phina stared at the man, who could have come from any number of Earth nationalities. He had interestingly shaped features but nothing far enough out of the ordinary to be memorable. His tousled brown hair looked like his fingers had run through recently, and it was sprinkled with white. His medium-brown eyes, not deep enough to be called chocolate or having sparkles of color to be considered hazel glinted with humor but also determination, and he stood close to four inches taller than her at 5'11." Perfectly ordinary and forgettable if you hadn't seen his personality seep through.

"You're Greyson Wells?"

"At your service." He gave a little bow with a grin on his face.

"This oh-so-famous diplomat I'm supposed to have heard so much about."

"The very same."

Phina scrutinized him for another moment, then shrugged a shoulder dismissively. "I don't see it."

"Ouch. Talk about prejudice, kid."

He scowled, then stopped himself as his eyes darted to the left. "Come along, my young padawan. Time to start your training."

He walked in the same direction as Phina stared after him and sighed. This guy was her mentor? She followed at a short distance until he motioned for her to catch up.

She fell into step with him just as they approached...a bar.

What kind of mentor took their diplomatic trainee to a bar?

They entered the large open room of All Guns Blazing. The crowd had picked up now that dinner was approaching. The uniquely large windows out to the universe drew her eyes, causing her to slow. Having lived on the station all her life, Phina had grown used to the sight of the stars and galaxies, but seeing so many at once with the larger view caused a tug within her. Shaking herself and finally turning away, she almost missed the familiar face of Todd Jenkins sitting at a table with some Marines and

Guardians. Surprisingly, the man had been watching her and nodded when their eyes met. She returned the nod, then continued following her new mentor as he threaded through the partially full tables and chairs. Finally, they reached a booth set toward the back but still in view of the room. As they'd moved forward, he had motioned to the bartender, who nodded and went to the tap.

They weren't sitting for long before a waiter brought a Coke for her and a dark beer that he set in front of...

"Here ya go, Greyson!" The waiter held up his hand for a fist bump as he grinned. "How long has it been, man?"

"A few weeks, I'd say, Bobcat. Good to see you. I thought you were done with your bartending days?"

The man gave a sheepish grin. "And Stephen and the women are doing very well running the place. When I am able, I come back to see Yelena and I help out when she's working. Hey, Grey, while you are here, you should check out my new recipe..."

Phina watched her mentor Greyson Wells talk beer with Bobcat. As she moved her eyes between the two men, she began to notice how friendly and open Bobcat was. He moved his hands quite a bit, his face was honest, and he had a grin on his face when beer was mentioned. He also shifted his position closer or farther away with the flow of the conversation.

In contrast, her mentor appeared friendly but he held back. His eyes were watchful, and he leaned forward as if interested, but he sat farther back in the booth, which gave him more distance. His body language was a study in contradictions and didn't say the same things to her as Bobcat's body language did.

She had heard about Bobcat, one of the founding members of Empress Bethany Anne's group and an integral part of the research team, BMW. The team had created many of their technological advances and also held part ownership of the bar they currently occupied, but Phina had never met the man. Apparently, she wasn't going to meet him now either.

"See ya later, Grey. I'll send out a tall one of that new dark for you to try." Bobcat politely nodded at Phina and walked back behind the bar.

Phina stared at Greyson and waited as she sipped her Coke. He didn't appear to notice, being engrossed in his enjoyment of his tall glass of beer. He murmured a few phrases as he savored the drink, but they made no sense to her in relation to beer, having only heard them in those chick-lit romance movies Alina liked to watch. She shook her head in confusion. Maybe he just really liked his beer.

After a while, they left All Guns Blazing and entered another place called Mac's Tavern and Bar that was located by the docking stations on the outer rim of the asteroid *Meredith Reynolds* had been built on. Her irritation grew since he never explained anything about who he was, what he did, or why they were bar-hopping. As she threaded her way between patrons, nudging a few hands that got a little close to her elbows, she heard her mentor being greeted by the bartender. "Stan! Stan the Man. How ya doing? Your usual?"

Phina frowned but remained silent. A few eye-rolling moments later, Greyson—or Stan—led her to a table near the back.

One by one, sometimes two at a time, people from

different parts of the bar came over to chat with "Stan," greeting him like long-time friends usually, though there were one or two who seemed irritated with him over some kind of cargo, she gathered. But though they all greeted the man in some way, by and large they ignored her. Greyson appeared to drink more than his fair share of beer, but she noticed he didn't drink as much as he acted like he did.

The whole thing was puzzling.

Also irritating.

Phina grew more agitated as time went on. The surprise of her new mentor had dimmed, but being around crowds, not knowing anything of why they were here, and being ignored stoked the irritation. At one point she made to get up and leave, being tired of it all, but he grabbed her hand and pointed both with his eyes and his other hand. "Stay."

She would have left anyway except she felt he was trying to tell her something with that look. While she didn't understand it, she sat back down in her seat with a huff.

Very irritating.

QBBS *Meredith Reynolds*, Anna Elizabeth's Office

Anna Elizabeth viewed her chosen protege with equanimity. Jace Anderson looked the part of an arrogant young man, but she had a suspicion about him and what made him tick. She was sure she was right about Jace. So sure, in fact, that she had staked her reputation on it.

She sat with her hands pressed together, fingers pointed up, with the tips resting against her lips as she regarded him. He tried to act casual, but beneath that air of arrogance, she could sense bluster and anger layered over despair and a hint of shame. This would take careful handling if she didn't want the young man to blow up in her face. She dropped her hands in front of her and clasped them together.

"So, Mister Anderson, here we are."

He stared at her with his lips pressed together, eyes pouting. Anna sighed and began to question her instincts on this course of action, then shook her head. This course could just as easily be the best thing to happen to this young man and the Diplomatic Institute.

Or the worst. No pressure.

"Jace, I understand you are disappointed to discover that Greyson Wells had chosen a student to mentor already and it wasn't you. I realize that this may be difficult for you."

Blinks were the only response to her words. She couldn't help having an edge to her voice as she continued.

"Between your decision to be upset about the state of things, voice your opinion of them, and sit in my office sulking, did you even notice who is listed as your mentor?"

"You."

Satisfied by his words—sullen though they were—that he would now be drawn into the conversation instead of sitting like a lump, she relaxed and nodded. "Yes. And do you remember how often I choose a student to mentor?"

His eyes showed a hint of more interest as he drew his eyebrows together in thought. Finally, he shook his head just as she began to nod hers.

"Correct. You are the first."

"Why?"

His shoulders lowered as he straightened. A brief glance at his eyes showed both curiosity and anger. She didn't think he would easily forget the dream he'd originally had, but she could give him something else to think about. Perhaps eventually he would thank her.

"Why you, or why are you the first?"

"Both."

Anna looked down and examined her hands. These hands were growing older as time marched on. Wasn't that really what irritated her when Grey teased her about being old? She had been grateful for the life extension Bethany Anne's blood had given her, but that extension had been wearing thin recently.

She stood at a crossroads, and she still didn't know which way she would choose: to grow old naturally or use the Pod-doc for another boost to her system that would extend her life for who knew how long as some of the others had. General Lance and those in the leadership barely looked thirty, but they carried twice and three times that number of years.

However she eventually chose, Anna Elizabeth had grown tired of dealing with the issues surrounding her position as dean as well as the role she fulfilled as Head Diplomat. It would take years after Jace graduated for him to be ready, so she needed to start now.

She finally brought her head up and looked at Jace directly in the eyes. "Because Greyson Wells and I hold two of very few positions that take a recruit for one reason only: to train our eventual replacements."

His eyes went wide with shock. She nodded at what she

saw within the young man, then mentally shrugged at the description. Jace was eight years older than Phina, but he still seemed young to Anna.

"Why me?" His voice sounded unsteady, though his eyes were now clear and focused on her.

Anna smiled, satisfied she had him hooked. "Because you are still relatively young, but you are respected by your peers—something I think you have come to realize this last week, I believe. You are smart, stubborn, possess leadership qualities, and can usually remain calm when under pressure."

She raised her eyebrow and his face flushed, no doubt thinking about how he had responded to Phina and Greyson Wells not that long ago.

"You also don't yet have the preconceived ideas current diplomats possess as to what my job entails. They would take the Institute in their own direction, so I need to make sure the person who steps into my shoes not just accedes to the vision I've put in place under Bethany Anne's direction but believes it with their whole being. The future of the Diplomatic Corps demands it. The Empire depends on it.

"Throwing your whole self into what you believe is something you do naturally. In short, you've shown flashes of being exactly the kind of person I need in this position. Now I need to make sure you do more than flash."

Anna leaned forward, eyes intent on Jace, trying to impress on him the importance of what he would be doing as well as ascertain where he now stood.

"Make no mistake, it will be a lot of work, but it can be very rewarding to know you are doing your best to expand

and protect the Empire as well as your fellow diplomats. Does leading and guiding the direction of the Corps sound like something that you can put your heart into? Can you see this work as equally rewarding to what you perceived to be Greyson Wells' role?"

She waited and observed the various thoughts and emotions flitting over Jace's face, which were much as she expected. Disbelief, amazement, yearning, regret, hope, pride, and appreciation all coalesced into determination. She nodded even as he spoke.

"Yes, Dean Hauser."

"Good."

She smiled, and a knot of pressure inside her eased. Now to help that attitude adjustment he'd just made become permanent.

Star System Near the Edge of the Empire, Tluedor, Planet of the Gleeks

Braeden sat with his eyes closed, meditating on top of the tallest rock formation outside of the largest commune on Tluedor, the planet of the Gleeks. It was small compared to other planets, but the Gleeks had made sure the planet could sustain life and provide for their needs.

Gleek - Image by Eric Quigley

If he were to open his eyes, he would see the commune below him, surrounded by the large fields and vineyards the brothers harvested to supply food and drink for their commune as well as to ship to other planets. Since the brothers brought back seeds and samples of plants from every planet they explored, their produce selection had grown exponentially.

The harvest always proved bountiful, thanks to tech the Gleeks had developed several hundred years ago to convert the gases the plants emitted. Those were pumped into the buildings, then circulated into another reservoir that mixed with the moisture in the air and additional minerals to become the best nutrients each plant needed. Nature and technology in perfect balance. If there was a code for how the Gleeks interacted with their environment, that statement described it perfectly.

Braeden's mind remained aware of everything in front

of him, even with his eyes closed. He sat on top of this particular rock formation often, letting his mind relax, open to his world and what it contained. It seemed to help since his mental reach had grown exponentially larger than that of most of his brothers, and not even they knew just how far.

Which was how he knew when a ship entered the atmosphere to descend to the spaceship landing pad some distance to his right. He also knew there were only twenty-two Gleeks aboard out of the twenty-four who had left. Not to mention that he hadn't expected these Gleeks back nearly this soon. They still had eight years left of their time on the Balderian planet.

He reached out with his mind to the leader of the Gleek party that had returned. *What has happened, Brother Traekor?*

"It is terrible news, Brother Braeden."

"Proceed to the main commune area, please. I will meet you there."

"Of course. We will all be there."

Though he had yet to open his eyes, Braeden could see in his mind the tiny figures who exited the spaceship and traveled along the path. When they had reached the halfway point, he knew it was time for him to join them.

Braeden opened his bright green eyes and stood up on his long slender legs. He stepped to the edge of the rock with his long feet that ended in four toes, then used his telekinetic abilities to lift and lower himself down. He landed on the hard rocky ground with his staff outstretched in his hand, brown wraparound shirt and knee-length shorts fitting his body well but loosely, his cloak fluttering around him in the gentle breeze.

He walked along the path until rocky ground turned to soil and then to the rich fields, pulling a few grapes off a vine as he passed the vineyard and popping them into his mouth. As the tart juice from the fruit spurted, he mentally connected with the other leaders of the commune and asked them to join in the meeting.

Braeden used the long walk to soak in and establish a peaceful balance in his hearts and mind. Since his telepathy had become so much stronger than most of his brothers', he already had some understanding of what had happened through connecting with Traekor's mind. His hearts grieved even as he processed his thoughts and emotions. He would do his brothers no good by allowing grief to blind him to the best course.

He entered the main commune building, simple and plain to provide no distractions in the Gleeks' quest for knowledge and understanding, and nodded at his brothers as he passed. Upon entering the room, the buzzing of conversation in his head as everyone strove to understand what had happened rushed full force to the forefront of his mind.

Peace, brothers.

His mental voice sounded quiet but carried an inflection everyone noticed, so one by one, they fell silent. He beckoned them to the circle some had already begun and they all sat together, joining their thoughts into a conscious whole. Present in the circle were the twenty-two Gleeks who had just returned, as well as the ten leaders of the commune.

Now, Brother Traekor, please share what has happened. We give you the circle.

Thank you, Brother Braeden. The news is the worst I can remember in recent history.

Thoughts began to buzz around the circle at that statement.

Please, my brothers. Let us hear the whole of the events that occurred first before we react. Brother Traekor, please tell us the facts. Later we can hear your thoughts on the facts you have presented.

Though Braeden felt his brother stiffen slightly, Traekor assented and related his news. In the end, they were all stunned, concerned, and outraged.

Peace, brothers. Please, let us confer and decide what must be done in recompense for this dishonor done to us. Braeden opened the circle to include the full commune in their mental conference, briefly explaining the facts as he knew them. He strove to keep his brothers calm and on task, an effort that seemed to fail worse with every voice that spoke.

Brother Traekor's mental voice broke through the rest, filled with fire and indignation. *I can see only one course to remedy this dishonor to us all.*

Only now did Braeden remember the reason Traekor had been sent out in one of the delegations instead of remaining home. His ability to balance viewpoints left something to be desired.

Should we send out investigators to ascertain the information that was lost? Perhaps we may not need to administer retribution to the fullest extent.

Braeden felt relief at Brother Kroeden's calm words. At least one person tried to think this through instead of reacting. Some voices reduced their intensity as they debated over the next hour, then began to rehash viewpoints already given.

Let us call the vote.

His earlier relief proved very short-lived.

QBBS *Meredith Reynolds*, All Guns Blazing

Finally, "Stan" made his goodbyes, throwing a wave here, a smile there, and a nod every so often. As they exited the bar, Greyson Wells, AKA "Stan the Man," walked off, throwing over his shoulder, "This way, my little apprentice."

Phina thought about just going home. However, since he was her mentor…

She pinged ADAM after having a thought and waited for him to get back to her as she followed the perpetuator of her irritation.

>>**Hello, Phina.**<<

"Hi, ADAM. Would you mind checking out the guy in front of me? I want to make sure he actually is who he says he is."

He responded after a brief pause. >>**Who did he say he was?**<<

"My mentor."

>>**Ah, yes. The man in front of you *is* your mentor.**<<

"ADAM, is there something going on?"

>>**There is always something going on, Phina.**<<

"Haha. I see through that very obvious deflection, ADAM. That's fine. If it's not something you can talk about, then I won't push you."

>>**Thank you, Phina.**<<

"You're welcome, ADAM."

Phina followed her mentor, who was meandering in what appeared to be no particular direction. By the time she realized the man was trying to determine if a spy had followed them, they had reached a hall off the more public areas. They walked into an office complex and turned down a side corridor. Her mentor pulled out a key card and swiped it on the reader to the side of the door.

After they went in, Phina was surprised by the upscale furniture scattered around the office. Down the hall, they reached a door with another key card access. Phina's eyebrows rose at the stairs they needed to climb and again at the complicated password exchange at the top.

Phina grew more excited as all signs pointed to some secret, mysterious place. What could it be? All sorts of speculation ran wildly through her head as they walked up the stairs. After pushing a few buttons and some whispered conversation, they finally entered the room, that oh-so-secret location, which was....

Another bar?

Phina's gaze darted around the room to ascertain if her eyes were deceiving her. Her shoulders slumped when she realized that she was really standing in another bar, one that had been hidden in a secret room. There were several other patrons in the cozy room, which was large enough that her classmates could all have seats, but not so large that it felt too open. The distance between the booths ensured privacy.

Various aliens and humans sat scattered around the room. A Yollin spoke to a human at a table on her left, his mandibles clicking. At another table, she noticed a Karillian speaking to a Torcellan, eyestalks waving about during the rather intense conversation. In the back of the room, an alien of a type she had never seen before sat looking straight and dignified as he waited. His light-green skin, though very different from that of the Shrillexians, made the red necklace he wore stand out in contrast. One large stone dropped to the middle of his chest, with smaller stones of some kind extending up toward his neck on either side. The strange thing was that all these conversations were completely silent. There must be some sort of technology keeping the conversations private in the booths.

Her eyes moved again and found…Greyson? Stan? He was standing by the bar, though his eyes remained on her. He raised an eyebrow, and she could practically hear him telling her to come over. Phina did so, though she remained quiet so she wouldn't interrupt the conversation that developed as she walked over.

"Hey, Smiley!"

"Hello, Mr. James."

"Ian, Smiley. You can call me Ian."

Phina's mouth dropped open. *Another name?*

"Of course, Mr. James. And the young lady?"

Phina heard someone open the door behind them and turned to see a tall human walk in and assess the bar. She became curious as he walked over to the right side and greeted the other human with a strange handshake, then a mutual cuff on the shoulder. She heard a throat clear and looked back to see that the man of mystery, or at least the man of the changing name, had turned to her with an expectant look on his face.

"Oh, I get to talk now?"

"Of course."

She waved her hand sharply in the air. "Fine, I'll have a Coke."

It wasn't until the bartender began to move that Phina realized something strange about him. She tilted her head in confusion as she tried to puzzle it out. She caught a movement in the corner of her eye and glanced over to see her strange mentor watching her with a satisfied smile as he pushed a button on the counter and the air around them felt muffled. Apparently, that was the sound-canceling control that kept all the conversations private.

"What?"

The bartender brought her Coke over and placed it in front of her. She played with the glass as she stared at her mentor's face, her own confused.

"You appear to be irritated."

Phina stopped moving as she gave him a look of incredulity. "'I appear to be irritated?' Really? I was in training this morning, then classes all day before being confronted by an arrogant fool. I leave irritated and go to meet my friend in the hope of having that irritation relieved when I'm accosted by the strangest man I've ever met and taken to not one, but two bars where I'm ignored by almost everyone before finally arriving at yet another bar that is the strangest place I've ever seen. Why would I be irritated? Being accosted by strange, arrogant men is my primary joy in life, and being ignored by everyone else is the second!"

She scowled at the man before closing her eyes and trying to shake it off. She opened them as he took a sip of his beer and savored it before swallowing. She reached for her glass and had just taken a big gulp when he casually spoke.

"Oh, right. I guess I also forgot to mention that all the regulars at Mac's think you're my sex kitten."

Coke sprayed everywhere.

CHAPTER TEN

QBBS *Meredith Reynolds*, Secret Bar

Phina froze in shock, Coke dripping off her, the bar, and everything else in a four-foot arc. She barely registered Smiley beginning to clean it up out of the corner of her eye. "I'm your *what?*"

"My sex kitten." His eyes danced with amusement, which lit a fire inside of her.

"I most certainly am not, you pervy old man!" She stood up and glared at Greyson or Stan or whatever his name had changed to now. Phina felt entitled to her outrage at his high-handedness.

Greyson grew still, his air that of someone who'd just realized they had made a tactical error. "Well, that's what they…"

Phina's control snapped at his deflection. "I don't care what they think! I care that it was what you told them!" She was so angry her face grew red. She hadn't been this outraged in years.

He put his hands up as if to calm her. "Now, Fee..."

"Fee? Oh, did you forget who you were talking to for a minute? Or have you had so many 'sex kittens' you can't remember my name?"

He opened his mouth to speak and stopped when she stepped within a foot of his face, her voice low and fierce.

"You tell me right now what's going on here and why you are being such a flake when everyone seems to think you're some kind of superman, or I'm walking." Even with the apparent situation, Phina hoped there would be an explanation she could accept. Still, this incident did not make her inclined to be mentored by the irritating man.

He nodded solemnly and spoke as normal. "As you wish, my dear."

Smiley held out a towel to her, and she grabbed it with an appreciative nod. She began to soak up the Coke that she had sprayed on herself while her assigned mentor escorted her past the gawking patrons to the back of the room, where they found a short hallway leading to several doors. He stopped at the very end on the right side and slipped a key card against the scanner. Once Greyson waved her inside, Phina walked into the room, not knowing what to expect. She was intrigued by the comfortable lounge in front of her, complete with soft chairs, a couch, and a long table with seats on either side. Against one wall lay a short bar where several bottles stood, partially empty. The air held the lingering odors of peanuts, beer, and something musky. Phina absently laid the towel on the end of the bar and turned quickly when she heard a loud noise.

Her mentor stood a few feet away clapping his hands, pride and satisfaction on his face once more.

"Brava, my young apprentice. Brava. "

Phina was confused. Very confused. Her gaze darted around the room as she tried to process his remark before returning to his brown eyes. "What are you talking about?"

"I'm talking about your performance out there. Nice job! I couldn't have done better myself."

Her eyes narrowed. "Are you telling me…"

"That everything is not what it seems? That I have been testing you and your responses? That there's a reason for my seemingly strange actions? Correct. You have done very well, my dear."

Phina couldn't believe what she was hearing. "This—all of this—was just an act?"

"Yes. You see…"

Phina forgot everything that was around her, why she was there, and even common sense in her anger. She shifted her body and shot her fist toward the man's face.

When Phina's thoughts began to register again, she had an up-close view of the floor, a heavy, unfamiliar weight on top of her, and a soft voice speaking next to her ear.

"Are you finished?"

"Get off me."

He moved, and she pushed herself to her feet. When she realized her irritation had decreased, she felt better until she saw his smirking face. Phina swung her fist again.

The floor did not improve the second time around. Neither did the weight on her back. Her irritation level, however, had become manageable. As Phina lay there, she began thinking about stress relievers and the need to find some that didn't involve her face and the floor.

"How about now?" Her mentor's voice didn't hold much in the way of emotion, so Phina didn't know how bothered he was about this situation. Probably not at all. Likely that takedown was as easy as pie to him. Really, that would just be her luck.

"I don't know; this floor really improves on further acquaintance. I might want to stay a while longer."

He snorted and moved his weight off her. She cautiously pushed herself to a crouch and warily viewed this strange man she didn't know at all. She needed to acquire an understanding of him and his reasoning, even if it felt like an exercise in futility. He lounged in one of the comfortable chairs a few feet in front of her and slung his leg over the arm.

The man in question grinned. "Want to go for round three?"

She drew a breath and rolled her eyes before shaking her head. "No, thanks. What I really want is to have everything explained so I understand what's going on because there seems to be more here than I would have expected with a diplomatic mentor."

He nodded, his face serious. "True, very true. And that, young lady, is one of the reasons why you were chosen instead of the kid you thoroughly put in his place. You understand when there is more going on and take steps to figure it out, even if you haven't the skills or knowledge to know what it might be."

Phina shrugged; that didn't seem like a big deal to her. Everyone should be doing that, in Phina's opinion. "You said, 'chosen.' What does that mean? It sounds like more than just chosen as your mentee."

"We will get to that."

Phina narrowed her eyes, though her face was otherwise empty of expression. "Seriously? Are you really going to eventually tell me what's going on? Also, what am I supposed to call you? I've heard three names so far. Are any of them your real name?"

Greyson nodded thoughtfully. "Call me by the name others are calling me when there are people around."

Phina muttered. "Right. Like that's not going to be confusing."

He shrugged a shoulder. "Needs must, kid. You'll let other people know something is off if you call me by the wrong name."

Phina snorts in amusement. "I'm not stupid. I can keep track of when I need to call you a different name. And what about when it's just us and we are training? Hey, you? Mentor Man? Stranger Danger? Peter Pervert?" Phina realized her irritation level was growing again and tried to calm herself down by breathing deeply. She stood up and walked over to sit in the chair across from him.

The man grinned. "Almost worth it to see what else you come up with. Call me Link."

"Link?" She tilted her head and squinted at him. "As in 'missing link'? You know, I think I might just see that."

He barked a laugh as she watched him.

"Is that your real name?"

He shrugged, though there was a small hesitation. "It's as good as any other."

She shook her head as she rolled her eyes in exasperation. "Really? Please tell me what the deal is here without any more equivocation."

He nodded and straightened in the chair so he appeared more serious than relaxed. "All right, here's the deal. Remember just about five weeks ago now when you were sitting in General Reynolds' office and Anna Elizabeth talked to you about your future?"

"Yes." Phina didn't know why he would remind her of something that happened in the past, but she wasn't about to slow down any coming answers by asking questions.

He nodded, then gestured toward the ceiling. "Meredith, screen, please. Play back Phina's interview with Anna Elizabeth, beginning when she's offered a job."

Phina saw a vid pop up on the wall several feet away. She was in the General's office with Anna Elizabeth as it began playing the conversation.

Link leaned toward her. "Now watch what Anna Elizabeth does as she talks, particularly when she leans forward."

Phina frowned, not certain what that had to do with anything, but studied the woman's movements. "Is she trying to tell me something without saying anything?"

"Yes. The first time she leans forward is when she talks about side work you might find interesting, which she later tells you has to do with spying."

"But then she said that was years away." Phina tried not to sound sulky, but she didn't think she managed it.

He smiled briefly. "And the next?"

"She's saying she thinks I'll have a satisfying career even if it's not what I wanted." Phina wasn't sure what he was getting at.

He paused the vid. "Here are your first two lessons. The first is that everyone always knows and means more than they are saying. They filter the meaning depending on the situation or the audience, but there is always more going on beneath the words than is actually said. This could be called subtext. You can ascertain a lot just by paying attention and minding the subtext.

"The second lesson is to always pay attention to body language since it tells you just as much as, if not more than, the words that are spoken. Leaning forward shows that something is important or she's serious about what she's saying. Leaning back would imply distance from what she's saying or that she's finished with the serious part. Shifting position from side to side or fidgeting can often mean they are uncomfortable with the topic. Moving frequently from front to back can show passion or agitation.

"The fun part is when their posture is conflicting with their words. That could mean various things, but usually that what they really think or feel isn't what they are saying. So, given this, what is Anna Elizabeth trying to tell you here?"

"That I'll find more opportunities to spy than I realized?" Phina's brain began spinning as she placed these lessons into her view of the world.

Link nodded with a grin. "Exactly."

"Does this lesson of yours apply to aliens too, or just humans?"

"As far as I've seen, it applies, at least in general, to all the species we've come across. However, that doesn't preclude a species where it doesn't."

"So, those aliens in the bar were definitely upset with

you over that cargo even though they were trying to act like everything was fine."

"Furious."

"And Bobcat didn't want you asking about his wife because they had a fight recently."

"Bingo!"

"And that it was about beer."

"Yes. Poor sap."

Her eyes narrowed at his look of superiority. "And that Torcellan female was coming onto you."

"Ah, what?" He looked startled.

Phina leaned forward with a gleam in her eye, "And you don't know what you feel about her yet."

He shifted in his chair. "Ah, well. I would say you've assimilated those lessons adequately."

"In that case, tell me why you found it necessary to tell people I am your...your...*sex kitten!*" Phina realized that part had bothered her more than anything else that he had said or implied so far.

"In my role as Stan, some months ago, when I knew you would be coming on as my mentee, I realized I needed a reason for you to be around me. Stan wouldn't have a mentee or a trainee, as he's much too independently minded and likes his freedom."

Phina raised her eyebrows. Link ignored her as he continued, "So, what to do? What reason could Stan have for a young girl to be around him? Well, the only real reason that occurred would be for some sort of lascivious relationship. So, enter Fee, the sex kitten. I talked you up the last couple of times I was there."

She looked at him incredulously. "Seriously? That's it?

Why not say I'm your niece, and while you hate the baggage of a young kid, you didn't want to leave me stranded? That at least would have been more palatable!"

He wagged his finger at her. "Ah, ah, but would imply Stan has a heart to care about what happens to said niece, and he does not. He's not completely heartless, but everything for him stems back to either business or pleasure, and a young niece doesn't fit either one."

Phina stared at him and tried to piece it all together in her mind. "Why couldn't realizing he had a niece dependent on him change that? It just makes Stan seem somewhat creepy. Bobcat didn't seem the type of person to be friendly with someone like that." She paused, then continued. "Although Bobcat knows Greyson, not Stan."

"Excellent. Now you are thinking. You are entirely correct about Bobcat's character, but he is also one of the few people to know about my cover as sleazy Stan. He helped me establish it."

She scowled at him, her thoughts still whirling. "I don't like it. A sex kitten? Ugh! That is the most opposite of me you could have imagined."

"Needs must, my dear." He shrugged and gave her a small smile.

Phina narrowed her eyes at him and shook her head, speaking decisively. "No. We're doing the niece thing. It's what makes sense, is believable if you explain it right, and I don't need to act too out of the norm for myself. If you really want someone to act like a sex kitten, then you need to find someone else."

He sighed as if he were really put out, but his grin belied the sentiment. "Very good, my dear. I can see we will get along famously. Yes, you are right; I can explain my niece well enough for Stan. Money is always a good motive, so he can get a chunk of money every quarter year to keep her with him. You have to admit, though, that your reaction was priceless." He flashed her another grin.

Phina rolled her eyes but nodded in satisfaction that she wouldn't need to do something so uncomfortable before realizing there were questions she had entirely missed.

"Hold on, you said you have been talking about me for months. It hasn't been months since I talked to Anna." Phina looked at Link warily. "What's going on?"

"Ah, I wondered if you would pick that up, and of course you did." Link eyed her appreciatively. "Let's just say that your spy skills were noticed, and I decided to seek you out. When I saw you really had some skills, I told Anna to add you to the program. You could say you're my recruit."

His eyebrows waggled as Phina frowned and ran over everything that had happened in this new context. "So, you were watching the entire time?"

"I was in the room when you flipped right over Todd's back." Link chuckled. "I've never seen him so surprised."

Phina tabled the rest of the implications of that revelation as she struggled with revealing her surprise and interest. Better to move on. "You talked about Stan being a role. Why would a diplomat have a role as someone in shipping?"

Her eyes grew wider. "Hold on. Ian James? Holy crumbs! You're Ian James, the information acquirer for the Empire?"

"The very same." He gave a little bow. "But just use 'spy,' kid. It's easier. I assume you saw my name on those documents you worked through as you assimilated those briefs about the Leath for the General? That was brilliant, by the way. Nice job."

Phina began to smile, then frowned in confusion. "Wait. You know about that?"

"Of course. I know everything. I probably am the only person in the universe who knows just as much about you as you do, if not more. Well, close enough." He smiled, probably meaning to be kind.

Phina's brain stopped whirling and she paled, her face expressionless. Everything?

Link watched the girl's face grow white, her eyes panicked. Poor kid. She was really messed up about her aunt, and he couldn't blame her. Not at all. Especially when...

He reined in his thoughts so he could respond appropriately. "It's all right, my dear. I know about your Aunt Faith. Don't worry, it doesn't change anything or what I think about you."

He stopped and retracted the statement. "Actually, it does change something because it lets me know that you are strong but can still adapt."

"I don't feel strong." The girl appeared startled by the thought. "I feel like I'm just getting by. Sometimes I think she loves me, and other times I think she hates me. It's...confusing."

"Understandable." He tapped his chin with a finger.

"Think about it this way. Every negative experience can either break us or make us stronger. The worse the experience, the further down either side of that spectrum we could come out of it. Do you feel like you are broken?"

"No." Phina looked thoughtful. "I don't think I'm broken. I think I came awfully close a few times, though."

"That's understandable too. It can be a hard thing to endure every day not knowing what will happen or when the next blowup will occur."

The kid scowled. "Like you would know!"

"I know."

"How can you possibly…"

He leaned forward, looked directly into her eyes, and spoke with restrained ferocity. "I. Know."

The young woman froze as understanding dawned on her. Finally.

Link relaxed in his chair and waved a hand. "Think of it like a butterfly cocoon or a sword being shaped and tempered. All your potential is hiding and waiting, being processed and forged in fire. Then, when you are done with your current shape and you realize how much it's holding you back, you'll burst forth into your final form, sloughing off the parts that aren't needed anymore and will be the strong being you always had inside you. Not broken, stronger. Make sense?"

She nodded, seeming to have put some pieces together. He knew she was a smart kid.

"You're right at the edge of it. I can already see it happening. You are much stronger than you think, my dear. Now comes the hard part."

Her eyes rose to meet his as if asking the question

without words. He grinned, hiding the constant ache underneath. "Believing it."

She snorted but looked thoughtful.

"Now there's something I need to tell you, a question to ask, and an answer you need to give me."

QBBS *Meredith Reynolds*, Secret Bar, Back Room

Wariness crossed the girl's face as she spoke. "Go on."

"You know I'm a diplomat, and you have correctly realized that I'm also a spy. What you don't know is that while there is an organization of diplomats, the Diplomatic Institute, and an organization of spies called SpyCorps, I'm the only one who is connected to both. Some in the know call me the Diplomat Spy, which is why ADAM calls me DS for short."

The girl smiled with a light in her eyes when he mentioned ADAM. Intriguing. He would have to ask ADAM about that if the recently recalcitrant AI would actually answer his damn questions.

"Why are you the only one? Wouldn't it make more sense to have, well, more?"

He shook his head. "The spies and diplomats are all over the Empire, but each of their focus is entirely different. Too many of both tend to be more difficult to wield effectively. Think of it like a knife honed to precision. It's a lot easier and more effective to just use one exactly where it's needed.

"Which is why I am involved in a lot of pies and stick my nose in many places that the diplomats do not, such as Stan in shipping. It's also why my attitude and the way I carry myself will be different depending on where I am and who I'm talking to. Just watch me and who I'm with, and you should be able to figure it out pretty quickly."

"Is that why Greyson is so arrogant?"

Link snorted in amusement. "You haven't met many diplomats yet, kid. They are all arrogant to some degree. Trust me, Grey slides right in."

Her eyes narrowed as she continued her interrogation. "And why Stan is so sleazy?"

Suddenly uncomfortable, he rubbed the back of his neck, then shrugged. "Some types of people will only talk to others if they think there's common ground. He fits a need."

She was quiet and Link eyed her warily, wondering about the direction of her thoughts. That startled him since he hadn't cared what people thought about him in a long time. Why had he even told her to call him Link? He hadn't used that name in… He shoved that thought aside. Finally, the girl shrugged and moved on, which filled him with relief. He didn't like it one bit and he scowled, not that it deterred the kid.

"So, what's this question you want to ask me?"

"I need to train someone else to be the new Diplomat Spy, and the person I have chosen to replace me is you."

Phina absorbed that for a moment as she watched him scowl in irritation before dropping all expression. He held himself perfectly still. Based on the lesson he had just taught her and having thought through the various implications and deductions about other behaviors, this made her think her answer was extremely important to him for reasons he hadn't named yet. Not that he had asked her a question.

So, she waited.

It wasn't very long until he frowned and turned his hands out. "Well?"

Phina blinked and smiled sweetly while she clasped her hands in front of her. "Oh, I'm sorry. I was waiting to hear a question."

"Smartass." Link scowled and said something in a language she recognized as Italian. She hadn't learned a lot of it, but what she could make out sounded like, "Heaven… me from kids who act older…their age."

That sobered the amusement right out of her. "If you 'know,' then you should also know that all of it ages you. I haven't felt like a kid in years. The closest I've come to it is when I'm with Alina."

"I do know." He nodded, and the gravity in his eyes caused him to appear his age instead of the perpetual youth look. "Having a difficult parent or guardian is hard, but when you have one and you never know how they will respond or react, it makes you constantly on guard. You never feel safe. The reality of that feeling ages you, weighs you down, and makes you feel like a planet rests on your shoulders. Of course it ages you when you have more serious things on your mind than the concerns most kids and teens do. Their thoughts are on comfort and fun; yours are on survival and making it through the day intact. Those are worlds apart when it comes to maturity. It's nothing to be ashamed of. Use it to your advantage and to make yourself stronger."

Phina felt uncomfortable but strangely relieved that someone knew and understood what she had gone through with her aunt. Not that it was the worst thing; it was not like her aunt beat her. Yet, hearing it out loud made it more real. Phina looked down and picked at her clothes until she heard him clearing his throat.

"So, Phina. Again, I am in need of training a replacement, and you have an interest in spying and helping the Empire. Would you please consider being my trainee, with the goal of becoming the new Diplomat Spy?" He looked at her expectantly.

Phina sat back and twaddled her fingers together as she thought. "Would I be able to become a regular spy instead?"

Link scowled, then mumbled curse words to the ceiling before shaking his head. He got up and began to pace as he muttered to himself under his breath, occasionally glancing at her. After a moment, he stopped next to her and pointed.

"Fine. If you really want to leave the Diplomatic Institute and be a spy full time, you can do that." Her eyes lit up but he waved a hand. "However, all spies in SpyCorps have to have some form of business or trade as a cover, so you will need to learn something in addition to spycraft. Is there some other profession that has caught your attention?"

Phina didn't even have to think about that. "No."

He spread his hands as if to say, "Well, then the answer's obvious."

She sighed internally, still debating her answer. She had always wanted to be a spy, and this was her chance to do so. Was he really offering anything different than what she had already accepted from Anna Elizabeth? Except now, she would have spying, too. Put that way, there was only one answer.

"Yes."

"Excellent."

He grinned and sat down. She thought she detected an air of relief but figured she'd imagined it. He studied her thoughtfully for a moment before leaning forward.

"Let's talk about your vow."

Phina narrowed her eyes and grew wary. "Why?"

"Tell me about it." His air of casualness belied the seriousness she saw in his eyes.

Phina's vow had been very important to her. She didn't want to share it and have him ridicule her or put it down. She also realized she had a hard time adjusting to all the new people in her life. Each person had an opinion about what she should do. *Particularly this man.* She looked at him sourly, and a feeling spurted up inside her. It was annoyance, she reminded herself as Link raised his eyebrows, waiting.

Finally she threw her hands up. "Fine. You're just going to keep asking if I don't tell you, aren't you?"

"Of course! Now you are getting it." He grinned.

She sighed. She didn't want to make it a bigger deal than it already was. "Basically, I vowed to make sure mistakes never happen again so that no loved ones would be lost. That I would become a stealthy information acquirer who passed on data to prevent death and atrocities."

Link appeared thoughtful, turning that over in his head before looking her in the eye. "And what happens to you and your vow when a mistake happens? Because, trust me, kid, mistakes happen all the time. Big, little, insignificant, they all happen.

"So, is your vow compromised because one person forgot to tell their teammate something and a person died? Or is it when a leader tells their unit information that they thought was true but proved incomplete, and half of them died while the rest were significantly injured? Is it Marine- or Guardian-wide only? Where do you draw that line of what information you need to be involved with and what you will assume is your fault because you didn't know?"

"You're just a little ray of sunshine, aren't you?" Phina was angry, frustrated, sad, and uncertain. She was on an emotional roller coaster and wasn't sure what to say or how to react. She realized she didn't like his question, no matter how valid. "I don't know."

"It's not bad, kid. We just need to refine it a little so you aren't assuming responsibility for things outside of what you can handle or control. That's the kind of thing that can crush a person if they aren't careful.

"How about we tweak it this way: 'To gain the best information available in the hope of saving as many lives as possible.' Would that allow you to keep the nature of your vow and hopefully your sanity later on? This is just the beginning, my dear. You don't want to drown yourself in impossible tasks right away." He smiled, and his eyes appeared kind.

Phina agreed though she added playfully, "I like to contemplate six impossible things before breakfast."

He flashed her a grin before continuing, "The last thing is that we will need to get you in the Pod-doc sometime this next week to be fitted with a new type of communicator that transmits faster and easier so there are fewer issues on missions. Would you be willing to do that?"

She nodded, her interest rising. New tech always got her attention.

He flashed her a grin. "Good. Oh, by the way, here in this location, your cover is as my spy trainee. The demonstration we gave everyone earlier has established that you aren't thrilled to be connected to me. For the near future, just continue that."

Phina let out a long breath. He was being considerate now, and she wondered if he wasn't as arrogant or sleazy as she had first thought. Of course, that thinking totally broke down with his next words, causing her to scowl.

"All right, my lovely little sex kitten...I mean, 'trainee.' It's time to see what you're made of. When we go out there, I need you to look none too happy with me."

"Trust me, that won't be a problem."

He winked as he stood up and moved toward the door.

She shook her head but followed him out the door, waited while he locked it behind them, and walked into the bar area. As they went to the outer door, she could hear Link, or rather Ian James, call to the bartender, "See ya, Smiley! Put some of that dark rum in the back, will you?"

"Of course, Mr. James."

"Ian, Smiley. Call me Ian."

"Yes, Mr. James."

While this exchange occurred, Phina glanced around the bar again, trying not to stare at the other patrons, who had increased by a handful while they had been in the room. She almost gave herself whiplash turning her head when she realized her Ethics teacher sat in a back booth on her left.

Link grabbed her arm and gave it a tug toward the door. She took a step before realizing she was supposed to be unhappy with him and jerked her arm away, giving him a scalding look before stomping ahead of him to the exit.

"Just so, my dear, just so," he murmured next to her as he put in the code to open the door.

They were silent as they retraced their steps through the office complex to the main area. Phina followed a step behind and to his left as they traversed the hallways. Finally, she couldn't hold her tongue any longer.

"Would you please tell me where we are going?"

"Very good, my dear! That took thirty seconds longer and was in a much better tone than I had expected." He winked at her, causing her to roll her eyes again, which in turn caused him to laugh.

"Now, kid, we need to talk shop on the way. Sort of a pop quiz, the outcome of which will determine how bad the next week will be for you."

He grinned at her dark expression. "You really need to learn how to control the emotions expressed on your face. Let's call that your third lesson. Everyone shows more of their internal thoughts on their face than they realize. As a diplomat, you don't want to show that you think the person you are talking to is an arrogant ass, even when they are. And in regard to the other profession, it can save your life to be able to keep your real emotions hidden.

"Right now, I can see your every expression flit across your face. Oh, you aren't as bad as some—your friend Alina for instance—and not everyone would notice. However, you could get in a spot of trouble or cause an incident if you weren't careful and completely in control of yourself. Best to avoid that."

Following him became much more difficult when they joined other humans and aliens in the crowded corridors. She suspected that had been why he had referred to being a spy in vague terms.

As she listened, she wiped all expression off her face. Lesson number three was a good reminder but wasn't needed. She just had to remember to show the emotion she wanted to express instead of what she felt.

In some ways, it felt like a relief to drop all emotion. After years of being around her aunt, she knew how to hide her emotions all too well. It had become normal. They were usually buried deep, and it took effort to tap into them. She tried to act normal around other people though, which meant showing what you were feeling.

Link nodded approvingly, though she sensed a sadness in him that made her wonder if he knew why it was easy for her. Since he had said he knew everything about her and it sounded like he had been in a similarly difficult situation, she wouldn't put it past him to know about her emotions, even though she had never told anyone.

"So, pop quiz. Did you see the two humans exchanging a clever little handshake back there?"

Only a small crease between her eyebrows showed she was thinking. "Before we went into the back room, there was one exchange. A strange sort of handshake and then a cuff on the shoulder."

"Excellent. What handshake did they perform?"

He looked at her expectantly, but she could only shrug. "I don't know. I've never seen it before."

"Ah, I would be very disappointed if you had, but take a note now. If you see that handshake again, you need to pay very close attention to them without appearing to do so. Most of the time, it will be members of Spy Corps and our trusted associates, who you will discover later. If he had not done that handshake protocol exactly right, I would have notified Reynolds to begin the process of shutting him down if he hadn't already done it himself."

"Wouldn't that be Meredith?"

"Nope! Reynolds is the man for all defense-related matters. Or the EI, I suppose I should say. Now, did you notice anything else about the members that were in the bar, both when we first got there and on our way out?"

"Well, yeah, my Ethics teacher was there. That was weird."

He looked intrigued. "Really? Who was that? I haven't checked the roster this year."

She shrugged. "I've never heard his name said, but the roster shows a listing for M.P. He is about your age, with darker skin and salt and pepper hair. He sat with a couple other people in the back booth on the left."

"Ah. Mr. Prez."

"Mr. Prez? That seems like a weird name."

"Yup, definitely. So Anna got the old man involved, eh?

Good on her." He mumbled this last as they turned a corner.

Phina struggled to keep up with and follow the strange man who was her mentor. She still didn't know where they were going but began to have a feeling.

"Anything else interesting, funny, or odd in the bar?" He spoke absently, as if he weren't paying attention.

"Well, there was this weird alien."

"Uh-huh."

"He sat all the way in the back."

"Right."

"He was green, but not like a Shrillexian. This was a lighter green."

"Good, good."

She wondered if he was even paying attention to her. "After we left, he got up and danced on the table."

He burst out laughing. "Now that would have been funny as hell."

Phina looked at him doubtfully. "I'm under the impression that hell isn't really supposed to be all that funny."

He raised his eyebrows. "It's just an expression, kid. Don't overthink it."

Phina followed Link into another hall. She knew where they were going now, which made her very curious.

"Was that all you noticed about this weird green alien?"

"Oh, no. I just wanted to make sure you were paying attention. He wore this big red pendant on a necklace with these other rocks around it."

"Excellent."

"What is it?"

"Which, the alien or the necklace?"

She rolled her eyes from a step behind him. "I would have said who for the alien, but now that you are asking, I am curious about both."

"Ah, well, that necklace has two different versions of it. One applies to their religious order, and the other is dispensed only to their assassination squad."

Phina's mouth dropped open as they stopped in front of the door. Her eyes went wide with alarm before she remembered she wasn't supposed to be showing emotions now, and she relaxed so as to appear only mildly interested. Her mentor's eyebrows went up though his eyes grew warm with approval. Phina felt warm inside at the affirmation. "Which one was this?"

"Did you see a black ring around the red pendant?"

She brought it back to mind. "No."

"Just so. He isn't an assassin. An assassin would have been too dangerous to steal a pendant from."

"Steal?"

"Yes, that man was an impostor. I notified Reynolds, but he was already aware."

She felt puzzled, not having seen anything weird aside from him being a green alien with jewelry. "How did you know?"

"Simple." He grinned. "A real member of their religious order wouldn't have been caught dead in a bar."

Phina stared at him, then shook her head. "So, why isn't all this in the databases? You would think the info would be widely useful."

The man grinned at her with unholy glee. "Oh, so you checked? Well, maybe you weren't checking the right labels."

Phina frowned, then quickly pulled out her tablet and did some searching. She began shaking her head as she realized he was right. The information *was* there, but you needed to know where to look for it to find it.

There were so many things she needed to learn about the various cultures, as well as what she needed to learn about being a spy. As she followed Link into the room, she ruefully thought of herself a few weeks ago when she believed she had already reached a top spy level.

Amazing what a difference in perspective a few weeks made.

CHAPTER TWELVE

Etheric Empire, Vermott, Planet of the Baldere

Geirik held a half-drunk glass of ale in his hand as he leaned against the railing on the balcony and watched the system's second sun sink toward the horizon. The dark ale was one of the best by-products of joining the Empire. However, in Geirik's mind, nothing compared to looking over the city on the best planet in the galaxy at sunset.

Strong but soft arms wrapped around his middle and caused him to amend that thought. He put his ale down on the table beside him and turned his head to see his beautiful bondmate smiling up at him with love in her blue eyes. He turned and enveloped her in his arms, resting his head against hers with a low sigh.

"Thinking about something difficult, hey?"

He laughed softly and whispered, "You."

"Aye, something difficult indeed," she teased as she pulled back to look into his worried eyes. "You're thinking about Velof again."

"Aye."

She closed her eyes and leaned her head against his chest. He knew she was smelling his scent since she'd told him before it was one of her favorite things and it centered her when she didn't know what to do. Since he felt the same way, he pulled her tighter against him and laid his head on hers.

"Is it our fault?"

Fastel lifted her head at his mumbled words, revealing surprised and confused eyes. "Is what our fault?"

"Velof."

Compassion softened her expression as she lifted her hands to his face, stroking with her thumbs. "No, my love, he is not our fault. Though we did play a part, it was Velof that cheated in the Jeskir games. We just didn't know until it was too late."

He looked down with troubled eyes. "He was my best friend, Fas."

"Aye, and now you've got a better one." She squeezed him tight.

"Halvad *has* proved to be a great friend." He reached behind her to run his fingers through her long hair.

She thumped his back and glared up at him, the slight upturn of her mouth revealing her amusement. "I meant me, you big oaf!"

He grinned as he reached behind him and took her hands. "I know."

She snorted but smiled. Tension released inside Geirik as he let himself be in the moment with his female. "Have I ever told you, Strength of My Soul, how happy I am that you chose me as your bondmate?"

Her eyes shone with love as she propped her chin on

his chest and peered up at him. "Perhaps once or twice, but it's getting kind of faint. Maybe you need to refresh my memory, hey?"

He grinned since her sense of humor and gentle teasing were just two of the many things he loved about her before looking at her with serious eyes. "I wouldn't change a single thing, Fastel. Losing Velof's friendship, even losing the games last time. Does that make me a terrible leader for our people, that I would choose you over them?"

"You're choosing them now, my love. Velof has gone too far." She frowned, thinking. "It's not wrong to want to believe the best of your best friend. As much as we pride ourselves on our strength, it is our hearts that make us who we are as a people, hey?"

Geirik began to squeeze her hands, but Fastel pulled away to pace the few steps the balcony afforded, growing more impassioned with every thought.

"When I chose you over Velof, he was the one who decided to cut off your friendship. He decided to become the Jeskir no matter what it took. He took everyone's trust and burned it to ashes when he turned to criminal activity against our people instead of protecting them. He was always weak inside, Geirik." She stretched her calloused hands out, palms up. "It's why I chose you over him, hey? His weakness is just now coming out for everyone to see."

He grunted in agreement and turned to catch the last light of the sun as it dropped below the horizon. She was right about everything. Geirik knew that, though it didn't stop his musings. His hand had almost reached his glass to drink it down when he heard Fastel's soft voice behind him.

"Do you blame me?"

He turned his head in surprise to see her beautiful face downcast, her body stiff with tension. In all their years together, she hadn't once asked him, though every so often, he had seen the question in her eyes. Given the Rikhar, he should have known this had been troubling her and given his love peace long ago. He let out the tension he had been holding and strode the few steps to stand in front of her, his hand reaching out to stroke her violet cheek.

"No, Fas. I've blamed myself. I've blamed Velof. I've blamed Drestin. I've even blamed our mothers for the way they handled our bondmatching, and our fathers for the pressure they placed on us, but never once have I ever blamed you."

He put one arm around her waist and the other held her head to him as his strong, fierce bondmate's eyes leaked on his shirt in relief.

QBBS *Meredith Reynolds*

Phina couldn't take any more. The dratted man was running her ragged, practicing diplomacy skills, spying skills, and fighting skills over the last several weeks between her classes and sessions with Maxim. Granted, she had been eager to learn a lot of the new skills and usually learned them quickly.

The subject matter wasn't the problem. She learned fast, often after seeing something only once.

It was the pace and Link's constantly changing attitude that were the problems. He had taken her to different locations on the station and expected her to adapt to that situation. That would have been fine if he had given her a clue about what she would be walking into.

Oh, no. Not Greyson Wells. Drat the man. She couldn't think of him as Link during those moments, as if his massive ego needed the full name to hold it. Link could almost be a friend at times, irritating though he might be. Greyson Wells was a slave driver.

Especially when he seemed to lack any compassion for her. "Sink or swim, kid. Sink or swim."

The arrogant, infuriating, pompous ass.

Phina decided she needed time to herself: no new skills to learn, no being on edge, just Phina. To that end, after her training with Link was done for the day, Phina had walked away and kept walking.

Eventually her steps had led her to a deserted hallway. A tingle of excitement ran up her spine as she grinned at the long, empty stretch. She bent over and extended her limbs to stretch her body. Finally, she popped up and ran down the corridor.

When her muscles had warmed up enough that they wouldn't cramp, Phina began one of the tumbling passes she performed in the halls. Since she had no padding to protect her body if she fell, she stuck to her tried and true favorites: cartwheel, front handspring, roundoff, back flip.

The airtime felt glorious.

After landing, Phina closed her eyes and took a deep breath, not even minding the dusty smell of disuse that permeated these corridors. She really wanted to climb around in the air shafts to feel more like her old self, but she didn't have her body suit. After another deep breath, she stepped forward and bent down into a handstand.

As she alternated between standing and walking on her hands, with part of her brain keeping track of how long she could stay up, Phina finally had the mental space to think things through.

She eventually came to two conclusions.

First, this was all training. Everything was training. She didn't doubt that a big part of Link's attitude was on purpose, to push her or to see how she would react. She needed to take everything in stride and adapt as quickly as she could.

And second, she really needed to do gymnastics more often. If only she had a set of bars she could use. She used to love flying through the air with only her hands to keep her from falling. It was freeing in a way she needed.

She remembered what Link had told her on their first day about sloughing off the fears and insecurities she had acquired by dealing with her aunt for years and realized that was exactly what she needed to do.

Phina had always wanted to go her own way. She wasn't one to fit in naturally or be a part of the norm. She wanted to walk to her own beat and not feel like it was necessary to apologize for it. However, her aunt had made her think she should be ashamed of herself, that she wasn't good enough unless she conformed to what her aunt wanted. That ended up making her feel like she had to apologize for being who she was, even if she didn't want to.

She paused her handstand, lowered her legs, and stood. Phina stared in front of her though she didn't focus on anything in particular.

Was it really so simple?

Accept who she was, don't apologize for it, and don't let

anyone's opinion make her feel like she was…less. It seemed easy in concept, but she didn't think it would be quite as simple in practice. After years of feeling like she needed to be less, it wouldn't just take one realization to make her feel like she could be herself, let alone become more.

Still, the realization made her feel lighter and cleaner. Perhaps a few of those layers really had sloughed off.

Phina closed her eyes and decided to just let go and relax. A song popped into her head and she started moving to that inner music, shaking off the nerves and turning stretches into dance moves. When her muscles had loosened up again, she opened her eyes and eyed the corridor as she stopped moving.

The music still playing in her mind, she took a deep breath and began to run. With the corridor clear, Phina closed her eyes and began a new pass, this one more difficult: cartwheel, front handspring, roundoff, back handspring, back layout.

She flew through the air, gaining momentum, hands and feet only touching the floor for brief moments. Phina felt relaxed and free for the first time in weeks. The final move was risky without a mat below her, but she could feel the movement in her body, the resistance in the air, and knew it would be fine. No, not fine.

Perfect.

Her hands left the floor and she flew backward, her body whipping around and her head missing the corridor's ceiling by inches, then her feet touched down while her body leaned forward slightly to help stop the momentum. Her feet slid a few inches, then stopped.

Phina jumped up with a whoop and a grin and did a happy dance. She knew what she needed to do now. She wanted that freedom in more than just the way her body moved. She would learn all the skills, experience, and tricks she could, internalize them to make them her own, and then figure out her own path in the diplomat and spy worlds.

Her heart felt lighter as she wandered home, not even changing when she saw Link leaning against the door to her suite with a smirk on his face as she approached.

"Come on, kid. We've got a situation happening tonight, and you need to come with."

He looked her up and down, appraising her appearance. "You should probably change clothes, though. You'll need something a little more formal."

Tensing again, Phina groaned inside. Dressing up was her least favorite part of being a diplomat so far. "So, this is a Greyson Wells situation?" It was always helpful to know which persona she was expected to interact with, even if he told her nothing else about it. If he decided to share that info.

He grinned. "Nope, Ian James. Just hold onto the attitude that you can barely stand to be seen with your mentor, let alone touch him, and you should be good."

Shooting him a look devoid of any expression except the glare, she walked past his grinning face of approval to enter her apartment and change.

"Just like that, my dear. Just like that."

As she let him in to wait for her, Phina remembered what she had decided not long before and felt the tension leave her body again.

Training. It was all training.

QBBS *Meredith Reynolds*, Receiving Hall

Jace had never worked harder in his life, and he had a niggling thought that perhaps this was all a big mistake. *He really should have been picked by Greyson Wells.* That some ignorant girl who didn't even know who Greyson Wells was or the bigger picture of the Empire shouldn't have gotten the coveted spot Jace wanted.

Granted, eventually becoming the Head of the Diplomatic arm of the Empire meant he would eventually become Phina's boss. He rather liked that part, and he did believe in a lot of the goals Anna Elizabeth had outlined for the Diplomatic Corps. The thought of helping his friends and fellow students and having their backs warmed him.

Still.

He'd never thought he would be helping organize the annual gala for the diplomats, the alien representatives, and the various leaders of the Empire. When he had recovered from his shock at the job request by Anna Elizabeth, he had asked if those leaders included the Empress. She had laughed, and in a moment of candidness, she'd said Bethany Anne would rather poke a sharp stick in her eye.

Jace was beginning to agree with that sentiment.

After running around all day attending to last-minute issues that absolutely had to be taken care of, Jace had finally gotten a moment to himself. He withdrew to the corridor outside the receiving hall that was empty now that everyone had gathered in the event room. He leaned against the wall near the corner of a cross corridor and closed his eyes.

They popped open again a moment later when he heard and recognized voices coming down the next corridor around the corner. Phina and Greyson Wells. Just his luck to have to face them now. He began to slink back down the hallway when their voices gave him pause.

"Why are we going this way? There's nothing here but that gala for the diplomats."

"Ah, my dear, that's why we've come."

"What? You told me this was an Ian James event, not Greyson Wells!"

"Of course, and it is. Or rather, it's both."

There was a slight pause. Their voices grew louder as they moved closer. He stepped back step after step as he continued to listen, but it sounded like they had stopped speaking for a moment. He hesitated since this sounded like a private conversation, something he wasn't supposed to know about. Who was this Ian James? He cringed at the thought of getting another scathing look from either of them.

"Oh, come now, my dear. Surely you knew it wouldn't be easy all the time."

"So, what you are saying is that you might not tell me everything I need to know, and I have to be prepared for anything no matter what you tell me because you might not tell me the truth or at least all the truth."

"Of course. As you *should* be prepared for anything."

"Being prepared for anything is one thing. Throwing me a curve like this makes it so that I'm not sure I can trust you. I need to be able to trust you if this is going to work."

A longer pause. Jace stopped moving in surprise, and he had to admit to some curiosity as he leaned forward to hear the reply. Had he backed up too far? He had lifted his foot to take a step toward the cross corridor when Greyson Wells answered.

"Fair enough. How about this? I promise I will tell you which personas we are walking into beforehand, even if I don't tell you anything else. Especially if there is more than one type of situation involved like there is in this one."

Another pause. He wished he could see if Phina was nodding. Body language made things much easier. He almost missed her answer since she spoke in a low voice.

"You're lucky I had a fancy dress to wear, thanks to Alina."

"And you look lovely, my dear."

Jace backed up quickly and leaned against the wall near the door of the receiving hall, trying to act natural as they strode around the corner and approached him. Greyson Wells' face was impassive, and his stride was easy. Perhaps his jaw seeming to be clenched was just a trick of the light. His dress clothes were fancier than normal but nothing out of the ordinary.

Phina, on the other hand, looked very different than normal. Gone were the t-shirt and jeans, the boots and the jacket. She wore a long dark-blue dress that sparkled in a pattern of some kind, but it wasn't discernible. Beneath the sparkles lay occasional streaks and clouds in faint blues, reds, and purples. It looked like a view of the depths of space layered over a dress. He tilted his head and stared, thinking it was cleverly made.

She wore glittery earrings and a silver necklace with a

pendant that didn't go with the dress but did suit Phina. Her hair, usually left down and barely brushed, had been pulled up and piled on her head, making her look grown up for once. It suited her, and he realized that since she appeared a little older now, her outside appearance now matched her eyes, which had always seemed older than her age and a little eerie to him.

"You're going to catch flies with that mouth, boy."

Jace blinked at Greyson Wells as he clicked his mouth shut. With a nod to both of them, he gestured them inside the hall. As they passed, he saw her eyes flick to her mentor as she pursed her lips. Taking another moment for himself, he drew a breath and let it out. He heard Phina speak quietly as they moved farther into the room.

"You didn't have to be rude to him."

"He was staring. It was rude of the boy to do it."

"Responding to rudeness with rudeness. Yeah, that always works out so well. Who's the famous diplomat now? Maybe you can introduce me. Apparently, I haven't met him yet."

Greyson Wells' response was lost in the noise of the room, but Jace turned to view them as they made their way to the beverage station. While Phina had placed her hand in the crook of Greyson's arm, she stood stiffly with her body as far from his as she could manage. Craning his neck to see over the crowd, he saw that Greyson stood easily, looking around the room and glancing down at the young woman every so often. He watched Greyson pour a glass and hold it out to her. Phina glared at him and poured a glass for herself while the older man shrugged and drank the one he had poured.

Their dynamic was…odd. And unexpected. And somehow worked.

The part of him that was still angry about being passed over for Phina lightened and another part was relieved.

Perhaps the mentoring decision had not been a mistake.

CHAPTER THIRTEEN

QBBS *Meredith Reynolds*, Marines' Workout Area

The past few weeks had been interesting—also irritating, confusing, and frustrating—and they had been long. She wondered what would happen today as she followed Link into the room she usually used when sparring with Maxim. Part of her just wanted to go home, and the rest couldn't have been dragged away by an angry Wechselbalg.

Maxim waited on the mat, though he moved through a fighting sequence that made it look like he fought an invisible person. He threw his whole self into every movement, and Phina was dismayed to realize how much he had been holding back with her.

Link didn't stop on the edge of the mat as she had. He continued to calmly and purposefully walk over to meet Maxim, who continued his strikes and blocks. The Guardian paused for a moment when Link drew closer.

"Don't stop now, boy. You were just getting to the good part."

Maxim stared at Link, causing Phina to wonder what

he saw in the older man's face. Link just stood there looking cool, calm, and unreasonably happy with himself, judging by the smirk on his face. After a moment, Maxim nodded, then continued on in his fighting movements, this time against Link.

Phina expected Maxim's fists and feet to connect with the other man, throwing him down or backward as she often had been. That never happened. Every time Maxim's fist or foot reached their extension, Link just wasn't there, having moved out of the way or moving the limb to the side away from him. The human kept the Were from connecting.

Huh.

After a couple of minutes of watching in amazement, she began to focus on what Link did specifically. Phina realized that he actually moved very little, just enough to deflect or guide Maxim's attacks to miss him. He never turned his movements into an attack, only defended. Most he deflected, though a few connected, judging by the grimace that appeared on his face. Once she began to understand Link's style, it changed.

Now as Maxim punched, instead of letting the attack slide to the side, Link grabbed the limb as he deflected the hit and pulled as he pivoted, throwing Maxim to the mat. Rather than his movement being arrested and falling into the hold the Were had shown her weeks ago, Maxim rolled as he fell, pulling Link with him. Link let go of the arm to prevent himself from falling, allowing Maxim to turn the roll into a move to stand and face him again.

Phina could see the sweat dripping on Maxim's body since he had barely stopped moving since before they had walked in, having been sparring for some time. Now Maxim moved to kick Link in the stomach. Link stepped to the side, grabbed his leg, and yanked as he pulled and turned, throwing Maxim to the floor. Maxim grabbed Link as he fell and took him down with him.

She assumed it would finish with one of them pinning the other, but Link must have broken Maxim's hold and rolled away from him since they stood to face each other at the same time.

"Good."

Maxim stared at the older man with curiosity and suspicion. "Who are you?"

Link smirked arrogantly, and Phina knew he had assumed his diplomatic persona. She shook her head. This name-changing thing could get confusing. Phina didn't think she wanted to have as many names and covers as Greyson had. How could he keep it all straight as to who knew which one, and how did he keep some from realizing others called him a different name? Something to think about later.

"I'm Phina's mentor Greyson Wells."

Maxim stood with his feet shoulder-width apart as he always did. His stance radiated purpose and contained movement as if he could burst into motion at any time. "Maxim Nikolayevich."

"That's not all of it, though, is it?" Greyson cocked an eyebrow at the other man. Phina thought it would take a lot of self-control not to try to smack that look off his face. Not that it had done her any good that day in the secret bar when *she* had tried to hit the man. She watched Maxim with new eyes. She didn't know how he could stand there and not punch the man in the face, though he hadn't had much luck just a few minutes ago. Still, it showed a lot of control and careful consideration.

Maxim's eyebrows drew in as if he were perplexed by the question. "I'm not sure what you are getting at."

"Sure. We'll go with that."

Greyson turned to look at Phina for a moment, likely noticing her arms were crossed and her feet were set slightly apart. She crossed her eyes and stuck out her tongue at him, eliciting nothing more than a glint of amusement. She sighed and wondered what his angle with Maxim was. The dratted man liked to poke buttons and see what popped out.

Maxim glanced at them, looking a little unsure. "I've wondered if I could meet you, but I'm not sure what is going on here."

"Ask, and you shall receive. If it works into my plans anyway!" Link grinned briefly before growing serious. "I told you to meet us here for a few reasons. The first was to demonstrate to Phina part of the style I want you to make sure she knows. It's easier to see it in action against someone else first. You might want to bring someone else in occasionally to demonstrate."

Maxim and Phina both nodded. It *had* been helpful to see the movements in action.

"The second was to meet you and make sure we are all on the same page as to what needs to happen with her training. You are teaching her Sambo, correct? She is doing well, but I want you to accelerate her training. Right now, she's a little too easy to put on the ground."

He turned to her with a wink that elicited a scowl from

her. Oddly, it seemed to delight him. Or not so oddly, considering she knew he liked to poke buttons. Maxim watched the exchange with a slight frown before Greyson turned back.

"Do you know Krav Maga? After Phina gets a little more acclimated to Sambo, begin adding some of those moves for defense and takedowns."

Maxim nodded and looked thoughtful, his eyes speculative as he glanced at Phina. She fought the urge to shift position, wondering what he was thinking.

"The third reason was to check in with you and find out if you both have what you need. I'll be gone for a week or so and want to make sure her training is taken care of while I'm gone."

Phina felt oddly deflated. He had been gone for a day at a time occasionally, but this would be the first extended trip since he had become her mentor. But since he was a diplomat and a spy, he would probably need to travel a lot. Maybe at some point, she could travel with him.

"She needs to practice her acrobatics, which requires specialized equipment we don't have. It's a skill she should hone since not many fighters have them and they are useful, given her size."

"Gymnastics." Phina and Grey corrected Maxim simultaneously, then she made a face at her mentor. He smiled. "Yes, I do pay attention to what you say. This is something you've mentioned wanting before, right?"

"Yes," she admitted. "I need to practice and stretch more."

"Switch out two trainings per week for gymnastics and

agility. You can decide together when those are. What equipment do you need for that?"

Greyson looked at her expectantly. She eyed the room and shrugged.

"For the absolute basics, the mat needs to expand to almost twice the size. The tumbling passes can get long. After that, I would need bars of some kind and perhaps a balance beam."

Phina held her breath and tried not to radiate her excitement. She had been wishing for a set of bars for years, and a balance beam as well as the larger mat would make it gymnastics heaven for her.

Grey looked up in thought a moment before glancing at Phina and Maxim. "The mat we can do, the beam we probably can do. I'm not sure about the bars. Maxim, could you get with ADAM and Meredith to see what materials and supplies we need to build them?"

Phina grew more excited. She tried to contain it but still did a little shimmy. *Yes!* Greyson turned back to her and she froze, though judging by his raised eyebrow, he had caught it. She gave him a smirk, and he responded by pulling his mouth to the side as if to say, "Nice try."

Maxim watched this exchange with confusion, but he nodded. "I'll check with him and see if we can get them made."

"Excellent." Link turned back to the younger man and looked at him intently. And it *was* Link this time, no personas or anything to dilute the man staring out of those brown eyes. Phina wondered what was going through his head.

Finally, he nodded his head. "Thank you for taking care of teaching Phina how to fight."

Maxim bobbed his head as well. "Of course." He hesitated, apparently considering.

"Spit it out, man. No need to stand on ceremony."

"May I ask why you are satisfied with my training her when you seem capable yourself?"

Link rested his hand on his hip as he leaned on one foot. "That's simple to answer. Aside from Bethany Anne and her inner circle, including Peter Silvers and Todd Jenkins, who is the best at training someone in combat?"

Maxim scratched his neck as he answered. "It's arguable, but probably me."

"There's your answer. I don't have time to do it myself." Link turned to the door.

"But why does Phina *need* combat training, and why at such an accelerated pace? Isn't she in the Diplomatic Institute?"

Link turned back and scowled at the younger man, his eyes narrowing as he took in the shift in Maxim's stance as he readied himself in case Link attacked. Maxim stared steadily back at him, his eyes unwavering. Finally, Link turned to Phina.

"Do you trust him?"

She looked at the two of them. Her eyes lingered on Maxim for a moment, then she nodded. "I think so. I've only known him for a couple weeks longer than I have you, but he's been straight with me and has treated me respectfully the whole time."

Link considered that, then turned back to Maxim. The

Were had been watching the two of them, never moving from his ready stance. Link waved his hand.

"Keep your shirt on, boy. I'm not going to attack you. Phina is in school at the Diplomatic Institute, yes, but that is not all that is in store for her future. She could be in a position in which she is by herself and surrounded by enemies, with no one else to rely on. There could be times in which words will not suffice and a stick is needed to bring sense to the situation, metaphorically speaking. Her avenues in such situations will be greater than those of her fellow diplomats, so she will need far more combat experience than they do. Thus, she deserves a teacher who is arguably the best.

"As for why an accelerated pace is needed, I fully expect Phina to exceed expectations and be ready for a hands-on experience before long. Better to have her as prepared as possible than to let her be caught off-guard, don't you agree?"

With that, Link turned again, gesturing for Phina to follow him and stand in front of the door. She glanced to Maxim in confusion, then shrugged and put her hands in her pockets as she walked behind her mentor. Link waited for her to step close, then spoke in a low voice.

"Is there something going on between the two of you?"

"Going on?" She frowned, then her face cleared. "You mean, like a relationship or attraction?" She shook her head. "Not at all."

His eyes steadily gazed at her while mulling that over. "You're sure there's nothing going on? Even just one-sided from his side?"

She snorted and smiled. "I think I would know. Trust

me, I can tell the difference when a guy is interested in me and when he's interested in my best friend Alina, who is definitely interested in him. He hasn't decided to do anything about it yet, though. He thinks she's young and infatuated."

"I see."

Out of nowhere, Link grabbed her arm and pulled her off-balance before using his foot to sweep her legs. Her hands tried to extend out for balance but got stuck in her pockets, which let him take her to the floor easily. She scowled, not happy about what had just happened.

"What was that about?" Phina spoke from the floor, glaring at her mentor. He grinned back.

"Lesson number four, always stand ready to defend yourself. This may mean you don't put your hands in your pockets, or you don't fold your arms in front of you, or anything else that hinders your movements and ability to react.

"And I will leave you with lesson number five, which is to always be wary of distractions. You were thinking more about the topic of conversation than what my body language told you."

Phina made a face at the man. Her head was barely able to turn since his hand was holding it in place. "Noted. Can I get up now?"

Her mentor looked at her blandly. "Can you?"

Eying the position Link was in as he leaned over to view her better, Phina decided to roll away from him a few turns before quickly pushing herself up.

"Excellent. Now you're thinking."

He nodded at the two of them and left the room. Phina

stood staring after him, not sure what she thought about that whole exchange. Link was a very confusing man, full of intrigue and surprises as well as being arrogant and intense.

"You ready to train?"

Maxim stood a few feet away from her, gazing at her uncomfortably. Didn't Wechselbalg have strong senses? She wondered if he had heard their conversation. If so, she couldn't blame him for feeling weird and uncomfortable.

"Don't worry, I'm not going to tell anyone else."

He seemed surprised and glanced out the door before focusing on her again. "About what?"

"About you and Alina."

The uncomfortable expression left his face. "There is no 'me and Alina.'"

"Right." She gave him a pitying look. "Keep telling yourself that."

He shrugged and turned back to the mat. "Coming?"

Phina began to put her hands in her pockets but stopped with a scowl. She made to cross her arms, then sighed. She was grateful to Link for taking the time to teach her, even if he irritated her sometimes. Strike that; he irritated her most of the time.

"Yeah, coming."

Phina thought about the lessons Link had taught her today and everything she had learned in her classes over the last few weeks. For the first time, she began to wonder if she would recognize herself when her training was complete. Somehow she didn't think so. She just didn't know if the change would be good or bad.

CHAPTER FOURTEEN

Star System Near the Edge of the Empire, Tluedor, Planet of the Gleeks

Braeden felt like he had stepped into an alternate dimension, one where everything he thought to be true had crumbled to pieces.

We can't allow anyone to disrespect us as the Baldere have! We are the Gleeks, the knowledge collectors of the universe. We should be treated as neutral because we only care about that knowledge, not selling it to the highest bidder like the Ixtalis! No, we should demand respect for what we do! If we let this stand, next time we visit a planet to gather information, they may kill us all instead of letting us go our own way!

Murmurs and cheers punctuated Brother Traekor's words. Where had he acquired this level of zeal and insistence? What had happened to the young Gleek who acquired knowledge for the sake of his love for it? And why would his fellow Gleeks go along with his rhetoric?

It made no sense to Braeden.

"He's quite the speechmaker, it seems."

Braeden turned, shocked that Brother Graeden had spoken out loud. The two of them stood at the back of the room in a rare meeting where all the Gleeks in the commune had gathered together. Traekor had had growing support since he came back from their ill-fated trip, and now it seemed they all would follow him or at least professed interest in his words.

"Apparently."

"You know our people won't survive if we go to war."

Braeden nodded. "We could physically survive, but our way of life as a people would be over. There are too few of us left to have enough brothers to train up renewed brethren after they perish and are brought back by the Mother."

"Precisely. Traekor can only blow smoke. Everyone will see the consequences of following what he's spouting."

"Where there's smoke, there's fire." Braeden shook his head sadly. "I fear everything is changing already."

And with his brothers no longer listening to his advice as they once did, if they got caught up in Traekor's fervor, there would be little Braeden could do to prevent it.

QBBS *Meredith Reynolds*, Diplomatic Institute

With her mentor gone for who knew how long, Phina threw herself into training harder and longer, as well as learning and studying hard in class and reading at night. Training became a relief from the brainwork, a place where she could push her body to its limits.

After being physically drained, she rested by reading texts like *Communication Principles*, which she had mentally renamed, *How to Make Friends Instead of Scowling and Crossing My Arms*, and *History of the Empire*, also known as *How Bethany Anne Saved Earth and Came to Space to Kick Kurtherian Ass*.

The more she learned, the more she enjoyed it, something that still surprised her since her high school work had been as boring as watching water drip since she had learned the whole four-year curriculum the year after her parents died. What else was an emotionally repressed but highly intelligent eleven-year-old with only one friend supposed to do? She had begun learning spycraft at twelve to keep herself from being bored.

Phina's classes went well, each one holding her attention, though she still had her moments of distraction and inattention. Since Karillian was the current subject of her Languages class and she already knew it, she worked ahead to learn Shrillexian. She formed the sounds in her head during class as she learned to read the language and practiced saying them out loud at night.

The trouble started when Phina was in her Current Events class two weeks after Link had left and one week after he was supposed to be back. Not that Phina had been counting. The students had each received a brief summary of the pertinent details for a particular planet. Their teacher droned on about details she had read in the packet during the first ten minutes of class.

Phina had begun to daydream and was wondering when Link would be back and what he might teach her next when her attention snapped back to her teacher.

"Excuse me, Professor Bergen. Would you repeat that, please?"

He looked at her with distaste in his beady eyes as he sputtered with indignation. "Why? If you can't be bothered to pay attention, then I can't be bothered to repeat myself."

Some of the other students snickered, which caused the back of Phina's neck to burn. This class wasn't just taught to the first-year students but to the entire student body. She felt the weight of Jace Anderson's conflicted gaze since he didn't appear to know how he felt about her at the moment. He had subsided in both his attentions and his skepticism. Phina hadn't known what to make of it.

Most of her classmates didn't seem to either but mostly avoided speaking to her since she had confronted Jace weeks ago. They seemed content to talk about her behind her back, even when she was in the room. However, what they thought didn't matter right now.

"Please, Professor Bergen. It's a matter of importance."

The teacher's mouth curled in scorn, but his ego apparently decided to show off as he finally repeated the words that had caught her attention. "I said, the planet of the Baldere has been so well-adjusted since its acceptance into the Empire eight years ago that it could be called a shining example of diplomacy."

"Thank you, Professor Bergen. That's what I thought I heard you say. I just couldn't believe what I heard was correct."

"What makes you say that, child?" He spoke to her in a condescending tone, but she thought his pride had been tweaked by the look in his eye. Still, it seemed he couldn't help but be curious.

"Well, because the Baldere are about to be at war."

QBBS *Meredith Reynolds*, Diplomatic Institute, Anna Elizabeth's Office

"I demand an apology! Her behavior in class was outrageous and preposterous! The girl is obviously seeking attention!"

"Yes, I heard you, August." Anna Elizabeth spoke firmly and with far more patience than Phina thought she would exhibit in her place. Of course, this was why Anna was the Dean of the Diplomatic Institute and Phina was still a student.

"Then you aren't listening!"

"August Bergen!" Anna Elizabeth glared at the man, her voice the iciest Phina had ever heard from the woman.

Professor Bergen flinched and grew quiet. Phina almost felt sorry for him, but he had proved to be one of the most arrogant and annoying men she had ever met. With Greyson Wells in the picture, that was saying something.

"Now, please tell me what happened and why in full detail, and I will decide what needs to be done." She looked at him expectantly.

"She interrupted my class and made wildly speculative statements that completely disrupted my classroom!"

"Yes, I have that bit, thank you. What I am looking for is the substance of the conversation and particulars."

Anna Elizabeth stared at Professor Bergen and waited while his mouth flopped open and closed like a fish's. Anna finally turned to Phina with a raised eyebrow that made her want to snicker. Phina wanted to be like Anna when she grew up. She spoke as seriously as she could manage.

"Yes, Dean Hauser. I sat in class listening to the professor when he said that the Baldere could be considered a shining example of diplomacy because they've been so well-adjusted. I…"

"That's when she said they were going to war!" He glowered at her, his face pinched and difficult.

"I see." Anna paused as she mulled that over. "No, actually, I don't see. How did you come to such a startling conclusion, Phina?"

"I read the handout the professor gave us earlier in class and noticed some peculiarities. The Baldere's imports are up, but their revenue doesn't seem to be reflecting what they are taking in. Even more concerning, however, are the census reports."

Anna Elizabeth blinked twice as she watched Phina. "The census reports were more concerning than money disappearing?"

"What important information about a war can you get from the census reports?" The professor huffed in irritation.

Phina tried not to let his dismissive attitude bother her, though she was extremely aware that someone hostile to her stood only a few feet away.

"The census records I'm concerned about are in reference to the Gleeks."

"The Gleeks! Those sanctimonious pricks—"

"August!" Anna Elizabeth's blue eyes blazed. "Perhaps I should be reconsidering your suitability as a professor, and perhaps even as a diplomat?"

He flinched, his mouth clicked shut, and his face blanched. He sat down and stayed quiet.

"Go on, Phina."

"Yes, Dean Hauser. The census records from one and two years ago show there was a small group of twenty-four Gleek living in the Baldere's capital city—in a sort of commune, I would imagine. However, the census taken just a couple weeks ago shows no Gleeks at all."

"You are right, that *is* concerning and something that slipped through the cracks of our attention, I'm sad to say. However, what causes you to believe they will make war on the Baldere? That detail doesn't seem to merit such a response. They could have simply gone home."

Phina took a deep breath. "I've been reading up on the Gleeks in the texts..."

"What? That's not covered 'til next semester! How did you get those?"

Phina and Anna Elizabeth ignored the professor's bluster. Phina thought she saw a hint of amusement in the dean's eyes.

"...and I believe that the Gleeks seek to understand above all else. They periodically send groups of their people out to various cultures and planetary populations and more rarely send one at a time for a specific task. These Gleek groups usually stay in that location for a minimum of five years, generally closer to ten, so to leave after only two years is a glaring difference in protocol for them.

"I also read that honor is one of the highest tenets of their society. An insult through dishonor must be satisfied. Not just desiring it to be satisfied, but imperative. If they believe recompense for a dishonor will not be granted, they will seek it to the fullest extent from the perceived injuring party."

"And you believe something like this occurred?"

"Why else would they all have withdrawn after being on Vermott only two years? Not just a few but all of them." Phina shrugged, hoping Anna Elizabeth believed her and she wouldn't get into too much trouble for accessing the texts for later semesters.

Anna Elizabeth tapped her desk as she grew lost in thought. Professor Bergen huffed in irritation but didn't say anything. Perhaps he had learned some wisdom. Finally, Anna Elizabeth looked at the both of them.

"What made you wait 'til the end of class to say something, Phina?"

"It took me some time to put the pieces together in my head, but I thought for sure someone else would have noticed already. I didn't realize no one had until the professor stated that the Baldere were well-adjusted and acquiring them within the Empire was a shining example of diplomacy. He obviously wouldn't have such an opinion if you all knew there was a big problem." Phina shrugged as Anna turned to Professor Bergen with an eyebrow raised.

"Really? A shining example of diplomacy, was it? I'm sure Grey would be so pleased to hear you say so, given that the last time you encountered him, you called him an arrogant, overqualified busybody."

"Well, I...I..." He looked alarmed and not a little taken aback.

Anna waved a hand and moved on, turning back to Phina. "Right now this is only speculation, but it certainly is suggestive. The Gleeks are not part of the Empire, though we have approached them and been refused once already. However, the Baldere are, and if the Gleeks have a problem with the Baldere, it will by extension become a problem for us. Phina, I'd like you to be involved in the fact-finding to determine if this is something serious or not."

"What! But she's only a student and a first-year at that!" Phina privately thought Professor Bergen sounded like a bird squawking and had a hard time keeping her snickers to herself.

Anna continued as if he hadn't spoken, though the woman's eyes warned her she needed to be more careful about masking her expressions. "Yes, I know you are a new student as yet, but I already know you have a good head for drawing out information that could turn the tide of a situation from your past briefs for the General. Your mentor should be back at any time. I'd like you to share this with him and see what you can come up with. In the meantime, check with ADAM to see what information you both might be able to access that could help you determine the situation."

"Of course. Thank you."

Professor Bergen huffed again. "And you are just going to let an infraction go? Even reward her for it!"

"Which infraction would that be?"

"Disrupting my classroom! If not that, then what about accessing the texts for later classes? Surely that's not acceptable!"

"Ah, but Phina has my permission to access those later texts when needed." Anna gave her a small smile before turning back to the professor. "I believe she may be one of the rare students who will be able to graduate early, though much of that depends on how well she does in her Communications classes."

She turned back to Phina and raised her eyebrows. Phina nodded, though she was slightly anxious. Learning facts and information? Piece of cake. Speaking to people she didn't know and needed to impress? She didn't see any way that didn't end with her in a gibbering puddle on the floor. She sighed and nodded again, meeting Anna Elizabeth's eyes. Phina was determined to do this and just needed to figure it out.

"You may rejoin your classes now, Phina. I believe you only have five minutes left of this period, so why don't you meet your classmates in the lunchroom?"

Phina nodded in agreement, then stood up and nodded in respect to the professor. No matter whether she felt him deserving of it personally, he remained her teacher. She stopped halfway to the door when the professor began to loudly complain that he still hadn't gotten his apology. Phina looked back to see if she should wait, but Anna Elizabeth shook her head and waved her on.

QBBS *Meredith Reynolds*, Diplomatic Institute, Dining Room

Phina left the room and was relieved to have a few minutes to herself before classes let out. She entered the dining room down the hall and found the meal already set up, the food in its dishes pristinely arranged since no one had yet come in to eat. She looked around but didn't see anyone in the room to ask if she could begin.

She shrugged and filled her plate, then found the table at the back where she usually ended up. Phina had just picked up her utensil when the first students began to pour in, raising the noise level from comfortable silence to an almost painful cacophony to her sensitive ears.

After a few minutes of eating and ignoring the students as they gave her side glances while they whispered, Phina heard the tap of Yollin claws on the floor as Sis'tael approached her table. She glanced up to give the young Yollin woman a smile when she saw Sis'tael's mandibles click in agitation as she sat down in the special seat designed for a four-legged Yollin.

"What's wrong?" Phina frowned, her eyebrows drawing in with concern. She hadn't wanted another friend, but shortly after introducing herself weeks ago, Sis'tael had cheerfully told her she wasn't going to give her a choice in the matter. Phina had reluctantly given in and now felt quietly relieved that she wasn't by herself when the other students began whispering. Phina had never seen the young female so agitated.

"I'm just furious about people's reactions to what happened in Professor Bergen's class. Some beings resent you, some admire you, but everyone is ignoring you! They will speak behind your back, but they won't talk to your face. I'm furious, but I'm also disappointed." Sis'tael's voice rose pointedly at the end as some conversations at the tables around them died down to whispers when those involved tried to hear their conversation. Some looked away in shame or irritation.

Phina struggled with her surprise at the assertion that some admired her and tried to cover it up by joking. "What, spending your day with judgmental, arrogant gossips is not your idea of a good time?"

"Well, it certainly wasn't my idea of the Diplomatic Institute!" Sis'tael's mandibles clicked a few more times, but the agitation had lessened enough for her to begin eating.

Phina shrugged, intensely aware of all the eyes on her. The weight of those gazes was almost enough to make her grab her food and go elsewhere for lunch, but she couldn't bring herself to do so and leave Sis'tael alone.

"I'm not here to make friends."

"You say that, and yet here we are." Sis'tael sounded like her quiet but cheerful self now.

Phina gave her a smirk. "In the dining room, surrounded by judgmental, arrogant gossips?"

"Yes!" Sis'tael pointed a segmented finger at Phina. They both laughed since the conversation around them rose and fell as normal.

Phina held up her fingers, counting as she spoke. "Here's how I see this. I have a few choices about how I respond. First, I could get angry. This does me very little good and usually just makes it worse in the long run."

Sis'tael nodded in agreement as she continued eating. Phina could hear the Yollin's teeth crunching her protein chips.

"Second, I could get depressed. Depressed doesn't do much for me and usually sucks my mind and emotions into feeling nothing, so I can't bring myself to do anything until I get out of it."

"I don't like that one. Depression sounds like zombies."

"Zombies?" Phina stared at the Yollin, surprised she even knew about the monsters from Earth's folklore.

Sis'tael nodded, slurping her soup before responding. "Yes. They eat your brains and you shamble along, not feeling anything except the desire for something to fill the emptiness."

Phina froze, her fingers drooping as that idea crystallized in her mind. "Wow, that's…brilliant."

The Yollin's mandibles clicked happily. "Thank you."

Phina shook her head before continuing. "Third, I could argue with them and tell them where they are wrong, but I haven't seen arguing change anyone's mind."

Sis'tael nodded, then looked sidelong toward the table next to them where some students were busy boasting and one-upping each other. "Agreed."

"Fourth, I can ignore them and just go my way in the hope they will leave me be."

Phina held up four fingers, then shrugged and began playing with the roll she had left on her tray. She avoided looking at Sis'tael.

Her friend clicked her mandibles. "I think you forgot one."

"No, I didn't." Phina shook her head, not wanting to hear it.

The Yollin's feet scraped the floor as she shifted forward to lean closer. "Yes, you did, Phina. You didn't mention that you can also confront them and show how their thinking is wrong like you did with Jace."

"And look how well that turned out!" Phina turned to

her friend sourly, then began to tear pieces off her roll and eat them.

Sis'tael stilled, then looked thoughtful. "Perhaps you added a little too much arguing to it instead of understanding or compassion?"

Phina sighed, thinking that as satisfying as it had been to tell him off, ultimately it hadn't solved anything. Sis'tael was likely right.

She didn't want to admit it.

QBBS *Meredith Reynolds*, Open Court

Phina walked through the corridors, thinking about the Gleek/Baldere situation, the other students, Jace, her aunt, and her departed mentor. The thoughts swirling through her mind were causing her head to ache.

Why did people have to come along and cause problems? Most of the problems in the universe would be gone if there were no people involved.

She snorted, startling a lone Karillian walking in front of her. He jerked his eyestalks around to look behind him in alarm, which caused him to notice the human girl. He bowed an eyestalk in acknowledgment and focused ahead before she could say anything in return.

Consumed by her thoughts and barely aware of the people she walked by, both human and alien, Phina didn't notice how far she had come until the hallways grew more crowded with foot traffic and the occasional transfer cart. Finally, she came out on the second level overlooking the

Open Court. The noise level pulled her from her thoughts and she went to the balcony railing.

Her mind stopped churning and calmed as her eyes raced around the huge open shopping and community area that stood five stories high around the open court in the middle.

Various resilient and determined Yollins marched past below Phina, alone or with a friend, their exoskeletons gleaming in the overhead light. More were visible around the court. A small handful of sneaky and clever spider-like Ixtalis sat at a tiny table in front of a cafe across the court-yard on the lower level. A Shrillexian walked past their table, his scarred green skin showing his fighting history.

Over in the corner, a small group of Karillians stood together, their eyestalks waving above their purple-hued bodies. Phina could see the Karillian she had disturbed in the hallway walking over to join them. Other species of aliens known and unknown to her dotted the large open area. Threading through the aliens were humans of different heights, shapes, skin tones, and Earth ancestry.

A child laughed as she got ice cream on her nose. A couple greeted each other passionately for all to see—if they happened to look into the couple's secluded corner. Friends chatted as they shopped in the store nearby. The ruckus of happy guests rose in All Guns Blazing across the deck as a band of Guardians and Marines entered. She absently wondered if Todd had joined them before her gaze moved on. A mother and son enjoyed time spent together for lunch at a restaurant to Phina's right. A small girl ran to her father, and he caught her and swung her up in his arms. Many different species coexisting as one large family. The Etherian family.

It was beautiful.

This was the Empire. This peaceful coexistence was what Bethany Anne had fought so hard for long before Phina was born and still fought for now. This was what her parents had fought and died for. This scene in front of her was what she needed to remember when her mind swirled with issues and she was frustrated with the problems people generated.

Her vow on her parents' memory had been made so a lack of communication and information never again caused the death of a loved one. Sure, it had been modified with Link's help, and she did understand the need for that, but the essence was the same. These humans and aliens, citizens of the Empire, were those loved ones and the families of the loved ones. They all needed protection because they each provided something that would be lost forever without every single one of them.

Yes, even the arrogant and annoying ones such as Greyson Wells, diplomat spy extraordinaire.

Phina didn't realize how anxious she had been until the feeling eased. Her mind trailed back to her earlier thought. It might be easier if no people were around, but it wouldn't be a better universe without them. Especially one person.

And Phina knew just where to find her.

QBBS *Meredith Reynolds*, Open Court, White House Designs

"Phina!"

Her head turned from perusing the various jackets, stylish tops, pants, skirts, and shoes that showed in the rolling viewing screen before her to see Alina bouncing down the aisle between the racks of clothes in excitement.

"What do you think?" Her friend stopped before her and spread her hands to indicate the boutique. "Pretty cool, right?"

Since Phina's only clothing considerations had ever been whether the garments felt comfortable and would let her be adequately sneaky, she wasn't able to share Alina's enthusiasm. However, anything that made her friend happy was a good thing in Phina's mind, and she said as much.

Alina looked amused but beckoned for Phina to follow her.

"Come on, you have to meet everyone!"

Alina pointed out items that caught her attention as they passed the large section of white clothing that gave the boutique its name on the left and an equally large section of black clothing on the right that Phina's eye lingered on, then through the aisles of clothing in various colors and designs.

"Look, this flirty and fun dress is amazing! And can you believe these amazingly adorable faux leather skinnies? Oh, look at those darling boots with the amazing peep-toes! Can you believe I get to work here and learn how to make my own designs? It's just so...so..."

"Amazing?"

"Yes!"

Alina squealed in excitement as she grabbed Phina's arm and drew her past bemused and disgruntled customers and clerks to the back of the shop. After the girls passed through the door marked Employees Only, Phina heard several people moving around completing tasks with one strident voice directing them.

"Liz, take that box of embellishments to the back room, please. Cherise, what were those measurements again? Open the order and check, will you? Nadine, you're cutting a little too close to the pattern. Make sure you allow enough room for the seam, or we'll all be sorry later."

The three women followed the directions, though Phina heard frustrated muttering from Nadine as the girl tried to fix her mistake. She was identifiable since she was the only one with a cutting implement. In the middle of the room stood a tall, slender woman, her hand flying across a screen as she rendered a design for an asymmetric dress with a metallic sheen. Hearing the girls come in, the beautiful woman turned to give them a wide smile.

"Hi, girls! Alina, who's your friend?"

"Mal, I'd like you to meet my best friend Phina. Phina, Mal is my mentor! Isn't this amazing?" Alina squealed softly.

Mal stopped sketching on the screen and took a step to reach Phina and give her a big hug. Phina's eyes widened, and she felt more than a little awkward. She was not used to hugs from anyone but Alina and occasionally her aunt, yet Mal had greeted her like she was family, a situation that hadn't happened to her before and she didn't know how to handle it.

Mal pulled back with a warm smile. "I feel I know you already, given how much Alina has talked about you. I'm so pleased to meet you, Phina."

"Really?" Phina's eyes strayed to Alina, her eyebrow quirking in a question before returning to the beautiful woman in front of her. "I know Alina has been really excited to have you as her mentor."

Mal gave Alina a quick smile. "She mentioned you are a student in the Diplomatic Institute. Perhaps you've met my father there. He teaches Ethics right now."

Phina felt a jolt of interest. Mister Prez was Mal's father? "Yes. He's a great teacher. I find the topic surprisingly interesting."

Mal's pleased smile contrasted with her dusky skin. "My father would be pleased to know that. Don't tell him I said so, but he thought he would hate teaching and only agreed because he was bored. Thankfully for everyone involved, he's a good teacher and really enjoys it."

Phina nodded with a small smile but didn't know what else to say, so she fell quiet. She didn't have to worry since Alina smoothed over Phina's awkwardness; being friends since they were toddlers came in handy. "Oh, Mal! Could I show Phina what I'm working on?"

"Of course, Alina. Just try to remember to get some work done too." She smiled, but Phina could tell Mal wasn't joking about the work.

"Absolutely!" Alina pulled Phina with her toward another room on the side. She carefully closed the door behind them and went over to the screen, where she slowed her movements toward reluctance as she brought up a few files for Phina to view

"Here they are."

Phina looked at Alina in surprise. "Really?"

Alina bit her lip and nodded, her eyes uncertain and just short of miserable.

"I was expecting something more…more…"

"Glamorous?"

Phina shrugged and nodded. "Yeah, like that. Isn't a lot of the clothing here made from rabbit hair the Etheric Academy figured out how to use without harming the rabbits? It just sounds more exotic than, you know…that."

Alina slumped before throwing her arms around Phina and speaking quietly though no less emotionally. "Phina, I just don't know what to do! Look at it. It's awful, but it's the first thing that Mal assigned me to design in the weeks since I've been here, so I have to do it. I can't just say no! I don't know what to do!"

Phina wrapped around her best friend, hearing the tears in her voice, as she turned her gaze to the screen to see…a pilot's atmosuit. Definitely not what Phina had expected Alina to be working on. Her mind turned toward the dress Mal had been designing, which seemed more to Alina's taste.

"What did she say when she asked you to design them?"

Alina sniffed and wiped her eyes as she stood straight and looked at the screen. "Not much. Just to create a functional pilot's atmosuit."

"Functional sounds like the only practical requirement."

"I guess so?" Alina looked at her questioningly, knowing Phina had a reason for asking. The diplomatic recruit tapped the screen carefully as she mulled it over.

"There's always more than one way to look at things. If

you have to make an atmosuit and functional is the only requirement, there's loads you could do with it to make it individual to the person. What if you made some in various colors or included other materials as accents? You could make the pockets have different colors inside if the atmosuit has to be all the same color on the outside. You could put on lots of kinds of sparkles, maybe? Or you could make the atmosuit reversible, one side for work and the other for fun if they don't have time to go home and change? Perhaps some looser and some skin-tight so people have options on which they prefer?"

Alina's eyes dropped their misery and grew more excited with each suggestion Phina gave her. "Oh! Those are all great ideas! I love it, Phina!" She threw her arms around her friend again, this time in excitement and appreciation. "Thank you so much!"

She pulled back and looked at Phina, unshed tears of relief brimming in her eyes. "Seriously, thank you. I had no idea what I was going to do. My panic and stress were overwhelming any creativity sense I have."

"You're welcome. Really. I'm always happy to help you, Alina; you know that. And you have much more creativity than you give yourself credit for." Phina smiled, pleased she could encourage Alina when she had given her so much in the past.

Alina's smile grew mischievous. "So, when I get them finished, would you be willing to try them on for me?"

Phina's smile faltered. Alina knew trying on clothes was not her idea of fun. Still, this was Alina's first big design project, and she wanted to support her. "If that will help you and make you happy, sure." She gave Alina her own teasing smile. "Why not ask Maxim to try on the ones for the guys?"

Alina's eyes widened. "Oh! Do you think he would?"

"It doesn't hurt to ask." Phina could already picture his face and smothered her laughter with another smile.

"Yes!" Alina danced around, showing her excitement before moving to the screen and bringing up a blank page. Her hand flew over the screen as she outlined her new creation.

Phina sighed. If only her tasks could be solved as easily.

QBBS *Meredith Reynolds*, Waters Residence

"So, how do we do this?"

"Do what, Phina?"

"You know..." Phina's mind blanked and she lost the words, so she gestured at herself and the ceiling as she continued to speak out loud. "*Do* this. I've never worked with you to try to find information, just looked for things on my own. So, where do we start?"

"Actually, we *have* worked together before. You just weren't aware of it." ADAM sounded apologetic as Phina frowned in confusion.

"What do you mean?"

"I mean that when you were accessing the systems to find information, Meredith, Reynolds, and I all helped you learn and figure out how to bypass the security measures."

"So, all those times I found myself blocked, it was you three doing the blocking?"

"Yes."

"And all the times I was able to access the information, it was because you three let me do it?"

"More like we guided you into figuring it out."

"But you still could have blocked me anyway?"

ADAM paused, wondering how she was reacting to the information he had blithely shared with her. "Yes?"

Phina felt like her feet had been swept out from under her and possibly would have fallen over if she hadn't been sitting on her couch. Hacking systems had been one of the things she'd felt secure about and sure of herself.

"Does this mean I am not really able to hack into the systems? Were you all doing it for me?" Phina's hands didn't know what to do with themselves as her anxiety level grew. They fluttered and tugged her clothing and body parts.

"Oh! No, Phina, you're one of the best in the Empire now. It's one of the reasons why we were helping you. We saw your potential. If it were any other group of systems but one with two EIs and an AI running through it, you would be flying past their security measures."

"What?" She lowered her hands and looked up in surprise. "I would be... I am one of the best?"

"Probably, yes. It's hard to tell who is best without having everyone compete against each other for the same information, but you are definitely in the top level."

Phina's shoulders sagged in relief as she covered her face with her hands. She couldn't wrap her head around being one of the best, but knowing that her skills were real and not a result of having help from the digital entities made her feel better.

"Phina? Are you all right?" ADAM sounded concerned.

"Just…give me a minute, please."

ADAM was silent as Phina worked through her thoughts. Part of her wanted to feel betrayed since he hadn't told her about it before, yet had a time to bring it up occurred since they had become friends? She had to admit that it hadn't come up in conversation, so it might not have occurred to ADAM to mention it.

On the other hand, the three of them had taken the time to train her and help her learn. Did they need to do that? No. And how many other people could say they had been trained by an AI and two EIs? She would bet not many. Speaking of which…

"ADAM? Whose idea was it to train me?"

"It was mine. The General and Bethany Anne approved it."

"The Gen… Bethany Anne knows?"

"And approved it."

Her mind reeled. This situation had become more than just knowing about her. This was investing time and attention into who she was and the skills she might develop.

"Thank you, ADAM."

"You are very welcome, Phina."

"Please also pass on my thanks to the General and… Bethany Anne?" She swallowed hard, wondering if she would ever be comfortable with people in positions of authority.

"Of course."

"Thank you both too, Meredith and Reynolds." They were listening, right?

"You're welcome, Phina." That same woman's light

voice came through the speakers just before the voice of a deeper, gruffer gentleman.

"You're welcome, young lady."

Phina felt a warmth inside her chest and wondered what the odd feeling meant. Just as she started to figure it out, the door buzzed.

CHAPTER SIXTEEN

QBBS *Meredith Reynolds*, Waters Residence

Phina opened the door to see Link waiting with a grin on his face. She had been irritated and concerned over the last weeks since he had been gone without notifying her that he was all right and when he would be back. She furrowed her brow and pursed her lips as if in deep thought.

"I'm sorry, who are you?"

"Haha. Very funny." He rolled his eyes dramatically.

"You look like you could be my mentor, but it's been a while. My memory is fuzzy."

He stared at her with his eyebrow raised. "Are you finished?"

"I don't know. Are you going to keep running off for days or weeks at a time with no notice and no message to tell me when you will be back or even if you are alive?"

He blinked and gave her a blank look before responding. "Possibly?"

Phina shrugged. "Then you are just going to have to deal with what you get when you come back."

He stared at her for another moment before grinning. "Fair enough. Can I come in now?"

She stepped aside to let him enter, then retraced her steps to the couch. "What are you doing here?"

He sniffed the air as he walked over to sit in the cozy chair her aunt usually occupied. "Is that a red sauce I smell? With garlic and...basil?"

"Yes, from my dinner. I made pasta." She waved her hand at the kitchen as she pulled her feet up on the couch.

"And you didn't save some for me?" He gave her puppy eyes.

She gave him a look. "If *someone* had told me they would be back tonight and that they would be coming over, then that *someone* might have had some pasta."

He put his hands up. "Understood, my dear. Fine. I will try to communicate with you better as to when I will be back. Just understand I've been doing things the same for longer than you've been alive, and it's not always easy to change a habit that long in the making. Try to give me some slack if I slip up, eh?"

His understanding and reasonable response were so uncharacteristic of what she had expected of him that Phina stopped and really looked at Link for the first time since she'd opened the door. His eyes showed strain and fatigue, his clothes were rumpled like he had slept in them at least once, and he carried himself stiffly and carefully like it hurt to move.

Yet, he didn't have the arrogant confidence of Greyson Wells, the sleazy wariness of Stan, or the casual debonair attitude of Ian James. He eyed her, his gaze questioning. "This is really you right now, isn't it?"

He didn't pretend to misunderstand her. "Inasmuch as anyone who is a spy can be, yes."

She brought her hand up under her chin, causing her head to tilt slightly. "It suits you." She paused before adding. "And has the added benefit of not making me want to punch you in the face every time you talk."

He grinned, though it was a tired one.

"Where have you been? Can you tell me anything about it?"

Link rubbed his face before speaking. "Do you remember the green alien with the stolen medallion?"

"Of course."

"I took care of that situation. It became more involved than I initially thought." He attempted a smile, but it didn't go very far. He shook his head, eyes bleary. "It's finished now. All wrapped up."

"How long has it been since you slept?"

He glanced at the ceiling as he recalled the last few days.

She shook her head. "Never mind. If it takes you that long to remember, it's been too long. Why don't you go to sleep?"

"Can't yet. There's a situation happening tonight. I thought you should come with me, so I came to get you." He raised his eyebrows in question.

"All right. What kind of situation? Diplomat? Spy?"

"A Stan and Fee situation." Link grinned and waggled his eyebrows. Or attempted to. It ended up looking like his face spasmed. He seemed too tired to be awake.

Phina made a face of utter distaste. "We're not doing the sex kitten thing, remember?"

He held up a hand lazily. "Relax, kid. I remember. Just poking your buttons."

She sighed and glanced at his weary face. "Can it keep for an hour?"

He shook his head. She sighed again and wondered when she had started caring about Link's health and well-being. Possibly around the time he had shown her something real.

"What about twenty minutes? There's a bed in the other room you could use. Would that be enough to refresh yourself without making you too sleepy?"

He considered that and nodded, then followed her into her aunt's room. He unceremoniously dropped on the bare mattress and fell asleep within two breaths. Phina shook her head and tiptoed out of the room to get ready since she assumed he would still want her to go with him after he woke up.

In her room, Phina got clothes out to change into when she had a thought.

"Umm, ADAM? Are you still here?"

"I have kept myself busy but had an ear out here for you, yes."

"All right." She shifted position and pressed her lips together, not certain how to ask.

"Is there a problem? Can I help with something?"

"I just wondered...well, you use the cameras to see, right?"

"In a sense, yes."

"So, you can see when people are changing clothes and such?"

He sounded amused. "I could if I wanted to, but being naked doesn't mean the same thing to me as it does to you. Clothed or unclothed, the only difference to me is that clothing appears to be more fun than being naked because you can choose many different options to wear."

Phina blinked, not knowing how she felt about that. "Okay. You sound very human at times, but I don't think a human guy would have had the same response. Anyway, could you just…not peek or something while I'm getting dressed? And the same with Meredith and Reynolds? Even if it doesn't mean the same thing to you, it still feels weird."

"Of course."

"Thanks."

She quickly changed her clothes and had just finished when her tablet beeped with an incoming message.

Phina, I hope you are doing well and haven't starved yourself or been seduced by one of those conniving students in your classes. I'm sure the reason I haven't heard from you is just that you are being inconsiderate and not because you've been kidnapped by a terrorist. I've attached a picture of the large apartment here as well as some of the many amenities you are missing out on.

If you change your mind, I suppose I can pay for a ticket on a ship heading this direction, though it would be a huge expense and inconvenient to pay for one now. If you decide to relieve my concern and get back

to me, I'll let you know how things are going here with work.

PS I don't want to hear you've been having wild orgies and parties in the apartment. I've put too much care and effort into keeping it nice to have it ruined now.

Phina was standing in her room, staring blankly at her tablet when she heard a knock on her bedroom door. She shook her head, but in her shock, she didn't answer. After a few seconds, the door cracked open.

"Phina, it's time to go."

She looked at Link with a lost and dazed expression on her face, her tablet held limply in her hand. "I…I…" She shook her head.

A hard light came into his eyes, then they narrowed, and he crossed the few steps to her. After a questioning look, he took the tablet she dropped into his hands before she turned and collapsed on the bed, feeling bewildered. These wild statements were far beyond what her aunt had brought up in the past.

"How could she say things like this? It's like she doesn't know me at all."

"The pox-eaten miserly old hag." Link muttered as he read, his voice angrier and harsher than she could remember ever hearing from someone, even her aunt. She looked up in shock.

"What?"

Link handed her the tablet, the anger in his face tempered by compassion for her. "If she can spout drivel like that, then you are correct—she doesn't know you. But if you haven't realized this yet, how she treats you is not your fault. It's not about you and only a fault with her."

Phina's heart warmed. She had come to that conclusion on her own some time ago, but she didn't realize how much she had needed someone to say it out loud.

"She's covering up her inadequacies by taking it out on you. I've already made sure she has to go to therapy and doesn't opt out of it this time. Still, this is not your fault, and she doesn't know you if this is what she really thinks."

Tears formed in Phina's eyes without permission, but she couldn't stop them. She launched up and threw her arms around him in one of the few hugs she gave anyone aside from Alina.

"Thank you," she whispered, not able to speak louder. He didn't smell the greatest—from the odors filling her nose, it had been a couple days since he'd showered—but right then, she didn't care. She couldn't remember anyone ever trying to alleviate her mind or her physical situation with her aunt, aside from Alina commiserating with her afterward. It felt amazing, though a little perplexing.

Link had initially stiffened but then recovered from the shock and carefully placed his arms around her, patting her back awkwardly. "You're welcome, my dear."

She pulled back, frowning. "Oh! Don't we need to go somewhere?"

Link took a step back and turned to the door. "You bet your bottom dollar we do!"

"What's a bottom dollar?" She wiped her face as she followed him. "If it's what it sounds like, why would I bet with it? Why not add it to my credit account?"

He turned back, incredulous, then shook his head. "You

don't know that quote? What are they teaching kids these days?"

QBBS *Meredith Reynolds*, Mac's Tavern and Bar

Phina was uncomfortable.

When she had grabbed clothes to change into, she had picked things that Alina had given her as a gift last year in the hope that she would dress more fashionably. While that hope had been unfounded before now, she had thought her use of the clothes to be brilliant when she was getting dressed earlier.

Now, she wore a dark-green thigh-high dress with a short brown leather jacket and boots with heels. Her legs were cold and awkwardly bare until her boots kicked in just above her knee. The only thing that made her more comfortable about the outfit was the leather jacket, even if it was disgustingly short by her standards. Also, a leotard the same color as her dress had been sewn in as a lining.

Phina could do gymnastics for quite a while in this dress, and it would stay in place. She could even roll around in a fight and her dress wouldn't get in her way. She snorted, picturing herself fighting someone in this outfit, but the idea of fighting anyone in heels was ludicrous to her.

Link and Phina had discussed that even though they were nixing the sex kitten bit, she still couldn't dress as she normally did when they went on Stan excursions since it wouldn't fit the image. Still, these clothes weren't her preference by a long shot. However, heels aside, it had been a thoughtful gift that Phina hadn't appreciated at the time.

Alina would be happy to hear she had worn the outfit but disappointed she hadn't worn it on a date. Well, she amended, glancing at Link, who was sitting next to her, a real date.

Earlier, Link had pulled up short just outside of the bar and explained to her how he wanted her to act. She had looked at him like he was crazy.

"I'm not doing that. We agreed we aren't doing the sex kitten bit, so I am not draping myself all over you and gazing at you adoringly."

"Fee is draping herself all over Stan and gazing at him adoringly." He grinned either to convince her it would be fun or because she had refused; she wasn't certain.

She gave him a flat look. "Stop poking the buttons. No sex kitten, no adoration. In fact, Fee is probably feeling some sullen aggression since her world changed and she has to spend time with her sleazy uncle now."

He eyed her appreciatively, clearly trying to use charm to change her mind. She just stared at him.

Link sighed heavily as if she were stealing all his fun. "Fine, but at least pretend you are on a date with someone you like and not someone you hate. Uncles and nieces do fun things together, I'm certain. Look at me often as we talk—hopefully with something positive in your eyes and not like you want to stab me with your heels—and hang onto my arm when we are walking so I can look more like a gentleman for the ladies and every so often while we are sitting down. If a woman comes up, you can back off and look bored. *Capiche?*"

She considered that, then nodded reluctantly. He offered her an arm, and she awkwardly wrapped hers around it before they started walking. "I'll try, anyway. I've never been on a date, so I don't know how they work."

"What? Never been on a date?" He paused to look at her in surprise, confusion, and some form of protectiveness. "Why not? You aren't that young, and there's nothing wrong with you."

She shrugged, then tugged on the hem of her dress with her free hand when it rose more than expected. This dress length didn't feel comfortable to her. "I've never really been interested or found anyone interesting enough to go through all that. This is not changing my mind, either."

He glanced down at her and muttered something under his breath that was lost in the increased waves of sounds coming from Mac's Tavern and Bar ahead of them. She could see a crowd of people even from a distance.

Since they had entered the tavern, Phina had been doing her best to act appropriately, but she couldn't help feeling bored as she took in the dim lighting and smoky atmosphere. The smokiness had to be on purpose and was worse than when they were here during working hours. Phina could attest that the air filtration system on the station was top-notch since she had used it as her playground for years. The customers varied between those who listened to the surprisingly skilled musician in the corner and those who seemed to want to forget themselves in their drink.

Across the room in a booth, she could see two figures making out, one practically on top of the other. Not that long ago, a rough-looking man had grabbed a woman walking by and gotten smacked for it, a group of aliens laughing drunkenly at the next table. Every so often, she could hear billiard balls smacking into each other in the back of the room over the din of conversation. Two big men passed in front of their table, visibly carrying weapons.

A rougher clientele for sure, and even more so than before when most of these patrons had likely been working. All in all, it was a far different atmosphere than All Guns Blazing.

What had happened to the urgency Link had implied earlier when he couldn't even sleep an hour? Her eyes kept moving in her boredom, though she strove to pay attention to what Link, or rather Stan the Man, said when he spoke to people or occasionally to her.

She was about to excuse herself to stretch her legs when Link stilled next to her, then relaxed. She leaned over to whisper while holding onto his arm for balance. "What's going on?"

He turned his face toward her and spoke as softly as he could manage and still be heard. "You see the alien who just walked in? That's who we came here to meet."

He made a face—likely realizing how difficult it was to speak in a loud bar and not be overheard—before widening his eyes in surprise. "Hold on a second. You got your upgraded implant while I was gone, right? I can't believe I didn't think of this earlier. ADAM? Could you create a designated channel for us to communicate through our implants? Yes, Phina and me. Fine, you too. Not like I could keep you out of it anyway."

Phina, in her surprise and interest, had straightened to her normal posture instead of the slouch she had adopted when they walked in. He gently nudged her with his elbow, but it took a minute for her to realize why and relax her position again.

"You hear me, Phina?"

"Yes."

He looked at her again, but this time he didn't move his lips, just his eyes. *It will be the same as when you talk to ADAM.*

Funnily enough, I figured that part out already.

Haha, you're hilarious.

As he spoke, he turned his head to see the purple-hued alien coming closer. He lifted a hand in greeting, then adjusted his position in the booth to wrap an arm around her shoulder, though he did not move as close as he would have if they were trying to indicate attraction. She stiffened, not knowing how to respond. It felt nice, more like a protective familial gesture.

You don't look natural when you go all stiff like that. Just keep breathing and relax.

Link's mental voice was a lot more easygoing than his physical one. The dichotomy between the two tripped her up in how she should respond. The change came across a little like Link's own self after he stripped away the personas. Still, there were some things she was going to have a difficult time with no matter which voice he used.

"You let that hand stray anywhere closer, and you're the one who's going to have a problem breathing."

Oh, really? The tone of his mental voice took her aback, especially when he shot a surprised but amused grin at her before turning back to the alien a few tables away.

She sent ADAM a query. "Do you know what he means by that?"

>>I believe he intended an innuendo of some kind. <<

It took her a few seconds since she wasn't used to thinking that way, then she responded to Link. *I mean, I'll punch you in the chest, you pervert! Holy crumbs, I can't go anywhere with you before you start insinuating things.*

Link realized he enjoyed poking Phina's buttons around the time the alien stepped into calling distance. As the young woman's posture relaxed and became more natural, he realized the relationship developing between him and Phina would become vital to him and his operations, just as he had hoped. He took a moment to mentally pat himself on the back for recognizing talent when he saw it before him.

He only had time for one more shot. *I believe you were the one to insinuate something, my dear.*

The look on her face was priceless. Still, someone had to be the adult here, and he had all the cards.

The violet alien stepped up to their table, the hard muscle on his athletic frame bulging through his clothing as he moved. The male wasn't wearing armor, but he was wearing a hard expression on his face as he greeted Link. Phina stiffened as she recognized something about him. Curious. Link nudged her again, though it took her longer to relax.

"So, you're this guy Stan, hey?"

"That's me. Care to have a seat?"

"What's there to talk about? We're here to deal, hey? We

have goods, and you're going to buy them. What's so hard about that?"

"Ah, but there are other considerations as well. What's your name again?"

"Brodin. What other considerations?" His eyes narrowed suspiciously as he reached up and scratched his head under the fringe around the crown.

Link tried to relax and appear to have few concerns except the conversation and the beer in front of him. He adjusted his position and realized he had forgotten his arm currently rested around Phina's shoulder. He pushed that thought aside, leaving his arm where it had become comfortable, and focused on Brodin.

"Why, the quality and quantity of the goods I am purchasing, of course. Quality is very important to me." He gave the Baldere a lazy grin.

"You don't need to worry there. The quality is the best, and the quantity will be more than enough. If for some reason there aren't enough goods for what you need, we can bring more for you in the next shipment."

"Can you indeed? Interesting."

"What makes you say that?"

"Just that the Baldere aren't known for their food exports."

He grew more alert when he felt Phina freeze.

CHAPTER SEVENTEEN

The Baldere are passing off food exports as their own? Phina tried to relax again, but she was now alert, so the task felt impossible.

You know anything about this? Surprise and a sense of "I should have known" shaded his question.

Yes, I realized there was a potential problem between the Gleeks and the Baldere earlier today and spoke to Anna Elizabeth about it. She told me to research it and talk to you and ADAM when you came back, but I figured it could wait since this seemed more urgent. While the Baldere are not known for their food exports, the Gleeks are.

The Gleeks? He paused in thought. *All right. Wait a few, then you can fill me in.*

Brodin scowled, his outraged eyes darting between the two of them. "We have plenty of food exports, hey? Are we going to make this deal or not?"

Link, as Stan, looked to be considering the matter as he absently tapped his fingers on her shoulder.

Would you like your hand smacked?

Link smiled in response, which he easily transitioned into Stan's agreement with Brodin. Phina didn't think she could be that smooth, but he did have decades of experience.

"Of course."

"Good. When will you transfer the funds?"

"Ah ah ah." Her mentor waggled a finger, then leaned forward, removing his arm from around Phina in the process. She immediately felt colder. "No deal until I see the cargo."

The Baldere's muscles tensed. "That's not the agreement we made, hey?"

"Well, I'm changing it." Link raised his eyebrows, clearly challenging the alien. "I'm perfectly willing to still buy the food from you. Just want to make sure the goods are in tip-top shape and worth the price. I still have to ship them to their destination, after all. Spoiled food is no good to me."

Brodin looked like he would rather disagree, but with food shipments, he was under a deadline to find a buyer just as much as Stan would be if he bought them. Pride or money, that was the question for the Baldere to consider in Phina's opinion. What she knew about them would have caused her to guess he would land on the side of pride, but then she had never heard of Balderian criminals before either.

"We'll deal, but you better pay up."

Link smiled easily. "Of course. As soon as I see the cargo is in top shape."

The Baldere agreed and led them out of the bar to the tram. Soon after stepping into the corridor, Phina realized how much smoke had filled the bar since she immediately felt relief from the cleaner air. She looked back and saw a haze of smoke layered over the patrons. She shook her head, not understanding why people thought breathing toxic air was a good thing.

>>**The owner of the bar received a special dispensation to adjust the filtration levels within the bar area.**<<

ADAM? Phina responded over her link to her friend's comment. *How did you know what I was thinking?*

>>**You were looking toward the bar, and your facial features indicated disgust. It was a logical conclusion.**<<

Ah, that makes sense. Thanks. I figured it was for ambiance. I just don't get why that sort of thing is attractive to some people.

>>**Yes. That is a thought I often have about humans, Phina.**<<

She shook her head then focused on the Baldere in front of her and Link beside her; he supported her occasionally when she stumbled in her heels. As they walked to the tram and traveled to the docking area, Phina used their implants to fill Link in on what she had figured out in class and from reading the textbooks and materials she had found in the secret files he had pointed out. While it was convenient for them to communicate over their implants on the private channel, it seemed more intimate than Phina felt comfortable with, no matter how different the real Link was compared to his cover roles. She wasn't used to that level of closeness with anyone. It didn't bother her with ADAM, but then the AI was unique in being both person and code, so it made sense for her as a hacker to be comfortable with him.

Intriguing. Phina, you believe that the Gleeks are planning on going to war with the Baldere over these goods that were stolen?

It appears that way, but I think there has to be more to it than that as stolen goods are not a matter of honor for them from what I have read. There must be something we are missing.

Very possibly. You are correct. From what I know of the Gleeks, war would not be an appropriate response for stolen goods. ADAM, have you looked any of this up yet to determine if this theory is valid and if there may be more to it?

\>\>I have looked into it, yes. While I can't confirm definitively that something more is going on, the goods carried by this ship did arrive from Vermott, the Balderian planet. Records indicate a shipment of goods from the Gleeks came in two days before this one shipped out.\<\<

How long ago would that have been, ADAM?

\>\>Not long before the census was taken, Phina.\<\<

The Diplomat Spy and Diplomat Spy in Training looked at each other as they followed the Baldere off the tram. The timing was certainly suggestive. Link patted her arm to tell her she had done a good job before looking at the approaching docks. A thought occurred to her.

ADAM, did you have a chance to look at those census reports in more detail?

\>\>Yes. The Gleeks left the city three days after this shipment.\<\<

When their glances met, Link's eyes were all business. That was not a coincidence.

Thank you, ADAM.

\>\>You're welcome, Phina.\<\<

Brodin led them to an area where several ships were connected and offloading cargo of various kinds. They passed mostly human shipping and loading crews, though some had Yollins and Shrillexians as well. By the time their contact stopped at a ship toward the end of the row, Phina was ready to throw her boots into a fiery grave. She surreptitiously changed which foot she stood on to give one foot some relief while she waited.

The cargo bay ramp opened to reveal two more Baldere, one of whom looked at Brodin in confusion, the other in irritation. They were dressed similarly and appeared close enough in their features to be brothers, though Phina could tell them apart since the confused one wore a blue shirt while the irritated one who began speaking wore green.

"What's going on here, Brodin?"

"Stan here is just going to inspect the cargo, Taulden."

"That wasn't the deal!" The Baldere's eyes narrowed as he focused on Stan.

"Yes, yes. We changed the deal so I could inspect the cargo. Nothing to worry about if the goods hold up, eh?" Stan waved his hand in a lazy fashion, seeming not to have a care in the world while his eyes took in everything and pointed things out to Phina in rapid-fire. The kid had to learn, even if it was by throwing her in the deep end.

Notice how even though Brodin is nominally the leader of this group, the unknown Baldere looks to Taulden for reassur-

ance. That means he is either used to taking his cue from him, or Taulden is really the person in charge here. See how Brodin put his hands out to placate Taulden and responded more as a subordinate than the person in charge? That means Taulden really is the real leader of this group. Interesting.

What?

I'm wondering why he sent Brodin to talk to us when he's really the one in charge of this deal. Ah...

Of course; they had been planning an ambush all along. Link wondered how many other buyers the aliens had approached before him. During the time he had been talking to Phina, Brodin had walked up the ramp and come to an understanding with Taulden. Brodin waved them into the hold.

"Come inspect the cargo. It's why you are here, hey?"

"Of course."

Phina lightly tugged on his arm, likely wanting him to continue his thought, but he figured she was smart and could pick it up on her own. *Sink or swim, kid, sink or swim.*

The two followed Brodin into the cargo hold, where specially made freezerators had been installed. Link approved since they were the best units to use for hauling food goods across systems without spoilage since the food easily thawed into a near-fresh state when removed. Brodin opened one freezerator unit for them and waved inside.

"Go on, then. Inspect away."

Phina took a step but stopped when she noticed Link hadn't moved yet, looking back at him with a question in her eyes. Link gave the Baldere a shark-like grin. "Nice try, bucko. I'm not going in there to be trapped when you shut the door on us."

Phina's eyes widened in surprise even as Brodin stared at him in confusion. "What's a 'bucko?'"

Link tapped his chin as if he were in deep thought. "You know, you're right. That's not the best word for you. How about a stooge? A chump? A patsy?"

The Baldere exchanged glances as they shook their heads. "Those words don't have any meaning for us."

Link sighed in disappointment. "What are aliens coming to these days? How about flunky, dupe, pawn, or pigeon?"

Brodin and the blue-shirted alien shrugged and continued to look confused, but the ineffectual leader became impatient. Link subtly moved away from Phina to give them space. She shot him a searching look.

What are you doing?

Just be ready to move.

Out of the corner of his eye, he saw Phina's face take on that focused look she got when she was thinking things through as she looked at the three Baldere and the still-open freezerator door. *Good girl. Put the pieces together.* She subtly widened her stance and became more alert. *Excellent.* He gave himself another mental pat on the back.

"Just get on with this. You made a deal, now give us the money." Taulden appeared to have run out of patience, which changed the demeanor of the other two Baldere.

"Ah!" Link held up a finger as they began to move, which stilled the three aliens. "I got it! How about pushover, fool, or puppet?" As he spoke, he pointed from Taulden to the other Baldere and at Brodin.

Brodin scowled. "I'm no puppet!"

"Really? You could have fooled me, especially considering Taulden back there keeps telling you what to do."

The unnamed blue-shirted Baldere finally woke up to what Link had said about him but was still confused. "I'm no fool, hey?"

Link pursed his lips and shook his head as the alien scowled. "I pity the fool!"

"Quiet, Jodin! You're as useless as your brother," Taulden growled. "Enough of this! He isn't going to give us the money. Just grab them and take them down."

QBBS *Meredith Reynolds*, Docking Bay

Phina tensed when she realized what Link had intended by saying, "Be ready." By the time Taulden shouted for his fellow Baldere to "get them," she was watching the Baldere for when they would jump the two diplomatic spies.

So, of course she missed seeing Link lunge forward and grab the closest Baldere, then launch him into the space in front of her. As Link turned to deal with the other two Baldere, Brodin scowled, stumbled forward a few steps, and recovered enough to throw a punch. She dodged, thanking Maxim for his insistence on repeating her punches and blocks until she could do them in her sleep, then used his extended arm to take him down as she had been taught.

If only it had worked. Brodin didn't go down at the right angle for her to pin him, instead sliding out of her grip and pushing back up. She tottered on her heels, wishing she had worn something more practical. Phina barely straightened in time to dodge another punch, though it grazed her side. Her stance wasn't right for taking him down, so she decided to follow with a blow to the chest to hold him back.

As she dodged another strike, she caught sight of the gaping doorway of the freezerator conveniently located behind him. Condensed chilled air exposed to the warmer temperatures had caused clouds to form in the unit, and its coldness had seeped out into the bay, chilling her legs enough to cause goosebumps.

"Leggings," Phina muttered, deciding to wear them next time she had to wear a short dress; she didn't care if it was fashionable. For her, practicality would trump fashion every time, and since her legs were getting so cold they were growing numb, leggings were becoming more prac-tical by the minute. Those freezerator units were not made to be sitting open like this.

Unfortunately, noticing the conveniently open door yawning behind her opponent had distracted her enough to miss blocking or dodging Brodin's next punch, which hurt as much as Maxim's punches when he wasn't being careful. Stumbling back, Phina realized she would be on the defensive unless she could quickly change the circum-stances.

When Brodin followed up with a second punch, instead of blocking or dodging, Phina dropped onto her knees below the male's reach and threw her fist into his crotch. Phina didn't know if it would work the same as it did with a human male, so as his upper body swung down in response to belatedly protect himself, she brought her forearm up to meet his chin.

Brodin swung backward, groaning incoherently as she pushed up and front-kicked him into the freezerator, stabbing him with her heeled boot. She stumbled back a step to get her balance. His angry but pain-filled eyes met hers, and his expression changed to panic when he slipped on the now-slick floor of the unit and landed on his back, moaning. She grabbed the door and shut it with the Baldere inside, sagging in relief before remembering Link was fighting two of the Baldere to her one.

Turning in alarm, she froze in place as she took in the scene. Jodin, the quiet Baldere in the blue shirt, whimpered in pain as he awkwardly cradled his elbow against his body; it looked like it had been either broken or dislocated. She blinked in surprise to note that his shirt had been pulled up in the back and was over his head, trapping the other arm behind him and effectively immobilizing him.

Taulden was sprawled on the floor not far away, his mouth gaping open. The large Baldere looked to be out cold, which impressed her. Phina could see a few places where a knife had slashed the Baldere, blood seeping out of the wounds. They didn't look serious, just uncomfortable and painful.

Link was leaning against the hull about ten paces away. His clothing looked even more rumpled and showed evidence of a knife being used against him at some point. Probably Taulden had started out with the knife, then Link had taken it from him and used it against the leader. Ah, she could see the tip of it just showing at the side of Link's body. He still held it in his hand while he stood with his arms crossed and a smug grin on his face.

Phina struggled with her irritation at seeing his smugness, then looked from the two prone Baldere to her mentor. She pointed at herself, then Link.

"We need to work on our communication."

CHAPTER EIGHTEEN

QBBS *Meredith Reynolds*, Diplomatic Institute, Anna Elizabeth's Office

"I don't think she should go."

"I'm telling you she needs to go, Anna. This doesn't work any other way."

"Grey, she's a student. She needs to be in class. Students don't go gallivanting across the universe!"

Phina sighed and shifted to her other foot, thankful she was comfortably dressed. She blew air into her cheeks and held it like those little animated chipmunks as she looked around the room. Anna Elizabeth sat behind her desk and was leaning forward, her folded hands resting in front of her. Link alternated between standing in front of her desk and pacing around the relatively spacious room, gesturing to make his point.

Phina glanced at Jace, who gazed at her…mouth?…with a smirk on his face and an eyebrow raised. *What's he playing at? Oh, right.* She blew out her cheeks, rolled her eyes, and paid more attention to the conversation.

"Anna, I'm telling you, every instinct I have says this conflict won't be resolved without her. She needs to come with me!"

"What's so special about her?" Jace's voice dripped condescension, which confused Phina. What had she ever done to him? Hadn't he been nicer to her lately? Or at least not hostile.

Link stopped pacing and pointed at Jace as he threw Anna a look of barely concealed impatient dismissal.

"What's he doing here?"

Phina wasn't surprised by the question. She had wondered the same thing. However, the flash of hurt that passed over Jace's face surprised Phina. What made Link's opinion so important to him? It made her wonder why her mentor seemed to dislike the younger man.

Anna shot Link a look of warning. "I'm his mentor. He's learning. As any student should be, particularly a trainee."

"I see." Link nodded. Phina recognized that tone and wondered what he was up to, turning her head to see his eyes grow calculating. Uh-oh. She had been on the other side of that look, and she always lost the argument.

"A student should be learning."

"Yes."

"And you want Phina to be safe."

"Yes!"

"She needs to be in class…why again?"

Anna gave him an icy stare. "To learn the material she needs for her job."

He nodded. "Of course."

Anna narrowed her eyes. "Why are you suddenly sounding reasonable about this?"

Link raised his eyebrows and pointedly looked at Phina, who leaned against the wall near the door.

"Phina, how many of the course curricula for the semester have you read?"

She sighed and grimaced. "All of them."

He almost looked bored as he continued to ask questions. "And for the next semester?"

She stared at him, not wanting to get in trouble. Still, Anna had said Phina had her permission, which should make it fine, even if she had read most of the materials before receiving it. "Yes."

"All of them?"

"Yes."

"And for next year?"

She shrugged and glanced at Jace in time to see his eyes showing surprise. "Maybe half."

"Of the first semester?"

She glared at Link, not liking how he was drawing this out and particularly his exposure of behavior she would rather keep to herself. "For the year."

"And how much do you remember?"

"Do you want me to verbalize it all or write it out for you?" She couldn't help the snark in her tone.

He waved magnanimously. "For now, we'll take your word for it."

She answered reluctantly. She had always kept how much she knew hidden from other people and was uncomfortable admitting how much she learned and retained. "Probably ninety-eight percent of it."

"Really?" He seemed disappointed, which caused Phina to grit her teeth. Just when she was feeling more kindly toward him, he pulled this stunt. "Why not the full hundred?"

"*Political Structures and the Laws That Created Them* was rather dry. I kept falling asleep."

Link barked a laugh. "I'm sure K'Kolorn will be thrilled to hear it."

"Grey." Anna's sharp tone held a warning. "You've made your point. Don't encourage the students to be disrespectful."

"Ah, so you agree Phina should come with me."

Phina held her breath as Anna's eyes narrowed. "No, you have made your point about whether she needs to be in class to learn the material. What you are proposing puts her in danger at the edge of the Empire. I can't in good conscience approve of her going with you."

Link's eyes held the dean's as he raised his voice. "Meredith?"

"Yes, Greyson?"

"Please play the feeds from the dock last night."

Meredith took a moment to respond. "Based on the context of the conversation, you are asking to review the fight that took place between you, Seraphina Waters, and the three Baldere?"

"Yes, Meredith. Start the recording three minutes before the fight began, please."

A screen in the wall displayed various angles that appeared to have been taken by small flying camera drones, based on the movement. Phina had not seen them last night. As the scene unfolded from multiple camera angles, Phina winced at seeing herself stumbling around on the heels and determined that she would ever after wear only footwear she could use effectively in a fight.

Out of the corner of her eye, she saw Link and Jace wince when she smacked the alien in his nethers, and she was surprised at the pride that grew within her when she kicked Brodin in the chest, causing him to fall into the freezerator. Phina was even more surprised to see a smile filled with pride on Link's face as he watched before he turned to the silent young man.

"To answer your misguided question, Jace, what's so special about Phina is that within two and a half months, she has learned ninety-eight percent of seventy-five percent of the written curriculum for the whole Institute, and if I know her at all, probably more." She smothered her annoyed glance at Link since he was correct. "She has learned enough in training to take out a Baldere on her own when many find them formidable opponents, knows four alien languages—"

"Five." She couldn't keep herself from correcting him even though it gave them even more information. Fudging crumbs. It was like she was becoming a whole different person.

Link turned back to her with his eyebrows raised. "Five?"

She shrugged a shoulder. "I learned Shrillexian during language class since I already knew Karillian."

Link turned back to Jace. "Speaks five languages, is extremely gifted, remembers just about everything she reads, and is one of the top hackers in the Empire. The entire Empire, not just those here on the station." He waited for a moment to make sure Jace took his point, then turned back to Anna. "Basically, she's backup, and not just backup, she's essential to this ending peacefully. She knows everything we do about each of the parties involved and can more easily gain the rest she needs to know than many others you could send with me. Not to mention that we wouldn't even have connected the two developing situations this soon without her."

Anna Elizabeth gazed at Link, then stared into space. Phina glanced over to see Jace looking at her with resignation and not a small amount of envy. She shrugged, not certain what else she could do. It wasn't her job to make sure he was all right, but she felt bad that something about her or her position with Greyson Wells caused him pain. Finally, Anna shook her head. "I don't even know where to begin."

"How about with saying she can go?"

Anna growled, "Grey, you are pushing me hard this morning. Please remember that I am still your boss."

"Of course you are, Anna. You and Stephen. However, a good boss listens to their employees when they have skills and instincts that are different from hers—"

She held up her hand to stop him and turned to Phina, her expression gentle but still carrying an edge. "Phina, do you wish to go? Do not say yes just because you know that Greyson wants you to go with him. Do you feel ready?"

Phina looked down at her feet so she could avoid the prying gazes of the people in the room. She wiggled her toes inside her shoes. Her regular boots felt much better than the ones she had worn last night, even though those were stylish. She could have easily distracted herself by thinking about it further, but the others weren't going to wait long. *Was she ready?*

She finally looked at Anna and nodded, her gaze steady. "Yes, Dean Hauser. There's book knowledge, and there's experience. I have a feeling that while I can learn a lot from a classroom and from the reading material, a lot of what I need to learn will come from hands-on experience. I don't know what…Greyson…" she glanced pointedly at him so he would know she had remembered to use the proper name before turning back to Anna, "did before he entered into his current role, but he likely had a lot of experience based on how the Empire did things before they left Earth, with snatching up those who are best in their fields. I have to play catch up, which means a lot of learning and gaining experiences I won't get here. I have no issues with going along and would like to learn more about how the Baldere, and especially the Gleeks, work as a people."

Anna Elizabeth held Phina's gaze, and the young woman did her best not to squirm or seem uncomfortable. The dean sighed and turned to Link with a resigned expression. "Very well, but you are taking even more backup with you. Phina's reasoning is correct that the Gleeks wouldn't have left just for stolen goods. The chances are good that those missing Gleeks were killed. You don't want to give the Baldere any reason to think you aren't strong enough to handle the situation."

"Of course, Anna."

"You will take a team of Guardians." Her hands flew over her tablet. "Maxim and his group are still here and available since he's been training Phina, so I will request them to go with you."

No sooner had she finished speaking than there was a ping from the door. It opened to reveal Maxim, Drk-vaen, and a sandy-haired man Phina guessed was Ryan Wagner.

"We got a message that you wanted to see us about a job?"

Anna lowered her tablet and glared at Link with exasperation. "Greyson Wells, you are incorrigible!"

Link just grinned. Maxim's eyebrows rose as his gaze moved between the two of them.

"So, was that a yes or a no?"

QBBS *Meredith Reynolds*, Spaceship Docks

"I can't believe you are traveling off the MR!"

Alina alternated between jumping up and down in her excitement and moping that Phina and Maxim would be gone for a while. Phina didn't know yet how she felt aside from being nervous. The whole situation felt much more real now.

The two friends walked together to the docks, Phina carrying her bag of clothing. As they approached their surprisingly large ship, they saw two Yollins and two humans standing outside. Phina wasn't surprised to see that the two Yollins were Drk-vaen and Sis'tael. However she was very surprised they were standing off by themselves and were far too close to each other for Yollins unless they had an intimate relationship.

While Phina waited for her brain to catch up and start working again, she missed Maxim introducing them to his other second, Ryan Wagner. The third of the Guardian team watched the girls approach with a grin on his handsome face, the sandy blond hair and blue eyes complementing Maxim's lighter looks.

"Well, hello, you two beautiful ladies! Looks like it's our lucky day, eh, Maxim?" Ryan elbowed the Were with a grin and received one of the few less-than-pleasant looks Phina had ever seen on Maxim's face. Ryan apparently took the man's response in stride since he just kept going, eventually drawing Alina to the side as they very obviously flirted with each other. Maxim stood with his arms crossed, alternating between glowering at Ryan and looking at Alina with longing and confusion.

Phina casually walked up to him, lowered her bag to her feet, and spoke just loud enough for his enhanced ears to pick up. "You know she's not serious at all about him, right?"

"What?" Maxim looked at her, startled but trying to keep his face devoid of expression.

She waved at the two attractive blond people standing a short distance away. They really did make quite a picture, but Phina knew looks weren't everything. Alina was too gone over Maxim to change where her heart had taken her.

"She's very obviously flirting. She does this often as one of her ways to show appreciation of people she finds interesting and attractive. However, you might have noticed that she doesn't do that with you."

Maxim gave her a flat look. "For trying to reassure me, you aren't doing such a great job."

Phina flashed him a grin while eying her best friend. "That's because you are still getting to know who she is. She can be excitable and even flighty at times, but when it comes to the serious things, she's all business. It's why she hasn't flirted with you that much. She doesn't want anything fake or put upon to interfere with a potential relationship that could develop between you two."

"And you know this….how?"

"Come on, we've been friends since we were in diapers. We could read each other's minds if we wanted to." She grinned at the tall Were, ignoring his grumpiness. "Plus, she pretty much told me the day you two met."

"Really?" His eyebrows were raised in speculation as he looked from Phina to Alina.

"Yes, really. I keep telling you to go for it. You guys should get to know each other better. As long as you don't hurt her, I'm all for you getting together."

"And if I end up doing so?"

"Did you see the video of the fight with the Baldere the other night?"

Maxim winced, not mistaking her meaning. "I'll keep it in mind."

Phina caught movement from the corner of her eye and saw Link striding toward the ship, pulling a transport cart behind him. He looked preoccupied, but as he drew closer, he called, "Five minutes, people! Get yourself and your stuff on the ship or get left behind."

Link picked up his bags from the cart and walked past them to board the ship. Maxim and Ryan moved to carry aboard a few bags that were still sitting around. Drk-vaen and Sis'tael joined Phina and Alina.

"Phina, was that your mentor?" Alina craned her neck to see into the cargo bay of the ship. "He's so handsome! He has that graying-with dignity-look to him like that really famous actor from Earth or even Mal's father."

"Mr. Prez? My ethics teacher?"

"He does look rather distinguished for a human male." Sis'tael spoke to them, but her eyes had followed Link as he boarded, causing Phina confusion.

"Who, Mr. Prez or my mentor?"

"Well, both."

"I think that's my cue to leave." Drk-vaen clicked his mandibles, then rested his hand on Sis'tael's shoulder, giving her a Yollin smile before walking up the ramp.

Phina introduced her friends to each other, then said goodbye. As Phina hugged her, Alina whispered, "Please be careful."

"What about Maxim?"

"Stars, Phina, I don't know what to do."

"Just hold on. I know he's interested, and it bugged him that you were flirting with Ryan."

Alina pulled back with her mouth open in shock, then frowned in concern. "I wasn't even thinking about that!"

"I know. Don't worry, I got you covered." Phina smiled as she gave Alina a final squeeze and turned to Sis'tael.

"So, you and Drk, huh?"

The Yollin female clicked her mandibles and shifted sheepishly. "Yes."

"We'll have to talk about that later." Phina smirked to let her know she was teasing, then picked up her bag and went on board. At the top of the ramp, she turned and smiled when she saw her female friends eying each other. Just before the hatch closed, she heard Sis'tael's voice.

"So, you and Maxim?"

CHAPTER NINETEEN

Etheric Empire, QBS _Stark_

Phina wandered through the big ship until she heard voices, noticing that the vessel appeared to be scuffed up and marked like it had been in action. She finally came upon the others in a lounge area that had straps to use when needed. It also proved to be the bridge, where the pilot sat to fly the ship. The console stretched on one side with seats for the pilot, the navigator, and the weapons specialist.

Drk-vaen attempted to use the seats made for four-legged Yollins in the lounge area. Since he stood taller than the average Yollin, he had difficulty with the height. Still, he looked up at her when she came in to give her a smile. Link and Ryan talked about their piloting experience, trying to one-up each other. Maxim stood to the side with his arms crossed, deep in thought. Phina believed his thoughts to be more preoccupied with Alina than who might be the best person to pilot.

Phina looked around the room and realized she was the

only female on board, as well as being the youngest person. She shook her head. They hadn't left the station yet, so it wasn't too late to change her mind. However, when she glanced at Link, she remembered his pride in how much she had learned and grown in just weeks. Phina still believed she needed hands-on experience to continue learning.

Her thoughts wandered to where they were going first, which caused her to think of the Gleeks and the Balderian people. Barnabas, the Empress' number one ranger and resident mind reader, had graciously offered to read the captured Baldere. He reported that they did not know much of note except that the food imports *had* been stolen from the Gleeks and the Baldere thought the Gleeks were weird, peaceful, and ineffectual. To a Baldere, this meant they thought the Gleeks wouldn't fight back or make a fuss about the stolen goods. They didn't know anything about the missing Gleeks, but they suspected the Jeskir's guards were involved in shady operations. If it was true that the Baldere were involved in serious crimes against the Gleeks, they had no idea of what they had unleashed.

She sighed at the weight of their task at hand and finally spoke up as she dropped her bag at her feet. "So, where are we going first?"

The males broke off what they were doing and looked at her in surprise. She hadn't thought she had been that quiet, but perhaps the sound of her bag hitting the deck combined with her question had been enough to startle them. Link recovered first.

"Excellent question, my dear! I believe we should head for the Gleek planet first since they are the ones who may be headed toward rash actions on a large scale. I sent a message asking them to wait for us since we have information for them."

"Sounds good to me." She shrugged. "How long 'til we get there?"

"Well, that all depends on Stark here." He leaned over and patted the bulkhead.

"Hey, guys."

The male voice coming from the speakers sounded relaxed but carried a slight tone of snark.

"Hi. Stark?"

"That's me."

Link introduced them all to the EI, but Phina was anxious to get moving.

"So, how soon are we leaving? Do I have time to put my stuff somewhere?"

Link broke in. "We will leave as soon as I get over there and get us going."

"I believe I mentioned I have more flight time and should pilot us instead." Ryan inched toward the console.

Link turned to him with a frown. "And I'm the one in charge, so I will decide who does what. I will be the pilot."

"Who has flown in battle and has a better reaction time, though? I believe that's me—young and speedy."

"Really, young and speedy? Watch what happens when older and experienced comes into play."

He sped to the console in time to trip Ryan, who grabbed Link on the way down, pulling him off-balance enough to fall to one knee. They had just finished a series of blocks and began to use grappling moves when Phina heard the ship powering up and going through all the processes needed to leave.

"Hey, dumbasses!"

Ryan and Link froze on the deck and looked at the console, which had begun lighting up on its own.

"You guys are forgetting that I don't need either of you. I'm my own pilot. Now sit down and buckle up, buttercups! We're hitting the road!"

Ryan began to snicker and sing off-key. "*On the road again!*"

Link smirked. "Roads? Where we're going, we don't need roads!"

Maxim rolled his eyes as he sat down in one of the seats and buckled himself in. "Great. Now there's two of them."

Phina walked over, sat down in another seat, and began to strap herself in. Link and Ryan had disentangled themselves, and now they clapped each other on the back in solidarity and grabbed seats of their own. Phina had Link on one side and Maxim on the other, with Ryan and Drkvaen across from them.

She felt a hand on her arm and looked over to see Maxim giving her an encouraging smile. "Don't worry, it will be fine."

Phina narrowed one eye and raised the other eyebrow in an exaggerated look of suspicion. "I didn't realize mind reading was in your repertoire."

"It isn't, but body language is, and yours shouts pretty loudly that you are nervous."

She nodded, feeling the ship detaching from the station. "I am, but I think it will work out fine." She smiled, mostly believing what she had said. He gave her another quick smile, then leaned over to talk to Ryan.

Phina felt the ship begin to accelerate as she leaned toward Link. From the corner of her eye, she saw her bag slide down the corridor. Oops! She would have to get that later.

"So, Stark. He seems kind of unusual."

"Ah, yes. You know ADAM likes to watch shows and movies from Earth?"

"Of course. We've watched a bunch of them together."

His eyebrows rose in surprise. "You've watched…" He shook his head as if to clear his thoughts. "Yes, well, Stark here was born during ADAM's superhero kick. He got a little too much influence as it were."

"I'm not sure what you mean." Phina's brow furrowed as she tried to puzzle it out.

Link smirked. "Well, he believes he's a superhero who lives in a metal suit."

"Oh!" Phina supposed that made sense. "Well, he goes with you to help the Empire, so isn't that kind of true?"

"Bam!" Stark's voice came over the speakers near them. "See, Wells? This girl knows. What's your name again? Kidding. I remember everything."

Link rolled his eyes. "Yes, yes, Stark. You're so amazing!"

"You know it, Sweet Cheeks!"

Link coughed and looked uncomfortable. "Yes, well, what were we talking about before? Right. How long 'til we get there?"

"Sure." Phina's eyes sparkled with amusement, but she tried to suppress her smile. Maxim and Ryan grinned at her mentor, and Drk-vaen clicked his mandibles and shifted in his seat.

"So." Link leaned forward to speak to all of them, resting an arm on the armrest between Phina and him. "Here's the deal. What I'm about to tell you can't be shared with anyone on pain of me and possibly the Empress herself coming after you. And trust me, there would be a lot of pain involved, particularly if it's Bethany Anne. You will talk about it with no one, even those here when we are not on this ship. Agreed?"

Phina looked around as they all agreed. The guys had their serious faces on now. It amazed her how they could flip the switch that fast, but given the work they did, they must be used to it. Work she was now part of, she reminded herself.

"Excellent. The QBS *Stark* is a Gate ship."

"*What?*" Maxim squawked.

Drk-vaen clicked his mandibles. "Like the QBS *Archangel II*?"

"Yes, but not quite as big."

Ryan frowned and leaned forward. "How does that work?"

"I got that." A holographic image popped up, showing a handsome man in his mid-thirties with dark hair. "Do you want the short answer or the long answer?"

"How about the short answer?"

"Ok, here it is. You ready? It does because Bethany Anne said it could."

"Yeah, thanks, Stark. I was looking for a bit more than that."

"Oh? Well, how's your mathematics and astrophysics?"

He gave them an explanation Phina only understood one out of every four words of and nothing that was material. Maybe she needed to read up on this stuff at some point so she had a measure of understanding. She put it on her mental to-do list.

"Okay, okay!" Ryan held up his hands. "I just wanted a simple explanation since I didn't know it was possible for a ship smaller than a battlecruiser to have a Gate drive."

"Well, this ship isn't exactly tiny. I walked by a bunch of rooms on the way up here."

Stark turned his holographic face to stare at Phina. "Are you calling me fat?"

"What? No."

He shook his head, his expression of disappointment looking odd on the holographic image. "And to think I was really starting to like you, Genius Girl. They gave us a Gate ship they conveniently and purposely didn't need anymore for my body, so it's what I'm working with right now. I'm going to get a new smaller body as soon as they finish it. An up-and-coming researcher named Anne has been working on it for a while. Then I'll be as slim and sleek as a Brazilian model. No, scratch that. A shiny silver corvette…"

Stark came up with a few more examples that gave the males some amusement. Phina turned to Link and whispered, "So, how long 'til we get there?"

"Likely three days."

Phina sighed as Stark gave them all the expression of an aircraft attendant. "You are now free to move about the cabin."

The guys got up and took their stuff to their rooms to

get situated. Phina pulled out her tablet, deciding to bite the bullet, as it were, and sent a message.

Hi Aunt Faith...

Star System Near the Edge of the Empire, Tluedor, Planet of the Gleeks

Braeden sat meditating in his favorite spot on top of the tallest rock formation. With all the turmoil of recent events, he welcomed a chance to relax and clear his mind as well as practice opening up his senses. He also waited.

Days ago, he had received a message from a member of the Etheric Empire. While the Gleeks were not Etherian citizens, the Empire commanded respect from many species, so when a representative asked to come and meet with his people to share some information on their current situation, he couldn't deny the request. Fortunately, the day-to-day running of the commune still fell to him and Brother Gloeket. If Traekor had taken that over as well, the request would likely have been rejected.

Only one situation out of all that faced the Gleeks on their planet could be of interest to the Empire, and it wasn't the recent lower yields in produce. Or that Braeden had begun to feel like a stranger among his own people.

No, the only situation the Empire would be concerned about was their coming conflict with the Baldere. His brothers were implacable about changing the course they had begun. Within a month, the population of the Baldere would be pruned back significantly. The brothers were just debating on the means to accomplish the task. The one concession Braeden had elicited from his brothers after much argument was to leave the young alone.

Braeden believed this situation to be the work of a small group of people, but his voice had been drowned out by Traekor's fervent insistence on leading their people to war—to enact justice, he called it. Braeden called it foolish fanaticism. He felt ashamed, dismayed, and heartbroken that he could not sway his brothers to a better course of action.

But perhaps these human aliens from the Empire would bring the evidence needed to mitigate their resolve about going to war. He desperately hoped so. Based on the message, they might arrive today. He decided to let his thoughts go and become one with his environment for as long as he could.

Stretching out his mind, he was aware of his brothers moving around in the commune below and on the farms. The plants gently swayed in the breeze. Small animals thrived around the commune, feeding off the healthy plant life. There were insects in the air and larger animals some distance away. His planet was beautiful.

Just on the edge of his awareness, he felt something unnatural descending through the atmosphere. He tilted his head toward the disturbance with his eyes shut and realized it was a spaceship and not one of theirs. The shape was entirely different. Ah. The representatives from the Empire.

Perhaps now they could get somewhere.

CHAPTER TWENTY

<u>Star System Near the Edge of the Empire, Tluedor, Planet of the Gleeks</u>

Phina was nervous as the shuttle descended. She tried not to show it, but she couldn't help feeling anxious about meeting an entirely new alien culture. Stark had stayed above the planet's atmosphere to keep anyone from being too nosy. He only gave them a little grief about staying behind but agreed that they didn't know enough about the Gleeks to trust them closer to their technology, particularly the Gate drive.

As the Etherians exited the shuttle, they were welcomed by two Gleeks who were almost identical. They were tall beings with elongated arms and legs and a skull that was higher in the forehead than a human's, as well as being elongated. Their skin tone was so similar to the dusty rock most of the planet appeared to be composed of that she presumed they wore clothing just to distinguish their forms. However, even their clothing was a similar shape and color. Phina wondered how she would ever tell them apart. As far as she could see, the Gleeks were practically twins.

"Greetings, Earthlings." He paused and blinked eyes that had no eyelashes. "Your pardon. Greetings, Etherians. We welcome you to our planet, to our commune, and to our people. May we work together as one." The Gleek on the left gave a slight bow of his head as he leaned over his staff. His voice sounded slightly raspy from disuse. "I am Brother Kroeden, and this is Brother Draeget. Please follow us."

Phina nudged Link, who walked beside her while the three Guardians walked behind. "They spoke English. How do they know how to speak English?"

"We have visited your planet Earth twice. One of those times was roughly one hundred and thirty-five of your years ago, many years before you all left Earth." Brother Draeget had turned his head at an awkward angle for a human, but on him, it seemed to work without much strain.

Link nodded. "Yes, I believe some Earthlings saw you and began a whole alien craze as a result, with UFOs and whatnot."

Ryan snickered. "So, all those times people were shouting 'Eeeek!,' they were really saying 'Gleeeek!'"

Maxim and Link chuckled while Drk-vaen clicked his mandibles, but the two Gleeks in front of them just stared at them as they continued to walk forward. The rotation their heads were capable of really looked strange.

"I admit, we had not prepared for the technological advancements that you Earthlings had developed so quickly since our prior visit roughly fifteen hundred of your years ago. Most humans at that point still had to ride your horses to get anywhere. After that unfortunate encounter you mentioned during our second visit, we had to withdraw and conduct our research more discreetly."

"So, you yourself went to Earth?" Link clarified.

"No."

"Oh? Then how do you know English?"

Brother Kroeden eyed them carefully before responding, "What one Gleek knows, all know."

That bombshell caused silence, but after a moment, Phina couldn't help herself. "What do you research?" Her curiosity drove her to know more.

The two Gleeks glanced at each other, and she felt a buzz grow in intensity within her head. They both responded at the same time. "Everything."

She rubbed her skull, the buzzing growing more severe as they approached the commune. She searched her companions' faces but saw nothing more than curiosity and interest. Strange. Just when the itchy buzz grew painful, Phina saw another Gleek stride up the path that angled off through the middle of the fields they had just walked beside from the landing pad.

The Gleek walking toward them looked a little different from the two they had met so far. The red cloak they all wore was of the same type and color, but this Gleek wore it more casually, not quite straight on his shoulders. His eyes seemed far more alert than the slightly blank stares of Kroeden and Draeget. Their eyes had the sense of people who were absent-minded, whose thoughts were elsewhere. This new Gleek appeared to be aware of everything.

"Welcome. I am Brother Braeden. Please follow us so we can commune together and discuss why you have come."

They entered a bland building that was empty of everything that wasn't strictly needed for practicality. They passed many other Gleeks and those gave each Etherian a slow nod, their bright green eyes staring. The buzz in her head increased from itchy and uncomfortable to somewhat painful to very painful. Phina wished she knew what it was. She had never experienced anything like it before, but she would really like the pain to go away.

Brother Braeden led them into a round room with several more Gleeks and encouraged them to sit in a circle on the floor. Drk-vaen found sitting on the floor difficult and stood behind the Empire's side of the circle. Finally, the buzz died down, causing her to sag in relief. Phina took deep breaths as she tried to puzzle out what was happening with her.

Brother Braeden spoke, his eyes on Link. "Your message mentioned you had information about our current situation. Would you please share your information with us?"

"Of course." Link glanced around the room, likely assessing the Gleeks' posture and expressions as they spoke. His eyes moved back to Brother Braeden, who sat across from Link and Phina.

"We know an incident of some kind occurred some weeks ago on Vermott. Would you please tell us what happened to cause all your people to leave?"

The buzz started again, which made her brain itch with

painful intensity. Phina reached up and rubbed her fore-head, causing Link to glance at her.

What's wrong? He spoke over their linked channel.

I don't know. I feel this weird buzz in my head every so often, and it itches.

Link's eyebrows rose higher than she had ever seen them and he was still as he glanced at the Gleeks.

Is that a problem? Well, aside from being uncomfortable for me.

He appeared lost in thought as he spoke absently. *It's very curious. I should have known you had even more surprises in store.*

Oh, yeah, that's me. Surprise Girl. I could be a superhero with Stark.

He glanced at her, his eyes showing amusement. He turned back to the Gleeks when Brother Kroeden spoke.

"We would prefer to hear the information that you spoke of first, but given our perception of your intention to help, we will tell you that we lost two of our brothers."

"Dead?"

The Gleeks all shook their heads at the same time, which was eerie.

"Worse."

Phina stared at them, barely noticing a shudder rippling over Ryan's body from the corner of her eye. What could be worse than death? Link nodded as if it made sense to him. She would bug him about it later.

Deciding that was enough to show good faith, Link began speaking. "We do have some information, but we do not have all that is needed to make sense of the whole situation. We would like to propose that you stop your war preparations and send a group with us to Vermott so that we all can gain the entire picture. What information we do have indicates this is a small group of people, not a population-wide issue."

This revelation and proposal seemed to startle the Gleeks, and the buzz intensified. Brother Draeget showed the most surprise. "How did you know our plans?"

Link nodded at Phina, which drew all eyes to her. She felt even more uncomfortable than usual about being the center of attention since the green, slightly unfocused eyes of the Gleeks combined with their hairless skin and elongated skulls caused them to seem all too alien. Only Brother Braeden differed as he tilted his head and focused his eyes on her.

As Phina explained how she had figured out what had happened between the Gleeks and the Baldere, she felt Brother Braeden's gaze on her. After she finished, the buzz in her head was painful, so she reached up to press and rub around her ears where it bothered her the most. Since it didn't really help, she lowered her hands, but not before she took note of his face.

If he were human, she would have said Brother Braeden looked astonished.

Braeden looked at the human girl in amazement. How could this be? He lost himself in his thoughts while the voices around him faded. It shouldn't be possible, yet here she was—assuming what he believed was true.

Mentally he reached out to her again, carefully

approaching her consciousness. In a normal human's brain, that consciousness was static and inflexible to his mind, with no resonance. He stopped reaching for her mind and reached out to two of the human male brains to check. Yes, they had the static inflexibility. He checked the Yollin's brain and found the expected flexibility but the same static state as the humans. The third and larger human male brain startled him in that it wasn't static, but there was no flexibility. Curious.

Yet, as Braeden turned back to Phina's consciousness, he could see quite easily that while the girl's brain was structurally human, there were many more connections being made than in a typical human brain. He wasn't sure how it had happened, but her consciousness was not static, nor was it inflexible. He wouldn't have been able to see even this much had he not honed his mental awareness to expertise. Even now, it was a strain to focus.

He relaxed his awareness and rested his consciousness next to hers. Her consciousness flared out, reaching, knowing his was there but not stable enough to make a connection. It was this instinct that caused her pain, and it wouldn't be resolved until she left the Gleeks or learned how to stabilize the connection herself.

Braeden gently withdrew from everyone so that he was isolated in his own mind. He couldn't deny he felt a certain relief at the lack of voices in his head, but there was also a sense of loss. He processed the options and realized he had only one ethical choice.

He just had to convince his brothers.

A hand on his shoulder shook him out of his reflections. He turned his head to view Brother Kroeden gazing at him impassively, though his eyes reflected concern. He felt a nudge on his consciousness and reached out.

"What is happening, Brother Braeden? Is there a concern?"

"Yes, definitely a concern."

"Then we will send the representatives of the Empire away."

Braeden grabbed Kroeden's arm as he turned. He could feel the surprise of his brother as he looked back.

"I mean, we have concerns to talk about privately before we decide who will go with them."

He viewed Braeden curiously. "You believe we should go with them? You think what they say is true?"

Braeden turned back to see the human girl watch their exchange with interested but pain-filled eyes. The older human male next to her was scanning them all confidently but with a narrowed gaze, as if trying to determine what the Gleeks would decide.

"Whether what they believe is true remains to be seen, but I'm convinced that we must go with them."

***

Phina observed the Gleeks, who were still communing on the opposite side of the room. The five from the Empire had withdrawn, and they were provided with finger foods, the most delicious fruits and vegetables Phina had ever tasted.

They also had been given a drink Phina had never imbibed. The only thing she could come close to was a drink that had all the sweetness of juice and the aftertaste that wine tended to leave but none of the heaviness, like a Coke without the bubbles. It was puzzling but very refreshing.

Watching the Gleeks proved similar to watching a lizard look around as it sat quietly, though without the reptilian stare. Their movements were economical and could have been easily missed unless you looked closely. A flick of the eyes here, a slight turn or tilt of the head there, or small movements in their hands were all that indicated something more than meditation was taking place as the Gleeks sat in their circle, almost motionless.

She felt someone stop just behind and to one side of her. Knowing who it was, she decided to venture a query. "Do you think they will agree to come?"

"They will."

A small smile played on her mouth as she moved her eyes in Link's direction though she couldn't see him. "You seem very sure."

"Of course."

She heard Ryan whisper behind her some distance away, likely standing by the table where the food waited for them. "Can we just hit something to decide for them?" The other Guardians laughed quietly with him, making it sound like an inside joke.

She let out a sigh, briefly closing her eyes. The itchy buzz was almost overwhelming. "Then we wait."

"A lot of diplomacy can happen while waiting."

She turned to see Link watching the Gleeks, though he smiled slightly to acknowledge her attention.

"Waiting is not my favorite thing."

He turned his head to look at her then, brown eyes searching, then he gave her a brief nod. "I know."

Phina sighed as she turned back to watch the eerie movements of the aliens they were trying to convince not to go to war. She remembered waiting years ago to hear that her parents were on their way back home from the war on the Karillian planet, only to be hugely disappointed.

"I hate waiting."

Though she whispered the words, she heard Link respond.

"I know."

***

You can't be serious!

I am very serious, Brother Traekor. She is showing signs of being twaen. *If you don't believe me, check her for yourself.*

You know I and most of us here do not have the skills in telepathy that you do, Brother Braeden. That makes it very easy for you to say whatever you wish and tell us it's true.

A third voice cut in. *If I may make a suggestion. Though I don't have the same level of skill, I believe my abilities are strong enough to verify it to be true, though it may pain the human female.*

Thank you, Brother Draeget. We should be careful, but I believe verifying this would be worth the pain for her.

Yes, fine. Traekor's mental voice sounded almost sullen.

Within a minute, their eyes were pointed toward the group of humans. The young female clutched her head in pain, then showed immediate relief as Draeget drew back. The Imperial males all reached out to her in concern while the oldest human male looked sharply at the Gleeks, his mouth tight.

I believe the evidence is now incontrovertible. She is twaen. Brother Klaeget's announcement was stated firmly.

How does this happen?

I'm not certain, Brother Bleuven, but I hope to find out more about her and ascertain some of the reasons she is able to do this on the way to the Balderian planet. Unless there are objections, I will also ask the female if she would like to be trained.

A female human... Traekor's words trailed off as he realized the rest were in agreement. He fell silent, but his expression made his displeasure known. Braeden was surprised but also grateful that they were now listening to his thoughts rather than ignoring them.

Brother Klaeget's eyes flicked to Braeden, responding to his words. *So, you believe we should send a group with theirs?*

I do. He nodded imperceptibly but spoke firmly now that they were finally accepting his thoughts. *It sounds like the Empire has some evidence that what they say is true and is trying to find more to come to a definite verdict. If there is a possibility that this involves only a small group of people, do you not think we owe it to the innocent to make sure we have the guilty parties involved? If we can avoid war, do you not think it's worth the time to make sure? War is costly. I do not think we are ready for another one.*

Silence fell as they all recalled the war three hundred years earlier that they were just getting over the consequences of in some ways. Even worse had been the loss of a number of Gleeks. With their population dwindling,

Braeden knew war was not worth the risk. He also knew Traekor wouldn't let it go so easily.

The Baldere insulted us and stole two of our number! I do not think letting that go is worth the risk either!

Of course not, Brother Traekor. Braeden had surprised himself with how smoothly he interjected. *Which is why going with these representatives of the Empire is the best move to make. Since the Baldere have joined the Empire, any move against the Baldere is a move against the Empire. Going with their people provides a level of protection as well as using their resources. It is logical and sensible. Also, do you really want to move forward with plans that put us against the Empire? Their Empress isn't known for letting insults go either.*

Half the group shuddered, and the other half put up a hand and made a warding motion. That caused Braeden to smile.

No one in these systems wanted to go up against Empress Bethany Anne after she had punished a whole planet's worth of Leath on Marrek for disrespect to a handful of her people.

Then again, there were some lines you just didn't cross.

CHAPTER TWENTY-ONE

Etheric Empire, QBS *Stark*

Phina padded down the corridor of the ship in bare feet. The metal felt cool but not unwelcome and rather soothing. She couldn't help feeling she had missed something at some point, and it bothered her. After tossing and turning to no avail, she decided a walk might help, and maybe talking to Stark for a while on the bridge. It felt odd to talk to the EI in her room in a way that it hadn't been for ADAM.

She heard voices ahead.

"I'm telling you, with that big brain of yours and my quantum processing power, we could discover new and amazing things that will blow minds away! Don't you want to figure out some of the mysteries of the universe?"

"Yes. This is why my people travel all over to different worlds. We seek knowledge and understanding so that we might know those mysteries."

Phina entered the bridge to find Brother Braeden sitting on one of the seats, talking to Stark. His bare feet shuffled every so often, drawing attention to his four toes. His elongated arms rested in his lap. Stark's avatar looked up as she approached. "Ah, Genius Girl. Come and help me persuade this tall, slim, and brainy alien to let go and live a little."

She arched an eyebrow. "You mean, to go discover new planets and civilizations? To boldly go where no alien has gone before?"

"Precisely." He grinned.

"I'm sure Brother Braeden knows what is best for him to do."

Stark shook his head as he tutted. "You're killing me here, Genius Girl."

"Actually, you could just call me Braeden. The term 'brother' is just used by us Gleeks."

"Ah, I'm sorry. I didn't realize."

Braeden nodded slowly. "Of course. We keep to ourselves when we aren't seeking out new information, so there aren't many who know more about us." He turned to view Stark's avatar again. "I must say that I find your EIs and AIs fascinating. We haven't interacted with many beings of your kind."

Stark struck a hero pose. "You know it, alien wizard!"

Braeden's green eyes turned puzzled as he dipped his elongated head to the side. "I am not a lizard."

"A wizard! Come on! You two are no fun." After pouting, Stark's avatar winked out.

"The Gleeks that met us at the shuttle, Kroeden and Draeget, told us you seek every kind of information. That seems like an awful lot. There isn't anything more specific?"

His bright green eyes assessed her as he tilted his head to the side. "There is, but it's not something we usually talk about with others. Perhaps at some point I'll share with you, but only for your knowledge."

Phina eyed the alien, confused as to why he might share information with her specifically, but she didn't want to pry if he wasn't ready to talk about it. He brought his long fingers together and looked thoughtful.

"Actually, I was hoping to speak to you about another matter of interest."

"All right." She sat across from him. Perhaps he would explain why he had given her those strange looks earlier.

His eyes grew even more focused, causing him to appear solemn and intense. "Earlier today, you were rubbing your head. Could you explain why you would do so?"

As Phina described the itchy pain she'd felt, he asked follow-up questions. He finished with a nod and what would have been a grunt in another male, but his voice didn't sound guttural enough.

"What I suspect is that your brain is sensitive to the mental wavelength my brothers and I use when we speak to one another."

Phina's eyes widened. The Gleeks were telepathic; that made a lot of sense. "So, I'm picking up those...brain waves? But what makes me sensitive to it when the others are not?"

"I suspect it has to do with how your brain formed. Do you find it easy to learn and retain information? Often at a much higher rate than those around you?"

Her hands tightened on her chair. "Yes."

"We have seldom found people outside of our species who can connect to us telepathically. However, the few who can share those traits with us. It has to do with how your brain receives and processes information. You are able to tune in to the same frequency that we do."

"If I am able to tune in to it, then why do I only have that itchy feeling instead of hearing you?"

He was silent a moment before responding. "Have you ever listened at a door to try to hear what other people are saying?"

"Yes."

"Depending on the door, you know people are talking, but you can't hear the specific words. Another example is a bubble. Inside the bubble are thoughts and words flying around. You are leaning up against that bubble, but you are not inside of it. However, if you were not leaning against the bubble, you wouldn't even know it existed. That is the state of most beings when it comes to our telepathy."

"I think I understand. I am aware of it, but I cannot hear it."

"Rather, you have the potential to hear it. You just haven't connected into it yet."

Her heart leaped with interest. "Yet? That means I could hear you and speak to you at some point?"

He nodded but paused as his penetrating gaze seemed to stare into her soul. "Yes. I could teach you if you would like?"

Phina was quiet. It might be helpful to have such an ability when they reached Vermott, especially if the Baldere were still intent on ambushing the Gleeks as they had the lost brothers.

"May I ask a question?"

Braeden nodded.

"Why do you refer to your brothers as lost? You mentioned earlier it is worse than death."

His serene expression turned downcast, and Phina mentally kicked herself for bringing it up. "I'm sorry. I shouldn't have pried."

He held up one of his four-fingered hands. "It is all right. It is not a secret necessarily, just not usually discussed. Our people are not born as you are, and when we die, it is not the end of us."

"You mean like—what's it called when you live again? —reincarnation?"

He tilted his head in thought before meeting her eyes. "I believe the concept is similar, but the practice is very different than what you mean. We live quite a long time, and when we die, our bodies are given to the Mother. It is our name for a machine that our people created long ago. The knowledge of how to create them has been kept a secret from all but one of our number and is passed on upon death. Such knowledge is one of the few things that only a single Gleek knows, and we don't usually discuss it with those outside.

"Back to your question. When our bodies are given to the Mother, they are broken down into their most basic components. The Mother builds a Gleek from the matter of the previous Gleek, infusing the new body with energy and life."

Phina didn't know what expression showed on her face, but she felt stunned and speechless. Braeden shook his head.

"It is a sad thing for our people to lose even one member, and it's been some time since the last unfortunate incident. To lose two of us is a terrible tragedy. There is no recompense great enough for that loss. It is why my brothers have been so adamant about going to war."

She couldn't even imagine how they must feel. Their way of living was very different from the human way, but it sounded beautiful at the same time. "I'm terribly sorry about your loss. We will do all we can to help you."

"Thank you. I know some of my brothers are still having thoughts about war, but I appreciate every opportunity to find any other option."

Phina could appreciate that as well. She just hoped they found enough evidence to change their minds.

Etheric Empire, QBS *Stark*

"What are you guys doing awake already?"

Phina started and looked up to see Link entering the bridge. His hair looked mussed as if he had just woken up, and the yawn gave a clue as well.

"It's morning already?"

"Well, you know it's hard to say out here in space, but I suppose you could call it morning since it would be considered so on the MR."

She shook her head, amazed at how quickly the time had flown, though she began to feel it as she too yawned.

"What have you been doing? Did you stay up all night?"

Phina explained as quickly and simply as possible the revelations she had found out concerning her, and that Braeden had taught her how to connect to their mental wavelength. It had taken hours to feel like she had gotten anywhere, but once she had it, a place in her mind clicked, amazing her with how right it felt. She had been having a mental conversation with Braeden and the other astonished Gleeks on the ship when Link walked in.

"Amazing! I suspected as much, but this is fantastic. Could I learn how to do it too?" Link seemed intrigued by the prospect.

Braeden shook his head. "I'm afraid not, Greyson Wells. As I told Seraphina last night, unless you are touching the bubble, you don't even know it exists. If your brain doesn't know it exists, then you won't be able to learn how to break through."

Link sulked a little. "But I know it exists now, so why can't I learn to find it?"

"You are familiar with the phrase 'tone-deaf,' correct? This would be where no matter what you try, you can't stay on the right pitch when you sing or try to create music. It is similar here. No matter what you did, you would not be able to figure it out because your brain just doesn't work the same way."

Drk-vaen had quietly come in during the explanation and sat down in his seat, seeming interested in the conversation. "It sounds like you are saying that Phina's brain is the one that doesn't work the same way."

Braeden nodded his head. "You could say as much, yes."

Phina hadn't really thought about it before, but this was yet another way she was different from those around her. She had gotten used to the loneliness of being the odd person out as she grew up. She had always felt like she needed to hide what made her different, but there was only so much she could do to hide her higher intelligence, agility, focus, and health. Even her strength was greater than it should have been, though it wasn't as pronounced as recalling most of what she read so she didn't need to study while the other kids were struggling. Alina had been the best friend and sister she could have ever had, but even her friendship couldn't stem the loneliness that came from feeling like she was different than the other kids.

She had come face to face with being different yet again since what she had declared in class about the Gleeks and the Baldere had become known. Her fellow students had begun calling her "the whiz kid." Phina could have kept silent, but some part of her had felt compelled to say something because she knew there was a problem. That basically summed up her life so far: stay quiet until there was a problem she could do something about, then figure out what she needed to do to solve it.

Was that the best way to live? It seemed reactionary now that she had been thinking about it and gained more experience in the last weeks. She had expanded the people she knew many times over since the fateful day Phinalina went on their final childhood mission together and met Todd, John Grimes, the General, and Anna Elizabeth. Link had been teaching her skills that would help her live as a diplomat and a spy, but while he kept himself apart a lot, he also never seemed to hesitate to pull people in when they were needed.

It certainly provided food for thought.

Even as she was drawn into her own mental musings, part of her stayed aware of the conversation around her. Situational awareness, of course. She had taken lesson number four to heart and tried to stand ready to defend herself no matter the situation. It was still sinking in, but she knew situational awareness was the first step.

Just as she was about to throw a teasing comment toward Link, she heard the ping that signaled a message and pulled her tablet out to read it.

Dear Phina, thank you for your message the other day. I'm glad to know you aren't dead or run off with an alien. I have to tell you something that may upset you. I feel it is my duty as your guardian and aunt, as well as what is best for you.

You need to drop your friendship with that Were you told me about. It's too dangerous! Those Weres are not to be trusted and I just know that something horrible will happen to you just as it happened to my brother, your mother, and my dear Simon! All the troubles in our family can be laid at their feet! You MUST cut all ties with them and stay away from them for your own safety!

Phina couldn't believe what her aunt was saying; she felt more confused than ever. Aunt Faith hadn't looked happy during their conversation, but she hadn't said anything to make her think her aunt had disliked the Wechselbalg that much. Granted, neither of them had had much contact with them before recent events, which she now realized had likely been by her aunt's design, but to say that Wechselbalg were not to be trusted? And all of them, not just certain ones in the species. It smacked of racism or speciesism or whatever the appropriate term would be for an enhanced human. And just how did her aunt "know" the Wechselbalg were responsible for their family dying? It didn't make sense.

She lost track of her surroundings as her thoughts swirled. She hadn't found any reason not to trust Maxim. He had taken every opportunity to show her he was kind and considerate, even wanting to be careful with Alina so he wouldn't be taking advantage of her. She had come in contact with a few other Wechselbalg over the years, and while she wouldn't want to be friends with all of them since she was still coping with the enlarged circle she currently had, they all seemed to have their duty and protecting their teammates forefront in their minds.

The very idea that Weres couldn't be trusted didn't compute for her. She slowly tapped her screen, not sure how to respond.

Etheric Empire, Vermott, Planet of the Baldere, Governing Center

Geirik and Halvad sat waiting to be called in for their appointment. Geirik couldn't help his eyes roving around the room in the newly constructed Governing Center, taking in the elaborate furniture, gaudy decorations, and tacky pictures. The material used in the building and its design showed off the owner's importance. It made Geirik feel sick to think about how much of their people's money had been used to create this beautiful monstrosity. This was not the Balderian way.

He heard faint steps approaching and turned to see a female in light armor with sheathed fighting discs on either hip. He saw the same coloring and fierceness in this female that he saw in his Fastel, but where his bondmate also had a warm and good-natured spirit, this female's face appeared closed and cold. He couldn't help wondering if Velof had tried to replace Fastel with an imitation, then felt bad that he was dismissing this woman as if she had no value of her own.

"Come with me." She gave them a look of disdain before turning to retrace her steps.

Then again, with that kind of attitude, perhaps she deserved a lesser estimation.

She led them into a room that was even more opulent than the one they had just left. Its design was focused on a wooden desk that seemed overly large for its purpose—just another example of wasting money on trivialities to show off Velof's importance. Geirik kept his senses trained on the woman behind them and was grateful when she left the room. He wouldn't have been able to concentrate on Velof if the woman had continued to stand behind his back. He knew how dangerous the female of the species could be.

The male watched the two from a chair as oversized as the desk he sat behind. He wore armor polished to a gleam and a black cape, both of which appeared extremely pricey. His expression was shuttered, as cold as that of the female who had shown them in, though without the fierceness. Seeing this display solidified Geirik's opinion of the Baldere in front of him. The man had grown greedy and weak and did not deserve to be the leader of the people.

"Sit down."

Halvad appeared surprised by Velof's cold, biting tone, but Geirik merely kept his eyes trained on the man set on ruining everything that he valued. Velof's eyes had shown him the truth: this man had become addicted to the power his position wielded. It was no longer about what the people wanted but what Velof wanted. That was not the kind of thinking Geirik desired in a leader, nor what his people deserved.

"I know what you are attempting to do, and it won't work."

Geirik stared at the male, holding his gaze and saying nothing.

"Did you hear me? I'm telling you I know!"

Velof leaned forward, gripping his desk with his hands. The lines on his face were more prominent when he snarled at the two Baldere who opposed him.

"I know about your plans for the Rikhar games, Geirik. Don't think I'm a fool! I've known what you planned for weeks now! I've set my own plans in place, and they certainly don't have anything to do with either of you winning!"

Halvad took his cue from Geirik and remained silent, which was a relief. Geirik had determined a few different ways to play this, depending on why Velof had brought them here. He had to admit that gloating and trying to poke holes in their confidence was not one of the options he had foreseen, but it did tell him something immensely valuable.

Velof was afraid.

"Well? Say something! I am your leader, and I demand that you treat me with the respect I deserve!"

The Jeskir's face showed aggression and anger, but his bondmate had been right. His eyes showed only weakness and fear. Geirik shook his head sadly. Velof's eyes narrowed, and his mouth turned up in a snarl. Geirik didn't pay any attention but held the other man's gaze as Velof sneered.

"How's your little bondmate? You are drawing close to the ten-year mark, aren't you? You ready to have your life invaded by a brat? How's it feel to know that the only reason she's with you is to get a kid?"

Geirik let his former best friend's comments pass him by. He knew Fastel from the inside out, just as she knew him. Their bond had proved to be one of the strongest of their friends and acquaintances. From the first moment he had seen her, he knew she was meant to be his bondmate. Balderian females were only fertile ten years after the bond had formed, which would happen just after the next Rikhar games. Neither Geirik nor Fastel could wait.

Finally, Geirik stood up and spoke. "I have seen your actions and the results of your actions, but never did I think to stand this close to you and see what I see in you now. You won't win, Velof. Your time as Jeskir of the Balderian people is at an end."

Velof rose and leaned forward over the desk, sneering. "*You* can't win, Geirik. I'll make sure of it! I'm stronger than I've ever been and train for hours each day. If you even make it to the games, I'll tear you to pieces. Fastel will be all alone and needing comfort, but don't worry. I'll make sure she's taken care of."

Though his rage burned at Velof's words, Geirik ignored him and turned to walk to the door, Halvad a step behind him.

"You hear me, Geirik! You can't win! I won't allow it!"

The female stepped back into the room and sauntered toward the desk. She ignored the two of them as they passed by, but he detected an air of disdain in the way she carried herself. They continued into the hall, but he paused outside and heard her words before the door shut behind them.

"Velof, we've had a message from the Empire. They're coming."

Etheric Empire, Vermott, Planet of the Baldere, Governing Center

Phina felt like she was out of place and in over her head. She had been fine for the past few days in the shuttle with the Gleeks. Once she had gotten used to being able to hear conversations in her head, she'd realized each mental voice sounded and felt different, which was likely how the Gleeks were able to tell each other apart, rather than by their physical appearance.

Braeden and Kroeden treated her kindly, which she appreciated, but Traekor was a jerk. Graeden had been somewhat stand-offish toward her at first, she assumed because he didn't know what to think about her being able to communicate with them mentally, but when he opened up, he had a dry sense of humor.

However, while Draeget was a fount of information, in some ways he was hilariously oblivious in social interactions. Sometimes Phina didn't know whether to laugh or try to explain things to him, so often, she did both. He took it well, and Braeden later confided that while the younger Gleek had learned everything in their information banks, this was Draeget's first excursion off-planet.

Phina felt she had some things in common with Draeget, so she understood and strove to keep her amusement in check. For the most part, the Gleeks got along with Phina and the guys on board *Stark*.

When they arrived at Vermott, Phina paused for quite a while as she took in the details of the massive city. Many of the buildings were tall, though not nearly as high as the skyscrapers she had seen in movies from Earth. Most buildings were only a few stories, though many of the public avenues were very broad. Link had pointed out where the Rikhar games would take place in several days, an arena so massive she couldn't keep her eyes off the building until it disappeared from view.

All in all, even though the tech was available in different ways for both of their cultures, the Gleek and Balderian planets were so different from each other that she couldn't help contrasting the two in her mind. The buildings the Gleeks had shown them had been simple and basic, which were two words that wouldn't be in a description for any of the buildings she had seen so far on Vermott.

The Baldere who had greeted them at the docks led them to the most elaborate building they had seen since they arrived. The furniture was oversized for humans, but since the Baldere were taller than the average human, that made sense. It did serve to make her feel like a child again.

Their party had been escorted to a large receiving room that displayed ornate decorations and furnishings so fancy Phina felt like she needed to take herself and her simple clothing elsewhere. Not that she wore her regular t-shirt and black jeans with her leather jacket. Oh, no. Those were deemed too informal for an assistant diplomat.

While Link wore something between a modified version of a military uniform and a suit, Phina wore a tunic dress of a similar style with leggings underneath. While there were many places for Link to carry weapons, the only places available for Phina, given the cut and fit of her clothing, were knife sheaths strapped to her thighs under the tunic.

Since Maxim had just started teaching her how to use blades, it had been impressed upon her that she should only take them out as a last resort for fear she might do more damage to herself than her assailant. Though she insisted it wouldn't be a problem, Maxim had not been impressed. Therefore, the sheaths sat like lumps she didn't know what to do with on her legs, and Phina struggled to refrain from waddling as she walked. The guys had snickered at her earlier, which had caused a traffic backup before she decided she would be the adult in the group and let it go…for now.

The receiving room they had congregated in was one of the most expensive and tackiest places Phina had ever seen. The Gleeks sat to her left, slumped awkwardly on chairs and couches they were too big for, while the three Guardians stood behind them, watching their back as it were. Phina didn't think they needed their backs guarded, but she had to admit that it made her feel better to know they were there for support.

She perched uncomfortably on the edge of a couch between Link and Braeden, facing two men she didn't want to meet in a dark alley. Well, the ambassador from the Etheric Empire to the Baldere appeared jovial but was arrogant. She found it very interesting that he sat on the couch facing his fellow diplomats rather than on their side facing the Baldere. However, the leader of the Baldere grabbed her attention. He rubbed her the wrong way almost every other sentence, and she couldn't put her finger on why since his manner and words indicated he was trying his best to be helpful.

"Of course we would be glad to help clear up any unfortunate misunderstandings between our people and the Gleeks. I can't imagine there would be an issue between our people, but I'm sure we can work it out."

The ambassador nodded eagerly. "Velof has been agreeable in all our dealings with each other. You can't imagine the lengths he has gone to make sure the Empire is pleased with his efforts."

Link waved his hand impatiently at the ambassador's pompous, ingratiating attitude. "Yes, yes, Charles. I would assume he has been agreeable enough since we have heard of no issues arising. No? Then let's get down to the issues that brought us here and see what we can iron out."

Both men's expressions changed as Link spoke. The ambassador straightened and leaned back, while Velof's eyes turned hard and his jaw set before he went back to his congenial expression.

Phina activated the direct channel between her and Link while the ambassador spoke stiffly of helping as much as possible. *Did you see that?*

You mean, did I see the ambassador imitate a stick while Velof completely changed his attitude?

All you had to say was yes.

What's the fun in that?

Phina huffed as her eyes rolled, then glared at him. *Fun for you, you mean.*

Of course, kid. What other fun is there?

Phina loudly said a whole lot of nothing and turned her gaze away from him while he spoke. "Actually, perhaps we should take a break for the day and reconvene for lunch so we can relax and interact more with you Baldere in the meantime? It's been a long journey here, and it would be really helpful to have our minds clear when we discuss this."

While Velof and the ambassador showed surprise and a little reluctance, they still agreed. Phina's head had turned enough to see Traekor's eyes narrow. He looked to be about to object to the delay.

Traekor.

His head jerked to her in surprise, though he still seemed angry.

We noticed there is something off that we can't put our finger on yet. We need more information before we talk to them about your brothers. If there is a possibility that Velof is involved, then we need to know more, or we are just going to get the run around from him. That doesn't help us.

He still seemed upset, but the other Gleeks chimed in with their acquiescence to the plan to wait. Traekor didn't want to wait, though, and continued to push. He didn't want to be put off.

Where are we going to get more information? And how?

Oh, don't you worry yourself about that, Phina replied with a smirk and twitched her fingers toward her tablet.

Etheric Empire, Vermott, Planet of the Baldere, Governing Center, Consulate

Ryan trailed after Phina into an open and empty room hours later. She paused to scan the interior, then sat down with her tablet at a small table on the far side of the room. Ryan passed her and leaned against the wall facing her. The better to see her and be seen by her. Oh, and watch the door, naturally.

He stood for a few moments, admiring the view. Velof was long gone. The Gleeks had gone out to search, though the aliens had little hope they would find their lost brothers. Greyson had the estimable job of keeping the ambassador busy. Maxim and Drk-vaen had stayed with them, and Ryan had accompanied Phina.

He couldn't complain.

In fact, he thought about thanking them. He would if the hot chick he was alone with wasn't ignoring him.

"What made you choose this lonely, empty room?"

"What?" Phina started and looked up from her screen, having apparently forgotten he was in the room with her. Well, that was a kick in the...ego. She grimaced, and he wondered what was bothering her. He didn't even entertain the notion that he was involved in the thoughts behind her expression.

"We're in a room together." His smile flagged as she continued to stare at him. He knew she was smart, but maybe she was too inexperienced to understand what he implied. Not one to just give up, Ryan tried again.

"We're all alone in an empty room." He raised his eyebrows, which made her snort as she realized his meaning. *Bingo!*

"Don't worry. I'll restrain myself."

"Well, that's disappointing."

She glanced at him and correctly realized he was only partly joking. "Sorry, bub, but I don't fall into random guy's arms just because they're there."

Ouch.

"What about a specific guy's arms?" She had turned back to her tablet and appeared to be trying to concentrate, but he let her hear a note of hopefulness in his voice.

"Nah, not those either."

Damn it. This was not going the way he had envisioned. If she wouldn't fall into the arms of a guy who clearly had an interest in her, then…

"Oh. So you would fall into a random girl's arms?"

She huffed and turned to face him. "No. No one's arms."

He blinked as he tried to process this unheard-of occurrence.

"No one at all?"

"No."

He scratched his head in confusion as he looked at her body. She wasn't as curvy as her friend Alina, but she still looked hot. However, she didn't appear to notice how hot she was or his interest in her. Ryan was perplexed and uncertain, not normal emotions for him.

"Okay…"

She raised her eyebrows, inviting him to ask what was

on his mind. Maybe she just hadn't understood the first time he'd asked.

"So, to clarify, you aren't interested in anyone?"

"Nope." She popped the P, looking more irritated by the minute.

Yeah, right, Ryan. Dismissing her intelligence was a great move.

"Why not?"

Crap on a cracker! It had slipped out before he thought about it. Still, he kind of wanted to know. He had helped Maxim gather intelligence on her when he had first been assigned as her trainer, and none of this stuff was in the bio.

She answered impatiently as she continued tapping on her tablet. "I'm not interested in anyone in any way right now, and I'm perfectly content to wait until that changes, if it ever does. I'm not the kind of person to do casual hookups either, so no falling into anyone's arms or whatever you had on your mind. Sorry. It's not you. While I recognize when people are attractive, I'm just not drawn to anyone in that way right now."

Yeah. He sighed and leaned against the wall, ready for a long and boring wait. Not how he had envisioned this conversation going.

Phina turned back to her tablet. After a minute had passed, she absently wondered if he had finally been stunned into silence. Or was he feeling hurt? She didn't have enough experience to know, but it seemed like his bruised ego was keeping him quiet more than hurt feelings. Ryan had been talkative on the ship and didn't seem to let too much silence build before breaking it, so this behavior was odd.

Before a second minute went by, she had forgotten about him, her mind focusing on her task. Her fingers flew over her tablet as she bypassed security measures one after the other and hacked her way into the system, making sure to cover her tracks and be able to back out of the system later with nary a ripple. The ease with which she accomplished the feat surprised her.

Huh. I guess ADAM might be right that I'm one of the better hackers in the Empire. This task would never have been this easy on the MR. Still, better to be cautious than complacent.

Phina set up the path she would use so it couldn't be easily traced back to her, laying down bunny trails to trip anyone who might be interested in finding her just in case. When Phina finally got to the location on the network she had been trying to reach, she ran searches for anything pertaining to the Gleeks or the Empire. She found one document in a folder containing video, audio, and text files. One marked Read Me Now caught her eye. Shrugging, she opened it after making sure her anti-virus and filtering programs were running.

My name is Terland. If you are reading this and you are from the Empire, then I am dead. I have succeeded in...

Several minutes later, she straightened quickly. "Fudging crumbs!"

Ryan leaned into her space, startling her with his presence as well as how close he was. "What? Did you find what you were looking for?"

She pushed his head out of the way. "Personal bubble, man. Respect boundaries."

He took an exaggerated step back as he rolled his eyes. "Fine. Did you find anything?"

"Yeah." She tapped her screen as a series of messages popped up. "I found a whole lot of something, and it's more involved than we thought."

She used her implant to notify Link, who was waiting to hear from her. He should still be in the receiving room across the building.

Tell me.

Phina explained everything she had found, getting the sense from his silence that he was angry, which was confirmed by the tone of his next words.

There's something else I need you to do.

As she finished his task, Phina's head filled with voices that were both alarmed and furious. Phina recognized one out of all the others as Braeden.

We're being attacked!

CHAPTER TWENTY-THREE

**<u>Etheric Empire, Vermott, Planet of the Baldere, City
Streets</u>**

Braeden followed Traekor as he led his brothers
through the city. They had been out for hours, searching in
vain for any sign of their lost brothers. It had been weeks
since Traekor and the other Gleeks had been in the city.
Their bodies were likely long gone, but Braeden and his
brothers still needed to try.

He shivered at the thought that Glaeken's and
Dreuved's bodies might have been discarded like trash.
Granted, not many knew Gleeks were returned to the
Mother and crafted into new bodies. A dead Gleek meant a
new one would arise in their place, but a lost Gleek was
gone forever, one fewer of their already dwindling
numbers. It was a terrible tragedy he had hoped might still
be avoided.

A presence broke across his mental awareness, causing
him to flinch. The rest of the people they passed were
preoccupied with their own business, mainly exuding

emotions that were normal in the course of the day. Anxiety, love, lust, and greed pushed at him and didn't cause any worry, but the presence now following them didn't feel benign.

Braeden had felt this mix of emotion once before when he had been attacked by a berserk Shrillexian who had tried to kill him and his brothers when they had visited the Shrillexian homeworld for research. Was this new person trying to kill the Gleeks or someone else? He waited, but when a second and then a third presence with the same emotions joined the first, he knew they were out of time.

Run!

Following his own advice, he moved faster, passing Brother Traekor.

What? Brother Braeden? What's happening?

If you want to live, stop asking obvious questions and start running faster!

Kroeden, Graeden, and Draeget kept up with Braeden, though they were a few steps behind. Each of them held their staff, cloaks swirling and streaming behind them. Traekor finally caught up as they slowed down at a crossroad Braeden didn't recognize.

Which way, Traekor?

I... The Gleek looked unsure and nervous as his eyes darted around. *I'm not certain.*

Braeden felt those who were following them come up behind them quickly, and he spun back toward the intersection they had just run through, his staff raised in front of him.

Then figure it out, quickly!

His brothers fell into fighting stances as the four Baldere approached them.

Is it them? Traekor mentally shouted from behind. *Could they be the ones that killed Glaeken and Dreuved?*

Braeden answered calmly. *So it would seem. Have you ascertained our direction of travel?*

Draeget glanced back at Traekor, his body in a position that allowed him to easily see in front and behind. *Perhaps he's directionally challenged.*

After a few moments of silence, Braeden risked a glance behind him. Traekor looked ashamed. *Figure it out.*

Only now did he feel frustrated that he hadn't heeded the advice of their new friends by taking one or two of the Guardians with them. He reached out to Phina, realizing her range likely wasn't great enough to hear them. *We're being attacked!*

Braeden! Where? And how many?

There are four of them, and we don't know. He described what he saw. Turning back to the four Baldere, he noticed there were even more behind them, bringing it to a total of seven. After a moment, he realized the reason they didn't feel the same was they didn't have the same intent in their emotions. They were eager to fight, but they weren't intending to kill the Gleeks.

Small mercies, but that made it even more likely that the first four Baldere were responsible for their brothers' loss. At least, they had been the hands that killed them. He didn't think it would be that easy that these were the only four Baldere involved.

Braeden, you said your range was larger and stronger than other Gleeks. Can you tell what direction you feel my mind in?

Now, why hadn't he thought of that? He shook his head as the Baldere drew closer. Mental communication was much faster than talking out loud, and he really appreciated that since the interaction between him and Phina took mere moments.

You are four blocks south of us and one block west.

On our way. Just stay alive!

Don't worry, we intend to.

Now that he no longer needed to worry about their location, he observed the Baldere as they approached. Their bodies looked very similar with their purple skin, athletic build, and heads that were bald and ribbed on the top, with fringes of hair along the sides. Their hair color and height provided the only differences. The eager looks on their faces and the cold light in their eyes had caught Braeden's attention. There would be no negotiating with these Baldere.

The Baldere were only paces away when anger ignited within him. These Baldere presumed to decide that his life and his brothers' lives were over. That whatever their goal, it was more important than the lives of these Gleeks. Braeden's body vibrated with anger and tension. Never again. They would be taking no more lives.

For Glaeken and Dreuved. No more.

What? Are you really considering...

Traekor's mental voice faltered as Braeden let out the anger and tension from his chest by emitting a sound that was somewhere between a roar and a sonic scream. The traditional Gleek war cry surprised him as much as the Baldere, who appeared frozen in shock. He would take any advantage he could get since they were outnumbered.

He rushed forward, bringing up his staff before him to jam the tip into the stomach of the lead Baldere. His momentum and the small amount of telekinetic energy he put behind the thrust were great enough that the blow caused the Baldere to fly back into the slower, shorter males behind him and knock them partway down the street. That would have to do for now.

Braeden twirled his staff to gain momentum for his strike against the Baldere to the left of him. Unfortunately, the shock had passed, and the Baldere blocked his thrust, though he wasn't fast enough to block the strike entirely. It clipped the back of his skull, and he staggered.

He moved to meet an attack from the Baldere to his other side, but Kroeden got there first, leaving Braeden to follow up with the one he had clipped in the head. Whipping his staff around, the Gleek hit the Baldere on the head again, this time a direct strike. Though the blow caused the Baldere to stumble, the purple alien recovered quickly.

"Brothers, avoid hitting them in the head. Their ribbed skulls must give them added protection. Aim for the soft tissue."

Braeden followed his own advice by striking the Baldere in the stomach, blocking the male's attack, and then whipping his staff into his opponent's chest where the alien's heart should be. Behind every blow, he applied a small amount of telekinetic force. Any more than that, and he would be too tired to continue if the fight lasted longer than he hoped.

His brothers did the same with their opponents, but they wouldn't be able to do it for long. Even the small amounts drained him since he had to focus and direct the energy to just the right place each time. Braeden's strike proved successful, and the Baldere fell to his knees.

Placing his staff firmly on the ground, Braeden used it to provide stability and momentum for a side kick to the male's throat. As the Baldere collapsed, unconscious or dead—at this point, he couldn't bring himself to care—he looked down the street to assess the situation and found that his fellow Gleeks had not fared quite as well. The Baldere were skilled opponents in their fighting style, as much as the Gleeks were in theirs, so it came down to strength and cunning. The Baldere had more strength, but he didn't think these had the cunning.

Kroeden still fought the Baldere he had kept from attacking Braeden, and while he was holding his own, it was obvious the older Gleek didn't have the strength to continue for long. Draeget seemed to be more inexperienced compared to the Baldere in front of him, and while he hadn't yet been defeated, the blood oozing out of his wounds proved he would soon be overwhelmed.

Graeden had done the best, having fended off two so far. Braeden saw that Traekor wasn't fighting his own Baldere but left those two to fight Graeden and nipped in with a strike here or there when he wouldn't be caught.

Braeden's jaw clenched, but he didn't have time to respond before the two Baldere he had struck with his initial blow were back. Soon he didn't even have time to think while fending off the attacks from both of them.

As Kroeden staggered to the side, about to be overwhelmed, he heard Phina's mental voice.

Incoming!

A moment later, he heard rushes of air and the impact

of bodies and weapons as one of the scariest monsters Braeden had ever seen ran into the fight, followed by Phina, Ryan, Drk-vaen, and Greyson. Within seconds, the tide had turned. The Baldere all stopped, their minds filling with fear, and ran away. Apparently, the Baldere were happy when they outnumbered their opponents but didn't appreciate the risk when they were on the receiving end.

The monstrous half-wolf, half-human-looking creature chased them, swiping with his claws every so often without any intent to kill. The rest of the group stayed to help the Gleeks. Braeden heaved a sigh of relief as he turned to Phina, who came to his side. He could hear the concern in her mind even though she hadn't formulated it into words. He shook his head at how strange it was to trust anyone outside of his brothers so quickly. He hadn't hesitated to reach out to her when he knew they were in trouble, and she and the rest of the team hadn't hesitated to help. It implied a level of trust he wasn't used to and was struggling to come to terms with. He patted the small five-fingered hand that touched his arm.

I'm all right, young friend. Just need to rest and heal ourselves.

He turned, and when his hip struggled to move, causing him to stagger, Phina ducked under his arm to support him. As he whispered his thanks, his eyes took in his brothers, none of whom were in great shape except Traekor, who had obviously stayed back the whole time, judging by the lack of visible wounds.

Brother Traekor.

Nervous but defiant eyes met his, though Traekor remained silent.

What kept you from properly fighting along with us?

He blustered a bit but finally got to the core of his complaint. *How do we know those Baldere were even a problem? They were just walking toward us when you ran at them.*

This was Traekor's issue? Braeden felt tired. Traekor had taken over much of the sway in the commune, insisting on taking their people to war, but when the time came to fight, he had held back. He had never realized that Traekor's bluster covered his cowardice.

Have you ever known me to attack someone without cause? No?

Then what makes you think this time is different? You told me Glaeken's babbling as he died indicated a dark presence of some kind. I felt it tonight as they approached. The four Baldere in front had the intent to kill us all. I turned to attack so that we might have even a moment's advantage.

Traekor's emotions turned from pride to shame, and Braeden knew he didn't need to say anything else.

Perhaps next time, you will trust your brothers instead of doing the bare minimum to keep us from dying.

Braeden was more disturbed by the lack of trust than he'd thought. There was a sharp contrast between the actions of Traekor and those of Phina and the males from the Empire, but Braeden didn't know what to do with that yet.

He turned away from Traekor to see Phina looking at him with interest as she stood supporting him. The rest of the brothers had field-dressed their wounds and hooked their arms around the humans' shoulders before they began their journey back to the consulate.

Phina, what was that frightening creature?

Phina looked up, then craned her neck to look behind them. *Oh, right. That was Maxim. He's a Wechselbalg who has a Pricolici form.*

Really? Braeden's interest was piqued, and a small rush of energy filled him at the knowledge he had just acquired. *We have heard of the Wechselbalg but hadn't interacted with those changed ones yet. The Pricolici form was just a rumor. Fascinating. He must have incredible strength and endurance.*

Braeden?

Hmm? He was engrossed in the questions filling his mind and barely heard her.

Did you say you could sense the Baldere's emotions?

Braeden blinked once as his mind returned to the present and ran her question through again before answering. *Yes.*

What about mine or Greyson's emotions?

Of course.

Phina's eyes lit up with excitement as she grinned and clutched his arm.

I could use your help.

Etheric Empire, Vermott, Planet of the Baldere, Governing Center, Consulate

Link and Phina stood at the side of the room, purposely keeping the conversation to nothing of consequence. At a lull, Link glanced around, viewing the cluster of Gleeks on the other side of the receiving room near an abstract painting. Eight Balderian guards were stationed at different points along the walls. The Guardians and Marines wandered around the room, stopping to talk to each other occasionally. Ryan had a surprisingly stoic look on his face, and Maxim and Drk-vaen looked serious. They all had their game faces on.

Link had a thought and turned to Phina. "My dear, I need you to do something for me."

Her eyes narrowed. Really, it was like she knew him or something.

"What is it?"

"I need you to let me do most of the talking."

Her face smoothed out as she relaxed. "Not that I want to talk in front of a group of strangers, but you were all gung-ho about me contributing to the conversation. 'Using my communication skills,' I believe you said."

Link coughed in amusement. "Yes, well, now that I've had more time to think about it, I realized we don't want to tip them off that you have hacking skills, let alone skills as high as yours, and I think we should keep your newly found mental skills completely quiet. So far as anyone knows, you are a regular diplomatic recruit with nothing special about you."

She squinted at him before raising her eyebrows. "You think anyone is going to believe that you have an entirely ordinary trainee when you are Mister Arrogant-and-Know-It-All Wells?"

With a side of Ian James, spy extraordinaire and Stan the Man, sleazy womanizer businessman. Phina added through their private link.

Link grinned at the young woman, acutely aware of Maxim snorting since with his sensitive hearing, he'd heard every word, regardless of how softly they spoke. He appreciated that she had remembered to speak that last part mentally. Pat on the back for him, of course, for choosing her.

"Rule number six, kid. Show only what you want them to see."

Phina had just opened her mouth to say something smart to Link when the doors at the end of the room flew open, revealing Velof. He stormed inside, dark cloak swirling behind him, and his thunderous expression blazed through his eyes and set jaw. A female Baldere followed him, but the cold look on her face and the way she moved made Phina feel uneasy.

Velof stopped in the middle of the room, the female only half a step behind, and sent piercing glares at everyone, ending with Link.

"You presume to summon me?"

Link stared at him for a moment, then assumed his Greyson hauteur. "You forget yourself, Velof. You are the leader of your people, but you have chosen to place yourself under the Empress' authority by joining the Empire. As her representative, I have full rights to summon any Imperial citizen, no matter their station. This was stipulated in the agreement we signed, I believe. You did read that document, did you not? It was rather lengthy. I can understand if you chose not to do so."

Velof's eyes narrowed and his hands clenched into fists as he glared at Link and the group of Gleeks. Finally, his mouth twisted into a sneer.

"Fine. Get on with it, then."

Link smiled pleasantly. "Not just yet, as not everyone is here."

Velof shot another glare at him before moving to sit in a chair that was shaped a little too much like a throne for Phina's peace of mind. The female with him stood behind and to the side of his chair, staring out into the room.

With the conversation effectively killed, they all stood waiting for another few minutes until the doors opened again, this time less forcefully. When she saw the ambassador enter the room, Phina smiled, then looked at Link.

"Rule number three, Phina."

She blinked and her smile faded. Control your emotions. Right. She nodded to indicate she understood his whispered reminder, then tried to relax as Velof waved a hand in the direction of the ambassador.

"Well then? We are all here now."

Link grinned at the Baldere. "Ah, but Charles was not the only person we are waiting for."

Velof scowled and drummed his fingers on the arm of the chair. The female could have turned to stone since she moved so little, but Phina would have bet she still took in the movements in the room. The Gleeks turned from facing each other in a group to facing the middle of the room, waiting. Maxim came to a stop near Link and Phina while Ryan and Drk-vaen took up stations near the five Gleeks. The ambassador hesitated, then sat in a chair positioned midway between Velof and where Link and Phina stood.

Phina found the placements and positions interesting and tried to think through the responses of each person to the news that would be shared.

It didn't take long for her to realize they wouldn't be leaving without a fight.

CHAPTER TWENTY-FOUR

<u>Etheric Empire, Vermott, Planet of the Baldere, Governing Center, Consulate</u>

Velof glared at the arrogant Imperial diplomat, then his eyes roamed toward the Gleeks. He didn't want to give them the time of day, let alone any attention. He figured they were here to discuss the reason their people had left weeks ago, and he couldn't be bothered about it.

He had more important issues weighing on his mind and wanted to get to it.

Polishing his armor, for instance.

When Velof found himself glaring at Greyson Wells again, he mentally cursed. As much as he hated the necessity, he needed to make nice with the man. His attention strayed to Charles, and he scowled at the ineffectual ambassador. Some big shot he'd turned out to be when this Greyson came and superseded his Imperial diplomatic authority. Really, what good was he?

Finally the doors opened, and Velof hoped whoever it was would be the last person so they could get on with this farce of a meeting. However, as the Baldere stepped into the room, Velof was shocked and felt like he had been cheated.

Geirik, Halvad, and Fastel walked farther into the room. The males were their typical annoying selves—tall, fit, and muscled.

But Fastel...the female was shorter and more delicate than the males, but the expression on her face showed just as much fierceness as theirs, if not more. Velof felt a sense of loss for the first time in a long while.

She should have been his.

Fastel's eyes narrowed as they honed in on Velof and Torel, his female bodyguard and companion. Her eyes met the Jeskir's as she moved into the room and stood next to Geirik, which caused Velof's muscles to tense and his fists to clench. His mind was still contemplating might-have-beens and what he would like to do to Geirik before taking Fastel for his own when Link stepped forward, holding his hands out and breaking Velof's focus.

"Ah, finally, we all have arrived."

Velof stood and glared at Geirik and Halvad, his face filled with suspicion. "What are they doing here?"

"All will be revealed in good time." Greyson gestured at everyone to be seated, but Velof alone sat down. Geirik, Halvad, and Fastel stood in front of the door with a couch between them and Velof, which was fine with him. Greyson Wells continued to speak, finally getting to why he had brought them here.

"Now, we have a situation we need to resolve today. A group of Gleeks came over two years ago and lived here until some weeks ago."

Velof forced himself to relax. It did him no favors to reveal his response to seeing Fastel. "Yes, I remember Charles telling me about this." Velof glanced at the ambassador, who nodded. "What does it matter that they lived here or not?"

"It matters. It matters a great deal. The last week the Gleeks were here on Vermott, they lost two of their members."

Velof gritted his teeth because now he had to deal with this, then spoke in an impatient and dismissive manner.

"So go find them."

Greyson pursed his lips before responding. "I don't think you understand the situation. They aren't mislaid somewhere. These two Gleeks were killed and their bodies hidden or discarded."

Velof glared at the man as he mentally cursed. Why did the Gleeks and the Empire have to come in and muck everything up?

Phina heard whispers from the three new Baldere by the door as they glanced at the five Gleeks, Link, and Velof, who frowned and narrowed his eyes.

"You know this for a fact?"

"Of course."

"And what, may I ask, is your evidence of this crime?"

Link grinned and splayed his hand across his chest. "So happy you asked! Phina, my dear?"

Phina felt a moment of shock before she spoke over their implants with a hiss. *What are you doing?*

Giving you experience. Go on.

You told me I shouldn't share any of my skills. That I should let you do the talking!

I didn't want you to be standing there nervous this whole time. Start moving, kid. They're staring at you. And you aren't sharing your skills. One of the other Gleeks is doing it, right?

I hate you sometimes.

No, you don't.

Fudging crumbs. She moved forward toward Link as he regarded her with amusement in his eyes and a smirk on his mouth. She resisted glaring at him only through supreme strength of will and because it would just amuse him more.

Stopping short of the man who loved to irritate her, she paused and drew a breath, then let it out and began to explain what had happened weeks ago when Glaeken died.

The ambassador interrupted, causing her to face him for the first time since they had met two days before. Charles Edwards could have been Link's younger and more dramatic-looking brother, with blond highlights in his brown hair and a slightly more prominent nose and chin. However, where Link's arrogance as Greyson was partly an act, Charles' was understated but appeared to be no act. Pompous arrogance was his natural mode, along with fawning over people he should exert his authority over.

"Young lady, how do we know you aren't making this up? Mentally reaching out to his...cohorts? Telepathy between aliens is rather far-fetched."

Having anticipated this, she had only to glance at Braeden and the Gleeks before Draeget crossed to her. She turned to Velof and Charles with a smile and an eyebrow raised. "So, which of you would like to speak to Braeden? You will share a phrase in a whisper, and he will send it to my friend Draeget here, who will announce it to you all."

Velof and Charles exchanged glances, each looking reluctant. Velof nodded at the newer Baldere with his chin. "What about them? One of them can participate in this parlor trick."

Phina glanced at the two males and the female. They all looked interested in the proceedings, though their posture and position indicated uneasiness. The male on the left curled his lip in disgust as he stared at Velof.

She turned back to the male in question to see him sneering back.

"Would you really take their word that it was true?"

He raised a ridge beneath the thick circlet resting on his head. Phina found herself staring at the spot where eyebrows would have been on a human but were absent on the Baldere. She shook her head to focus just as Velof responded that the female would do.

Phina blinked as she realized one of the things that bothered her was that he spoke more like humans in his mannerisms and wording than his own people. No wonder he was having problems. The Baldere were very national- istic or whatever term was the equivalent for an alien species. She shook it off before turning to the female Baldere, asking for her name and if she would mind help- ing. She received a bright but wild grin.

"Fastel. Sounds fun, hey?"

Braeden stood waiting for the female to walk over to the group of Gleeks. He nodded and held out his hand in welcome. He stood a head taller and his elongated limbs caused him to seem even larger, though the Baldere had more muscle mass. Even though her grip was strong, he couldn't help thinking of the female as delicate.

Fastel gave him a quiet greeting and began to speak in a voice so low that no one else could hear. As he listened, his heart beat harder, and he pressed his lips together to repress a smile. Clever female. He couldn't have chosen a better phrase if he tried. He gladly sent it to Brother Draeget and Phina.

Since Phina had been leaking a little mentally—he made a mental note to help her with that—he had caught that she would be hiding her skills, but he still wanted her to know what was said. Draeget was amused when he received the message and spoke clearly and strongly.

"The lazy man only loses himself, the proud man endangers his honor and his heart, but the greedy man stands to lose everything since he will go too far."

Almost before he had finished speaking, Velof stood and glared around the room, pausing on the Gleeks and then on Link and Phina. His female companion placed her hands on her weapons. The ambassador leaned back in his chair but watched Velof and Link. Fastel, who had moved back toward the door, and the two males she had come with looked very interested in Velof's angry reaction.

For that matter, Braeden was very interested himself. The Baldere leader appeared to be reacting defensively to the notion of a greedy man. A guilty conscience, maybe? Perhaps now all would be revealed and they would find peace again. He found himself both relieved and disappointed by the thought.

"Wells, you will tell me what you mean right now! You dare to come to my planet and my city and accuse me? Get on with it before I get tired of dealing with all of you!"

Link and Phina exchanged glances before turning back to Velof. Link was cautious. Though he had been the one to bring the Baldere into the Empire several years ago, he still had difficulty navigating their volatile emotions.

"Fair enough."

He explained about the cargo that had come to his attention in his role as Stan, though he didn't include using his alternate persona. He had just gotten to the part where he knew the Baldere who had come to meet them had been carrying food stores when he saw fear cross a Baldere's face.

But it wasn't Velof. It was one of the guards who had been placed around the room.

Intriguing.

He skipped over the part where he and Phina had realized these food stores were likely stolen and moved on to the events that had occurred in the cargo bay. At that point, his eager listeners became resistant questioners.

"How dare you accuse us of theft!"

"You are telling me that you and your apprentice there were able to defeat three Balderian males?"

The question had come from Geirik, and while he had

sounded interested, his face revealed that he didn't quite believe Link's story.

Good thing his belief wasn't required, though it would have made this whole thing easier.

"That's preposterous!"

Halvad leaned over to Geirik, Link listening to the lowered words as he turned to Velof.

"What's preposterous is that Velof knows the word and how to use it."

Geirik hushed his friend, though if he were Link, he would have been mentally cackling at the dig. Turning his attention to Velof, Link assumed a pleasant expression.

"What would be preposterous, Velof?"

"That you would have us believe you and your small female over there defeated three of us Baldere, aside from the accusation that we stole the goods in the first place, which I won't even touch since the idea is ludicrous."

"And what would you have us do? Prove it, as we did with our little telepathic demonstration earlier?"

Velof seemed surprised, then recovered, assuming a shrewd expression as he smiled.

"Yes, let's have a demonstration. Taben can fight you, and your female can fight Torel."

He gestured at the largest Baldere in the room, who was standing guard in the back, and the Balderian female standing silently beside him. The two Baldere both looked over at those words, eagerness lighting their faces. They appeared to love fighting, no matter who it was.

Yeah, no.

Link smiled pleasantly. "Here's an idea. How about Phina spars with Tape Head, and I'll spar with Toro?"

Maxim and Phina shot him looks of surprise and disbelief, but Taben snorted, then was still. Maxim recovered quicker, but his posture showed he was not happy about the suggestion. Velof turned his head to shoot Taben a look that suggested pain in the Baldere's future for daring to make a noise. The big male paled.

Are you crazy? Phina couldn't believe what she had heard. *You just made fun of their names. How is that diplomacy? Do you really expect me to be able to defeat the biggest guy here? I'm seriously confused right now that you are the one teaching me diplomacy.*

She turned to Velof. "As much fun as it would be to have a little sparring match, that's not why we are here."

Relax, he's not going to go for it. Even so, you need to have more confidence in yourself.

Are you sure we won't be fighting? How do you know? She ignored his comment about her self-confidence, although he might have had a point.

Look at his eyes. He's weak, no matter what shows of strength he gives us, and he doesn't know what to make of us. He will only go for what he thinks is a sure thing.

Velof eyed the two of them before turning back to Link, expressing false concern.

"Oh, we weren't thinking anything as banal as a little sparring match, but if you aren't up for it, then we will move on."

See? Weak. No wonder people have lost confidence in him. He still had some strength left when we signed the accords.

"We appreciate your forbearance." Link inclined his head, keeping his eyes on the Balderian leader.

"Of course."

"We do still have a problem, however."

"Oh?" Velof pulled out a tablet and appeared distracted. "What might that be?"

"The fact that you ordered four of your guards to kill anyone who stumbles onto your business in the warehouses here. The fact that weeks ago, your guards found a Gleek named Dreuved looking into the food stores you had taken and were selling without paying the Gleeks. The fact that two days later, those same guards killed another Gleek named Glaeken. And the fact that last night, you ordered those same Baldere to find and kill all the Gleeks who came with us."

Geirik spoke up. "You also unfairly take a cut from your own people's businesses, letting your guards push around females and children and twisting the governing system to line your pockets."

Velof had been trying to pull off looking casual as Link listed the relevant crimes, his only reaction a tightening of his jaw, but at Geirik's words, he leaned forward and hissed.

"Lies!"

Link shook his head. "No can do, honey pie. We've got evidence on you fair and square."

Velof's lip curled in disgust. "What evidence?"

Subtly, Phina tapped on her tablet, bringing up a video on a screen in the room. Shown clearly in the video were five Baldere moving cargo from a storehouse to the cargo hold of a ship—a cargo hold Phina had become familiar with not that long ago. She glanced to the side and found all five of those Baldere in the room with them, standing along the wall. Fudge in a bucket. Two cents would get you five that those were the ones who had attacked last night too. They had disappeared too quickly for her to get a sense of them, and these hadn't been here until just before the meeting. Possibly keeping out of sight. Hmm.

After a minute of transferring cargo, the Baldere on the screen all looked up to view something off-camera. Within ten seconds, all the Baldere ran off-camera in the same direction. A few more buttons and the screen flickered through a series of images showing the Baldere running after a Gleek. The final image showed the Gleek injured on the ground. A Baldere had knocked him off his feet and spoken to him, then pulled his weapon across the Gleek's throat.

"Dreuved."

Phina could feel the emotion that slipped through her mental connection with the Gleeks, but it was muted. If the raw burn of sorrow and anger passing through to her was only a fraction of the emotion Braeden felt, she didn't want to feel the whole of it since it felt like it would scorch her mentally and emotionally.

Velof yawned and sighed. "Very well, but this only shows why those Gleeks are here and that some Baldere did it. There's no connection to anyone else."

Phina held herself still so as not to react, though she really wanted to. The sanctimonious prick knew those Baldere stood behind him and was lying to their faces!

Link grinned. "Oh, we've got more."

Phina tried to breathe normally as she surreptitiously tapped and played through several more clips, one showing the Balderian guards chasing Glaeken through the streets and crushing his skull after shooting him in the back, and two more cargo acquisitions. Through them all, Velof's body grew tenser, his jaw clenching, fingers digging into the arms of the chair, but he never acknowledged that it had anything to do with him or any of the Baldere in the room.

Finally she turned to Link, her eyes questioning, and he gave her a subtle nod.

Her finger tapped the screen.

CHAPTER TWENTY-FIVE

Velof seethed as he watched the videos featuring his male warriors, clearly showing that the Empire was on to them. *Vrukk!* All his plans were coming undone before his eyes, and he was scrambling to figure out a way through it. All he could think of was to deny it had happened in the first place. Anger and fear wrapped around him, almost paralyzing his mind.

No.

Was he not Velof, Jeskir of the Baldere? He was the strongest, best, and most cunning warrior. He let go of his fear and fed his anger. How dare they come and ruin his plans! How dare they come to his city and his planet and tell him what to do!

Velof gripped the arms of his chair as the video ended. He began to push up so he could give these interlopers a piece of his mind and hope something came to him that might distract them from their line of inquiries, but the next words froze him in place.

"We have quite a collection of evidence that we've

acquired from a rather brave and astute Baldere named Terland."

Velof mentally cursed. That sewer scum he had dealt with weeks ago was causing him problems from the grave! He should have taken more time to thoroughly express his displeasure before the final blow.

"Terland? The name doesn't ring a bell."

Greyson's eyes bore into him, and Velof felt the eyes of Halvad, Fastel, and especially Geirik watching him. He had a feeling they knew he was lying. He set his jaw and his mind. If he was going down, he wasn't going alone.

And it wouldn't be without a fight.

Link had watched Velof's face as they talked and tried to follow how his mind worked. What would his next move be? They had tried to anticipate all the ways this could go.

Phina, what's Braeden picking up from everyone? Anything that might help?

After a minute, he got his answer.

Braeden says the guards feel pride, indifference, fear, and greed, and most of all, a desire to fight. Our three guests are mostly showing determination and disgust, likely at what the videos revealed. Velof is showing a heavy dose of fear and anger, and our co-conspirator here is feeling unease, concern, and some fear, but also sharp anger.

About what he expected. Time to go for the throat. He told Velof about the evidence Terland had collected.

"Terland? The name doesn't ring a bell."

Velof's hand tightened, and the tablet he held cracked. He glanced at it and threw it to the side.

Link, Braeden says Velof lied about recognizing the name but that he's only showing anger now, and it's tipping toward reckless and violent.

Really? Link felt like grinning even though Phina had sounded concerned. *Let's throw in the rest.*

Is that wise? Aren't we supposed to...you know, parlay in diplomacy rather than push them toward violence?

My dear, you will find that there are all kinds of ways to practice diplomacy.

Phina looked at him in disbelief. *What way is this?*

He tossed her a grin and didn't care if anyone else saw it at this point. *Push them until they admit what they know.*

He turned back to Velof with raised eyebrows and an expression designed to look challenging. "So, Terland gave us a lot of interesting tidbits in his notes and files. One file listed every crime he had witnessed and who was present, as well as who had ordered it. We know you are involved in this whole thing as he captured video of everything in your system long before you thought to wipe it when you knew we were coming. Nice try, that! Sorry it didn't work out. Our people have better skills than your people and we found everything, so we know you ordered the deaths of Dreuved and any other Gleek who found out. You are involved in these crimes up to the ridges on your purple head. However, the thing he told us that especially caught our attention was that you had a co-conspirator. Care to share?"

Velof slowly pushed to his feet, his body tense and

unyielding, his face set and glaring. Link knew what he would say before the words came out.

"Only this. Guards! *Kill them all!*"

Ah. It was so nice to be wanted.

Phina couldn't believe Link had purposely pushed and tried to aggravate Velof into confessing. It seemed reckless and pointless. She had only a second's warning from Braeden along with her own assessment before Velof shouted for the guards to kill them.

What?

The situation threw her until she realized that had been the point of Link's pushing. He wanted to cause Velof to act rashly in a way that made it easier for them to act in response and remove the problem. Sneaky, tricky man.

Within ten seconds, the guards inside the room were fighting the five Gleeks and the three Guardians and Marines. There were only two extra guards if those fought one each, and Maxim fought two at once, bringing it down to one.

That left Velof, his fierce companion, and the spare guard for Geirik, Halvad, Fastel, Link, and her, which was manageable since Geirik and Halvad vaulted over the couch in front of them and went for Velof while Fastel ran around to meet Torel. Link ran past her to attack the last guard, surprising her by drawing a knife from a sheath that was hidden on his back under his shirt.

Phina took a breath and observed the fighting, trying to decide where to join in as she tucked her tablet away.

Everyone held their own against the Baldere. Halvad and Geirik took turns against Velof. In their exchange over the past two days, which had been initiated by Phina at Link's request, they had expressed in no uncertain terms that Velof had to live to compete in the games. Their people had to see Geirik win as the leader before Velof died. That made the fight more complicated since Velof had no compunction about harming *them*.

She turned to Charles Edwards to see what he would do in the midst of all this, and the doors crashed open, and five more guards ran into the room.

With only her free to fight them off.

She drew her knives from their sheaths on her thighs and took a shaky breath at the sight of the incoming Baldere with their fierce and determined expressions as they drew their weapons, all of them much larger than her knives.

"Uh, guys? Little help?"

Braeden and the other Gleeks had spread out to each meet a Balderian guard. As the fight went on, he thought it felt like a repeat of the night before. He moved his staff quickly, connecting with the Baldere's weapon hand, shocking it to release his weapon, much to the guard's shock and dismay.

He had just turned his staff and was preparing to knock him out when he felt Phina's emotions jump in shock and alarm. Whipping his head around, he took in the five guards about to attack her, then turned back and assessed the group in a glance. His fellow Gleeks were fighting beside him, having twisted around a little. Draeget took a step to his left, Kroegen took a step forward, and...ah, perfect.

Braeden quickly moved to the side of the Baldere he had just disarmed, and much like the night before, he shoved his staff into the Baldere's belly with even more kinetic force behind it. The impact threw the male back into the Baldere fighting Kroegen, who didn't even have time to brace himself before they both landed on a third Baldere who was fighting Draeget. This freed up Braeden and Kroegen to help Phina.

"Knock them out and disarm them, Draeget!"

Braeden gestured for Kroegen to join him in speeding over to rescue Phina from the guards who had just surrounded her. She wasn't doing too badly, but with five to her one, she was getting overwhelmed. The Gleeks' elongated limbs made their gait ungainly but they covered ground much more quickly than Baldere.

Within seconds they closed in, but it was too late to keep Phina from harm if he didn't act immediately.

Duck!

He threw the order to Phina, who dropped into a crouch. Good enough. Using as much as he dared, he thrust his hand forward and forced the kinetic energy out, aiming for the guards' chests. The force exerted was greater than he'd thought it would be, and the Baldere had no chance to brace themselves. Only one even saw him coming. As a group, the Baldere flew into the wall near the double doors.

The two closer Baldere had been flung into those

behind them, which gave them a slight cushion. However, the two Baldere at the back of the group hit the wall hard with their heads, just missing the ridges, so they had no protection from the effects. Both were knocked out. The last Baldere had hit the floor hard, just missing the wall. He wasn't unconscious, but the force seemed to have broken something inside that helped to maintain equilibrium since he appeared to be dizzy.

A figure flew in front of them toward the guards.

When Link had heard Phina's uncertain voice asking for help, he had been toying with the guard. Why not? It barely gave him exercise to fight, but it was the most action he'd had all day. Her uncertainty gave him pause since Phina had always sounded confident, and if not confident, then she had attitude.

Phina uncertain? That didn't bode well. Swerving to miss being hit by the Baldere's strange-looking sword with a slit in the middle and barbs on the edges, he sidestepped and glanced over to see five Balderian males advancing on her.

No!

He focused on the Baldere in front of him, ducked, twisted, and shoved his knife deep into the thin slot between the male's arm and his chest protection. He jiggled the knife from side to side and withdrew it as quick as you could spit, then turned to run to Phina just in time to see the Baldere fly toward the wall.

Braeden, Braeden, what large teeth you have…

Seeing Phina crouched gave him pause, but when her head popped up to see the aftermath of Braeden's push, he felt like he could breathe again. If something had happened to her…

But it hadn't. *Focus and finish the job, man.*

He turned his run to Phina into a run toward the fallen Baldere, dashing past the taller Gleeks while he moved his knife from one hand to the other, flipping the point around so he could use the hilt on their skulls. Two taps to each head where their necks met their skulls did the job nicely. The ribbed armor on the top of their head didn't help them there, but he saw a few slices on their bodies and knew they were from Phina's knives.

Heaving a breath, he turned to examine the young woman. She had a gash on her leg and a large slice on the opposite arm, neither of which was deep enough to be life-threatening but were concerning enough that he stopped and pulled off his coat.

Phina blinked up at him, confused. "What are you… Oh!"

Taking a quick glance at the fight told him the Gleeks and Guardians had the guards under control, which was a relief. The three Guardians ran over as Link applied his knife to the jacket, taking strips off the bottom, and began wrapping them around her leg over the wound, which seemed slightly worse than the arm. After tying one off, he did the same with the slice on her arm. Throughout his ministrations, Phina remained quiet, just watching him and wincing every so often. Maxim was muttering curses under his breath, apparently thinking he should have been faster to lend aid.

After Link finished, he rested a hand on her shoulder. "That should do it, but you need to see this out from a chair."

When she made to push herself up, he lifted her in his arms, eliciting a small noise of surprise from her before one arm slid around his neck and the other gripped the opposite shoulder. He waved off Maxim's offers to carry her and glared at Ryan when he attempted to take her from him. By the time he had deposited her on the couch facing away from the door, her face was red from the attention.

"Thank you."

He nodded and turned to view the state of the others in the room. The guards had all been knocked out and disabled or killed. The large Baldere Velof had called Taben sat with no weapon and two Gleeks holding their staffs toward him.

Charles Edwards had moved to the side of the room and was looking around with impassive eyes. The only ones still fighting were Velof and Geirik and Fastel and Torel.

It didn't seem to be going well for Fastel.

Fastel had noticed the Balderian female as soon as she entered the room with Geirik and Halvad. As the others had talked, her attention had strayed to the female she had later learned was named Torel. The name wasn't what drew Fastel's attention. No, that had been entirely because of the way she looked.

Torel could have been Fastel's sister, they looked that much alike.

Shaking her head, she had viewed the male who had sought to be her bondmate years before and knew she had made the right choice. Velof had shown a few redeeming qualities when they were younger, but she had seen a core of weakness in him that came out eventually. That weakness had done so in the form of all the sneaking around he had done to gain wealth and power over the past ten years, quietly slaying those who opposed him or found out about his machinations.

It sickened her to think she might have been tied to him if life had turned out differently. No, she had made the best choice, and it wasn't on her that he had committed all these crimes after she had chosen Geirik over him. Those acts had been his choice alone. Fastel hadn't realized how much she had needed to recognize and understand that. It felt freeing.

After she had been volunteered to do the little telepathy project, she felt the weight of someone's glare and looked up to see Torel's eyes burning into her. Ah, jealousy. Perhaps she had realized who Fastel had been to Velof after he volunteered her. Torel's eyes had remained on her until Velof suggested she fight the young girl from the Empire.

The human girl had looked startled. Torel had looked both eager and disgusted that she had to spend any time on the young girl, then returned to her stoic and sullen but proud self when the topic was dropped.

It didn't take long for Fastel to feel the rumblings of a fight about to break out. Once Velof had shouted for them all to be killed, Fastel ran to fight the opponent she had chosen—Torel, who looked so very much like her.

Perverted bastard.

As Fastel ran around the couch toward Torel, she saw that the other female had an excited light in her eyes and was eager for a fight. They wouldn't have a lot of space for maneuvering between the furniture, but there was enough to move around. Fastel pulled her short swords, which were flaumag—wavy blades with sharp angles and curves on both the tip and the flanges just below the hilt. Perfect for slicing things to pieces.

"He will never be yours, *pahka!*"

The venom in Torel's tone didn't surprise Fastel but the words did. She stopped a few paces back, considering the other female.

"I thought I made it clear years ago that I didn't want him."

"Lies! I saw the way you looked at him earlier."

"You mean when I showed pity and disgust on my face? That was all for him, but I would have thought it would tell you I don't want him. He's nothing to me now."

"I see in his eyes when he's thinking of you. You still have a hold on him somehow, but it will end with your death!"

The female lunged forward, pulling out her weapons and engaging with Fastel's swords. Fastel felt pity for the younger female, that she wanted to believe it was she who was the villain here instead of Velof.

That didn't mean she was going to lay down and die for her.

CHAPTER TWENTY-SIX

Fastel was good.

She could hold her own with Geirik in skill; she just lacked his endurance, strength, and strategic mind to determine how situations could play out. However, where Fastel was good, Torel was vicious. Fastel had heard of her. Any small opening her opponent gave, Torel took and then hammered until the other person gave up. However, Fastel hadn't ever been one to give up, and she wouldn't start now.

Turn, strike, strike, strike. Nothing existed but the need to keep fighting, looking for every opportunity to slash and slice. Fastel ducked, whirled, lunged, and dodged as she tried to avoid and block the strikes of the other female as well as push back.

She ignored the grunts and cries around her about trouble with the extra guards that had come in. She ignored Velof fighting with Halvad and her bondmate. She ignored it all and focused on the female in front of her. She had to. Fastel could feel the burns of the cuts she had received from Torel's weapons, which were shaped like metal disks with a slice taken out, leaving a thicker bar with holes for the female's fingers to fit through. The weapons were called rhinghur disks, and they moved like an extension of Torel's hand. The circular blade made it so very easy to slice from any angle.

As evidenced by the number of cuts on Fastel's body. The Baldere had the ability to heal quickly, but the more there was to heal, the slower the recovery and the slower she moved while she waited for the cuts to heal. Fastel had done damage to Torel, but those cuts were fewer, though not as easily healed since the barbs on the tips of Fastel's swords tore as much as sliced.

Fastel realized she was in trouble. She needed an opening to get past Torel's defenses. She blocked one strike and batted away another, but doing so left her open to Torel's other rhinghur disk. Torel's eyes ignited with glee when she realized Fastel wouldn't be quick enough to block her strike to a vital part of her body.

As Fastel moved forward in a thrust of desperation, Velof bellowed a cry of outrage and dismay, causing Torel's attention to search him out in alarm. Fastel's move was too quick, her blade too sharp, and Torel's movement was arrested.

The blade slid deep between the female's heart and her lungs. There was no changing the mortal strike. If Fastel pulled out her blade, it would tear the other female's body more. Torel's rhinghur had sliced Fastel's hand, causing her other sword to drop, but that gash was nothing compared to the wound Torel now bore.

Fastel let go, leaving herself with no weapons, but Torel wouldn't be able to take advantage as she sank to the floor, fingers reflexively opening and letting her disks slide down her fingers. Her face spasmed between emotions, choking and gasping, though she reached a trembling hand toward Velof.

Fastel stood back and watched the female bleed out. She was uncertain about the feelings running through her, but she knew that despite the criminal activity Torel had been involved with, she cared about the man at the heart of the corruption.

Whether Velof reciprocated those feelings remained to be seen.

Geirik and Halvad had flown over the couch to meet Velof as he drew his hagrund. Since Geirik's skalax wasn't suited to this type of setting, doing better in an arena or a practice area, he had brought his secondary weapon. It was more easily sheathed—a sword similar to Fastel's two wavy blades, though larger and better suited to his size and strength.

Halvad had pushed forward to meet Velof with a ferocity that surprised the Jeskir. Halvad had always been easygoing and less ready to jump into a fight. His friend had confided to Geirik on their way to the station that when the communication from the Imperial representatives arrived, it had stated that much of their evidence came from Terland—who had asked Halvad to be contacted since he knew the potential next Jeskir, a Baldere who had disappeared and was presumed to be dead. It was the last straw.

Terland had been Halvad's childhood friend, and though they had lost touch over the years, especially while Terland had worked for Velof, he had still been important to Halvad. Since it appeared all but certain that Terland's death had been caused by Velof, Halvad had finally decided that not only did Velof need to be deposed as the Jeskir, but he needed to die.

They had agreed Velof needed to be alive to legitimately compete in the Rikhar games since many of the people loved him and had no idea about his corruption, though Halvad had been reluctant. Now Geirik not only needed to defeat Velof without killing him so he could fight and kill him later, he needed to let Halvad fight Velof and keep his close friend from killing his former friend.

How had his life gotten so complicated?

Velof easily met Halvad strike for strike and blow for blow. Though his friend was eager and had skill, he didn't have the natural killer instinct or desire that gave Velof his edge. Eventually, Halvad began to flag.

"Halvad."

His friend blocked Velof's strike, pushing it back harder than he might have otherwise, and sprang back. Geirik leaped forward to take his place, swinging to hit areas that would disable the Baldere for a moment but where the wounds would not be deep enough to kill him. Velof blocked and struck back, and Geirik sidestepped and dodged even as he blocked the blows.

After a time, Geirik realized he and Velof were too evenly matched since Geirik couldn't use any killing blows. He also realized he would need help to overcome the Jeskir and keep him prisoner until the Rikhar games.

"Halvad!"

His friend cut in from the side, slicing into the outside of Velof's weapon arm as Geirik ripped from the inside. It couldn't have gone better if the two friends had planned it. Velof's arm spasmed, his fingers opening reflexively. He was not able to grip his hagrund anymore, and it fell to the floor with a thud, barely missing Geirik's foot.

Velof bellowed his outrage and dismay. "No! You can't!"

He bent to reach for his hagrund with his other hand, only to have Halvad step on the weapon, his large foot keeping the device on the floor as he growled at the defeated male.

"No, you don't, you bastard!"

Geirik sheathed his sword, then wrestled with the Jeskir to pull his arms behind his body, only to realize he had nothing to tie them with.

"Anyone have anything we can use to tie up this villain?"

He looked around to find all the guards knocked out or tied up or both. Two of the Gleeks were on opposite sides of the room, watching the guards to make sure they didn't move. Two others were standing near the human female who had been injured. The other Imperial males had congregated there as well. The last Gleek stood off to the side, looking as uncertain as a Gleek could. Charles Edwards had been standing off to the side. He had now backed up to the doors and was about to push through.

"Someone grab him." Geirik pointed at the fleeing human by the door.

The alien Yollin used his four legs to jump over the couch, almost tipping it over to the surprise of the human female sitting on it. She yelped as the Yollin leaped over the back toward the ambassador. Charles looked up in fear and dismay to see the ferocious Yollin bearing down on him, then ran out of the room.

The Yollin chased the human male down the hall and roared as he reared up and knocked his quarry over with his front feet.

"Got him!"

Charles Edwards couldn't think about anything except the Yollin who had just jumped over the couch and now raced toward him. He forgot everything in his desperate hope to leave without being caught. He had been so close! After pushing through the doors, he ran out to try to get away. Perhaps it wasn't too late.

He was halfway down the hall when he heard Drk-vaen a step behind him. He turned around and gazed with horror at the large alien who had reared up on his back legs with a roar, his savage spiked face frightening, mandibles spread to their fullest extent. The front legs reached toward him, sharp claws extending from three long toes, causing Charles to shriek in alarm and push his hands out in a futile attempt to keep the Yollin back.

He was going to die!

Charles winced and closed his eyes as if blocking the

sight would prevent the act. He felt a hard impact on his chest, then a harder impact when he hit the floor.

"Got him!" Drk-vaen bellowed to the occupants of the room they had just left.

Charles squinted up at the alien towering above him and whimpered.

"Please don't hurt me!"

As he leaned over to look at him, the Yollin's mandibles clicked, causing the man to flinch and put his arms over his face.

Drk-vaen shook his head and spoke, the words translated by Charles' implant. "You are so disappointing. How did you get to be a diplomat? You see a Yollin and think I'm just a bloodthirsty beast, don't you?"

The ambassador lowered his hands and peered up at the alien. "So you aren't going to kill me?"

Chuckling, the Yollin bent down and grabbed Charles' hands to draw him to his feet and yank him back toward the room.

"Oh, I didn't say that. Just that I'm not going to kill you right now."

***

While Geirik watched the Yollin, his hands didn't maintain a tight grip on Velof, who caught sight of Torel lying on the floor. With a bellow, he yanked his arms out of Geirik's grip and lunged over to the mortally wounded female.

He laid a hand on her neck and must have failed to find a pulse since he pulled it back quickly. Velof peered at Fastel, who was standing off to the side, looking beautiful even with spatters of violet blood dotting and streaking her body. She had a number of cuts that had bled, though they seemed to be healing.

She stared steadily at the man who would have had her years ago and had sworn off friendship with either of them when she had refused him for Geirik. For his part, Geirik had never been prouder of her. Velof seemed conflicted in his thoughts and barely acknowledged Geirik when he walked over and pulled the male's arms behind him again.

A hand held out a few strips of fabric to him. Geirik reached for them and followed the arm to the face of the representative from the Empire, Greyson Wells, who gave him a nod.

"Thank you."

Geirik began wrapping the strips around Velof's wrists to hold them together just as the male seemed to wake up from the daze he had entered. After a few tugs and some angry muttering, Greyson stepped over and pinched Velof's neck in a particular spot, causing the Baldere to freeze and twitch in place. Geirik nodded his thanks and finished binding the Jeskir with the strips.

As he straightened and stepped back, Greyson grinned. "The pinch hold. Works every time for any creature with a nervous system. You just have to find the right spot."

Geirik smiled in amusement. "I'll remember that."

Velof could only throw himself around, and without his arms out for balance, he had difficulty staying upright. He glared at Charles Edwards and thrust his chin out at the man.

"This is all his fault!"

After Drk-vaen had almost toppled the couch—*thanks for that, Drk*—Phina had decided it would be better to stand. Surely the cuts had slowed down their bleeding and it wouldn't be that bad.

Her leg hurt when she stood and was difficult to walk on, shooting out twinges of fire since the makeshift dressing pressed into the wound with every step she took. Okay, maybe sitting had been better. She had just settled back down on the couch, turned at an angle so she could see what was going on better when Velof accused the ambassador.

Ah. Right on time.

Charles stood at an uncomfortable angle since Drk-vaen held the now-former ambassador's arm higher than was comfortable for the shorter human. He appeared surprised by Velof's accusation and lifted his free hand to cover his heart, giving off an air of being confused and affronted.

"I beg your pardon? I have no idea what you could be meaning."

Link barked a laugh as he stood near Geirik, who still had hold of Velof. Maxim and Ryan had stayed with Phina, while the three Gleeks who weren't watching the guards, Braeden, Kroegen, and Traekor, had spread out between her couch and Link, facing Drk-vaen and Charles Edwards.

"I sincerely doubt that, old man."

Insult crossed Charles' face. "Who are you calling old? You're older than I am!"

"Not by much." Link waved a hand, "That's not important. What is important is that you betrayed your Empress and the Empire. That…that's very serious."

"What proof do you have?"

"Proof!" Velof's face twisted in anger and disgust. "You were there making decisions with me and for me every step of the way, you arrogant human!"

"It's his word against mine." Charles spoke calmly as if he were talking about nothing of consequence.

Phina sighed and readjusted her leg. He really was an arrogant fool.

Braeden.

The Gleek didn't mistake what she was looking for since it had been the third thing she had asked his help with since last night.

"This male has been emitting deception ever since he opened his mouth. He enjoyed it when everyone fought, felt delight when we were pushing Velof, and when we tested the guards this morning, every time his name came up, they all had similar reactions—secrecy, distrust, and not a small amount of fear."

Velof laughed low, but it turned manic as it went on. Everyone stared at him, then eyed each other uneasily.

Link cleared his throat. "Yes, Velof's testimony, Braeden offering a telepathic empath's testimony as to the state of your emotions and intentions, and this."

Phina had pulled her tablet out again, anticipating his request, and brought up the last major video they had gleaned from Terland's collection of files. She pushed the sound up so it could be heard very clearly.

The longer Charles watched the video, realizing he had

implicated himself, the more he sweated and turned pale. When it finished, Link turned to Charles with raised eyebrows and a smirk on his face that said, "Gotcha."

"Anything to add?"

"I...I tried to minimize Velof's actions so they weren't as bad as they could have been."

Link scoffed. "What, you think this is some kind of trial where you can get off easier for good behavior? No!"

Charles took a deep breath and seemed relieved until Link leaned forward with a hard look on his face.

"No, Charles, this is the kind of trial where we already judged you guilty and sentenced you to death. The Empress is not happy. You're lucky she's not here as she takes treason and betrayal *very* seriously. You conspired to kill Etherian citizens. You conspired to kill others who were doing nothing wrong. You conspired to perpetuate brutality and the subjugation of the Balderian people. You contributed to defrauding both the Balderian people and the Etheric Empire. I wouldn't be surprised if we found more money than Velof here believes you have from your operations.

"These are all betrayals, Charles. Betrayals that are treason because you are an Etherian diplomat acting against the Empire. And although you failed to take note of current events, you should have remembered what Bethany Anne does when one of her citizens is disrespected. For this betrayal? You are lucky that the General, Anna Elizabeth, and every single one of the Bitches convinced her to let us handle this. What were you thinking, man?"

Link sounded curious and a little bewildered. He really

didn't understand how Charles could turn against the Empire and the Empress. Phina was curious too, but she thought she understood a little more than Link did since she had been angry with the Empress herself at one point, even though the emotion had been misplaced. She had been eleven years old and grieving the death of her parents, after all.

"Do you know how long and hard I've worked to further the ends of the Empire? Years!" Charles sounded both pleading and aggravated, which gave his voice a curious tone. "I looked at my life and realized I had nothing! No spouse or kids, no one special or important in my life. My best years were given to the Empire, and I received very little in return! Certainly not access to the inner circle or being given the opportunity to advance in my career. I've been doing the same thing for the last two decades! Why wouldn't I try to get more so I could live comfortably and be able to retire?"

Ok, she had been wrong. She *didn't* understand.

Phina pushed her way to the side of the couch and stood up to hobble over and stand in front of the arrogant, ignorant man. Link had been about to speak until he saw her moving.

"Is this worth breaking open your wounds?"

Phina waved a dismissive hand toward him. She had to do this. She stared into the man's blue eyes and saw arrogance and disdain. He looked at her and saw a young girl who didn't know anything. What he didn't know was that thanks to Anna Elizabeth, Jace, Link, Sis'tael, Maxim, Drkvaen, the Gleeks, and even Velof and Charles himself, she finally understood exactly what being a diplomat for the Empire meant.

"'The diplomat's primary allegiance is to the Empress and the Empire, and they will do all in their power to uphold honor and Justice throughout their service.'" She spoke softly as she eyed him. "'The Diplomatic Corps was established to facilitate the introduction of alien species into the Etheric Empire and protect Etherian citizens.' That is written in the manual given to every diplomat trainee."

"How dare you stand there and lecture me, child! I..." His voice cut off from the combination of her next words and Drk-vaen's pressure on his arm. He subsided and listened to her with a sheen of perspiration on his face.

"Honor. Justice. Protection." She dropped the words like hard pearls that had been growing for weeks inside her, as indeed they had been. "That is what it means to be a diplomat for the Etheric Empire. Did you forget your purpose, sir, in your desire for vengeance for your perceived slights?

"When you went along with and even encouraged Velof to kill Gleeks, Baldere, and others we have yet to learn of, did you ever stop to think that those Baldere were the very people you swore to protect? That the Gleeks and any others you were involved in killing could be future Etherian citizens?

"Did you even once think our Empress isn't one to force those to serve who don't believe in the mission and purpose anymore? Had you gone to Anna Elizabeth at any time and said you wanted out, you could have retired and moved on to something else that didn't require so much of you. She would have understood your choice—and make no mistake, this was all your choice.

"You chose to betray your Empress." Her clipped words landed like blows as he jerked against the grip Drk still had on his arm, his eyes growing more desperate with each sentence she spoke. "You chose to betray your Empire. You chose to become the very thing you were supposed to protect the people against. You, and only you, are to blame for this.

"'A diplomat's primary allegiance is to the Empress and the Empire, and they will do all in their power to uphold honor and Justice throughout their service.' Your actions, sir, were neither honorable nor just. You threw everything away for money. You changed your allegiance. You've shown where your allegiance lies—it is not to the Empire, and it is certainly not to the Empress!"

Phina finished speaking and felt satisfied but drained. She went to move back to the couch but was stopped by Link's hand grasping her shoulder.

"Well said, my dear. Well said."

He stepped closer and leaned over her as she flushed with elation from his words. Though she also felt a little lightheaded. Perhaps it was a good thing Link had a hand on her shoulder to help keep her upright.

"Charles, you have already been sentenced to death in the Empire. However, the Gleeks have requested that we turn you over to them, and we have granted that request. They will do as they like with you as they choose, whether it be death or slaving for them for the rest of your life. The only two caveats we agreed on with them were not to use torture, and if they let you live, that they not mistreat you, though believe me that those conditions are very narrow."

"What?" Charles struggled against the hand holding him, with his eyes bugging out. "You can't do this!"

"It's done."

Etheric Empire, Vermott, Planet of the Baldere, Rikhar Arena

Skalax struck hagrund before Geirik swung up his shield to break the other male's wrist, but Velof pulled his arm back quickly enough for it to miss. Phina found herself tensing every time Velof's strikes came close to hitting Geirik. A hand on her shoulder startled her into turning to meet Link's calm face.

"Relax. Geirik is the better fighter. The outcome is all but certain."

Phina shook her head even as she tried to take his advice to relax. Geirik might be the better fighter, but Velof was sneaky. Didn't Phina have plenty of examples where sneakiness won over skill? Geirik and Fastel had told them Velof had cheated to win ten years ago and that he'd tried to escape twice in the two days since the fight in the consulate. The outcome wouldn't be certain until the match was over.

Link stayed beside her, leaning against the barrier

between them and the arena as her eyes were drawn back to the fighting. Geirik swung with his shield, catching the hagrund in Velof's hand and pushing it to the side before swiping at Velof's chest with his skalax. Metal, cloth, and flesh were sliced open, droplets of violet blood spraying the two fighters. The now-familiar spicy scent of the blood had begun to permeate the air. Unfortunately, Velof had taken a step back at the crucial moment, so rather than the match being almost over, the cut only caused pain instead of serious injury.

Even from a distance, Phina could see both men tightening their jaws for different reasons. This match was the last chance for them. One of the two wouldn't leave here alive. There were a few options available for the loser, but with this much animosity and jealousy on one side and intolerance for dishonor and greed on the other, death would be the only end. However, Link, Phina, and the Empire needed Geirik to win, not to mention the Balderian people themselves.

The two warriors swung and sliced at each other while the thousands present in the stadium around them roared encouragement. Phina couldn't tell if the crowd rooted for Velof or Geirik since the cries all ran together. Perhaps they didn't know or care which Baldere won. The two males pressed each other back and forth across the field, each looking for any small advantage. Phina saw they were tiring, though their strikes were still almost as powerful as when they had begun.

Geirik will win, don't worry.

Phina still started whenever Braeden spoke in her head. She supposed it would take time to get used to the feel of someone speaking mentally. It was very different than when she heard Link or ADAM speak over the implant. That felt almost like she heard the words with her ears, but they were not audible to anyone else. However, when the Gleeks spoke, she felt the words more than heard them. The thought was just there in her head, but with a different tone than her own mental speech.

The group had questioned all the guards and finally found where the two Gleek bodies had been disposed of, so Braeden and the other Gleeks were more at ease now, knowing their brothers were not lost. There was a marked difference in how the Gleeks came across. The familiar ease between them all was less strained, and even Graeden had cracked a smile. Braeden, in contrast, had grown quieter and more withdrawn. Phina thought he had a lot on his mind.

Really? She tried to see what Braeden had in their actions, but though the two were slower than they had been a few minutes ago, there was no real change. *How can you know?*

I feel it. Geirik has felt resolve throughout the whole fight, and while he may occasionally grow alarmed if the fended-off attack was a close one, he has not wavered in that resolve. Whereas Velof's feelings are tinged with desperation. He started off confident but wary. Now his desperation has grown and his confidence has flagged.

Interesting. Thank you. She mulled it over, marveling at how much Braeden could understand about the people around him by feeling their emotions.

Her attention was drawn back to the fight when Velof swung his hagrund at Geirik's head. Geirik lunged to the side under the battle-axe and bypassed the shield to thrust his skalax into Velof's exposed chest, piercing his body in two deep punctures. Given how deep the blades had sunk, Phina thought the Jeskir would die, but though he stumbled and knelt, he didn't fall over.

Geirik used the opportunity to knock the hagrund out of the other male's hand while he was weakened, then put his shield under his arm while he grabbed Velof's shield and tossed it over his shoulder to land several paces behind him. The crowd inexplicably quieted.

"Do you yield?"

Geirik's tone was calm, showing a steady strength she hadn't thought to hear after they ran around the arena. Velof glared at Geirik as he clutched his chest. They all silently waited to hear the answer. After a moment, Geirik prodded him with his skalax, eliciting an icy growl.

"Fine."

"The words." Geirik stared at Velof, waiting, his tone even without any note of gloating or excitement that he had won.

"I yield." Velof bit off the words as his eyes narrowed.

The crowd cheered, the roar building, but Geirik held up the hand that still clutched the skalax, his eyes not leaving his enemy and former friend before him.

"Do it."

Before Velof's face could do more than crinkle in confusion at Geirik's words, Phina tapped a few buttons on her tablet and piped the audio through the arena's system.

"Ziver, you take Narvid, Vodin, and Gaudun and take care of that Gleek snooping around. I don't want anything to come back on us. We need those food shipments coming in, and I won't tolerate anyone stopping us."

"We still get our cut, hey?"

"Of course, Ziver. Now go."

After a few seconds, Charles' voice spoke.

"Velof, you know this isn't sustainable. We will only manage a few more shipments anyway. Perhaps we should stop with what we've attained and move on to a different type of cargo. Once this Gleek is gone, the others will become suspicious anyway."

"Come now, Charles. You aren't growing weak now, are you? Because that's what I'm hearing. You're being weak, just like these Gleeks, and just like those Baldere who can't do anything without direction and reassurance. These people think they know what it's like to lead? They know nothing. The only thing that will keep us at the level of wealth and power we have grasped is to take more, whether it be from our allies or the people themselves."

The crowd, which had murmured at the beginning, was roaring by the end. Phina stopped the recording they had shown Charles. No one would have heard it anyway with the level of noise the crowd had attained in expressing their displeasure.

Velof stared at Geirik, his face a sickly pale lavender. He knew his fate was sealed. Geirik raised his skalax again for silence. It didn't take long for the crowd to quiet down, though a few hurled curses at the disgraced former leader for another moment. Geirik turned to face them, and they stopped. His voice rose, strong and commanding.

"My people, you have heard evidence of some of Velof's crimes. Stealing cargo for his own gain. Ordering the deaths of two visiting Gleeks and attempting to kill five more. Conspiracy to commit criminal acts against our own laws. Attempting to defraud the Etheric Empire we have become part of. Disgracing the name of the Baldere and our entire race!"

At this, many in the crowd shouted angrily, while others booed and hissed.

Velof sprang forward, pulling a knife from his belt as he lunged for his nemesis, his eyes glittering with hate. "You've taken everything from me!"

Geirik raised his shield and backhanded Velof across the face with it, then kicked the knife out of the male's hand. Velof staggered back, then fell when Geirik slammed the edge of the shield into his chest, compressing the air from his lungs. He curled in on himself, trying to catch his breath.

"Kill the coward!"

A voice rose from the stands, eliciting raised shouts of agreement. Geirik raised his skalax again.

"The authorized representatives of the Etheric Empire and I have gathered, heard, and witnessed the evidence of all these crimes. You have heard the words from his own mouth. His accomplice, the Imperial Diplomat Charles Edwards, has already been appropriately dealt with by the Empire." He nodded at Link and Phina. "The Imperial sentence for treason is death.

"We are here now to determine this Balderian male's fate. So, my people, do you find Velof guilty or innocent?"

The crowd roared, "*GUILTY!*"

"What sentence do you give him?"

"*DEATH!*"

No sooner had the pronouncement been given than Geirik dropped his shield, drew the male up by the body-suit layered under Velof's armor, and sliced deep across his throat—too deep to heal before he bled out.

The crowd went wild as Phina sank against the barrier between her and the arena. She felt Link to her left and Braeden to her right.

"This is diplomacy?"

A few moments went by before a somber Link responded, "Sometimes."

She heard the jeers for Velof and the cheers for Geirik as she watched the new Baldere leader close his eyes for a moment before seeking Fastel. "It's done," he mouthed. His bondmate nodded, her eyes full of love and sorrow. The new Jeskir slowly walked to meet her as Phina turned her eyes toward the two males with her.

"It's not what I thought it would be."

Phina felt Braeden's mental presence wrapping her in comfort. Link's hand covered hers for a moment and squeezed.

"Life rarely is."

Geirik felt Velof's blood gush over his hand as he sliced the male's throat. Though he should be proud that he had ended Velof's treasonous and criminal activities, he couldn't help the thought that the death of his former friend had been a waste.

Choices had led them to this moment—Velof's choices, Fastel's, and his own. Although he had never blamed his bondmate, Geirik knew they had all contributed to the decisions Velof had made. Even the choices of his people who filled the arena and were now screaming Geirik's name had led them to this moment.

He hated that it had been his hand on the knife, no matter that Velof's death was just or deserved. They had to do better as a people to guide their younglings so they would be as strong in spirit as they were in body. The Balderian people couldn't handle another Velof.

He opened the eyes he didn't realize were closed and saw that all life had left Velof. Geirik turned to find the one person who always helped him make sense of the universe. Fastel stood on the inside of the arena by the gate, without tears, and with the remainders of her own victorious fights proudly represented by bloody stripes on her body, though the wounds were already healed. Her face full of compassion and sorrow—for him.

"It's done." He knew she wouldn't be able to hear him over the crowd, but he needed to get it out.

His bondmate nodded and held out her hand to him. Focusing on her blue eyes, he walked toward her, dropping his skalax just before reaching her so he could hold onto her hands and lower his head toward hers. After a moment of breathing her in and ignoring the quieting cheers of the crowd, he told her what was on his mind.

"This was a waste, my love. We need to do better with the next generation, hey? There have been too many Baldere in our path lately that didn't have the strength to step up and say that Velof was wrong. We let this happen by not standing together and saying no. We have to do better."

His voice hadn't faltered, though his heart had bled all through the words. Geirik was so wrapped up in his musings that he almost missed his bondmate's words in return.

"You will have plenty of time to practice with our own youngling, then."

Startled, he pulled his head back to stare into her mischievous, smiling face.

"You are serious?"

"Mmhmm." She lifted one of their clasped hands to her heart. "I solemnly swear that by this time next year, we will have a youngling of our own."

It wasn't until the crowd roared their approval and congratulations for their new Jeskir that he realized everyone in the arena had heard them through the microphone that had been placed on his bodysuit before the match.

Fastel took it all in stride as she looked around the arena. "Oops! Well, I guess the news is in the wind now." She turned her deep-lavender face back to his and grinned.

Under the cover of the cheers, Geirik whispered into her ear, "Has it really been ten years since the last games?"

"Only just, but then we didn't exactly wait until after the games now, did we?" She winked with a grin on her face, which ignited a core of happiness within him. They had too much trouble and strife behind them. Now they needed to live and make better choices.

With a roar, he lifted the female he loved and whirled her around, their laughter blending with the excited cheers of the crowd.

. . .

Etheric Empire, QBS *Stark*

"Ow. My head." Maxim moaned as he slumped in his seat.

"Your head?" Ryan complained. "What about my chest and back? I feel like I got pounded."

Drk-vaen weakly twitched his mandibles. "You did get pounded."

"Oh, yeah." Ryan sounded puzzled, as if he wasn't firing on all cylinders yet. "Those Baldere really pack a punch."

Maxim nodded in agreement and winced at the renewed pain. "Neven's right hook was a beautiful thing."

"Not so beautiful on the receiving end." Ryan hissed as he attempted to sit up, felt like a truck lay on his chest, and flopped back down. "Vinger had a nice kick, though."

Drk-vaen rubbed his legs with a frown, making sure they were still attached. "Don't remind me." He shook his head, then began to chuckle. "Did you see his face when he landed on his back on the table, then slid to the ground? He twisted once to try to land better, but it went wrong. So worth getting hit."

"Yeah, man." Ryan's tone lightened as he grinned and held out his hand for a fist bump. "Totally worth it."

"Yes." Maxim agreed and fist-bumped the others.

Phina grinned at the exchange, watching as she sat sideways in her seat on the bridge, her legs propped over the armrest. Her wounds were healing quickly and didn't hinder movement, though they itched fiercely. She had her eyes open now but stared at nothing in particular. By the time they returned to the *Meredith Reynolds,* it would be just over five months since that conversation with Anna Elizabeth in the General's office.

She had more friends than she knew what to do with now. Gone were the days when the Phinalina duo sought adventures alone. Her life had become far more complicated. Being honest with herself, though, she had to admit that while she missed spending time with Alina, she enjoyed getting to know other people better as well.

Life had grown more complicated but also more interesting. While she knew a lot more now, she still had a lot to learn. Phina had a feeling Communications was the class that would not come as easily to her as the rest, what with translating abstract thoughts into practice and speaking in front of people. This trip had helped, but she still thought of herself as someone to keep in the background and not stand in the spotlight.

However, when it came down to it, she hadn't done too badly. She thought back to her little impromptu speech to Charles Edwards. *"The Diplomat's primary allegiance is to the Empress and the Empire, and they will do all in their power to uphold honor and Justice throughout their service."* That, for Phina, was the heart of what she had learned.

Even if Anna Elizabeth still intended to uphold the deal she had made at the beginning—to give Phina a blank check to pursue her dreams—she knew she wouldn't take it. There was no better place to fulfill her vow. The Diplomatic Corps and becoming the Diplomat Spy was right where she wanted to be.

Her tablet indicated a message had been received, breaking her train of thought. She tapped it open to read.

Phina!!!! Maxim just sent me a message to ask if we could message and talk to get to know each other

better! It sounds kind of old-fashioned, but at this point I'm okay with it! Can you believe it?? I'm so thrilled, Phina, you have no idea!!! I had almost given up hope, but that hope is now restored! When are you getting back? We've got to talk about this rooming thing! See you soon!!! You're my bestest friend ever!

Phina smiled in amusement at Alina's excitement. Her best friend always made her feel better. Good for Maxim. She hoped this meant they would stop being broody over each other. Closing out the message, she saw another had come through while she read the first. Her back stiffened when she saw who it was from, but she opened it anyway.

Phina, I don't know when it will be, but I hope to visit soon to discuss this matter of the Weres that you seem to fail to take seriously. If you won't take it seriously for yourself, then there will be consequences. Please take care of yourself and watch your back until then.

Shaking her head to try to clear the confusion, Phina read the message again, but it still didn't make sense. Why would she need to watch her back? Her aunt's idea that Maxim couldn't be trusted seemed over the top. And what did Faith think she could do that Seraphina couldn't do herself? Her aunt hadn't ever been and would never be a fighter. The thought of her challenging Maxim was laughable. And what consequences? Phina was an adult now. It wasn't like she could be grounded in her room.

Irritation swept her, but she couldn't dwell on it anymore. She needed to calm down. She directed music toward her implant, then got up and moved to the small gym on the ship so she could practice her fighting positions and forms. As she went through the motions at quarter speed in deference to her still-healing wounds, half her mind focused on her movements while the other half dwelled on the haunting harmonic melody from her music class. The combination of high, middle, and low tones in perfect sync swept over her.

QBBS *Meredith Reynolds*, Secret Bar, Back Room

Two Weeks Later

Phina sat at the long table, a feast for two laid out on one end, complete with cloth napkins and glasses filled with wine. Steam rose from a few dishes, wafting aromas toward her that caused her belly to rumble with hunger.

She turned to examine Link, using the skills he had taught her, and she realized he was both nervous and a little reluctant to talk and was not sure if he wanted to be farther away or closer. Something must be really bothering him to forget to control his body language like this. Her heart beat faster even as she took even breaths to calm herself.

"Link, what's going on? What aren't you telling me?"

He stopped eating and placed his fork on the table, looking down for a moment to gather his thoughts. When he looked back up, Phina was startled to see the look in his brown eyes turn from slightly lost to resolved and determined.

"There are many things I haven't told you, my dear. These past five and a half months have been just the beginning, with much to come. Before we discuss that, though, there's something you need to know."

She looked at him with suspicion but he ignored it, giving her a smirk. Back to normal then, no trace of his prior uneasiness. She let out a breath of relief. Perhaps his news wouldn't be too bad.

"What's that?"

"The Empress."

Phina tried to swallow but found it difficult because of the sudden dryness in her throat. Her heart raced as she struggled with her nerves and lost. A growing sense of excitement and anxiousness filled her.

"What about her?"

"She wants to meet you."

The End

Seraphina's story continues with *Diplomatic Crisis*, coming soon to Amazon and Kindle Unlimited.

Claim your copy today!

Thank you so much for reading, not just the first book in the series of The Empress' Spy, but my first book ever! :) I'm soo excited that you finally have it in your hands!

It's been quite a journey to get to this point. First, before I go any further I need to thank a few people because without them this book wouldn't have been written.

I'm back! I moved them all to Acknowledgements because... well, the list kept growing... and growing... so, it needed its own section! Shh! Just don't forget to read it before you go because those amazing people deserve others to know how awesome they are. :)

Did I mention I'm super excited that you are finally here and have read Diplomatic Recruit? I hope you enjoyed it and are looking forward to the next book!

Who am I?

S.E. Weir is short for my name, Sarah Elizabeth Weir. If you know personality type things (which I love!) then you will know a lot by my telling you that I'm an INFJ 9. In a nutshell that means I'm an introverted, imaginative, feeler and planner who likes (practically craves) peace and quiet, dislikes conflict, and wants everyone to be their best self while letting everyone else be their best self. 😄

(Note to editor: does this sound pretentious? 🙃 Just want to make sure....)

I'm married to a hardworking and amazing man named Steve who works tirelessly in arts and technology (He paid me to say that... just kidding! 😅 It's really all true). We have two super active and imaginative boys who love to build and do things. No, really, I mean they like to do all the things **all the time**. Do I get peace and quiet? 😳 No... no, I don't. Not until everyone is blissfully sleeping away at night.

Why has it taken so long to get Phina's story in your hands?

Well, first there's our boys. It's really hard to write when I'm constantly interrupted. Yes, you read that right. Constantly. Interrupted. 😶 Some days they are relatively fine and other days they need a lot more attention. So, I haven't really had a consistent block of time to write except for when after everyone is asleep. And then I'm exhausted.

Still, I wouldn't trade our boys for anything. Out of all the things I'll ever be a part of creating they will always be the best. 🖤

Sadly, I also have health issues at play here, mainly fibromyalgia and carpal tunnel. Fibro symptoms include lovely things like extreme fatigue, pain, and brain fog. So, there have been days when I feel perfectly fine… ish. Basically as good as I'm ever able to feel (I love those days). And other days when I could barely function enough to take care of myself and my boys (I loathe those days). Most days are somewhere in the middle where I just do what I can when I can do it.

Through this whole process I have had to learn a lot about myself and how I work when it comes to writing. They say the first step is acceptance and I've had to accept that I'm never going to be a super fast writer who puts out a book every two weeks. I'm sorry if that is a disappointment, but I just can't. I might eventually be able to do one every other month, but I'm really not going to count on that happening because that's not where I am right now.

What I *can* do is write the best book I'm able to do in the time I'm able to do it. That's going to have to be enough for me. I hope it will be enough for you as well because I have a lot of characters and stories in my head waiting to come out, both for Phina and many others. :)

Where did the idea for The Empress' Spy come from?

It really started with a short story that was released in January 2018 called Last Adventure First. That short story was developed after I saw a call out in the author notes of one of Michael's books for anyone interested in writing fan fiction. This was around August 2017. Since earlier in the year I had decided to devote my free time to writing it caught my attention.

Once in the group I met Nat, who you may know as N.D. Roberts. I'm always wary about meeting new people but there weren't many active in the group at the time and we got to talking a bit. I found out she was a new writer herself and an extremely lovely and beautiful person. I had been struggling with a book I had been trying to write and was getting a bit discouraged. Still, I knew I had stories in my head and she gave me a spark of encouragement to just try and see how a KGU short story would turn out.

That spark caught onto a scrap of an idea about two best friends. I saw that first scene in my head so clearly where they were arguing about the next step in their adventure. One friend was an outgoing boy crazy older teen girl who loved clothes and people, and the other an introverted intellectual who loved spy stories and gymnastics. These two were loosely and somewhat based on my sister Becca and I. :) We had been best friends growing up with her being outgoing, boy crazy (wicked smart though!) and liked dressing up, and myself being introverted, bookish, and interested more in creative things. We both had taken gymnastics though for a while. :)

Well, the spark and scrap turned into a flame that gave me one of the best writing days I've ever had (still!) and wrote the whole first draft in one day. I seriously could not put the words on the page fast enough. It felt amazing! 😊

After editing and adding a bit more the short was reviewed, voted on and eventually published in the first KGU fan fiction anthology— And people liked it!

It was just a story that I had written in one day about two best friends and their resulting adventure. Before then I didn't even know whether anything I wrote was actually good or not. I had hoped for sure, but I had no way to be objective enough to really know since anything I had previously written had only been read by friends and family (who are wonderful but kind of biased so it was hard to know how others who didn't know me would receive it.)

Almost two months later Michael invited me and two others to continue our stories into a published series! 😄 It took three and a half years, but it's finally here!

Haven't I seen some of these characters before?

Yes, if you've read Michael's main series, The Kurtherian Gambit, there will be a number of cameos spread across the series. Bethany Anne, his main character, will appear at least once in each book as well as occasionally others from her immediate circle. Drk-vaen and Sis'-tael's stories began as part of Michael's books Never Surrender and Might Makes Right respectively, though Drk makes an appearance in MMR too.

If you've read The Etheric Academy series written by TS Paul and continued by Nat you will have recognized a few characters as well, especially Maxim. The other kids from the series will show up in book three. You may also have read a bit about Greyson Wells at the end of book four since he recruits Masha into SpyCorps, a group that you learn about as The Empress' Spy progresses.

You also may have seen a glimpse of Phina in the future as well as some of her group of friends in The Kurtherian Endgame, Promises Kept. It doesn't give away many secrets for what happens in between now and then (though there are hints for the clever and speculative), but it does show a few things you could have guessed at after reading this one. Don't go reading it again now! Wait till after book three or four and you will pick up a lot more. :)

What's next for Phina?

Secrets, surprises, suspicions, and songs lead to a perfect storm of significant changes for Phina; changes that will last forever.

Phina definitely won't have it easy in book two, but she's definitely going to be the woman for the job! :)

Phina isn't the only one experiencing changes in book two. For book one I kind of instinctively felt my way through writing since it was my first completed novel. It wasn't till book two that I began to be more intentional about where everyone and the plot was going and how everything fit together between books one through four.

As a result, the next book becomes a bit more streamlined with more dialogue and action and a bit less of Phina's internal thoughts. Hopefully everyone will be happy with that as the series moves forward!

Book two should be out soon so it won't be long! I have to say that it may be my favorite though I do love them all!

Till next time! :)

Thank you for not only reading this story but to the end and these author notes as well.

For those who have never read a book that I am involved in, here is an introduction:

Who am I?

I wrote my first book *Death Becomes Her* (*The Kurtherian Gambit*) in September/October of 2015 and released it November 2, 2015. I wrote and released the next two books that same month and had three released by the end of November 2015.

So, just at five years ago.

Since then, I've written, collaborated, concepted, and/or created hundreds more in all sorts of genres.

My most successful genre is still my first, Paranormal Sci-Fi, followed quickly by Urban Fantasy. I have multiple pen names I produce under.

Some because I can be a bit crude in my humor at times or raw in my cynicism (Michael Todd). I have one I share with Martha Carr (Judith Berens, and another (not disclosed) that we use as a marketing test pen name.

In general, I just love to tell stories, and with success comes the opportunity to mix two things I love in my life.

Business and stories.

I've wanted to be an entrepreneur since I was a teenager. I was a very *unsuccessful* entrepreneur (I tried many times) until my publishing company LMBPN signed one author in 2015.

Me.

I was the president of the company, and I was the first author published. Funny how it worked out that way.

It was late 2016 before we had additional authors join me for publishing. Now we have a few dozen authors, a few hundred audiobooks by LMBPN published, a few hundred more licensed by six audio companies, and about a thousand titles in our company.

It's been a busy five years.

Let's talk about Sarah!

I get the opportunity to see a few results of crazy and wonderful stuff I did back in the day. Usually that means decades ago, but right now, it is about four years ago.

One of the things that Sarah is not mentioning is that she, Nat (ND Roberts), and Erika (Erika Everest) all supported and helped bring out the second and third Fans Write anthologies that brought many new authors into the world.

Now all ladies of the three Kurtherian® musketeers have released stories on Amazon, so please go check them out sometime when you are interested to see what they have accomplished since meeting during that fateful first anthology of Kurtherian Gambit fans.

I heartily support Sarah's dogged determination that no matter what life threw at her (and it threw a lot), she kept working toward the goal of getting her first books out into the wild. Just know that we already have three of her books and the fourth (I think) almost in hand or already delivered.

You don't have to worry about not getting this series! Sarah understood her challenges and allowed the stories to sit on the shelf until she knew she was not going to leave our fans in the lurch.

That is the mark of a professional.

So, let me be the first to officially welcome (at least in print) Sarah E. Weir to the level of published professional author.

You did it once with a short story. Now you will have four full books in short order up on your author shelf!

CONGRATULATIONS.

Ad Aeternitatem,

Michael Anderle

ACKNOWLEDGMENTS

They say it takes a village to raise a child. Well, it also takes a village to write a book even though it appears to be a solitary endeavor! 😄

First, thank you Michael Anderle for giving us such a fun universe to read and play in! When I first read the series you had written (up to around book fifteen or so) I seriously think I read them all in five days. Yup, I completely devoured them and couldn't wait for more!

Thank you Steve Campbell for allowing me to join JIT and find an amazing group of people to enjoy this universe with! Not only that but you've been awesome with helping me learn how to use scrivener and organizing everything for publication. If anyone in the LMBPN universe is like ADAM for the Etherian Empire, I think it's you. :)

Thank you Nat Roberts and Erika Everest for a whole pile of things from sounding board, brainstorming, alpha reading, encouragement, and probably a lot I've forgotten! I love you and you both are amazing! 🩶

Nat, a special thank you to you because I'm not sure

Last Adventure First, which started all of this, would have been written without you. Not to mention all the questions, brainstorming, canon checking and generally keeping me sane when I'm about to go off the deep end! You always give me encouragement at just the right time and help me believe I can do it. If you have a superpower, I think it's that one. You help people believe in themselves because you believe in them.

Thank you Lynne Stiegler for your awesome editing, encouragement, and being so welcoming! :) When we went to Vegas for the conference that first year I was really nervous but they went away like *magic* after spending some time with you. I always appreciate my conversations with you regardless of the topic!

Thank you again Michael for me inviting me to become an author in your world and shaping this series with me! I've often dreamed of becoming an author and because of you that dream is coming true. Maybe you are a fairy godfather in disguise... It's certainly feels that way sometimes!

Thank you so much to all my beta readers (listed at the front of the book) who gave me such great feedback! You helped with at least one if not more significant changes in each book as well as a number of smaller ones. You all are awesome!

Special mention to Jim and Larry as you have stuck with me since the beginning, reading every draft, and gave me considerable help over the last few years. Thank you, thank you, thank you!

Thank you Steve, my husband, for being wonderfully supportive and helpful in encouraging me to write! You've also been my #1 fan telling everyone about my books and how things are going with the road to publication. 😄 You are amazing and I love you!

Thank you Becca Griffin, my sister, as without you I wouldn't have had the memory of best friends and sisters that set this story in motion! I love you sister! (And yes, I really did play barbies with you when we were kids! 😜 It definitely happened.)

Thank you Rachel Heise, my amazing sister, for being writing buddies, always willing to talk story and be a sounding board when I'm stuck or panicking! :) I love you!

Thank you Lynne Stiegler, Randy Barber, Tracey Byrnes, Tom Dickerson, Tracy Martin, Charles Wood, Randy Bork, and Lois Alston for helping me with many of the names listed in this book and the next three to come. I always check the list first when I'm coming up with names! :)

Special mention to you, Kelly O'Donnell, for suggesting several I've used but especially Greyson Wells! :) It was absolutely perfect.

Thank you to those in my role playing servers, especially Brian, Alice, Ian, Goose, Alex, and my fellow goblins who have helped me really grasp how my characters work and interact. You've all helped me tell a better story and I'm very grateful.

Thank you Kelly O'Donnell for being absolutely amazing and the perfect person for the job! You've helped keep everything straight and been so helpful whenever I have questions, and I often do! :)

Thank you Mihaela Voicu for the beautiful covers! 😊 I absolutely love them!

Thank you Eric Quigley for the spectacular illustrations of Geirik the Baldere, Braeden the Gleek, and Drkvaen the Yollin!

Thank you to all the JITers (listed at the beginning of the book) who are always on top of things and giving of your time to make our books better! You all are awesome!

Thank you Judith, Grace, David, Micky, and everyone else behind the scenes at LMBPN!

Finally, Michael thank you again for everything but especially understanding my writing pace and all that goes with it! :) Your graciousness is definitely one of the biggest reasons that this series is finally being published.

www.ingramcontent.com/pod-product-compliance
Lightning Source LLC
Chambersburg PA
CBHW020528110726

47899CB00004B/1298